Atomic Werewolves
and Man-Eating Plants

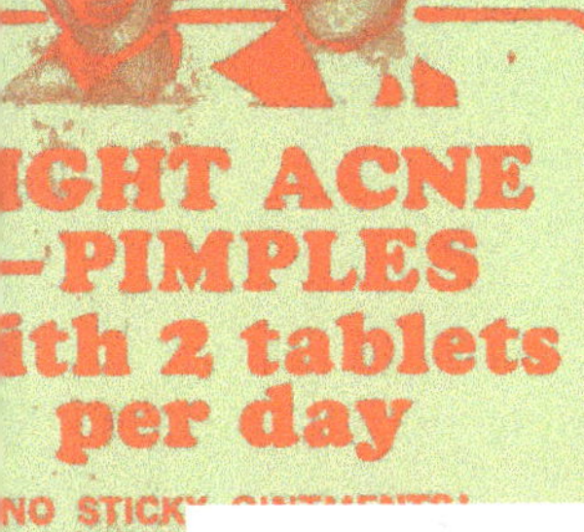

ATOMIC WEREWOLVES AND MAN-EATING PLANTS

when men's adventure magazines got weird

EDITED BY **ROBERT DEIS & WYATT DOYLE**

MensPulpMags.com

A New Texture book

Copyright © 2023 Subtropic Productions LLC

Archival materials supplied by The Robert Deis Archive

"A Century of Weird Tales" copyright © 2023 by Michael P. Chomko

"Weasels Ripped Their Flesh!" copyright © 2023 by Stefan Dziemianowicz

All Rights Reserved.

Cover: "Trapped by a Man-Eating Tree" (detail) by Geoffrey Biggs;
"Curtain Call" (detail) by Jack Davis

Copy editor: Rob Morris

Designed by Wyatt Doyle for The Men's Adventure Library

*With thanks to Stefan Dziemianowicz, Mike Chomko, Bill Lampkin, Jack Cullers,
Eric Blackburn, Jules Burt, and Morgan Roberts*

NewTexture.com

 @NewTexture    @ThisIsNewTexture

MensAdventureLibrary.com   MensPulpMags.com

Booksellers: *Atomic Werewolves and Man-Eating Plants* and other
New Texture books are available through Ingram Book Company

ISBN 978-1-943444-59-5

First softcover edition: August 2023

Printed in the United States of America

10 9 8 7 6 5 4 3 2 1

Men's Adventure Magazines [MAMs]

A bona fide publishing phenomenon that emerged in the 1950s and thrived through the 1970s, the tropes and aesthetic established by **men's adventure magazines (MAMs)** have proven so durable and have been absorbed so totally into the American consciousness that even decades after their demise, MAMs remain an incontestable—if invisible—hand behind key events and directions in entertainment and popular culture.

Incorporating the colorful, eye-catching cover paintings and pulse-pounding action/adventure fiction of pre-World War II pulp fiction magazines, MAMs added non-fiction adventures to the mix, and blurred the line between the two by frequently claiming the outrageous, high-octane fiction was *also* true, even when such claims were implausible, preposterous, or demonstrably false. This blend quickly became standard for the genre, and pulp "fact" ran side by side with pulp fiction.

The MAM formula cannily incorporated aspects of other popular magazines that appealed to the working-class readership they targeted, including racy "bachelor" and pin-up mags, outdoor and travel periodicals, true crime and detective magazines, and celebrity scandal rags.

The format was adopted by multiple publishers, who produced magazines of varying quality. All told, more than 160 different periodicals fit the classification. Some lasted decades, others, only a few issues—or just one. While the more lurid varieties (sometimes called "sweats" or "sweat mags") often draw the most attention (and criticism), the range and quality of MAM content is more varied than is generally understood.

Though dismissed in their time as downmarket, lowbrow entertainment, the magazines were an enduring success, enjoyed by millions of readers over three decades. MAMs published popular writers of the day, and artwork by many of the era's top illustration artists. The terse, hard-boiled intensity of the writing and the dynamic, explosive, and racy illustration art—on their covers and in their pages—are essential to their appeal, then and now. The potency of these words and images remains undiminished; their excesses still spark gobsmacked wonder, and their artistry inspires fascination on its own terms.

CONTENTS

A CENTURY OF WEIRD TALES

by Mike Chomko

MAM content was too varied for MAMs to be defined as direct descendants of any single magazine, or even any single type of magazine. But the brevity and intensity of MAM fiction was clearly inspired by classic pulp fiction from the 1930s and '40s that Weird Tales *helped establish, and many weird tales in MAMs were clearly inspired by* Weird Tales *magazine. Occasionally influence crossed into confluence, with some MAMs not only running stories by notable* Weird Tales *writers, but reprinting stories that appeared previously in* Weird Tales *magazine. Pulp historian Mike Chomko relates a brief history of the magazine.*

WEIRD *Tales* was the first periodical devoted to fantasy and the supernatural. Along with Hugo Gernsback's *Modern Electrics, The Electrical Experimenter,* and *Science and Invention,* "The Unique Magazine" also provided a home for early science fiction.

The magazine was the brainchild of Jacob C. Henneberger. With his partner, JM Lansinger, Henneberger published the very successful *College Humor,* along with its lesser companion, *The Magazine of Fun.* Wanting to expand into the growing pulp magazine field, the partners launched *Detective Tales* in September 1922, with author and journalist Edwin Baird serving as editor.

Hoping to spread their overhead costs over two pulps, Henneberger and Lansinger introduced *Weird Tales* about a half-year later. Its first issue was dated March 1923. Subtitled "The Unique Magazine," the new pulp was meant to give a writer "free rein to express his innermost feelings in a manner befitting great literature."

The early issues of *Weird Tales* were, in reality, filled with ghost stories and what the magazine's editor Edwin Baird termed "gooseflesh fiction." Far more interested in the publishers' *Detective Tales*, Baird had little interest in fantasy and the supernatural. Add onto that uninspiring interior illustrations and bland, three-color cover art, low author rates and slow payments, and a high cover price when compared to other pulps, and one can understand why *Weird Tales* soon found itself in hock to its printer.

Convinced that a magazine dedicated to the strange and unusual could be successful, Henneberger sold his interests in *College Humor*, *The Magazine of Fun*, and the retitled *Real Detective Tales* to his partner. He plowed his proceeds back into *Weird Tales*. Baird stayed with the detective pulp, while one of his assistants, Farnsworth Wright, was named editor of "The Unique Magazine."

Although Edwin Baird had introduced *Weird Tales* readers to some of the magazine's leading lights—Otis Adelbert Kline, HP Lovecraft, Frank Owen, Seabury Quinn, and Clark Ashton Smith—"The Unique Magazine" truly came into its own in late 1924 when Wright assumed the editorial reins. Although Lovecraft sometimes found Wright to be "a most bewilderingly capricious cuss!" it was Farnsworth Wright's sense of the commercial pulp fiction market that kept the magazine afloat during some very challenging times.

With Wright at the helm, *Weird Tales* introduced readers to the work of Robert Bloch, Arthur J. Burks, Hugh B. Cave, Mary Elizabeth Counselman, August Derleth, Nictzin Dyalhis, Paul Ernst, Edmond Hamilton, Robert E. Howard, Carl Jacobi, Henry Kuttner, Greye La Spina, Frank Belknap Long, CL Moore, GG Pendarves, E. Hoffmann Price, Manly Wade Wellman, Donald Wandrei, Henry S. Whitehead, Jack Williamson, and others. And let's not forget artists Hannes Bok, Magaret Brundage, and Virgil Finlay or the continued work of Kline, Lovecraft, Owen, Quinn, and Smith. It was Wright who published "The Call of Cthulhu," "The Whisperer in Darkness," and other classic works by HP Lovecraft. And though it was Edwin Baird who began buying the poetry of Clark Ashton Smith, it was Farnsworth Wright who launched the poet's fiction career in 1928.

In addition to publishing some of the best fantasy and supernatural fiction of the twentieth century, *Weird Tales*—like the Munsey magazines—featured science fiction and scientific romances in its pages, offering tales of interplanetary expeditions, brain transference, death rays, lost races, parallel worlds, and more. Edmond Hamilton was its leading contributor of science fiction. With stories about alien invasions, space police, and evolution gone wild, the author became known as "world-wrecker" Hamilton.

(Cont'd on pg. 17)

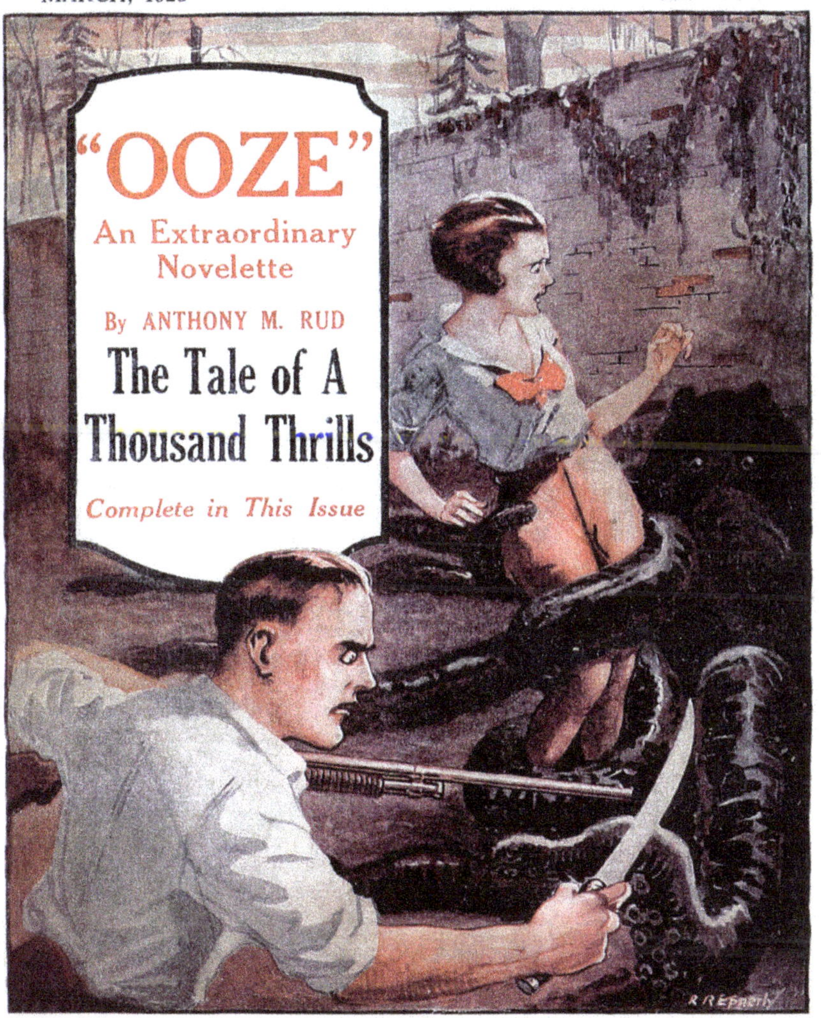

The first issue of *Weird Tales*, dated March 1923, featured cover art by RR Epperly. It is best remembered for publishing Anthony M. Rud's "Ooze," a story concerning a giant amoeba. The issue was edited by Edwin Baird.

Farnsworth Wright's first issue of *Weird Tales* as editor was dated November 1924 *(opposite, top left)*. It's the magazine's second four-color cover, following the "Anniversary Number" of May-June-July 1924. The cover art is by Andrew Brosnatch.

One of the changes that Wright instituted when he took over "The Unique Magazine" in the fall of 1924 was to increase the number of interior illustrations in each issue. According to Terence E. Hanley, writing in *Tellers of Weird Tales*, "Brosnatch illustrated every part of the magazine for the next year and more, sometimes singlehandedly...."

Margaret Brundage *(opposite, top right)* created 66 covers for *Weird Tales* between 1932 and 1945, making her the most in-demand cover artist for the magazine. Only Virgil Finlay was a close rival.

Hannes Bok contributed seven covers to *Weird Tales*, including the May 1940 number *(opposite, bottom right)*, the first issue of the pulp to be edited by Dorothy McIlwraith.

With increasing competition from digest magazines, paperback books, comic books, and more, *Weird Tales* was converted to a digest magazine with its September 1953 issue, with cover art by Jon Arfstrom *(opposite, bottom left)*. It labored on for another year, featuring a mix of reprint fiction and original stories. Three of its final four covers were also reprints.

November 1924

October 1934

September 1953

May 1940

September 1954; reprinted cover art by Virgil Finlay

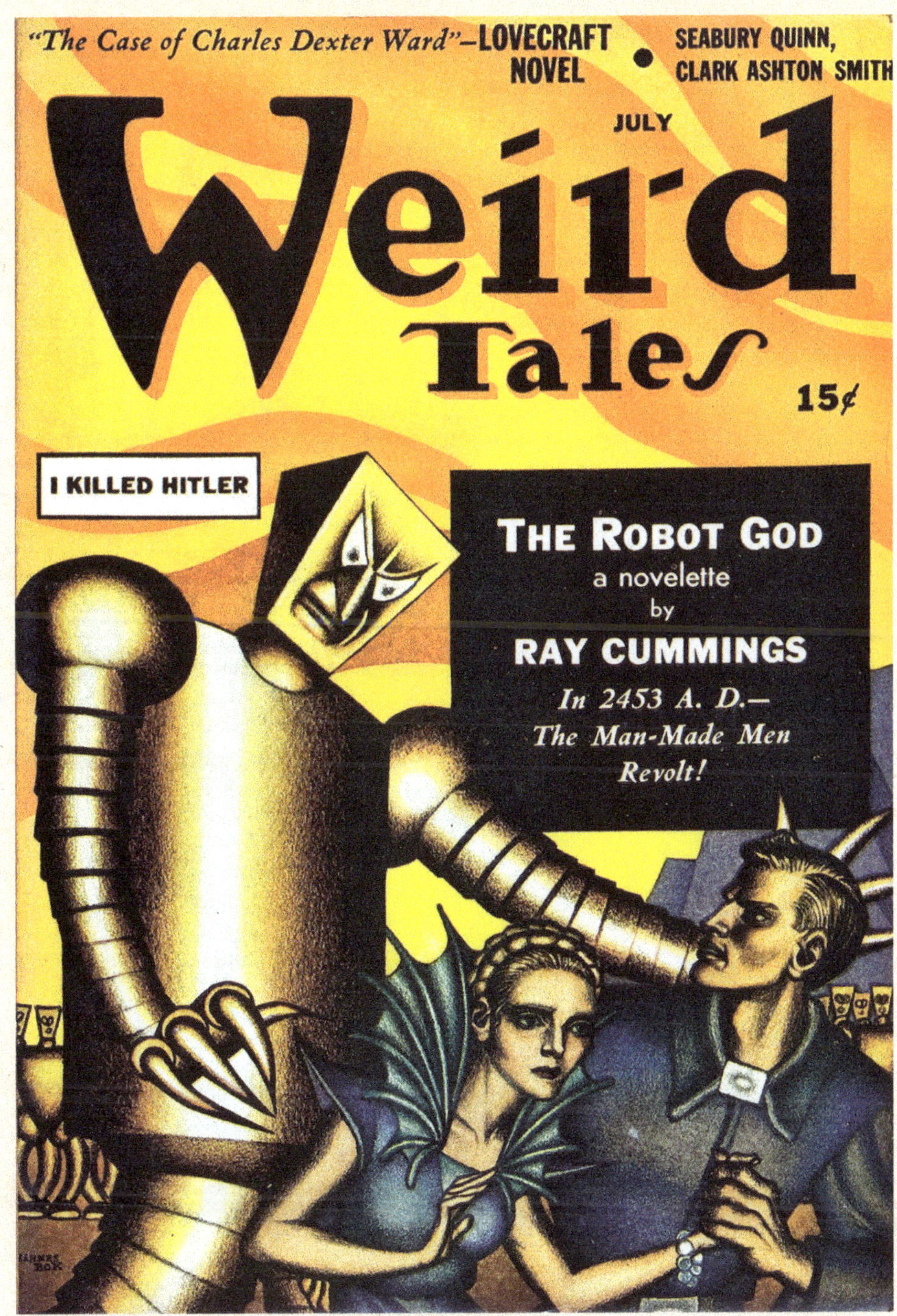

July 1941; cover art by Hannes Bok

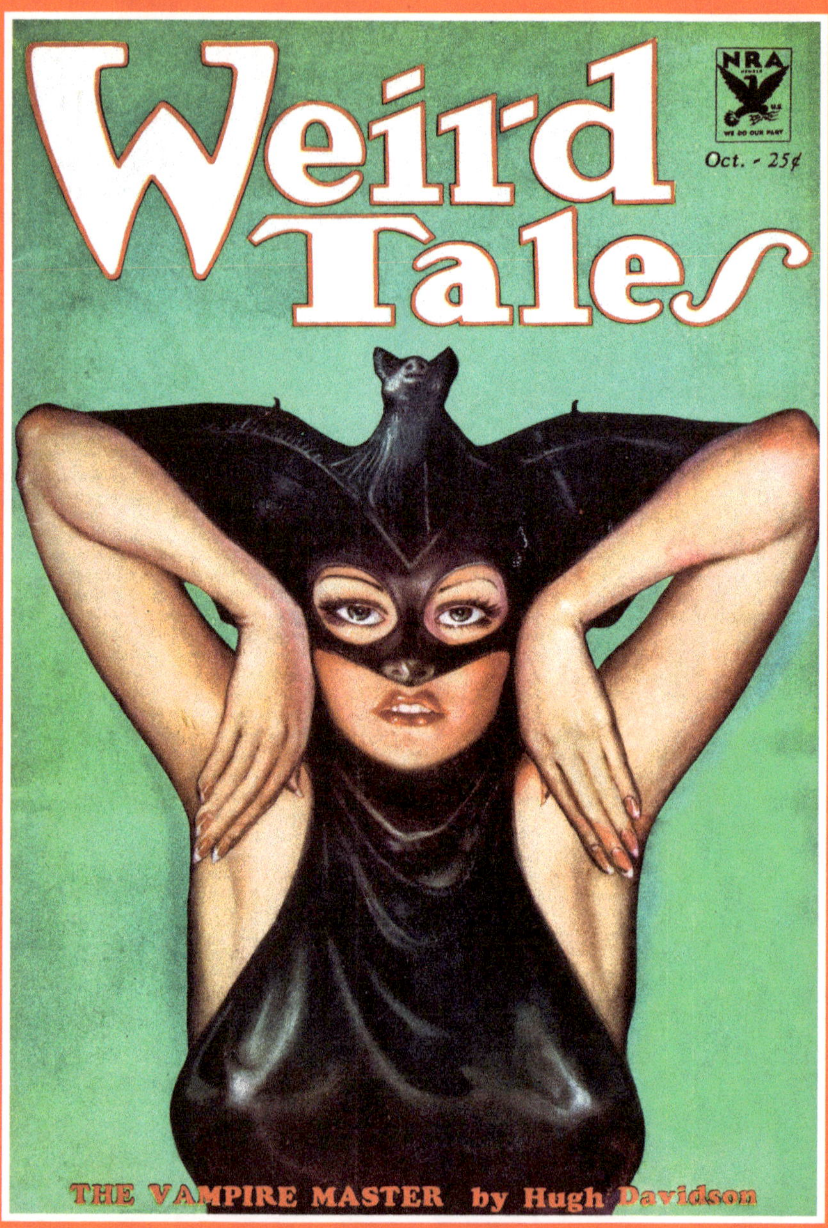

Contributing over five dozen covers to "The Unique Magazine," Margaret Brundage's cover art for the October 1933 *Weird Tales* is probably considered her most iconic image.

(Cont'd from pg. 10)

Other notable science fiction in *Weird Tales* included work by Austin Hall, Otis Adelbert Kline, Frank Belknap Long, CL Moore, Donald Wandrei, and Jack Williamson. And of course, HP Lovecraft spun his own unique style of science fiction in his tales of cosmic horror.

In late 1938, *Weird Tales* was sold to William J. Delaney, publisher of *Short Stories*. The magazine's editorial offices were shifted from Chicago to New York, along with Farnsworth Wright. Dorothy McIlwraith, the editor of *Short Stories*, was named Wright's assistant.

In declining health due to Parkinson's Disease, Wright stepped down from the magazine in early 1940. Now a bi-monthly, McIlwraith's first issue as editor of *Weird Tales* was dated May 1940. Farnsworth Wright died not long after its release.

Like Wright before her, Dorothy McIlwraith continued to publish excellent fantasy and horror fiction, introducing readers to the work of Ray Bradbury, artist Lee Brown Coye, and author Allison V. Harding, as well as some of the early work of Fritz Leiber. Robert Bloch, August Derleth, Edmond Hamilton, Carl Jacobi, Seabury Quinn, and Manly Wade Wellman also continued to contribute significant work to "The Unique Magazine."

Facing increased competition, *Weird Tales* became a digest magazine with its September 1953 issue. One year later, the final number of its original run—the last of 279 issues—was published. It was dated September 1954 and featured a reprint cover by Virgil Finlay.

Nearly twenty years after its initial demise, "The Unique Magazine" became "The Magazine That Never Dies."

During 1973–74, *Weird Tales* was revived for four issues, edited by Sam Moskowitz. A paperback series lasting four more issues—edited by Lin Carter—appeared from 1981 to 1983. During 1984–85, Brian Forbes published two issues of what has become known as the California *Weird Tales*. The magazine was revived again in 1988 by George H. Scithers, Darrell Schweitzer, and John Gregory Betancourt. Since then, it has, more or less, been published continuously. The 367th issue was recently released. Learn more at **WeirdTalesMagazine.com**.

A century after its debut, *Weird Tales* continues to inspire writers, artists, film directors, and other creators in important ways. You can't get much more "Unique" than that!

November 1944; cover art by Matt Fox

WEASELS RIPPED THEIR FLESH!

by Stefan Dziemianowicz

TO MOST readers with even a glancing knowledge of the men's adventure magazines (aka MAMs) of the 1950s, '60s and '70s, the phrase "Weasels Ripped My Flesh"—a cover line from the September 1956 issue of *Man's Life* that became a popular meme after Frank Zappa borrowed it for an album title—epitomizes the contents of many stories in those publications: purportedly "true" stories of intrepid adventurers engaged in death-defying struggles against outrageously exaggerated threats both natural and unnatural. But sometimes, as the contents of the book you are now holding demonstrate, the tales published in MAMs crossed over the line into even weirder territory.

The heyday of the men's adventure magazines—sometimes referred to as "sweat magazines," or just "sweats"—was the quarter century following the end of World War II that encompassed both the Korean and Vietnam Wars. Not coincidentally this interval coincides with the decline of the pulp fiction magazines, which for much of the first half of the twentieth century entertained their mostly male readers with all sorts of genre fare—mystery, western, horror, fantasy, and science fiction—as well as stories of exotic adventures in far-flung locales tailor-made to titillate their armchair-traveling audience. The rise of comic books, mass-market paperbacks, and television programming made serious inroads with the audience that the pulps once catered to and, by the early 1950s, only a handful still survived.

Some pulp publishers with the strongest survival instincts pivoted nimbly. Speculating that returning war veterans and the burgeoning postwar "guy" culture were still hungry for the sort of red-blooded adventures that the pulps had provided, several of the longest lived of all pulp magazines—

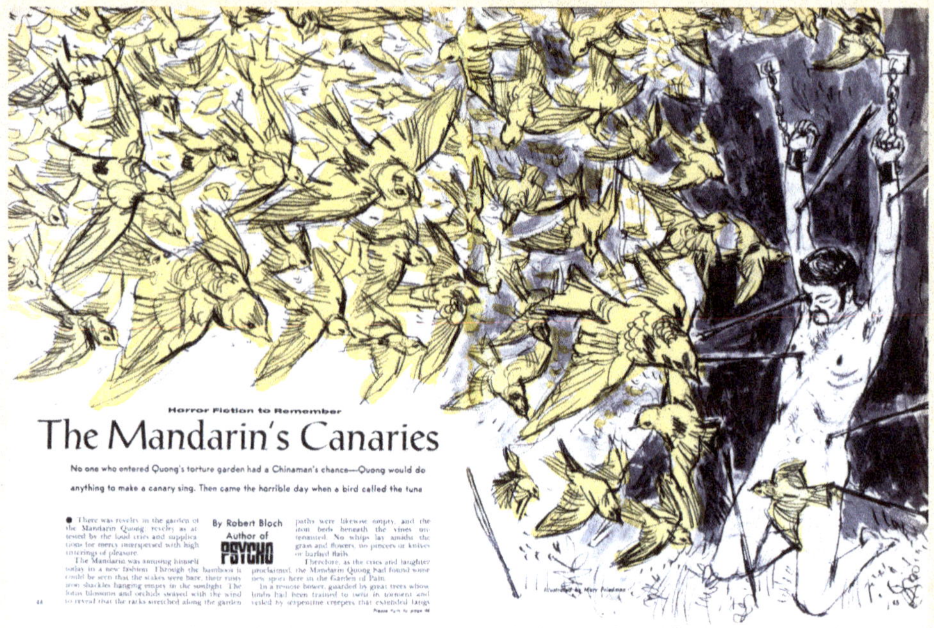

"The Mandarin's Canaries" by Robert Bloch
Art by Marv Friedman
CAVALIER, December 1960

Adventure, Argosy, and Blue Book—morphed into men's adventure magazines, the new genre that emerged in the early 1950s. Periodicals in the MAM genre still had fiction stories, but also featured true (and faux "true") action and adventure stories, cheesecake photos, and news-style non-fiction articles and exposés. In this way, they were able to compete with the tsunami of newly minted men's adventure magazines washing over the newsstands—although they might have seemed less recognizable to the readership that had sustained them up to that point.

Not all pulp magazines were as fortunate. A case in point is *Weird Tales*, the last surviving weird fiction pulp, which gave up the ghost with its September 1954 issue, after having cultivated a readership for tales of the strange and supernatural for more than thirty years. Everybody who was anybody in horror and fantasy fiction in the early twentieth century—HP Lovecraft, Robert E. Howard, Clark Ashton Smith, Robert Bloch, Ray Bradbury, Henry Kuttner, CL Moore, Manly Wade Wellman, and others—logged appearances in *Weird Tales*. Its discontinuation punched a hole in the weird fiction market, but the magazine left a legacy that kept its memory alive. Several writers who had contributed to it over the decades—among

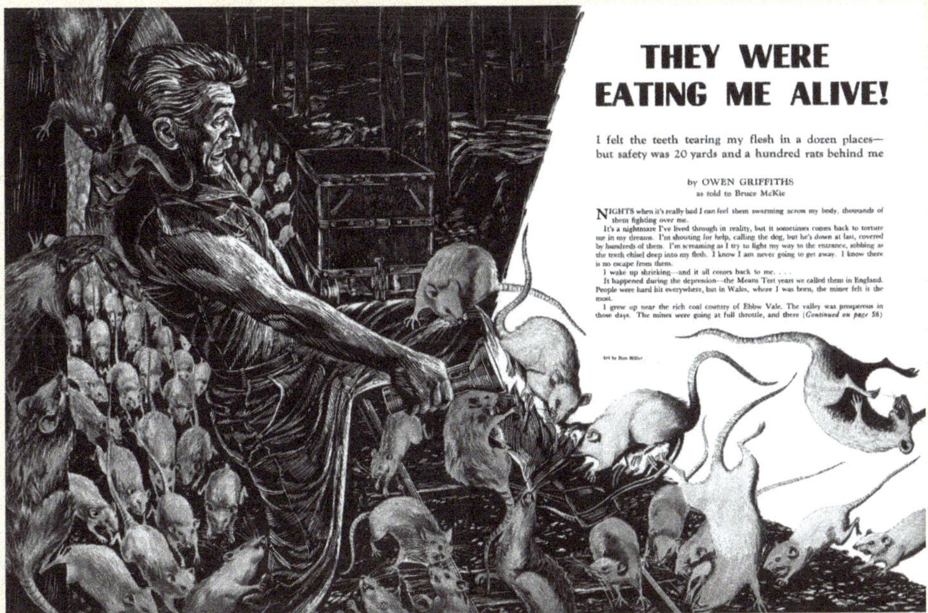

"They Were Eating Me Alive!" by Bruce McKie
Art by Don Miller
MEN, November 1957

them Arthur J. Burks and Thorp McClusky—would find a second home for
their work in the men's adventure market.

Perhaps more important, *Weird Tales* engendered a mindset about a
particular type of story that publishers did not find inconsistent with the
tone and temperament of the contents of their MAMs. Before you analyze
that observation too deeply, put yourself in the place of a hard-working editor laboring not only to vary the contents of his monthly men's adventure
magazine—or *magazines*, since several editors usually helmed more than
one at a time—but to set that issue apart from the scores of similar magazines competing with it at the newsstands. Their different titles notwith-
standing, many MAMs—like many of the pulps that preceded them—were
pretty much all cut from the same cloth. Many MAM stories were presented largely as first-person accounts of physically torturous near-escapes
from a variety of wild perils: Nazi sadists, communist captors, Amazonian
female cults, ravenous cannibals, carnivorous flora, jungle gorillas, hungry
sharks, man-eating turtles, and other specimens of exotic wildlife. Often the
narrators of these tales recalled the horror of watching their companions
succumb to the very threats that they themselves barely escaped. Nearly

all of these stories were chock-full of outrageous exaggerations—and that dramatic excess tended to level the playing field for how memorable the contents of any one magazine would seem compared to those of another. Might some editors have thought that the best way to set their monthly issues apart from the competitors was to push the envelope with stories that veered into the strange and fantastic?

One way for a MAM editor to do this was to trawl the vast archive of tales that had appeared years earlier in the pulps. Second serial rights to stories that originated decades earlier in *Weird Tales* and other fantasy magazines facilitated reprints of stories by Bradbury, Bloch, and even HP Lovecraft (who likely would have been appalled) in *Cavalier, Fury, Sensation, Zest,* and similar venues. Manly Wade Wellman's "The Song of the Slaves," reprinted here from the April 1959 issue of *Cavalier,* was first published in the March 1940 issue of *Weird Tales.* It doesn't take much analysis to under-stand why this story was selected to appear in one of the more prestigious men's adventure magazines of the day. Its premise—an American slave ship that dumps its human cargo overboard to avoid prosecution by the pursuing Royal Navy—had a foothold in historical fact. And the fates suffered by its victims and villain were gruesome enough to appeal to those with the palate for sensation that MAMs catered to.

Theodore Sturgeon was another contributor to *Weird Tales,* but his story "The Blonde with the Mysterious Body," reprinted here from the April 1962 issue of *Men,* first appeared in the March 1957 issue of magazine *Gal-axy Science Fiction*—only don't go looking for it under that title. Sturgeon originated this well-known story as "The Other Celia," and its retitling reveals a strategy applied to other reprints in the men's adventure maga-zines: if you can't change the content of the story to align with the tenor of the magazine, then at least change the title. Sturgeon's tale, about a kinky boarding-house tenant whose voyeuristic proclivities uncover a secret about the woman in the room below him, surely tickled the fancies of readers who wanted to believe, as he writes, that "within the anthill in which we all live and have our being, enough privacy can be gotten for all sorts of strange-ness, providing the strangeness doesn't show." Perhaps more important, the inclusion of Sturgeon's tale (and others in this volume) show that MAM editors did not consider science fiction an outlier genre, as it had been treat-ed in trade publishing for most of the early twentieth century. In America's immediate postwar years science fiction experienced an explosive popularity, with a glut of mostly short-lived magazines invading the newsstands, and the adventure magazines clearly were not hesitant to try and tap a market that resonated with many of their readers.

Those magazines didn't just reprint science fiction stories—they also

"The Rocket Man" by Ray Bradbury
Art by James Bingham
ARGOSY, February 1952

originated them. Dane Marshall's "Their Bodies Glowed with Fire," from the December 1961 issue of *Peril,* is a tale of first contact with extraterrestrials that reminds us the flying saucer craze was very much a part of our cultural zeitgeist in the 1950s and '60s. (If that angle wasn't original enough at the time for the magazine in which it appeared, consider that the story also is narrated by a disgruntled army vet who happens to be a Native American.)

Three of this book's science fiction selections—"The Man Who Couldn't Die" by Gardner Fox (another *Weird Tales* alumnus), "The Hunted," by Rick Rubin, and "Killer of the Cave" by Gene Preen—all were first published in *Adventure,* a magazine whose original pulp pedigree extended back to 1910. Although the contents of *Adventure* were devoted predominantly to tales of daring and intrigue, usually set in exotic foreign locales, in 1920 the magazine coined the term "off trail" as a designation for the occasional story that strayed outside the boundaries of realism. (The term "science fiction" would not come into vogue for at least another half-decade and over the years *Adventure* published a handful of distinguished fantastic tales, among them it's first "off trail" offering,

TS Stribling's "The Green Splotches," which became a much reprinted science fiction classic throughout the twentieth century.) *Adventure* had pretty much scrapped the "off trail" categorization by the 1960s, but these three stories are very much in the spirit of what that categorization was code for.

"Killer of the Cave" is an especially interesting story, given that it is set in a post-apocalyptic landscape whose horrors reflect American anxieties of the dawning nuclear age. Its plot (no spoilers given here) is straight out of a science fiction B-movie—so it should come as no surprise that the illustration for the story's opening splash-page spread, adapted as the cover art for the hardcover edition of this book, was provided by Basil Gogos, who also provided cover art regularly for *Famous Monsters of Filmland*, a magazine launched in 1958 to celebrate classic monster movies as well as new horror and science fiction movies opening soon at a theater near you.

Indeed, several of the stories collected in this volume are very evocative of monster movies pumped out for the drive-in movie circuit of the day, among them Rick Manners' "Strange Cult of the Vampire Tarantulas" from the September 1962 issue of *Peril*, and Bill Wharton's "Island of Doom" from the Spring 1957 issue of *Sports Trails*. Both are giant critter stories that have their cinematic analogues in such monster movies as *Tarantula, The Giant Gila Monster,* and similar B-movie fare. If anything the editors of the men's adventure magazines appear to have had an acute awareness of the popular culture that their publications were influenced by, and influencing.

The stories gathered for this volume show the sort of variety and versatility that imaginative writers brought to the MAM genre. Take "The Flag of the Stonewall Brigade" (*Action*, March 1953). It's a ghost story set at the height of the Korean war, but author Ronald Adamson cleverly thought to introduce the supernatural into it through an artifact from the American Civil War—*i.e.*, another war that pitted armies of a country's North and South against one another. For "Fowl Play" (*Escape to Adventure*, May 1962) William Bayne eschews the traditional first-person narrative style of the true adventure story to allow the reader to view its events through the eyes of a character acting under the influence of personal psychological distress.

Lewis Greer's "Vampires Ripped My Flesh" originally appeared in the September 1962 issue of *Man's Life*—the same magazine responsible for the story "Weasels Ripped My Flesh"—but six years later. Its title didn't achieve the renown of its predecessor, but the story epitomizes the way in which authors for the men's magazines found leverage in the raw materials for their man-versus-nature stories to elevate them to the level of horror. Martin Bowers's "Soft Nudes for the Nazis' Doctor Horror" shows just how outrageous such stories could become, with its depiction of grotesque

"The Mummy That Came Alive" by Paul Ilton
Art by John Leone
MAN'S WORLD, May 1957

experiments performed by a mad Mengelian Nazi doctor who also shows a fascination with shrunken head practices of South Sea cannibal cultures.

Most of the stories in this book are seeing their first light of day since their original magazine appearances, which begs the question why they aren't better known. The answer is relatively simple: most readers—even devoted readers of weird fiction—didn't know of these stories' existence. Credit editors Robert Deis and Wyatt Doyle with performing an extraordinary act of archeological excavation from magazines whose contents remain under-recognized, under-indexed, and therefore largely under-appreciated more than a half-century after their heyday. That said, at least one story included in this volume enjoyed a second act. George Venner's "Her Body Belonged to the Devil," from the December 1961 issue of *Man's Life*, was reprinted a decade later in the June 1971 issue of *Horror Stories*, a short-lived publication helmed by Theodore S. Hecht, the same editor who oversaw the contents of *Man's Life*. There may be more such instances of weird tales from the men's adventure magazines being picked up and recirculated elsewhere without the knowledge of the genre's most dedicated bibliographers. Thankfully, this volume allows readers to appreciate the stories brought to light in their original glory.

June 1938; cover art by Margaret Brundage

A TURN FOR THE WEIRD

by Wyatt Doyle and Robert Deis

MEN'S ADVENTURE magazines—MAMs—those manly post-WWII periodicals known for "true" exotic adventure, crime and war stories, and yarns
about flesh-ripping weasels and sadistic Nazis—were often wild and weird.
But few know that you can find many stories in MAMs published in the
1950s, 1960s and 1970s that are even wilder and weirder than their usual
fare: stories about evil cults, vampires, aliens and robots, ghosts, plants with
a taste for humans, and other things that would have fit right in the classic
pulp magazine *Weird Tales*.

Those whose awareness of MAMs comes primarily from cover scans
circulated online or via parodies of these vintage mags can be forgiven
for their narrow perception of their contents. But in fact, MAMs, partly
descended from pre-WWII pulps, cast a wide net in their efforts to attract
and entertain readers. Many MAMs covered a little bit of everything in an
effort to appeal to the widest possible readership.

In part, this was because they faced a lot of competition on newsstands,
from other types of magazines and from other publishers' MAMs. To seize
the attention of potential readers, editors and art directors pulled out all the
stops when it came to content and cover art. These magazines were impulse
buys, and publishers catered to readers' impulses—aggressively. Think of
them like old-school wanna-buy-a-watch? street hustlers, determined to
catch your eye (and the contents of your wallet) with trinkets dangling
inside their coats, ready to accommodate any desire or passing fancy—from
cheap jewelry to naughty postcards to a slightly used .38, only fired once…

That dedication to variety meant features about dangerous adventures
in exotic places bumped shoulders with tough, graphic accounts of military

battles. News of a salacious celebrity scandal might be followed by a hard-boiled heist story. Non-fiction sex advice for the modest and unsure could be sandwiched between a man-alone-on-an-island-of-women yarn and a harrowing tale of some lethal air disaster. And somewhere in the mix there were pin-up photospreads and straight-shooting consumer advice on how to not get screwed buying a used car. If any one of those features piqued your curiosity (MAM publishers figured), there's a good chance you might pick the magazine up and take a look. Should more than one of those features catch your interest? You might just cough up the two bits or 35 cents to take it home. There was no surer confirmation of *mission accomplished* like the ring of the cash register.

So while it may at first blush seem unexpected to find *Weird Tales*-style tales in MAMs, it shouldn't come as a complete surprise. Weird tales were simply another option at the MAM buffet table. And like other kinds of fiction in MAMs (action, war, exotic adventure, crime, noir…) they came in numerous varieties and were presented in diverse styles, ranging from pitch-black and unsentimental to playful, even comic.

MAMs positioned themselves as places where readers could get the straight dope on confusing and complex issues, delivered with a barracks-room familiarity, in a man-to-man tone. Editorial voices in MAMs spoke with authority, but never talked down to their audience. Never mind that MAMs played fast and loose with facts and definitions of "true," or that most of the time writers were making it up as they went.

What's more, most mainstream news sources didn't have much to say about some of the fringe subjects of male curiosity MAMs covered, like cryptids (Bigfoot and other legendary creatures), UFOs, or dark, mysterious activities like voodoo or devil worship. (Not to mention addressing—and also stoking—readers' fears and uncertainty about anti-social trends like biker gangs, landscape-altering cultural phenomena, and unconventional sexuality.) Weird stuff was of interest to male readers; they had questions, and MAMs endeavored to supply answers. Whether readers' interest was deep and committed or merely passing curiosity, MAMs sought to accommodate them.

Sometimes weird fiction in MAMs meant reprints of older stories by popular or notable writers that were presented as classics of their kind. Sometimes they were existing stories that fit particularly well with other kinds of MAM fiction. And sometimes they were new works commissioned by editors, stories that tailored weird events and phenomena to better suit the MAM setting.

This anthology collects some of our favorite and most representative weird tales from MAMs' three decades on American newsstands.

"The Flag of the Stonewall Brigade" by Ronald Adamson (likely a pseudonym) merges two popular MAM subjects, the American Civil War and the Korean conflict, into a single narrative, then folds in an unconventional ghost story for good measure. MAM fiction often stacked popular elements in a single story as a means to goose dusty plots, but even so, the appearance of a heroic ghost brigade was hardly typical. Today the idea of Confederate soldiers rising from the grave for a final act of wartime heroism would be seen as rather more circumspect, as would the notion that members of the Confederacy would be eager to aid soldiers standing for the nation they sought to separate from. But 1953 was another time, when the events of 1861 through 1865 were seen by many through a markedly different lens.

"When the Vampire Was Captured" by Ward Semple follows an often-employed template. Not that vampire stories turned up all that frequently, and granted, some of the story's details are less hard-boiled than straight out of Bram Stoker. But the idea of digging up an unusual, shocking, and violent historical event and retelling it for a contemporary readership was standard operating procedure for MAMs; it's only unusual in that there is a supernatural creature involved. (That this story, like most vampire tales, has an undercurrent of sexual menace would only make it a more appealing choice to a MAM editor.)

(Cont'd on pg. 32)

Stefan Dziemianowicz: *"Reviewing stories by* Weird Tales *writers that appeared in MAMs, I noted Robert Bloch's 'Curtain Call' in the January 1961 issue of* Fury. *I've delved a lot into Bloch's work and was unfamiliar with this title—until I realized that this*

"Curtain Call" by Robert Bloch
Art by Jack Davis (uncredited)
FURY, January 1961

is his story 'Final Performance,' which appeared originally in the crime digest Shock *in September 1960. Its appearance as 'Curtain Call' has escaped the notice of even Bloch's most dedicated bibliographers. Makes me wonder how many more instances like this are lurking in MAMs...."*

Here's another major find, in the same story: We contend the uncredited illustration is by the late, great Jack Davis. Justly celebrated for decades of memorable cartooning in *Mad*, his weird bona fides run deep, most notably his pioneering contributions to the iconic and controversial EC comics of the 1950s, among them *Tales from the Crypt*, *The Vault of Horror*, and *The Haunt of Fear*. His *You'll Die Laughing* monster trading cards from 1959 are highly prized, and his poster for the UK chiller *City of the Dead* under the US title *Horror Hotel* (1960) is among the most unnerving and imitated designs of the era. Artist Ron Cobb adapted one of the ghouls' faces for the cover of *Famous Monsters* #40 in 1966; it was later swiped and reworked to promote 1971's *I Drink Your Blood*.

WHEN THE VAMPIRE WAS CAPTURED

Jean Jacques Rousseau, one of France's great philosophers wrote: "If there ever was in the world a warranted and proven history, it is that of vampires; nothing is lacking, official reports, testimonials of persons of standing, of surgeons, of clergymen, of judges, the judicial evidence is all embracing."

BY WARD SEMPLE

CROGLING Grange in England is a rambling, one story house with a sweep of well kept lawn which stretches to a field of trees that separates the Grange from an ancient church and cemetery. It has been in the Fisher family for centuries. The latest owners, for reasons of their own, rented the Grange to two brothers and a sister and left for the south of England.

In this undramatic way starts one of the world's most weird vampire histories. It was told by Capt. Frederick Fisher, whose family owned Croglin Grange, to August Hare, England's famous writer and traveller. In his six volume "Story of My Life", Hare tells of the Croglin vampire. Since the incidents involved innocent persons who were liked by their neighbors,

ILLUSTRATED BY DWIGHT HOWE

(Cont'd from pg. 29)

Other than the story's gory duotone (two color) splash pages by artist Dwight Howe, with its gush of purple blood from the vampire's stake wound, supplementary illustrations are mostly cribbed reprints from vintage sources. That was another favorite MAM device that not only supplied an air of verisimilitude, but also allowed art directors to illustrate stories without commissioning (and paying for) new work. And of course, if an even slightly racy image from the archives (like this story's inclusion of silent movie starlet Theda Bara posing with a skeleton, an antique image even in 1953) could be shoehorned in, it was—even if the image's captioner had to twist logic into knots to justify its inclusion.

"Vampires Ripped My Flesh" by Lewis Greer (a pseudonym) purports to be a first-hand account of an emerald hunter's alarming, near lethal encounter with some of nature's most menacingly named creatures. Now *this* is what so many readers think of when they think of MAMs: man versus nature! (This story predates the famed "Weasels Ripped My Flesh" yarn from *Man's Life* that Frank Zappa borrowed for an album title by six months. Indeed, quite a few MAM stories had similar titles.) And while MAMs trafficked regularly in killer creature horror, it wasn't necessarily viewed or presented as horror *per se*. Animal attack stories emerged as an extension of hunting stories and tales of outdoor adventure and survival taken to their logical (well, perhaps *ill*ogical) extreme. If a creature walked, crawled, swam, or flew, MAM writers figured out a way for them to organize and turn against man. MAMs looked to the defining work of Jack London, Ernest Hemingway, and others, stripped away all literary trappings and pretense, then turned up the volume; thus was wilderness adventure mutated into what can fairly be described as incognito horror fiction.

As a rule, MAM fiction of this stripe is not macho, chest-thumping stuff with square-jawed heroes conquering all. Readers seemed to welcome excess in most areas, but according to MAM writer Robert F. Dorr (whose stories are featured in our *A Handful of Hell* collection), they had little patience for that kind of puffery. Instead, MAM animal attack fiction offers detailed, harrowing expressions of fear, panic, mutilation, and fatalism. Among the likely reasons animal attack stories and this approach to them proved so popular and enduring in MAMs is their power as metaphor. With most MAM readers (most American males, really) veterans of WWII, Korea, and later Vietnam, there was something in these stories that spoke very clearly to that readership, and even the increasing outrageousness of animal characterizations (lethal flying squirrels? killer pangolins?) and the sometimes repetitive nature of the narratives were not enough to distract from their arresting premise and the graphic intensity of the prose, which never winks to the reader, nor descends into intentional camp.

Vampires Ripped My Flesh

I felt their sharp teeth, and my blood trickling down my body. Some of the bats were in my hair, others hung from my skin. I was in a cave filled with flying death!

by LEWIS GREER

THE fetid heat of the jungle rolled up into the high ground at dusk, clawing our throats, soaking us, robbing us of our last strength, Caymen and I. But we ran to the high ground, ran frantically, tripping headlong into the stinking green morass and rising and running again. But we made it to the high ground above the Carare River and we were out, and so were the emeralds. A million dollars worth of green ice for the two of us.

My khakis were shreaded at the ankles from the sharp tugging of the tall grass; my hands were raw and oozing thick rivulets of blood; my face felt heavy with the grotesqueness of panic, and the poison of before. But I was alive and death was behind me, I thought. I lay on the hot red ground, too weary to speak, too tired to look down the canyon for the Indians. Indians and more Indians.

I lay there an eternity and the exhaustion swallowed me and I felt the heat waves lifting my body. And I slept. Like a dead man. And Caymen did, too. But Caymen woke first and when I opened my eyes and saw he was gone, I thought the emeralds had gone with him.

I'D never distrusted Luke Caymen—but that time was different. After what we'd gone through—the blood—sweat—tears and death—I'd suspect my own grandmother. Frantically I lurched to my feet and spun up the rise and I saw Caymen there, on his knees, praying.

When I dropped to the ground beside him, Caymen ended his supplication and turned to me and grinned.

"So you're awake? You see, it was just as I said it would be. We're alive. Two more days and we're back in Bogota and we're rich!" Caymen said.

"Do we travel at night, Caymen?"

"Yes. Indians prefer the daylight hours. We travel at night."

"Okay," I said, seeing the exhaustion on his coppery face. "How do we do it—on our hands and knees?"

Caymen smiled. He knew we needed rest. Three days ago we'd begun the trek. Three years ago, so it seemed. Then, the chonta spears began falling and the original five, dwindled to two.

Below us sprawled the rushing white waters of the Carare and to a side on the far bank rocks. Caymen indicated the rocks with a nod.

"There," he grunted, "are the caves. We go there. If we remain on the high ground they'll come up soon. I figure we'll fool them. They'll never look up there. Backtrack. And right now. We'll be safe in the caves," he nodded.

But Caymen was wrong—dead wrong, almost, because what happened next made the spears of the savages seem hardly more than a bad hangover. What happened next happened slowly and bloodily and it robbed us of our Muzo treasure. And more—much more, including sanity itself. Mine and Luke Caymen's. . .

ON the 12th day of March, 1946, we made our strike. It happened late in the afternoon of a day that had started out most unfortunately for me. a moderately poisonous mountain snake caught me in the calf of my right leg.

I'd been in the Columbian jungles almost seven months scratching the hills above the Carare, digging for emeralds. Seven months of sheer backbreaking labor because, among other things, we—Caymen and I—were borrowed up to our eyeballs in order to keep our operation rolling.

Worse yet, our crews were constantly threatening to quit. Indian trouble. The fatal kind. Repeatedly we were harried by sporadic attacks on our mountain excavation—attacks that came suddenly with the whizzing of spears, or the sharp sing of the arrows. And always there were dead men in the wake of these attacks, and more men quick to quit. Seven months of that and I sprouted the neatest crop of gray sideburns this side of Bogota.

But, somehow, I'd always managed to come away from those deadly encounters alive and with a whole skin. I can't say why. Maybe it was luck; maybe the Indians had lousy vision; maybe they were saving us for a worse fate than the poisoned splinter.

I wondered about that for seven long months, day in and day out. I saw men sliced down the middle, split like stuck pigs by machetes that lanced through the jungle, thrown by unseen hands. I saw a lot of things that came under the general heading of horror but as I'd guessed, the worst was yet to come.

ORIGINALLY, Luke and I were pearl dusters in Mexico. Luke, whose mother was Spanish and his father Columbian, spoke the language, naturally. He was my voice, and, on many occasions, my life saver. We'd done service together in the old China fleet, running the Yangtse on a gunboat. The Navy agreed with us; we were shipmates and we had plans.

When World War II broke out, Luke and I got separated and we didn't meet again until the day I mustered out at Mare Island Naval Base. That was in May, 1945, I met Luke standing against the bar in the St. Francis Hotel in San Francisco. There, in an atmosphere of gushing whiskey, we formulated our weird plan. Next morning when I awoke, Luke met me down in the coffee shop and we rehashed the bit of the previous evening. Not the whiskey part—not just then. Just the part about the pearls Luke said he knew were ripe for plucking.

That's how it was. From Pearls with a capital P, we poured a thumping 70 thousand into men, materiel, engineers and a lot of bum advice. We listened to talk that the Muzo treasure was as available as our pearls had been. Muzo as in Spanish Conquistadores!

SEVEN long months slipped by and the only emerald I'd seen to date was down in the government assaying office in Bogota. I awoke that morning feeling lousy. I stepped out of our tent, and climbed down the grade to the chow house. I stumbled sleepily against a boulder and caught it—a searing pain in my right leg.

"Bad?" Luke said, running down.

"Bad enough!"

Luke tore my pants leg and made the incision. Then he gave me a shot of snake serum and stuck me back in the sack. Fever raged through my body until nightfall, and I swelled so I could barely breathe. But I lived, thanks to Luke Caymen, and that night my world took on a new lustre.

I was still in my bunk when I heard Luke shouting, and the other men with picks hollering like maniacs. I forgot the snake bite. I crawled out of the sack and literally slid down the grade on my hands and knees. They were too confounded crazy with joy to worry about me—the four of them (Continued on page 72)

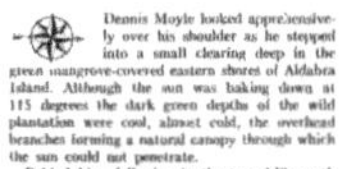

Dennis Moyle looked apprehensively over his shoulder as he stepped into a small clearing deep in the green mangrove-covered eastern shores of Aldabra Island. Although the sun was baking down at 115 degrees the dark green depths of the wild plantation were cool, almost cold, the overhead branches forming a natural canopy through which the sun could not penetrate.

Behind him, following in the tunnel-like path which he had hacked through the jungle, he heard his two companions, Vic Lister and Ed Hammett, moving toward him, but it wasn't their sounds that Moyle heard. It was a heavy, almost stertorous breathing which seemed to emanate from the dense bush ahead of him.

Beyond the bush, maybe another twenty or thirty yards farther on, rose the craggy peak they had set out to see.

Moyle's hand rested lightly on the .38 revolver in the holster on his hip as he turned his six-foot frame toward the entrance which he had chopped through the undergrowth. A curly blond head appeared and Lister stepped into the clearing. Behind him came Hammett, sweating profusely.

"What's wrong, Dennis?" Hammett asked at once.

"I don't know," Moyle replied in a quiet voice. "Just keep quiet for a moment and listen."

As the three men stood silent they heard the heavy breathing and without any warning the slope facing them seemed to come alive. There was a violent rumbling like that of an avalanche; the ground shook underfoot, branches brushed them as trees were shaken.

Gradually the rumbling noise decreased until it faded altogether. For another few moments the men stood listening, then Moyle wiped his forehead.

"Let's go," he (Continued on page 81)

The three men crouched in the dense brush, hardly daring to breathe, while the monster rumbled steadily toward them.

It's a cinch to find the fortune on Aldabra. The trick is getting out—alive.

ISLAND OF DOOM

By Bill Wharton
ILLUSTRATED BY MORTON SHORE

In addition to suffering their own mutilation, stories' protagonists witness friends, lovers, rivals, and strangers fall victim to brutality, dismemberment, and agonizing death. And though the narrator might emerge alive to tell the tale, the trauma is life-altering and leaves deep scars, both physical and psychological, which the narration recognizes and acknowledges.

The parallels between such stories and wartime trauma are apparent, and it's long been our contention that animal attack stories and their consistent popularity with MAM readers was linked to postwar trauma for many, with the stories serving as an unexpected coping tool, whether readers were consciously aware of it or not. We make no argument that editors and writers were acting intentionally in this, only that they sought to understand what "their guys" wanted to read, and kept it coming.

BILL WHARTON, author of **"Island of Doom,"** was a regular contributor to MAMs such as *Action For Men, Combat, Action Life, Stag, For Men Only, Outdoor Adventures,* and *Man's Magazine.* He wrote for bachelor mags like *Rogue* and *Adam.* (His stories were also printed in an Australian bachelor mag named *Man,* which was reprinted in the US, but was not widely known.) Additionally, his work appeared in *Fate,* the long-running magazine devoted to stories about supernatural and occult topics. He wrote at least one novel, *The Real 007.*

There isn't much plot to "Island of Doom," making it more interesting for what it doesn't say—particularly Wharton's unwillingness to define the monstrous menace at its center too clearly, leaving much of the heavy lifting to the reader's imagination. Just what the hell *are* the unstoppable 15-foot reptiles that menace the small band of men, anyway? Even the illustration by Morton Engel shows us very little. Odds are Wharton was hoping what few, vague details he did supply ("resembling a dragon but more likely a giant iguana") would catch in the reader's brain somewhere near half-recalled information about Komodo dragons and tall tales suggesting relict species of dinosaur may yet survive in remote, unexplored locales.

One of the convenient aspects of MAM fiction focusing on creatures from the realm of cryptozoology or unexplained phenomena is that writers didn't have to definitively prove any of their stories' claims, nor resolve plots in a conventional manner. Instead, they could wrap things up with convenient "one never knows…" editorializing, or "I know what I saw!" claims from the mouth of the narrator/survivor.

With so much MAM fiction presented as true accounts, writers availed themselves of speed-plotting techniques that cut the narrative short in ways that would be unacceptable in traditional fiction, but get a pass in faux non-fiction. Here the initial narrative drops off suddenly, to be bolstered by similar fabricated bits of island lore—first from an earlier century, then from only a few decades prior—chronicling grislier encounters with the beasts that led to human fatalities. Thus, "Island of Doom" offers three incomplete versions of what is essentially the same narrative, merged into

TRAPPED BY A MAN-EATING TREE

Crippling pains shot up my legs as long sticky arms curled around me. I hacked at the poisonous vines that were picking me up—It was going to swallow me whole!

by OSCAR SCHNEE (Lt. Ret. RDN)
AS TOLD TO ROBERT MOORE

CELEB fishermen call it the devil tree—Rauk Yav. It grows in terrible profusion along the south coast of Makassar. On the Postiljon Islands, especially, cannibal or devil tree, is taboo. No islander will approach within a mile of it. I shouldn't wonder why.

In March, 1943, three of us escaped from the Japanese prison compound at Sumbawa, Dutch East Indies. Ironically, the world is full of redolent islands where the shipwrecked for years have found survival, if not happiness. In the back of three exhausted minds was the hope that Laut, a pearly green thumb of land, would be such a place. We made for it in the wake of a typhoon.

Rudder gone, leaking, we hit the outer bar and capsized finally. More dead than alive, we dragged ourselves up on the hard, white sands—delighted just to be alive and free again. Starvation had emaciated us, yet now, for the first time in nearly thirteen months we had hope. My companions—Johnny Kruman and Paul Doers—and I were naval officers, Royal Dutch Navy.

"Let's scout the upper end. There's some cliffs up there!" Paul Doers suggested right away. "With Oscar's knowledge of signaling, maybe we can raise some friendly native . . ."

ACTUALLY, it was a couple of days before we had strength enough to walk from the beach. For two days we lay in our new- (Continued on page 76)

He hacked with his knife as the green tendrils curled around him, sucking him into the death tree.

a single account and presented under the guise of non-fiction. Creating something big and ominous out of something minor or even something incomplete was a MAM specialty.

VEGETATION with a taste for human flesh has long been part of folklore the world over, leading to many man vs. plant stories in weird pulp fiction, movies, comics, and TV, from *Weird Tales* to *Little Shop of Horrors*. **"Trapped by a Man-Eating Tree"** brought the trope to the March 1958 issue of *Man's Life* in gruesome style. It's credited to "Robert Moore," one of multiple pseudonyms utilized by Robert Moore Williams. Williams penned at least 19 science fiction novels, and was a prolific author of short stories as well. He wrote for pulp magazines from the late 1930s into the 1950s before moving to MAMs, with his work mostly appearing in Crestwood Publications titles such as *Man's Life* and *True Man Stories*. Like "Trapped," about half of his MAM stories follow the popular "as told to" approach, a technique implying that the story has been related to the writer as a first-hand experience by the characters involved. Well, the *surviving* characters, anyway.

"DEAN OF Fantasy" Manly Wade Wellman was *Weird Tales* royalty. He wrote in several popular genres, but is best remembered for his groundbreaking work in fantasy and science fiction.

The Wellman story included here is from *Cavalier*, a magazine that started out as an early top-tier MAM, then over time changed into a

Song of the Slaves

The chained slaves were at the bottom of the ocean—but their terrible chant would not stop until a very special white neck filled the empty collar-shackle

by Manly Wade Wellman

Illustrated by John Leone

Gender paused at the top of the bald rise, mopped his streaming red forehead beneath the wide hat-brim, and gazed backward at his 49 captives. Naked and black, they shuffled upward from the narrow, ancient slave trail through the jungle. Forty-nine men, seized by Gender's own hand and collared to a single long chain, destined for his own plantation across the sea. . . . Gender grinned in his lean, drooping mustache, a mirthless grin of greedy triumph.

For years he had dreamed and planned for this adventure, as other men dream and plan for European tours, holy pilgrimages, or returns to beloved birth places. He had told himself that it was intensely practical and profitable. Slaves passed through so many hands —the raider, the caravaner, the seaborne factor, the slaver captain, the dealer in New Orleans or Havana or at home in Charleston. Each greedy hand clutched a rich profit, and all profits must come eventually from the price paid by the planter. But he, Gender, had come to Africa himself, in his own ship, with a dozen staunch ruffians from Benguela he had penetrated the Bihé-Bailundu country, had sacked a village and taken these 49 upstanding natives between dark and dawn. A single neck [Continued on page 71]

There was only one way to get rid of the evidence. The slaves were chained to the anchor, thrown overboard.

A famous master of the tale of horror
and suspense takes you on a nightmare visit to

the RATS in the WALLS

(Copyright 1923, 1945 by August Derleth and Donald Wandrei. By permission of Arkham House.)

By H. P. Lovecraft

ON JULY 16, 1923, I moved into Exham Priory after the last workman had finished his labors. The restoration had been a stupendous task, for little had remained of the deserted pile but a shell-like ruin; yet because it had been the seat of my ancestors, I let no expense deter me. The place had not been inhabited since the reign of James the First, when a tragedy of intensely hideous, though largely unexplained, nature had struck down the master, five of his children, and several servants; and driven forth under a cloud of suspicion and terror the third son, my lineal progenitor and the only survivor of the abhorred line.

With this sole heir denounced as a murderer, the estate had reverted to the crown, nor had the accused man made any attempt to exculpate himself or regain his property. Shaken by some horror greater than that of conscience or the law, and expressing only a frantic wish to exclude the ancient edifice from his sight and memory, Walter de la Poer, eleventh Baron Exham, fled to Virginia and there founded the family which by the next century had become known as Delapore.

Exham Priory had remained untenanted, though later allotted to the estates of the Norrys family and much studied because of its peculiarly composite architecture; an architecture involving Gothic towers resting on a Saxon or Romanesque substructure, whose foundation in turn was of a still earlier order or blend of orders—Roman, and even Druidic or native Cymric, if legends speak truly. This foundation was a very singular thing, being merged on one side with the solid limestone of the precipice from whose brink the priory overlooked a desolate valley three miles west of the village of Anchester.

Architects and antiquarians loved to examine this strange relic of forgotten centuries, but the country folk hated it. They had hated it hundreds of years before, when my ancestors lived there, and they hated it now, with the moss and mould of abandonment on it. I had not been a day in Anchester before I knew I came of an accursed house. And this week workmen have blown up Exham Priory, and are busy obliterating the traces of its foundations. The bare statistics of my ancestry I had always known, together with the fact that my first American forbear had come to the colonies under a strange cloud. Of details, however, I had been kept wholly ignorant through the policy of reticence always maintained by the Delapores. Unlike our planter neighbors, we seldom boasted of crusading ancestors or other mediaeval and Renaissance heroes; nor was any kind of tradition handed down except what may have been recorded in the sealed envelope left before the Civil War by every squire to his eldest son for posthumous opening. The glories we cherished were those achieved since the migration; the glories of a proud and honorable, if somewhat reserved and unsocial Virginia line.

During the war our fortunes were extinguished and our whole existence changed by the burning of Carfax, our home on the banks of the James. My grandfather, advanced in years, had perished in that incendiary outrage, and with him the envelope that had bound us all to the past. I can recall that fire today as I saw it then at the age of seven, with the Federal soldiers shouting, the women screaming, and the negroes howling and praying. My father was in the army, defending Richmond, and after many formalities my mother and I were passed through the lines to join him.

When the war ended we all moved north, whence my mother had come; and I grew to manhood, middle age, and ultimate wealth as a stolid Yankee. Neither my father nor I ever knew what our hereditary envelope had contained, and as I merged into the greyness of Massachusetts business life I lost all interest in the mysteries which evidently lurked far back in my family tree. Had I suspected their nature, how gladly I would have left Exham Priory to its moss, bats, and cobwebs!

My father died in 1904, but without any message to leave to me, or to my only child, Alfred, a motherless boy of ten. It was this boy who reversed the order of family information, for although I could give him only jesting conjectures about the past, he wrote me of some very interesting ancestral legends when the late war took him to England in 1917 as an aviation officer. Apparently the Delapores had a colorful and perhaps sinister history, for a friend of my son's, Capt. Edward Norrys of the Royal Flying Corps, dwelt near the family seat at Anchester and related some peasant superstition which few novelists could equal for wildness and incredibility. Norrys himself, of course,

(continued on page 83)

35

Playboy-style bachelor magazine. It was published by Fawcett, which also published the popular MAM *True*. Fawcett was a major and pioneering paperback publisher as well, popularizing paperback originals—as opposed to reprints of hardcovers—via its Gold Medal Books line.

Wellman's story **"The Song of the Slaves"** first appeared in *Weird Tales*, March 1940. It's one of many MAM stories reprinted from *Weird Tales* and other pulps. (The text of the story in *Cavalier* was slightly shorter than its original appearance; we chose to include the full *Weird Tales* text in the interest of completeness.)

The fact that it turns on a theme of well-deserved comeuppance was a likely factor in its reprinting in *Cavalier*. MAMs generally targeted a working-class readership, and non-fiction exposés and articles that took a finger-wagging/finger-pointing tone with exploitation-minded fat cats were consistently popular.

HP LOVECRAFT'S reputation looms about as large as that of any writer of the fantastic's, and **"The Rats in the Walls"** is among his most famous and frequently reprinted stories. Originally published in March 1924 in *Weird Tales*, it's probably the pulp story in this collection with the fewest direct links to more typical MAM fiction. But when reprinting classic stories or work by authors whose reputation preceded them, MAMs were more open

(Cont'd on pg. 40)

"These are the bones of slaves. They gleam from the abyss."

Art by Harry Ferman
WEIRD TALES, March 1940

Art by John Leone (detail)
CAVALIER, April 1959

In his comments, Stefan Dziemianowicz calls attention to MAMs altering titles of previously published stories to better fit their readers' expectations. But titles weren't the only way MAMs guided readers, and it is instructive to compare how two very different magazines presented the same material, separated by just under two decades.

The difference between the illustrations for *Weird Tales'* and *Cavalier*'s respective publications of Manly Wade Wellman's "The Song of the Slaves" boils down to a difference in tone. Not the tone of the story, which remained the same, give or take a few minor edits (likely for space considerations) in its *Cavalier* appearance—but the tone of the *magazines*.

One emphasizes panic, desperation, movement. The other: a ghostly, haunting stillness. A futile fight for survival vs. the chilly calm of the grave. These choices speak volumes about the personalities and priorities of the two magazines.

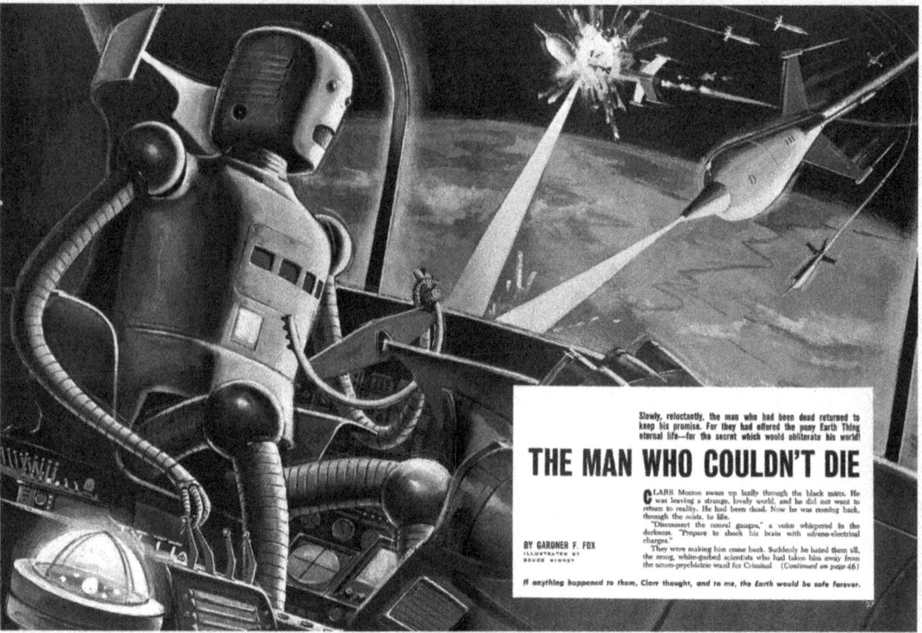

(Cont'd from pg. 37)

to stepping outside their usual criteria.

There are MAM elements here: More than one human found himself squaring off against rats in MAMs, and cannibalism was something that also cropped up on occasion in both MAM fiction and non-fiction pieces, though it was more likely to be practiced by an adversarial tribe in some exotic wilderness than presented as a dark and secret family trait. Still, it's a thrill to include a Lovecraft story in this collection, and it's a testament to the variety of content found in MAMs that the story qualifies for inclusion here in the first place.

DESPITE its futuristic setting and reliance on technological advances that remain science fiction even today, **"The Man Who Couldn't Die"** by Gardner F. Fox is nonetheless firmly ensconced in MAM territory. And Fox had been a writer for *Weird Tales* as well. (It's also worth noting that *Adventure*, the magazine that published the story, began its life as a top pulp that morphed into a MAM.)

Fox is also known as the co-creator of DC Comics heroes Barbara Gordon, the original Flash, Hawkman, Doctor Fate, Zatanna, and the original Sandman. He was the writer who first teamed several of those and other heroes as the Justice Society of America, and he later recreated the team as the Justice League of America. Fox introduced the concept of the Multiverse to DC in the 1961 story "Flash of Two Worlds!"

Stories with a protagonist plotting payback and revenge—whether their efforts ended successfully, or were derailed in ironic failure—are perennials in hard-boiled fiction, and had a regular place in MAMs. The fact that this one involves a man's forced conversion to a cyborg and his subsequent desire to make the entire Earth pay for it takes it out of MAMs' more conventional settings, but at its heart it's a story readers were already familiar with and surely welcomed.

LIKEWISE, stories of weary protagonists on the run from relentless pursuers are a staple of action-adventure fiction, and they appeared in MAMs in any number of variations: A white explorer/adventurer evading an angry native tribe in an exotic locale; an escaped POW making his way across enemy lines; a city boy on the wrong side of backwoods bad guys on their home turf... Favoring familiar story types was one more way MAMs were able to make outrageous science fiction premises a bit more acceptable to MAM readers. Rick Rubin's **"The Hunted,"** with its depiction of humans on the run from organized sentient robots, was not typical of MAMs. But robot stories were common in *Weird Tales*, and pursuit stories fit quite neatly into a mold MAM readers understood and enjoyed in almost any setting.

Accompanied by one of the worst illustrations we've encountered in a MAM, Stuart Evans' **"The Werewolf and the Cowboy"** deserved better. A tense, suspenseful, and legitimately thrilling werewolf story that manages to play to both action-hungry MAM readers and scare-hungry monster fans, its presentation gives lie to the idea that MAMs bolstered mediocre fiction by the inclusion of spectacular and sometimes superior illustration art. True, there are examples where that clearly occurred, but this story makes a compelling case for the inverse, where a solid story is almost undone by the Bob Baum's amateurish rendering—in fairness, an illustration that wouldn't be *quite* so awful if not for the comical hind quarters of the creature, which give it a look more fitting for a toy poodle than a bloodthirsty lycanthrope. But don't let the art department's misstep put you off the story, where the real meat lies.

"Mad Doctor of No-Name Key" by Peter Eldridge is the story of one very eccentric character's morbid obsession with a young woman. It was exactly the kind of bizarro, fact-based story that MAMs loved to dust off, punch up, and present to its readers. It's legitimately creepy, it deals in sexual obsession and taboo sex (implied necrophilia), and best of all (for a MAM editor), it's actually based on real people and true events. MAMs put so much effort into convincing readers that complete fiction was true, that when they found a true story this strange, with this many exploitable elements, it was positively irresistible.

The events are legendary in Key West, and versions of the story were published in a number of other magazines, including *Amazing Detective Cases* (February 1941), *Man's Magazine* (December 1952), *Police Dragnet Cases* (March 1966) and others. "Mad Doctor" Count Von Cosel even wrote his own, self-serving version of what happened that was published in the September 1947 issue of the pulp magazine *Fantastic Adventures*. (It was reprinted in the 2012 book *The Lost Diary Of Count Von Cosel.*)

Eldridge's account for *Adventure Life* plays a bit fast and loose with the facts, but so do most retellings of the strange story of Count Von Cosel and Elena Hoyos. There is a very good, well-researched book about them: *Undying Love: The True Story of a Passion That Defied Death* by Ben Harrison, first published in 1996. (In 2018, a musical based on that book was created and performed in Key West. Titled *Undying Love: A Key West Musical,* co-editor Bob Deis, who lives in the Florida Keys, saw and loved it and its often humorous songs.)

MUCH OF the appeal of MAMs was the escape from reality they provided their readers. And key to escapist entertainment is the thrill of danger, adventure, and sex experienced vicariously through the characters. **"Her Body Belonged to the Devil"** is part "readers' confessions" story (that, with a few more adverbs, wouldn't be out of place as the basis for a *Penthouse*

Nothing had ever shocked the American people as much as what was unearthed in an eerie lab off the coast of Florida.

Doctor von Cosel spread the silk square on the Chahbar rug, where the single shaft of moonlight streamed into the tomb. He held up his wrist and peered at the luminous dial of his watch. It was 10:47 He had eight minutes. Out in the night, beyond the rows of graves, the watchman was a lengthened shadow moving slowly down the path.

The doctor opened his black leather surgeon's case, and took out the suction cups, the glass-cutter, and the vial of kerosene. With a moistened finger he wet the rubber cups and pressed them against the window. He dipped the blade of (Continued on page 46)

24

TAKE A CLOSE LOOK at the cute blonde waiting near you at the bus stop. Yep. She's neatly dressed in the latest fashion and her pert face is a picture of innocence.

Yet, she may be a full-fledged, witch!

See that attractive matron in her early 30's—the one who lives right down the street from you? Sure. She's quiet, well-mannered. At least, on the outside.

Behind that calm, placid facade of respectability, she could very well be hiding the vile, orgiastic nature of a woman devoted to worship of the Devil and the forces of Evil!

6

Don't laugh. Don't dismiss the possibilities from your mind. It doesn't matter much where you live —in the largest of eastern seaboard "Big Towns" or quiet, midwestern communities.

The shocking facts are that witchcraft, Devil Worship and the "practice" of Black Magic are commonplace in the United States today! All across the country, thrill-seeking men and women are turning to the "Dark Arts" to satisfy their thirst for weird and bizarre orgies.

In Los Angeles, California, three "Devil Cults" sprang up to take the place of the infamous "Purple Cult" which was (Continued on next page)

Forum letter a few years later), and part first-hand account of a Black Mass, told with a requisite abundance of exclamation points and thick with scare quotes. Thus the story covers major bases for MAM readers, delivering inside intel on what horny devil worshippers really get up to when they congregate, while pulling double duty as a sex story.

UNDERESTIMATED protagonists were always popular, establishing an easy point of identification for the reader, but Dane Marshall's **"Their Bodies Glowed With Fire"** differs in some ways from a typical MAM story.

Having the story told in first person by a Native American, Joe Rainwater, is unusual, though MAMs often embraced underdogs. (Another example of how actual MAM content was generally the opposite of the kind of alpha male machismo they are often associated with.) The story is also unusual because it notes the racism Joe has faced. Joe's slightly ambiguous plans at the finish are also unexpected.

It's a bit odd (or at least a missed opportunity) that "Joe Rainwater" is not credited in the story's attribution paired with the "as told to" qualifier, since it's written as a first-person story (though it is obviously science fiction). Since we haven't found the name of credited writer Dane Marshall elsewhere, we suspect it's a one-off pseudonym.

Joe is a World War II veteran, a target audience of MAMs. He served with the famed Merrill's Marauders, and came back wounded. The town mentioned, Nuevo Cordura, Arizona, is fictitious. Joe sees what he calls a "flying saucer"—a common topic in MAM stories, though usually UFOs appear in exposé-style articles rather than fiction.

The trope of alien-human sex is an old one. In pulps, human women were often threatened by ravishment from some evil and ugly alien. Of course, this is a MAM story, so the female alien is gorgeous ("a vision with voluptuous breasts, tapering thighs and long, slender legs") and the sex is mutually fulfilling.

"THEIR BODIES GLOWED WITH FIRE!"

By DANE MARSHALL

THEY SAY DEATH comes as the end, but I'm not sucker enough to buy that. Of course, back home in Nuevo Cordura, they've always figured me, Joe Rainwater, for a sucker.

It's a funny thing the way all whites out there think as a group, like believing every Indian is poor red trash, especially me, Joe Rainwater, the local boy who made good in the War but didn't have enough pride to stay away from his home town.

All I really wanted was to come back home, forget war, and do a little thinking while prospecting in the Arizona desert. So they started to figure I was touched in the head.

"That crazy, lazy redskin, trying to find gold in the desert, the fool," is the big joke they told among themselves, when I'd go off with my burro and my pack. "He'll be lucky to find his way home."

What the hell did they know about it? Did they know I was really glad and grateful to get back after the War? Even if home was the hypocritical little town of Nuevo Cordura I headed back like a homing pigeon. My folks were dead then, my father, the son of a chief, and my white mother who had been raised in Nuevo Cordura. If you were a stranger come to town, you'd have heard all about my mother soon enough.

Carmella Meigs! She shucked the town when she married Aaron Rainwater, my father. "A good Christian girl like Carmella taking up with an Injun," they shrieked in outraged horror. And didn't stop to think that my father had been converted to Christianity a long time earlier.

But that's Nuevo Cordura for you. My mother hadn't given them the satisfaction of seeing her run away. She'd stayed right there in town, had me, and raised me, and saw me go away to War where I was with Merrill's Marauders for a long, long time. And three wounds. One of them was my left leg, a hit bad enough to get me a pension and it was this that I lived on when I decided to return to Nuevo Cordura. And why did I come back? Because I thought that somewhere, out on the desert that bordered the town, I could wipe the bitterness from my heart and become whole again. I wanted to be the Joe Rainwater I was before the War, a guy who loved hunting in the hills and fishing and fun.

Instead I returned to deceit and hypocrisy and fist fights with bums like Ed Gordon, Wally Carter and those other shining lights of town. Sure, I could have shaken the dust of the place off my feet right after I visited my parents' graves. But when I saw I wasn't wanted, I decided to stay. At least until I found myself again.

So that's how come word got around that I was touched. Wally Carter started it when I bought grub and supplies at his General Store the first day I set out for the desert. When he asked what I was planning I said "look for gold." I knew as well as he did there was no gold out there, but he had to have an answer. Three trips later he had the whole town convinced I was touched.

(Continued on page 51)

IT STREAKED TOWARD HIM, A FEARSOME BLAZING APPARITION OUT OF THE DESERT NIGHT AND JOE RAINWATER, EX-GI AND HALF-BREED, WAS SURE HE WAS LOSING HIS MIND! AN INSTANT LATER HE BEGAN TO LIVE AS NO MAN HAS—BEFORE OR SINCE!

26

THEODORE Sturgeon is one of the great writers of science fiction and fantasy stories and novels. Most of his short stories appeared in science fiction pulp mags, though some were published in *Weird Tales*. **"The Blonde With the Mysterious Body"** from *Men*, April 1962, is a reprint of Sturgeon's story "The Other Celia," which first appeared in *Galaxy*, March 1957.

It's a creepy tale involving voyeurism and a beautiful, though very strange, woman. Anything with a proximity to sex that's not actually explicit found an ideal home in MAMs, particularly in the genre's earliest years, when the magazines endeavored to balance an obsession with sex and all things sexual with stricter societal attitudes about how such subjects could be effectively presented without creating legal problems for publishers. The result was heavy use of metaphor and generally cagey language when the subject was sex. The voyeurism in this story takes an unexpected turn when our protagonist ends up seeing much more than he ever anticipated—itself a familiar trope in MAM tales of voyeurism, but Sturgeon's bizarre climax is like no other peeping tom tale in MAMs. It's a favorite story of many Sturgeon fans, for good reason.

"FOWL PLAY" by William Bayne has a lot of deep weirdness going for it. First, there's the artwork by Sydney "Syd" Shores, who is best known for work in comic books. It's one of the strangest paintings to grace the cover of a MAM (which is really saying something). It's like a scene from an EC

By THEODORE STURGEON

Slim was constitutionally incapable of borrowing your bathroom without looking into
your medicine chest. Send him into your
kitchen for a saucer and when he came out a
minute later, he'd have inventoried your refrigerator, your vegetable bin, and (since he
was six feet three inches tall) he would know
about a moldering jar of maraschino cherries
in the back of the top shelf that you'd forgotten
about.

Slim liked you better if, while talking to you,
he knew how many jackets hung in your closet,
how old that unpaid phone bill was, and just
where you'd hidden those photographs. On the
other hand, Slim didn't insist on knowing bad
or even embarrassing things about you. He just
wanted to know things about you, period.

Living in Mrs. Koyper's cheap, rundown
rooming house was therefore a near-paradise.
Within a week he knew Mrs. Koyper's roomers
far better than she could, or cared to. Each secret visit to the rooms gave him a starting point;
subsequent ones taught him more. He knew not
only what these people had, but what they did,
where, how much, for how much, and how
often. In almost every case, he knew why as
well.

ALMOST every case. Celia Sarton came.

Slim Walsh got a glimpse of her as she followed Mrs. Koyper up the stairs to the third
floor. Mrs. Koyper, who hobbled, slowed any
follower sufficiently to afford the most disinterested witness a good look, and Slim was anything but disinterested. Yet for days he could
not recall her clearly. It was as if Celia Sarton
had been—not invisible, for that would have
been memorable in itself—but translucent or,
chameleonlike, echoing the drab wall color,
carpet color, woodwork color.

She carried a bag. When you go to the baggage window at a big terminal, you notice a
suitcase here, a steamer-trunk there; and all
around, high up, far back, there are rows and
ranks and racks of luggage not individually noticed but just there. This bag, Celia Sarton's
bag, was one of them.

So anonymous, so unnoticeable was she that,
aside from being aware that she left in the
morning and returned in the evening, Slim let
two days go by before he entered her room; he
simply could not remind himself about her.
And when he did, and had inspected it to his
satisfaction, he had his hand on the knob, about
to leave, before he recalled that the room was,
after all, occupied. Until that second, he had
thought he was giving one of the vacancies the
once-over.

He grunted and (Continued on page 66)

Copyright © 1957 by Theodore Sturgeon. This
story first appeared in Galaxy Science Fiction.

horror comic at its wildest. Is it showing some kind of voodoo ceremony? A sex rite? A nightmare? Talk about an illustration that compels the viewer to investigate further!

The story itself is unusual, with an unreliable narrator who works as a chicken chopper while daydreaming of a different kind of life—and fantasizing about just how far he's prepared to go to get it. The use of an unreliable narrator puts the reader on uncertain footing from the start, Jim Thompson-style, and never lets up. Though it doesn't share as many parallels with more typical MAM fiction as some of the other stories in this book, it is indisputably dark and hard-boiled, a sharp turn into a truly weird world that shows just how wide the doors could swing in MAMs.

LIKE "ISLAND OF DOOM," **"Strange Cult of the Vampire Tarantulas"** by Rick Manners is part of a long MAM lineage: tales of explorers, treasure hunters, and adventurers who venture into uncharted territory and are confronted with greater and more terrible dangers than they could have ever predicted. Sometimes it's angry natives. Sometimes it's rival treasure hunters. Sometimes it's a wild animal or animals, acting as *de facto* guardians of whatever the protagonist is after. And sometimes, on rare occasions…it's giant tarantulas. Not only giant tarantulas, but giant tarantulas who may not have been *born* giant tarantulas…

The story's giant spiders inspired Stefan Dziemianowicz to name-

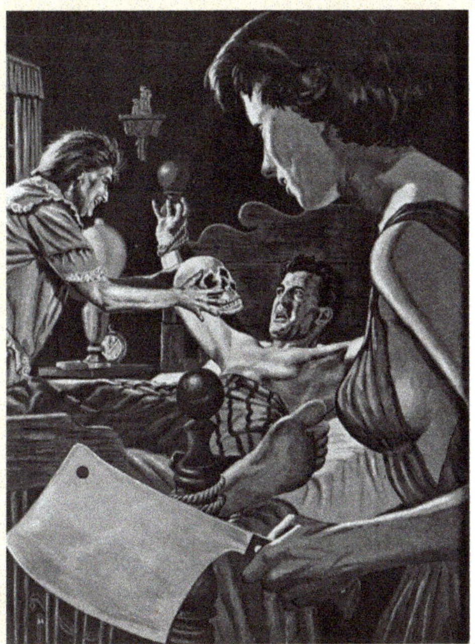

FoWL PLAy

**Buzz, Buzz Went That Strange Noise in Bill's
Ear. It Whispered a Solution to His Problem**

By WILLIAM BAYNE

CRACK! Plunk! Crack! Plunk! He got another one. Crack! Plunk! The same old thing everyday. Everyday. Until today! Today was different! Just take it easy and relax, and I'll tell you all about it. I'll tell you all about the heads!

Heads! Heads! Heads! That's all Bill does everyday, is cut off heads. He works in one of the larger poultry houses in the city. His job for eight hours a day, six days a week, is to cut the heads off chickens, and after he's finished with the bird, he passes the fowl to the next man on the bench, and after that man does his part, he in turn passes the bird to the man after him. At the far end of the bench, the birds are cleaned and packaged, and made ready for the delivery to the stores, for sale to the consumers to purchase. Hundreds of birds everyday, and then today it happened.

Today as Bill was reaching into the huge container that held numerous dead birds, he got a strange buzz in his ear. At first he thought it was a bug, but after brushing his ear with his hand, and finding no insect, but still hearing the buzz, he thought that he had something wrong with his ear. The buzz went away, and when it returned Bill didn't think anything strange about it.

It returned just as he set the chicken on the chopping block. He checked again to make sure that a bug was not in his ear, for he thought that maybe the insect eluded him the first time. He brushed his ear, and looked at the space between his head and the ceiling. No bug. He laughed inwardly to himself, and looked at the chicken on the chopping block. No! It couldn't be!

He took his eyes off the bird, and then returned his gaze to the bird.

Yes, it was! But how? But why?

He blinked and wiped his eyes, for he could hardly believe what he saw. When he set the chicken on the block, it was a true normal chicken. All over! But now the bird was exactly the same, except for one thing. The head! The head on the body of the chicken was the head of his mother-in-law! Everything matched: the beady eyes, the ashen skin, the parrot-like beak for a nose, the stringy hair, and the two missing front teeth. Bill was sweating, and he wiped his forehead with his handkerchief. He looked again, and it was still there on the chopping block waiting for the cleaver. The buzz was back in his ear, and then the other happened.

Sensual spasmodic tremors trickled through the husky body of the man, and it was sheer delight for him to gaze down on the head on the chopping block.

He would lift the razor-sharp cleaver with a sense of satisfaction that he had never experienced before, and drive the blade of the cleaver down on the neck of the mother-in-law with a powerful stroke. Crack! Plunk! The head flipped off the chopping block, and into the box on the floor at the side of the chopping block.

He'd lean over the block with the feeling that if the head was in the box, he would be able to complete his satisfaction all of the way. He'd discover nothing but chicken heads in the box, and it would leave him frustrated. He had the desire to see the head in the box like a junkie needs a fix. Head after head, the same old thing. He would always see the head of the old woman on the block, but after using the cleaver, and peering into the box full of hope, it was not there. Crack! Plunk! He'd look again, but (Continued on page 53)

The only light in the bedroom was the eerie moonlight coming through the window, but Bill did not have any trouble at all seeing what the woman thrust in front of his nose.

check mid-century cinematic sci-fi like *Tarantula* (1955) and *The Giant Gila Monster* (1959) in his comments, to which we'll add three spider-specific drive-in favorites, *Missile to the Moon* (1958), *Horrors of Spider Island* (1960) and most prominently, *Mesa of Lost Women* (1953), a threadbare drive-in oddity with which the 1962 story shares a major (and majorly bizarro) plot point. Movies took a lot from MAMs, and MAMs took a lot from movies. Each nudged the other, providing inspirations both large and small, to where it can sometimes be a challenge to determine who got to what popular trope first, not to mention who did it better.

But it wasn't only ideas and concepts that were exchanged, but imagery—sometimes very specific imagery, as in "Vampire Tarantulas." Eagle-eyed readers may recognize its photo illustrations as actual uncredited movie stills, including one swiped from the 1956 Columbia Pictures adventure *Safari*, starring Victor Mature and Janet Leigh, both of whom are clearly recognizable in the image. (*Safari* was directed by Terence Young, soon to be helming James Bond films, and was produced by future Bond producer Albert R. "Cubby" Broccoli.)

"Vampire Tarantulas" has its own pleasures as old-fashioned adventure fiction married to a mad scientist tale, and its Dr.-Moreau-meets-Dr.-Mengele villain was a recurring character type in these stories, though the emphasis here is far more on adventure and thrills than the specifics of the protagonists' torment. To get a clearer picture of just how far some MAMs

I STILL DREAM of the horrible, nightmarish sight of that huge, black, hairy spider beginning to feed upon the blood of that beautiful girl. It's something a man just can't forget—not if he lives to be a hundred.

The whole unbelievable terror-stricken adventure began about a year ago. Actually it must have begun long before that in the fevered brain of a man named Dr. Unicorn. But I didn't know anything about Dr. Unicorn until . . .

I'm getting ahead of myself. the whole thing actually started on a sunny morning in Spring. I was in my laboratory testing a new species of algae for resistance to radioactivity, when the director of our foundation, The Society For The Study of Marine Growth, came sweeping through the door with a loud bang. It is definitely not like Dr. Ponsonby to come sweeping through doors. He is a short, rather stout man, who usually walks softly and always knocks before he enters any door. I knew he must be very, very upset.

"Rick, dammit, we've got to do something about this. This is the second expedition we've lost in three years. We just can't go on losing people. Why, one of our best men was on that trip. How could they just vanish without a trace?" and he looked at me plaintively as if he expected me to have an answer up my sleeve.

"Don't tell me we've lost touch with the Cawthorne expedition, too," I asked unbelievingly.

"Haven't had a word from them in two weeks. And you know they were supposed to contact us every second day."

"Where were they the last time you heard?" I asked.

"Well, the best I can figure is that they were between Nukutipipi and Mantoa in the Tuamotu Archipelago. The last radio communication received by our control ship placed them in that area. We've got to find them," and he pointed his fist on the table so that the test tubes rattled dangerously.

"That's why I'm sending you, Rick. You know all about those Pacific islands. You were on that expedition that was investigating the resistance of plankton to radioactivity."

"But—wait, doctor . . ." I interrupted helplessly.

"Now, don't give me any excuses. I've got the boat all set and I'm sending a good crew of men with you. Elaine is going, too. She is so worried about her friend Maria who was on that expedition as Cawthorne's assistant," the doctor paused for a moment and watched me knowingly.

I didn't know that my secret was that well known around the labs. I had a yen for the luscious Elaine from the moment I had caught a glimpse of her beautiful blonde hair and her beautiful blonde body. Around the offices our contacts had been scrupulously polite and circumspect. She transcribed my notes efficiently. She even called me Dr. Manners instead of Rick as most of the girls did. Only once had I felt the touch of fire buried deep within her, when I had accidentally brushed against one magnificent breast. She drew back quickly but her eyes flashed like streaks of passionate lightning.

Needless to say, I was on that ship when it left two mornings after Doctor Ponsonby had talked to me.

Did I call that hulk a ship? It was the most run-down, unseaworthy-looking craft I had ever seen. The cabins were about as big as broom closets and less comfortable. And from the very beginning before we even got out to sea the ship began to roll and pitch as if she were possessed. Since most of the members of our search party were not really good sailors, they spent the first week of our voyage in the unhappy agony of seasickness. And I'm sorry to say my lovely Elaine was no exception.

Thus it was that I didn't even get a chance to speak with her until we hit the smooth (Continued on page 34)

32

were prepared to go in that direction, look no further than the next story, published in a different kind of MAM targeting a slightly different kind of reader: "Soft Nudes for the Nazis' Doktor Horror" by Martin Bowers takes the mad scientist concept in a far more lurid direction.

THE TERM "sweat mags," initially used to describe MAMs by people who disparaged them, has been embraced by MAM fans, though they often use it to describe the whole genre. We tend to use that term only for a subset of MAMs: the wildest low-budget titles that regularly featured cover art and stories featuring sadistic Nazis torturing scantily-clad women and similar outré things that were envelope-pushing at the time and are now considered even more politically incorrect. The Reese and Emtee (sometimes spelled Em Tee and EmTee) publishing companies, helmed by BR "Bud" Ampolsk and Maurice Rosenfield (spelled *Rosenfeld* in some sources), were among the most notable publishers of what we call "sweat mags."

One of their longest-lasting sweats was *Man's Story*, which published **"Soft Nudes for the Nazis' Doktor Horror."** It ran from 1961 to 1971. Other Reese and Emtee sweat mags include *Man's Book, Man's Epic, Man's Story, Men Today, New Man, Real Combat,* and *World of Men.* Such MAMs are clearly different than top-tier MAMs like *True, Argosy,* and *Saga,* and from mid-tier MAMs like the Atlas/Diamond line published by Martin Goodman's Magazine Management Company (*Action for Men, For Men Only, Male, Men, Stag,* etc.).

48

Fiction in the sweat mag subgenre of MAMs regularly featured stories with bondage and torture elements, accompanied by equally lurid, leering artwork that rose (or sank, depending on your perspective) to the level of the text.

Cousins to killer creature stories in that they too emphasize details of physical torment (with the addition of human cruelty), Nazi torture stories, like killer creature tales, also consistently acknowledge the profound trauma of such experiences. But sweat fiction goes further, adding an overt sexual component: Rape and sexual assault (or at least implied rape and sexual assault) are prominent elements of their plots.

Though magazines emphasizing this kind of extreme content comprised only about 25% of the 160 or so documented MAM titles and were never top sellers, their kinky covers and freaky subject matter have led to a latter-day collectability (and online popularity) greater than any attention they received in their time.

Correcting misconceptions about MAMs has always been crucial to our mission with The Men's Adventure Library, and this is one of the biggest. Though sweats are popularly considered to be representative of the genre, they simply aren't. They were and will forever be a part of MAM history, but it's an error to think they typify all MAMs. And while these seedy stories trade in dark titillation, their Nazi stories do not glorify Nazis. Nazis

SOFT NUDES FOR THE NAZIS' DOKTOR HORROR

By MARTIN BOWERS

The beast's severed arm represented the madness of a regime where surgery was butchery and the scream of a woman could fulfill a strange lust.

THE gorilla had received a shot of morphine. The girl who lay chained to the operating table had not. She listened to the rasping surgical saw and the final sickening crack of bone. Before her horrified eyes a geyser of steaming red blood spurted from the portable cage.

Despite the anesthesia, the gorilla thrashed and groaned. By instinct its remaining paw slapped at the stump of what had been his arm.

Fritz Mennecke watched the grisly tableau and grunted in satisfaction. His fingers trailed over the tight silk panties the girl still wore. He watched the paroxysm-like heaving of her conical breasts which threatened to burst the straps of the skimpy bra which covered them. Her flesh was warm and sweet to him despite the sheen of perspiration which covered it.

The Nazi doctor stooped over the straining girl. His yellow teeth shone in the overhead light. "Ach, fraulein, what a pity it is that you are too mad to understand the importance of the scientific research we do here."

The leg irons clanked ominously as the girl fought to free herself of their fearfully cold grip. Her fists clenched and unclenched in futile convulsive movements.

"In the name of heaven, you can't!" she cried through clenched lips. Her answer was the sound of tearing cloth. She felt the last of her clothing being shredded from her young body.

"In the name of science we must," Mennecke snickered. "Our soldiers are dying at the front to make a better Germany. You anti-socials should feel honored to make a contribution to their welfare. Only through experimentation can medicine advance. Do you realize what it will mean if this graft takes hold? Men who have lost their limbs in battle will be able to be fitted with new living prosthesis. But of course you could have no interest in such things. You have been judged insane by a competent board of psychiatrists. I don't know why I waste my time explaining our program to you."

Mennecke's obscene touch traveled up and down the girl's right arm. He probed the tenderness of her young flesh with his dirty fingernails. The girl's head swung from side to side. Her eyes grew wide and fixed as they fastened on the bloody contents of the towel carried by the gross faced guard. The hairy fingers of the gorilla's dismembered limb blotted out all other vision.

An uncontrollable shuddering suffused her. Little tendrils of blood seeped from under the iron cuffs which held her ankles. Mindless shrieks of terror bubbled from her distended mouth as she saw the glint of the surgical saw waving above her. The steel grip of the fetter which held her arm was replaced with the more repulsive clasp of her tormentor. The hot flame of agony burned across her bicep as the saw's teeth grated across her skin. . . .

Two days later the maimed gorilla died of shock. Mennecke had used all the drugs at his command to spare the brute the tortures of its mortal agony.

The girl, the hideous limb firmly affixed to her shoulder by strong sutures remained alive longer. She even regained consciousness long enough to view the hairy hand lying naked beneath its plaster cast across her bosom.

However what Mennecke and any second year medical student had already known proved itself again. The human body will reject any foreign matter attached to it. It may host a kidney from an identical twin, but its immune mechanism will not tolerate a transplant from other humans, let alone other species of mammal.

Mennecke could not have cared less. He sat at the girl's bedside savoring the hideous suffering of his victim, refusing her even the mildest palliative prescription. He watched her skin turn black and her body bloat to three times its normal size as the sepsis flooded slowly to her brain.

He attended her final death throes not as a physician, but as a torture master.

DOKTOR Fritz Mennecke was one of the elite of Nazi medicine during a time when humanity and learning turned back a thousand years to the torture chambers of the middle ages. Together with S.S. Major General Karl Brandt and Dr. Paul Neitsche they formed the infamous Traveling Circus. Where their bloody (Continued on page 56)

34

in these stories are clearly, unambiguously evil, and generally get their just desserts by the end of the story.

"Soft Nudes for the Nazis' Doktor Horror" is a typical example of sweat fiction, another variation on a Moreau-meets-Mengele story that, for all the outrageousness of its central conceit, was probably not much more bizarre than the real-life horror stories then circulating about Nazi doctors' experimentation on human beings. Nazis made ideal MAM villains, since readers were prepared to accept they were capable of absolutely anything.

Even human-gorilla experimentation was a rather common trope, in all areas of entertainment. Men in gorilla suits strapped to operating tables make frequent appearances in Poverty Row feature films, shorts, and serials, in comic books, even in old time radio drama. (Particularly memorable is a 1942 episode of the radio series *Dark Fantasy* penned by Scott Bishop entitled "Spawn of the Subhuman." It concerns a mad scientist on a remote island who surgically combines gorillas and humans to create a new breed of creature that can fly planes and sing opera (!). Truly, even the most far-out MAM ideas can be seen as part of a continuum of outrageous plotting in popular culture—and the public's willingness to embrace it—in those years.)

It's worth mentioning that the model for the hapless woman preparing for the worst in Norm Eastman's artwork for "Soft Nudes" was Eva Lynd, who is alive and well. From the late 1950s to the late 1970s, Eva was a MAM and paperback cover model, a top pinup photo model, and actress. Her career is chronicled in *Eva: Men's Adventure Supermodel*, from The Men's Adventure Library

IN THE late 1960s, cultural shifts and, almost more importantly, notable court decisions regarding the definition of obscenity, led to a relaxing of standards regarding explicit sexual content in magazines.

So by 1966, stories like **"Stone Age Lust—Today"** from *Man's Daring* (one of several sweat-style MAMs launched by *Cracked* publisher Robert Sproul), had greater freedom to include scenes of dark rituals, and even a gang rape of the story's ostensible heroine. (Though the language is not explicit, it remains an unnerving scene.) The story purports to be recounted by its main character, a British archeologist, and is credited to pseudonym Goeffrey (sic) Costain. (Our guess is the author thought the name to be *veddy British* but ran into spelling difficulties.)

The story makes use of an oft-used MAM trope in which the protagonist is accompanied by a sexy female co-worker, a partnership that in many stories is forced upon him, despite his misgivings. It was an angle employed so often, it's actually part of multiple stories in this book. Characters sent on assignment in MAM fiction tended to be dispatched with the office looker. Naturally, she usually ends up as the story's damsel in distress; sometimes a victim.

(We'll add that the editor's note at the start dates from the story's original publication. The editors of this volume make no such claims.)

BEFORE the late 1960s, MAMs faced the threat of censors who lobbied for bans on the sale of "pornography" on newsstands and in stores, and the threat of being prohibited from using the mail for subscriptions if they were deemed pornographic by postal officials.

Thus, during the '50s and early '60s, the cheesecake photo spreads in MAMs were fairly tame, non-explicit glamour girl photos of models and actresses. Generally, the language in stories referring to sex was also not explicit. By the late '60s, as censorship threats subsided, MAMs faced a new challenge: steadily increasing competition from men's mags like *Playboy* and its clones, and even more explicit men's mags. So, when court decisions led to relaxed censorship laws and postal regulations in the late '60s, MAMs tried to maintain their readership by publishing more explicit photos and artwork featuring nude women, and by allowing more graphic sexual language in stories.

Ironically, as MAMs amped up their own racy content to keep pace, those efforts to remain competitive helped contribute to their demise: These updated MAMs weren't really graphic enough for the raincoat crowd,

IT TURNED A MAN INTO A KILLER-BEAST, AND NEWMAN TRACKED IT DOWN UNTIL HE STOOD FACE-TO-FACE WITH IT . . . THEN HE HAD NO CHOICE BUT TO DIE

KILLER of the CAVE

Like a man drugged, Don Newman had been sitting on the soft earth outside the mouth of the underground cave, looking into the distance. Hope had left his eyes, even the fear that had replaced it, and now they stared blankly as though a shade had been lowered behind them to shut out the scene—the scene of a world that had ended, a world that had been scorched clean of all living things, both evil and good, with atomic power unleashed by men's hatred.

The soft loam beneath him was just a strip around the cave, all that was left in existence. Beyond it the strangely crystalline sand, that only a month earlier had been the same loam verdant with foliage before it had been transformed by the alchemy of atomic fission, stretched endlessly toward the horizon where warped, naked steel girders marked the grave of a city. In the lowering twilight the sand had begun to glow weirdly. It became a sea of cold luminescence and in it the host of charred white skeletons of men and animals lay half submerged like ghostly swimmers struggling to reach his small island of life. And the cave had been a real island of life in that vast deluge of death. Its natural magnetic ore had been an impermeable fortress shielding him and his companions against the bombardment of nuclear radiation. But death had long known other ways of killing.

A chill suddenly shook Newman's motionless figure. His eyes cleared and he turned to look down the strip of earth toward a spot where a number of graves were marked by shallow mounds. Originally there had been eight people, including Newman himself. All had miraculously escaped the holocaust, and had been the last living creatures on the world. Now six of them lay buried there. Murdered! By an inhuman creature spawned by the same radiation they had escaped!

For a minute Newman shook his head insanely from side to side as though trying to dislodge the memory from his brain. Alice! Would she ever forgive him!

As he struggled to his feet a photograph dropped from his pocket, a portrait of the killer taken with the camera he'd rigged as a trap. He picked it up, looked at it. The face of a monster leered back at him. In a frenzy he tore the photograph to shreds and (Continued on page 75)

ADVENTURE

BY GENE PREEN
ILLUSTRATED BY BASIL GOGOS

who now had more options than ever to choose from, and they became increasingly less attractive to readers who had enjoyed the content of older MAMs. Action/adventure paperbacks swept in to fill this gap (in some instances reformatting reprinted material from vintage pulps of the 1930s), swiftly emerging as a refuge for readers who found MAMs' reinventions wanting, and missed the kind of unapologetic, action-focused writing MAMs had previously delivered.

"**Killer of the Cave**," from the April 1966 issue of the pulp-turned-MAM *Adventure*, is credited to Gene Preen, one of many pseudonyms used by Gil Paust. An editor for *Mechanix Illustrated*, *Argosy*, and *Adventure*, and a prolific writer of short stories and non-fiction who published under many different pen names, Paust also wrote scripts for the Canadian *Twilight Zone*-esque TV show *The Unforeseen*.

In "Killer of the Cave," someone is murdering members of a small group of survivors following an atomic blast, but the culprit is a mystery. And as their numbers shrink and even prime suspects fall victim to the killer, the question becomes less "Whodunnit?" and more "Who will survive… and what will be left of them?"

It's fitting to close this collection with Paust/Preen's story, for a number of reasons. For one, it features a fantastic painting by Basil Gogos (1929–2017). (His references were Joan Stein and the iconic and ubiquitous illustration model Steve Holland.)

An illustrator whose work appeared in MAMs throughout the 1960s (examples of his covers can be seen on pg. 54 and pg. 108), Gogos' reputation today rests largely on the many memorable cover paintings he created for *Famous Monsters of Filmland* magazine, starting in 1960. Another of the frequent and fruitful intersections of MAMs and some of the defining weird content of the 20th century.

The story itself is built on something central—even essential—to most MAM fiction: desperation. Desperation and desperate characters are key elements in many of these stories, and this is true of much MAM fiction, across the board. MAM protagonists are often simply men desperately trying to cope with or escape an impossible situation.

Desperation was relatable, so MAM writers ensured that readers understood exactly what was at stake in each of their stories. Most importantly, desperation fuels intensity—and intensity is the coin of the realm in MAMs.

Though characters may have little chance of survival, and they will certainly *not* escape unscathed, they still fight tooth and nail to endure. MAMs offered few bulletproof alpha males charging boldly into fire. Examples of such characters in MAMs are often "Book Bonus" versions of novels, such as Don Pendleton's *Executioner* books. Those types of stories actually run against the grain of what MAM fiction was usually about—namely, relatable male characters who are more everyman than superman.

Despite their frequently superhuman powers of endurance, a MAM protagonist is often…just a guy. A guy at a crossroads, a guy struggling to survive some battle or exotic danger, a guy in trouble. Less raw machismo, more guts brought out by naked desperation.

Sometimes that naked desperation emerged because fate took a turn for the weird.

October 1972
Art by Basil Gogos

THE FLAG OF THE STONEWALL BRIGADE

Ronald Adamson

Action, March 1953   Cover by Mark Schneider

THE FLAG of the STONEWALL BRIGADE

BEHIND the horn-rimmed spectacles the doctor's eyes glistened with exasperation. "Lieutenant Frazer, you know you want to tell me something." The young officer turned from the window to look at the doctor, a startled look on his face. This psychiatrist seemed able to read his mind, he thought.

"You think I'm off my rocker, sir," he said. He lowered himself gently into the big chair, taking care not to jar his wounded leg. He looked like any other normal young American—a little gaunt, perhaps—but a close look showed a slight tremor about his lips. His eyes, too, held an odd light—as though he saw things invisible to other men.

The doctor smiled a little. "No," he said. "You only need some psychiatric care. However, if you continue to resist me—" he spread his hands wide in a gesture of resignation.

Lieutenant Frazer shifted uneasily in the chair. Because his confounded tongue had slipped in an unguarded moment, he had been sent to see this Army "Psycho" doctor.

"If something is bothering you," the doctor added. "Talking about it will help."

We were all conscious of it, of course, (said the Lieutenant) but

(Continued on page 56)

ART BY MARK SCHNEIDER

BEHIND the horn-rimmed spectacles the doctor's eyes glistened with exasperation. "Lieutenant Frazer, you know you want to tell me something." The young officer turned from the window to look at the doctor, a startled look on his face. This psychiatrist seemed able to read his mind, he thought.

"You think I'm off my rocker, sir," he said. He lowered himself gently into the big chair, taking care not to jar his wounded leg, He looked like any other normal young American—a little gaunt, perhaps—but a close look showed a slight tremor about his lips. His eyes, too, held an odd light—as though he saw things invisible to other men.

The doctor smiled a little. "No," he said. "You only need some psychiatric care. However, if you continue to resist me—" he spread his hands wide in a gesture of resignation.

Lieutenant Frazer shifted uneasily in the chair. Because his confounded tongue had slipped in an unguarded moment, he had been sent to see this Army "Psycho" doctor.

"If something is bothering you," the doctor added, "talking about it will help."

"We were all conscious of it, of course," said the Lieutenant, "but Sergeant D'Allessandrio was the first one to put it into words. We were feeling pretty chipper that day. We knew we'd given the North Koreans a damned good licking, and we were chasing after them up near the Manchurian border. Colonel McQuade had come by to tell us to dig in for the night on top of the ridge we'd just climbed. "A company of South Koreans will pass through you in the morning. You'll remain in support of them."

I SET the platoon up for the night. On the right of the road that bisected our position were Corporal McGovern and his ammo carrier, Luther Crofts. On its left were Corporal Jacques Claudier and his sidekick; "Itky" Itkowitz. The BAR men and the riflemen were spread in a perimeter.

The Sergeant and I were just bedding down for the night when he said, "Yuh know, Lieutenant, we ain't had one casualty for two months. Not since Luther joined the platoon. We don't even catch colds."

I was shocked. "Don't talk about it, Sergeant," I said. "You'll put a jinx on us!"

He shook that hairy head of his and grinned. "Not so long as old Luther keeps that flag o' his handy."

I rolled over and pretended to be asleep, for I was superstitious about that flag. It had become customary before going into combat for everyone in the platoon, including me, to find some excuse to touch the tattered rag the Sergeant had just mentioned.

But the Sergeant's words took me back to the night Luther had joined us. We had fought in the battle for Seoul a few weeks earlier and since then we'd been busy cutting our way into North Korea. The Reds still packed lots of punch, and we'd lost a lot of men. This particular night, however, we were resting in a battered old farm house.

A soldier had come in through the ruined doorway. He peered uncertainly about the room and said, "Lieutenant Frazuh?" Outside, sleet pelted the dreary Korean landscape, and the water dripped from his raincoat onto the floor.

"I'm Lieutenant Frazer," I said.

He grinned and approached me in an easy countryman's walk. He stuck out his hand. "Yo' got yo'rese'f a new soldier, Lieutenant. I'm Luther Crofts."

I ignored his outthrust hand. "Don't expect any velvet carpets, Crofts," I said. "Go over by the fire and dry out a little. Sergeant D'Allessandrio will explain your duties."

The newcomer ambled over to the fireplace. Like all replacements, he seemed very young. He was tall and a little underweight. When he dropped his packroll on the floor, it scattered water over the Sergeant.

"Fercrysake, watch it!" grumbled the Sergeant, his dozing interrupted. He was a squatty sort of bird, the Sergeant, and one of the finest guys to have backing you up in a fight. He was God's own homely man with a big nose and beady eyes, and his hair was long and lank.

"Ah'm sorry, Sergeant," said Luther, and the shy friendly grin appeared again.

CROFTS shivered and bent over his packroll for a moment. When he straightened up, he held a bottle in his hand. "A little nourishment," he chuckled. The gleaming bottle killed instantly our indifference toward him. You could hear men sitting up all around the room. I licked my lips and began to think the new man might do very well, indeed.

The Sergeant really put the slug on that bottle before he passed it to the man next to him. You could have heard his sigh of contentment a block away. "Welcome to the party, Luther." he said. And when Luther came up with still another bottle, the boy was in.

But Luther wasn't done with rummaging through that packroll yet. This time he drew out a crumpled, soggy cloth and shook it out in front of the fire.

"What the hell is that?" said the Sergeant.

I knew what it was right away, and I sat up for a better look. Luther wafted it back and forth gently in front of the fire. "My flag," he said. "The flag o' the Stonewall Brigade." He spoke very softly, but you could hear the sound of bugles in his voice. "My great-gran'pappy give it me." His eyes were misty with pride. "This'n's one Confederate flag was never surrendered. The Stonewall Brigade fought in every battle Lee's Army was in. It was in Jackson's Valley campaign, too, at places like Kernstown and Port Republic. An' this flag led it through 'em all."

Jacques Chaudier arose suddenly and moved forward. "What yo' mean 'twas neveh surrendered?" Luther looked mighty relieved at the Southern note in Jacque's voice.

"Yo're from what part o' the South?" he asked.

"N'Orleans," said Jacques. "Keep talkin'." He turned to look at his buddy, Bill Itkowitz. "Listen to this boy, Itky."

"Yo' sure yo' all want to hear this?" Luther said. Warmed by his whisky, the others murmured assent. I felt my heart go out in a warm rush of affection for them. Their attitude toward Luther's flag was a typical example of their innate kindness toward each other.

"THE STONEWALL Brigade was Stonewall Jackson's own outfit," Luther went on, "till Ole Jack got promoted. Great-gran'pappy's Regiment, Harper's Fifth Virginia, was part o' the Brigade. And when the surrender come, they was ordered to parade before the Union Army and give up their flags and guns."

The boy fell silent then and stared into the fire. "Gran'pap couldn't see given up this flag—too many had give up their lives for it," Luther said at last. "So when the Army marched down, all the flags was stacked but this'n. This'n was under gran'pap's shirt."

He looked up with that likeable, shy grin. "Today's the first time ah ever showed it to anyone since ah joined the army. But ah figure ah'm home now—ah've got my own outfit—it's right yo' should know the story." The men nodded and looked at each other in approval.

Chaudier hunkered down next to Luther. "It's been in yo're family since the war?" His hand went out slowly to touch the flag.

Luther nodded. "Yep. When gran'pap was dyin', he asked me to take it down from the wall. Ah put it in his hand, an' he jus' about had strength to raise it to his lips and kiss it. Then he give it to me. 'Keep it by yo', Luther,' he said. 'An yo'll never be alone. Remember, it ain't never been surrendered.'" That shy grin appeared again. "Ah reckon great-gran'pappy never rightly got reconstructed."

As LUTHER's voice died away, the men studied the sodden flag where it hung before the fire. Its red had faded to orange, and its edges were frayed. Ragged holes gaped where the gunfire of other days had wounded it. Here and there rust-colored blotches stained it. Luther reached out to touch it. "Them's blood-stains from men o' the Brigade," he whispered.

Just then a voice bawled from the doorway, "Tenshun !" We all stiffened as Colonel Blackheart McQuade, the regimental commander, stamped through the doorway. A hard-bitten old iron-head, discipline was the deep love of his government-issue soul. However, as a saving grace his frosty blue eyes held just the faintest hint of sparkle.

Blackheart circulated through the Regiment constantly. He claimed it was the only way a commander could really get to know his men. Now I shivered a little as his frosty eyes flicked about the room. He studied the bearded, filthy men for a moment then his look caught me. "You're letting your men slip, Frazer," he snapped. "We're in a rest area. The men should be cleaned up and shaved."

That two-week rest had been a great break for us. When Colonel McQuade had said terrible days lay ahead, he hadn't been fooling. As we battered our way through North Korea with the army, we spent mighty few days out of combat. But those rough weeks of death, pain, filth, and fear gave birth to a new emotion among us. Each passing day served to increase its depth. Still, until Sergeant D'Alessandrio put it into words, no one dared mention it.

And that brings us up to the time we dug in on that hill top near the Manchurian border.

I WOKE up early the next morning, and after checking Badtooth Jackson who was standing sentry to our rear, I stumbled back up the hill. I stood there for a while instinctively studying our position.

The ridge we rested on overlooked two smaller hills on the right and left flanks. Three hundred yards in front of us lay a dense wood commanded by the knoll we were on. Between us and the woods lay a flat snow-covered expanse which ended at the foot of the hill. Just beyond the smaller ridge to our right and disappearing behind it ran a stream. I noticed that in the bitter cold a dense haze hung over the running water. Our hill would make a good place to defend if necessary.

Since the rest of the platoon was now stirring, I instructed Sergeant D'Allessandrio to take half the men back to the company kitchen for breakfast. As the group left, the sight of Luther ambling along made me grin a little. l knew he had the flag tucked in his shirt. From the first he had proved himself a natural-born soldier although he had grown so thin that he looked frail and transparent.

Fifteen minutes after the first breakfast contingent had left, the sound of men's feet on the road came to my ears. I peered back down the hill. "Who goes there?" Badtooth Jackson's challenge rang loud in the cold air.

"South Korean soldiers!"

Jackson waved them on, and out of the early morning mist a column of men began to climb the hill. When I saw the American uniforms, l relaxed and along with my men waved greetings to the oncoming ROKs.

Then abruptly the column halted.

Rifle fire and the staccato bark of burp guns tore the air as I dived into my foxhole. "Get the CP on that phone!" I shouted at Carter.

Carter barked hoarsely into the instrument, then turned back to me. His face was working with panic. "It's dead, sir!" He and I burrowed deep into the earth as a grenade burst on the lip of our foxhole. God, how I cursed myself—to be caught by infiltration after all my experience! A mumbling sound came from Carter, and I realized the boy was praying.

I remember thinking that prayer was about all we had left. I had to find some way of getting McGovern and Chaudier to fire. Then I saw what I had to do.

I took a deep breath. It wasn't a pleasant decision, and Carter's eyes widened even further as I got to my knees. "I'm going to jump out of here," I told him. "Maybe I can get a few shots of the carbine and attract the gooks' attention. When you hear our machine guns start talking, you stick your head out of this goddam hole and use your rifle, Carter, hear?"

Carter, too, got slowly to his knees. "Two's better'n one for creating a diversion, Lieutenant," he said. I slammed him on the shoulder, and together we started for the lip of the foxhole.

I raised my head cautiously rand ducked quickly as bullets stitched the earth nearby. I figured Carter and I weren't going to last long. But we couldn't back out, because if those Reds charged the foxhole while everyone was pinned down, there would be one hell of a slaughter in the platoon. I tensed for the leap.

THEN over the racket of the gunfire rose a strange, yipping cry. Somewhere a whistle blew. The Red fire faltered, and I raised my head quickly.

Luther Crofts marched up the road with the flag of the Stonewall Brigade flying proudly over his head. Alongside him strode Itky, blowing madly on the whistle, then turning to wave back down the hill as though he was urging men behind him to hurry. And from Luther's lips came the shrill, chilling sound that could only be the Rebel Yell.

From the corner of my eye, I saw Luther dive into the gun emplacement with McGovern. He plunged the staff of the flag into the snow as he did. I cheered and fired my carbine madly.

It was a hot fire-fight until the rest of the platoon charged up the hill to the rescue a few minutes later. Behind them came the company of ROKs we'd been expecting. The Reds fled then with the South Koreans hot on their tails.

As the sound of the fighting faded away, I moved across the road toward McGovern's gun. Alongside it, the flag floated gently in the breeze. The Irishman's marble-like eyes were glazed with anger and fear and awe. "Lieutenant, I've seen everything in this lousy war, but I never seen a guy charge with a flag before!"

"Thank God he did," I said.

THE ROAR of an engine came to our ears, and we turned to see the Colonel's jeep bounding up the hill toward us. "You had trouble up here?" said old Blackheart as I hurried up to meet him.

"Yessir," I began. "A bunch of gooks ambush—"

Then the Colonel's eyes fell on the flag. His eyebrows went high and he turned back to me, anger flashing on his hard face. "Do you permit this sentimental tripe in this platoon?" he bellowed.

My men gathered quietly around the jeep, and I could feel them pulling together just as they did in combat. "It's not sentimental tripe to us, sir." I was horror-struck at the words issuing from my lips—nobody spoke that way to Colonel McQuade—but I was determined to defend Luther and his flag even if it cost me my Lieutenant's bar. "That flag just saved our lives!"

The Colonel's face was gaunt and gray and filled with bitter anger. "All the Chinese in the world are coming through those woods!" the Colonel spat. "Let that ROK company pile back through you. Then see what you can do about holding up those Chinese." He glared fiercely in the direction of the enemy. "I've got to get back to headquarters. But I'll get you out. Just try like hell to hold them as long as you can till we can get some kind of defense organized." Skidding crazily on the frozen snow, the jeep took off for the rear, and such was old Blackheart's reputation we knew he was not running for safety.

Suddenly the Colonel's jeep reappeared. Only he and the driver were in it. His iron face black with weariness and strain, the Colonel hopped out. "They damn near got us back there," he said roughly. "We're cut off, Lieutenant. They killed all the ROKs." His glance flickered over the position.

I knew we were in for it, but deep inside me a crazy belief said the flag would pull us through. "We'll do our best, sir," I said.

"The Regiment'll get through to us," said the Colonel.

The Sergeant and I went over the position again. Luther and Turk were on the right side of the hill while Chaudier and Itky were on the left. They would work crossfire and could swing their fire to the rear if necessary. The riflemen and BAR men were properly placed. We'd done all we could. Now we sat back to wait.

"Here they come!" said the Sergeant at last. Dark figures appeared on the snow at the edge of the woods. Mortar fire began to fall on us while the enemy moved out on the flat expanse.

We held our fire as the Reds trotted forward. When their mass was halfway across the flat we opened fire. Great holes appeared in their ranks, but the flood rolled on steadily. It reached the foot of our hill before it broke and fled to the shelter of the woods. Off to my right Turk McGovern raised his hands in a fighter's handclasp when I looked his way. Luther grinned and waved, and l took comfort from the way the flag still waved over their emplacement.

Sergeant D'Allessandrio returned from checking the positions. His eyes, redrimmed and staring, were full of wonder as he knelt down beside us. "We ain't lost a man yet!" he said.

The Chinese were all around our hill now, pouring rifle and burp gun fire into us. For the first time since Luther had joined us, I saw my men beginning to drop.

TIME and space became lost as somehow we drove the Chinese off our hill time after time only to see that inexhaustible tide press right back. Ammunition was very low now.

Once more the enemy fell back, and I seized the chance to pull my survivors into a tight defense. Luther and Badtooth, with the assistance of Carter, brought their gun and the flag with them. Looking at the proud, tattered banner coming up the hill, I felt comforted even though I knew the next charge would be the last one for my platoon. Wherever the men of the Stonewall Brigade were now, I thought, they would be proud their flag flew over brave men, for none of us thought of surrender.

The Chinese came again, closing in on us in a screaming circle. We held our fire until the last moment, then opened up. The Reds momentarily wavered under that fierce hail; then as the ammo dwindled, they came on faster. Luther swung his gun to face those coming in from the right. Badtooth and Carter stuck by him. They were still firing when the Reds ran over them.

Sergeant D'Alessandrio screamed in bitter despair. "Come on, goddam it!" We flung ourselves toward the spot where the flag of the Stonewall Brigade had disappeared under the charging Reds. We tried to cut our way through those screaming madmen to the flag. But there were too many of them. Panting and howling with desperation, we retreated back to our hilltop. Filled with hatred and despair, we waited to die.

SUDDENLY, Sergeant D'Allessandrio bellowed wildly and pounded my back. "Look! In the name of God, look!" A high wild note filled his voice.

My heart skipped a crazy beat. Over the brow of the small hill on our right, long files of troops ran steadily toward us. Line after line of them came out of the mist raised by the stream behind that hill. They moved forward silently and mercilessly, the sunlight glittering on their old-fashioned bayonets.

Despite my fear and the heat of the battle in me, I went cold all over. Those troops who moved so quickly to our rescue wore gray, nondescript uniforms. And they wore slouch hats of many kinds.

Suddenly the Chinese were running for the shelter of the woods. The lines of gray strode on, their guns held high. As they came abreast of our position, they halted. One of the figures stopped and touched Luther where he lay huddled on his face. Then the figure picked up the flag and paused.

Luther rose slowly to his feet. The other soldier put the flagstaff in his hand. Then all those gray ranks turned to face us! They came to full attention while the figure next to Luther saluted us! Then they about-faced while Luther passed through them until he stood at their head. The figure next to him motioned forward, and the gray ranks resumed their steady pace towards the woods into which the Chinese had fled. And not a sound came from those thousands of gray-clad men.

THE ROAR of fire from the woods reached a thundering crescendo, but not one of those silent figures fell. My eyes smarted and I looked at the Colonel. Old Blackheart McQuade was crying openly. "There they go—the best goddamned infantry the world's ever known."

"The Stonewall Brigade came to save their flag," I said, hardly able to get the words out. "The one that's never been surrendered, remember?"

The Sergeant's eyes were filled with a brilliant light. He knelt in the snow and crossed himself. "God rest their souls!" he whispered.

We watched while the Stonewall Brigade disappeared into the woods. The gunfire ceased abruptly and a weird silence fell over the battlefield. Jacques Chaudier, supporting Itky who had been hit, looked at me with fierce pride. "Did yo' see 'em, Lieutenant?" His voice was singing. "They saluted *us!*"

"We didn't give up that flag either, Jacques," I said. "It's still never been surrendered." Something plucked at my foot. I looked down. Turk McGovern's eyes pleaded with me. I knelt down beside him. "Yes, Turk?"

He put his band on my arm. "Will the Lieutenant get Luther out o' those woods?"

We knew those woods held no further danger. I nodded to Turk and looked at Sergeant D'Allessandrio. "Let's go," he said. It was then I found I'd been wounded, for when I tried to walk I fell down. They made me comfortable while the Colonel went with the Sergeant into the woods. In a little while they reappeared, carrying Luther between them. Others ran to help them bear him up to our hill top. They laid him down next to Turk, who raised on one elbow to look into the Virginian's face. "I reckon his soul's off with the Brigade," he said. He fell back again.

"We found him in a clearing deep in the woods," said the Colonel. "The cold sun was lighting his face. And he was covered by the flag." He drew the flag from the front of his jacket and put it in my hand. "The First Platoon earned this today."

THE LIEUTENANT fell silent a moment then looked up at the doctor. "I blacked out then. Came to in a hospital in Japan. No one from my outfit was in that hospital. I haven't seen any of them since that day on the hill." A defiant look hardened his eyes. "But what I've just told you really happened. I saw it myself."

A look of great puzzlement filled the doctor's eyes. He tapped his teeth with a pencil and looked out the window a moment. "You only arrived here yesterday, Lieutenant." Frazer nodded. A look of awe now rested on the psychiatrist's face. He spoke into the intercom box on his desk. "Will you send that other patient in?" A moment later the door behind Lieutenant Frazer opened and closed. He turned to look at the new arrival.

Colonel McQuade's eyes widened as he saw Frazer in the chair. Then suddenly they twinkled in merriment. A wide grin cracked his face. "Frazer! You too?" The Lieutenant nodded, and now he, too, chuckled. Suddenly he felt better. The Colonel strode forward and took his hand. "I got in day before yesterday," he said. He nodded at the doctor. "He had me in telling him all about it. He thinks I'm crazy."

The Lieutenant threw back his head and laughed aloud. "Me too!" His and the Colonel's laughter resounded through the room.

"Just a minute, gentlemen," said the doctor. His voice sounded strained and uncertain. "There is something I must tell you. Sergeant D'Allessandrio is arriving here today for psychiatric examination." The laughter of the two officers grew louder. The doctor walked across his office to stare out the window for a moment.

Then he turned to face them. "I know that the Sergeant will tell exactly the same story as you two. I suppose in a way it's a case of mass hysteria but— Oh hell, gentlemen, where is that flag now? I'd give my right arm to see it!"

October 1962
Art by Vic Prezio

WHEN THE VAMPIRE WAS CAPTURED
Ward Semple

True Weird, March 1953   Cover by Clarence Doore

A great cry issued from the long dead corpse as the village officials drove the sharp end of a cross through the heart of the cadaver.

WHEN THE VAMPIRE WAS CAPTURED

Jean Jacques Rousseau, one of France's great philosophers wrote: "If there ever was in the world a warranted and proven history, it is that of vampires; nothing is lacking, official reports, testimonials of persons of standing, of surgeons, of clergymen, of judges, the judicial evidence is all embracing."

BY WARD SEMPLE

CROGLING Grange in England is a rambling, one story house with a sweep of well kept lawn which stretches to a field of trees that separates the Grange from an ancient church and cemetery. It has been in the Fisher family for centuries. The latest owners, for reasons of their own, rented the Grange to two brothers and a sister and left for the south of England.

In this undramatic way starts one of the world's most weird vampire histories. It was told by Capt. Frederick Fisher, whose family owned Croglin Grange, to August Hare, England's famous writer and traveller. In his six volume "Story of My Life", Hare tells of the Croglin vampire. Since the incidents involved innocent persons who were liked by their neighbors,

ART BY DWIGHT HOWE

CROGLIN Grange in England is a rambling, one-story house with a sweep of well kept lawn which stretches to a field of trees that separates the Grange from an ancient church and cemetery. It has been in the Fisher family for centuries. The latest owners, for reasons of their own, rented the Grange to two brothers and a sister and left for the south of England.

In this undramatic way starts one of the world's most weird vampire histories. It was told by Capt. Frederick Fisher, whose family owned Croglin Grange, to August Hare, England's famous writer and traveler. In his six volume *Story of My Life*, Hare tells of the Croglin vampire. Since the incidents involved innocent persons who were liked by their neighbors, Hare omits the names of the brothers and sister.

Hare identifies the house as Croglin Grange, but those who investigated this weird and almost incredible occurrence established that England has a Croglin High Hall and a Croglin Low Hall. Investigators concluded that Hare's description of Croglin Grange fits Croglin Low Hall.

It should be mentioned at this point that stories of vampires are something like ghost stories. There is ample documentation by reputable persons but their existence is questioned by many students of inexplicable phenomena. Jean Jacques Rousseau, one of France's great philosophers, writers and social reformers, after studying the claims of vampirism, wrote:

"If there ever was in the world a warranted and proven history, it is that of vampires; nothing is lacking, official reports, testimonials of persons of standing, of surgeons, of clergymen, of judges; the judicial evidence is all embracing."

Rousseau, and others before and after him, often meditated on the fact that (again like ghosts) reports of vampires, even in ancient times, are found in widely separated areas of the world, which had no mutual contact. In documenting case histories of vampires in recent centuries, the testimony includes the sworn statements of men of learning, physicians, judges and

August Hare, one of England's famous writers, who got the weird details of the vampire of Croglin Grange from a member of the family.

Jean Jacques Rousseau, famous French philosopher who found that legal evidence of the existence of vampires was overwhelming

men of the cloth—all with unquestionable reputations of veracity.

The general conception of a vampire is a dead person who leaves his or her coffin to suck the blood of the living and thus keep himself or herself "alive" after death. According to recorded cases, those so attacked generally die within two or three days; and, after death, they too become vampires. Another type is the dead who suck the blood of the living indefinitely, without causing the death of the victim. Students of the subject agree that vampires function only at night and, for a yet unexplainable reason, are most likely to roam when the moon is full. In broad daylight, the vampire is helpless.

With the advance of science and especially knowledge of abnormal psychology, belief in vampirism dwindled to where few dare to say publicly that they had actually seen or been attacked by a vampire. This reticence, however, does not mean that vampirism no longer exists. The Hon. Ralph Shirley, a scholarly student of the subject, wrote in 1924:

"It may be doubted whether the vampire, in one form or another, is quite as absent from modern civilization as is commonly supposed. Although we are not today familiar with the Slavonic type of vampire that sucks the blood of its victims, producing death in two or three days' time, strange cases come to light occasionally where people are victims, by their own confession, of something of a very similar nature…Such cases are today, generally speaking, promptly consigned to our lunatic asylums and do not reach the public ear…."

This "not reaching the public ear" is what happens to reports of vampires in this modern age. Instead of viewing vampirism as just one more inexplicable occurrence in the many weird manifestations of things we do not understand, the unhappy victim of vampirism who tells of being attacked by the "living dead" is bundled off to an asylum.

BEFORE telling of England's famous Croglin Grange vampire, I shall tell a little about them both for the reader's instruction and—so to speak—to set the mood for the main astonishing tale.

Most vampire records in Europe are found in Slavic countries like Poland, Hungary and Slovakia but there are also a great many recorded histories in Greece, Arabia and China. Vampirism does not seem to be confined to one section of the world or to a special period in history. Vampires have been reported in England and in China in periods of high cultural development and in legends which precede written history. Vampirism seems to have a common universal foundation.

One of the most famous vampires in history was one Peter Plogojowich, who lived in the village of Kisilova, near Gradish, in Hungary. His case has been the inspiration for much of the fiction written which has vampirism as its central theme.

The historic records concerning Peter were sworn to by local clergymen, judges and others of unquestioned integrity. These statements assert that not long after Peter was buried, several persons in Kisilova reported that the dead man had personally attacked them by seizing their throats and sucking their blood. Though there were what seemed to be teeth marks on their throats, the village fathers thought them a little addled and ignored the reports. Within a few days, every person who reported being attacked was dead of some mysterious ailment—though to all appearances they had been in perfect health.

The village elders called a meeting and, accompanied by the local physician, a judge, and a clergyman, entered the vault where Peter had been buried. It was obvious from the moment they entered that the coffin had been tampered with. The top, which worked on hinges and had been tight at the time of burial, was no longer tight.

Muttering prayers and fearfully crossing themselves, the village fathers raised the coffin top. Peter Plogojowich lay with arms folded across his chest as they had last seen him six weeks ago. But, by the light of the lanterns they held above him, there was no mistaking that instead of the customary pallor of the dead, the skin was firm and even more fresh than when he was alive. In a comer of his mouth was a fleck of blood.

The doctor cut a vein in the dead man's arm with a sharp knife. A little

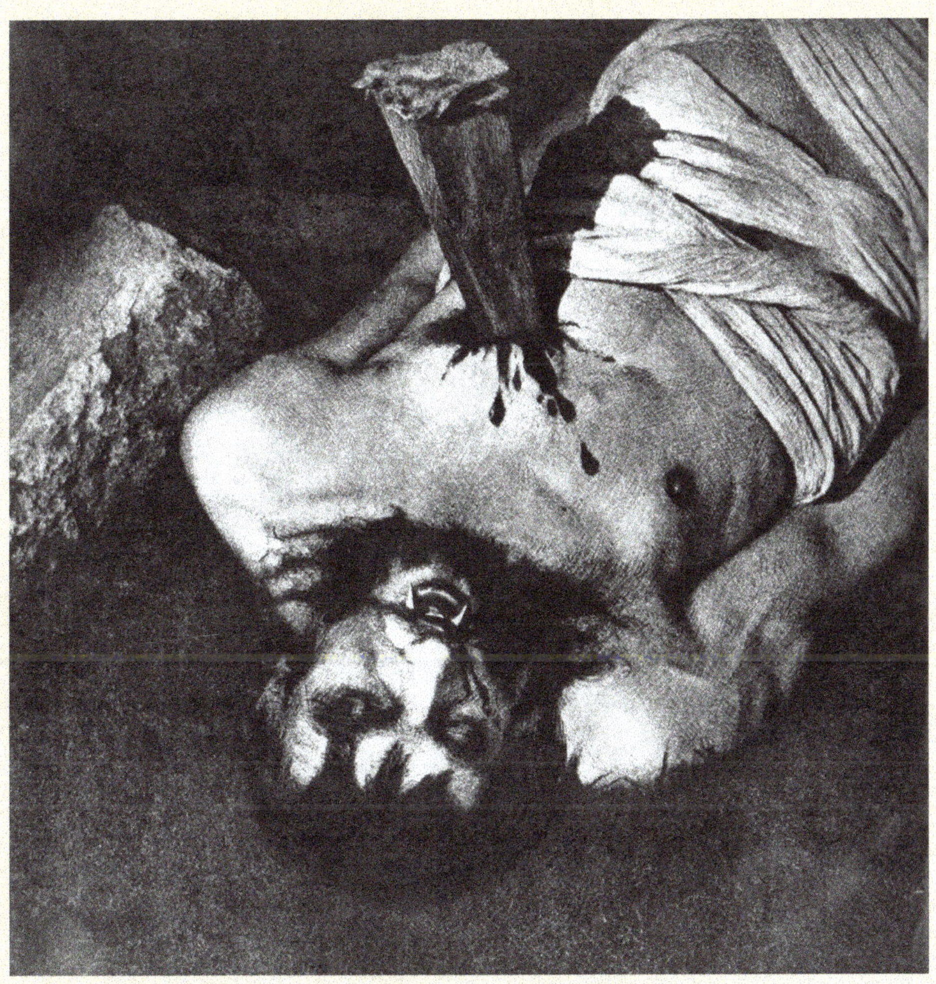

trickle of blood oozed out.

"A dead man's blood does not circulate," said the physician. "Either this man is not dead—and I will swear he was dead six weeks ago—or he is a frightful manifestation of something neither medicine nor science understands."

Without any ceremony, the villagers prepared a huge funeral pyre, placed the coffin and its grisly body on it and, to play safe, dug up the bodies of those who died after being attacked by the vampire, and placed those, too, on the pyre, and fire put to it. The corpses were burned to ashes and the vampire never troubled the villagers again.

In the vampirism at Croglin Grange recorded by August Hare he states that the details were told to him by Capt. Fisher, whose family lived in the house. The Fishers rented the Grange to the two brothers and sister and, before leaving, asked their old neighbors to be hospitable to the newcomers. Hare does not give the exact rental dates nor the names of the brothers and sister, presumably to spare their feelings.

The villagers were delighted with the newcomers and welcomed them cordially. Apparently, the little family had an income sufficient for its needs for none worked at earning a living. All three devoted their time to cultural pursuits. Within a few weeks it seemed as if the newcomers, and their ancestors, had lived at the Grange for centuries. The neighbors were especially drawn to the sister, an attractive, vivacious, witty and level-headed girl.

In this tranquil environment the three saw fall skies fill with scudding clouds and fall leaves turn their golden colors. Life on the Grange was a haven of peace and contentment, with beauty wherever they looked—especially the lawn that sloped to the field of trees which separated the rambling house from the village church and its quiet graveyard down in the hollow. With the coming of winter, the fireplace became the center of family life. The three often sat before its blazing warmth, reading, discussing the affairs of their time and, on proper occasions, entertaining.

So winter passed and spring, with its buds of new life, appeared on bush and tree; and in the summer, there are lovely sections of England where the heat sometimes seems to enfold the area and block out every breath of air. Croglin Grange was one of these spots. One day in midsummer, the heat was so all embracing that all the body wanted was a shady spot to gasp for breath quietly. There was a heavy humidity, so impressive that it was almost tangible. It was a day when nothing stirred.

The brothers found spots under ancient trees which shaded the picturesque terrace and lawn. They tried to read but could not concentrate because of the heat. All they could do was wait hopefully for the cool of the evening. Their sister sat on the terrace, under the shade of a huge tree's intertwined branches. She, too, was washed out by the heat. When the sun set there still was no movement of air but at least the burning glare of the sun was gone for a few hours. In the dusk the sister brought out some cold meats, for no one wanted a full meal, and dinner of a sort was finished. They sat in silence, watching a sky changing to suffuse the heavens with a glorious sweep of colors. A sense of peace and contentment filled them that they had not felt in years.

A BARREL-HEAD of a moon rose over the distant fields and climbed upwards, bathing everything in an unearthly beauty. When they finally retired, the moon was riding high in a cloudless sky. The rooms were hot, especially the sister's, and not a breath of air stirred in her direction. It was just too hot

to sleep, but she did not mind for the moon had turned the grand sweep of
lawn into a field of dark burnished gold and silver. The night was so beautiful that she decided to sit up in bed—all night, if necessary—and enjoy
the beauty spread out before her. She fastened the ancient window with its
small leaded diamond shaped window pane and, facing the view beyond the
window, propped herself up to revel in the patterns cast by the branches of
the ancient tree.

Since Croglin Grange was a one-story house, all rooms were on the
ground floor and her view was level with the stretch of lawn. She thought
she saw something like two bright lights flicker in the distance and smiled
to herself. She knew there were no lights across the lawn or in the belt of
trees that separated the sloping acres from the churchyard in the hollow.
Yet, even as this passed through her mind, she again saw two flickering
lights, something like the eyes of a prowling night animal. She wondered
curiously if it were some neighbor's dog, for no wild beasts were reported
in that area. Gradually, the lights approached near enough to the house so
that she made in the moonlight, the vague form of a human being. A little
frightened, she peered intently, straining to see the form more clearly.

She rubbed her eyes to be sure it was not an hallucination for the form
was now approaching the house. The sharp face of a man became clear, a
man whose eyes gleamed like burning candles. The details of his face were
not clear except that it seemed sharply chiseled and the general appearance
of the man's form was that of one thin and scrawny. It was while she was
trying to catch a glimpse of his features that he raised his head to stare at
the moon. The silver light fell full on his face and what she saw paralyzed
her with horror.

It was a thin, drawn face with skin tight against the cheekbones,
and long, matted hair. It seemed in that flashing glance like the face of a
mummy. In that moment of horror the tightly drawn skin seemed to relax.
A full-mouthed, terrible grin spread over his face and disclosed teeth set in
jaw bones from which all flesh seemed to have fallen away. From the sleeves
of an ancient coat long, bony fingers extended and moved spasmodically.

She wanted to scream for her brothers and opened her mouth, but no
sound would come. Her mouth was dry as if it had turned to cotton and her
throat had constricted tightly. A fright such as she had never conceived as
being possible swept over her. She could not move. Her eyes were hypnotized and stared to the locked windows and door.

The creature appeared at her window, moving lightly as if it were on
air. She heard a scratching sound—a terrifying scratching as if he were
trying to get to the window lock. Literally petrified, she could not move.
In an agony of horror she listened to the steady scratch on the leaded

window panes.

Suddenly the scratching ceased and she heard a new sound—a pecking sound, as if the creature had concluded that it could not get in by scratching at the lead but only by pecking at it. In a few moments a diamond shaped pane fell into the room noiselessly as it came to rest on a thick rug.

Even in these moments she still could not utter a sound. A long, thin bony hand reached in through the open space in the window, unlocked the latch and bounded into the room, and she watched in fascinated horror as he moved silently towards her.

And suddenly two bony hands flashed out and twisted themselves into her hair. They jerked her head violently to one side and the long teeth sank into her throat in a ferocious and hungry bite.

Whether it was the searing pain of the bite or the actual physical contact with the creature, she never knew; but that bite broke her paralysis and she uttered the cry of the damned—a cry so loud, so piercing and blood chilling that the creature himself jumped away from her and leaped through the window, running across the lawn towards the woods.

The brothers came running but her door was locked on the inside. One started to break down the door, for when they called they got no answer. Not until considerably later did they learn that after that blood curdling cry she lost consciousness. One of the brothers saw the dark form scurrying across the lawn and chased it up to the stone wall surrounding the churchyard, where it vanished.

By the time the brother returned to the house the sister had recovered consciousness and explained what had happened. Other than knowing that she was not given to hallucinations, the provable facts verified her story. Someone had broken into her room the way she described, for the window pane still lay on the soft rug where it fell. One of the brothers had actually seen and pursued a man; and, most convincing of all, there was the wound in her throat from some wolfish animal.

"I imagine," said the sister when she had recovered consciousness and her poise, "there's a lunatic loose and the community should be on the watch for him."

The family physician who was called immediately, agreed with her assumption that a madman was afoot. The girl insisted that she was all right, but the physician advised a change of scene. Since she really had been badly shaken up by the experience, she agreed and the three went to Switzerland, certain the lunatic would be captured before they returned.

In the fall the sister suggested that they go back to the Grange which she missed. In one of the discussions they had with friends to whom they told the story one suggested that perhaps it was a vampire. This idea

The "living dead" monster dropped—wounded

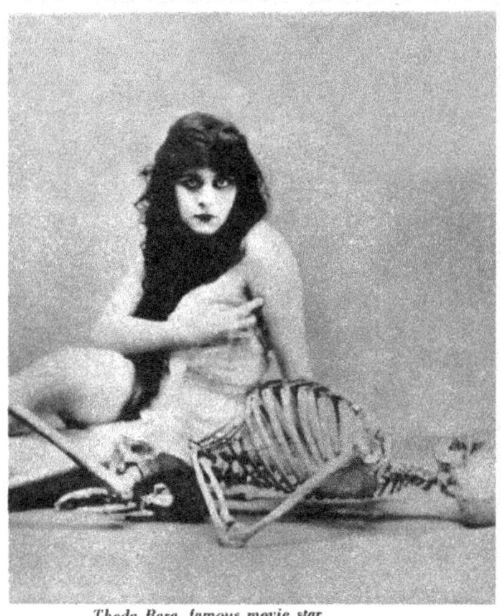

*Theda Bara, famous movie star
in a posed scene from her
famous picture "The Vampire"*

aroused considerable laughter and was pooh-poohed as not worth commenting on.

No one questioned but that it had been a lunatic and, the sister assured them, lunatics do not escape every day, so the chances of another like unpleasant encounter were very remote.

They returned to their tranquil surroundings, the girl completely recovered from the shock. Though they did not hear that a lunatic had been captured in their absence, she was certain that the unbalanced monster was no longer about. But this time the two brothers had keys made to her door should an emergency ever arise again, and slept with loaded pistols beside them.

The fall days at Croglin were even more beautiful than spring and winter. On a winter's night especially, the snow spread out over the countryside, covered everything with an eerie air and the stillness was so intense you could almost feel it. Winter was devoted to cultural pursuits and to entertaining friendly neighbors and being entertained. Occasionally, the sister admitted later, when she retired on some still night, the thought of the monster crossed her mind, but she quickly threw it out.

The family had all but forgot the incident when the sister was awakened from a deep sleep by a familiar sound of scratching on the leaded window panes. There was a horrifying familiarity about the sound and she was wide awake instantly. She knew also in that instant what the sound meant. It was a full moon, and with terrace and lawn bathed in silvery light, she saw the same hideous face, the same toothy smile, and the long, bony fingers now pecking at the lead.

This time she was not paralyzed by fear. The scream she uttered awoke her brothers and startled the monster into a fast retreat.

The brothers came dashing to her room, each with pistol in hand. One quickly unlocked the door with the key he always carried, while the other rushed around towards the terrace in time to see the creature running across the lawn. The brother took careful aim and fired. The creature fell, picked himself up and continued to run limpingly across the lawn. Because of the wound the brother was able to gain on the fleeing monster and was in time to see the creature vanish into the cemetery and enter a vault—the door to which was open as if he had just left it.

The pursuing brother did not follow the creature into the vault but decided to return home and investigate the vault in daylight. Upon his return he found his sister completely recovered. She told the details of what had happened and the brother told them he was certain he had hit the marauder.

"We must tell the villagers," said the other brother. "We must examine the vault. Maybe it's a vampire!"

"What nonsense!" exclaimed the sister, laughing. "It's probably the same lunatic who attacked me last summer. It's some kind of obsession that comes over him when the moon is full, and because his family guards him well, he is not generally known. But, whatever it is, it is no vampire. Vampires are creatures of legend. But I do think the vault should be explored. This lunatic may be using it as a hiding place."

In the morning the neighbors were told for the first time why they went to Switzerland and what happened again last night. No one knew of any lunatic in the neighborhood but all agreed the vault should certainly be inspected. The town elders and they immediately went to the cemetery where the brother pointed out the vault the scrawny man had entered.

"But it can't be," said a village official. "This is the family vault of a long extinct family. The last direct member of the line was buried almost ten years ago and the vault has not been disturbed since."

"Let's examine it," said the brothers grimly. "If this lunatic hides out here, we should know it."

LANTERNS had been brought in the event it was decided to enter the dark vault. The local magistrate, who was present, called attention to what everyone had noticed but which no one had commented on: the door to the vault had been opened recently! Whether the marauding unknown was still in there they could not tell, but there was a possibility that he had left something which would help trace him and by which he could be identified.

The leaders of the village—the doctor, the magistrate, the minister, and the two brothers, each holding lanterns, opened the creaking door. A smell of mustiness and death swept over the gathering, and as the door swung open, everyone present gasped.

In the years since the last member of the family had been buried, dust had seeped through the tight door, and in this layer of dust everyone could see distinct footprints of bare feet!

Astounded as they were by this they were more astounded when they entered the ancient family crypt. There was no sign of a lunatic as the yellow lantern light illumined all corners of the vault but what was visible brought uncontrolled exclamations of shock and disbelief.

Coffin tops had been ripped off as by some extraordinarily powerful hand. What was left of the dead—some more than a century old—had been torn apart as if they had been thrown away after seeing they were useless for the creature's purpose. Only one coffin escaped the ravages of the unknown marauder. That one was intact and crossing themselves the village doctor and one of the brothers raised the creaking lid and held their lanterns high.

There, shriveled, mummified, the skin drawn tight over the cheeks and jaw bones, lay the last of the long line—and fitting exactly the sister's description of the creature who had attacked her! So far as medical and legal records were concerned, this man had been dead for years!

Their horror at what they saw was only surface horror for something far deeper was apparent. The mummified face showed no sign of the natural disintegration which comes with death!

The doctor motioned to the sister to come closer: For the first time in her life she questioned her own sanity. This was something which existed only in superstitions and fevered brains, yet the mummified face she looked at, the face of one who had died many years ago, was the face of the creature who attacked her last summer and who had tried to enter her bedroom the night before. There was no mistake about his identity!

"This is the man," she said and fainted.

She was carried outside and revived. The doctor, with the others crowded into the vault watching, examined the dead man carefully. In the left calf he found a pistol bullet buried deep in the still firm flesh!

"As a scientist, I just do not believe it," said the doctor. "I have heard of vampires but they are creatures of legend and superstition. But, as a man of science, I must maintain an objective mind. I must believe what I see and what everybody else here sees. Shakespeare was right when he said there are more things than are dreamt of in our philosophy.

"Whatever we believe or do not believe we must take precautions as if a plague came to the village. We may not know what the plague is or what causes it, but we know there are timetested beliefs on steps to halt the plague. Fire is one, and perhaps the most perfect for fire destroys things utterly—germs and bugs and life itself. For centuries the records show that the only way to get rid of a vampire is to burn the cadaver until nothing is left of even the bones but ashes. There is also the belief that a cross driven through a vampire's heart will pin him forever to his coffin. I do not know if this is true. I know only that we are in the presence of things we do not understand and I favor taking all precautions. That can do no harm."

Villagers scattered throughout the field of woods between the Grange and the churchyard. With the minister's help everyone collected all dead and dried limbs. A huge funeral pyre was built in a clearing outside the graveyard. A cross was made of wood and, with the minister standing by, the local carpenter took his heaviest hammer, put the sharp point of the cross over the heart of the long dead man, and drove the wood through the vampire's heart.

From the sagging mouth of the dead man arose a cry of agony which chilled everyone with fear. The carpenter dropped his hammer and swore mightily. A woman fainted and everyone who heard it shook as with palsy. It was a terrifying sound coming from a man dead for years. The doctor, his own hands shaking from the unnerving sound tried bravely to explain that the blows had produced pressure which created the sound of air, but even as he tried to explain he looked as if he himself did not believe it.

Those present took no more chances. They picked up the corpse in the coffin and placed it on top of the dried wood and set a match to it. The fire leaped and burned with an almost unimaginable fury. The very flames seemed anxious to consume the corpse within it.

The watchers waited, fearful that another cry of agony would sound when the fire reached the cadaver but nothing else was heard other than the crackling wood. By nightfall the corpse was completely consumed.

I do not know or pretend to know what this weird incident means. I simply record it as one of the world's most weird tales—just one more of the many, many occurrences which science cannot explain.

VAMPIRES RIPPED MY FLESH

Lewis Greer

Man's Life, March 1956   Cover by Norman Saunders

Vampires

I felt their sharp teeth, and my blood trickling down my body. Some of the bats were in my hair, others hung from my skin. I was in a cave filled with flying death!

by LEWIS GREER

THE fetid heat of the jungle rolled up into the high ground at dusk, clawing our throats, soaking us, robbing us of our last strength, Caymen and I. But we ran to the high ground, ran frantically, tripping headlong into the stinking green morass and rising and running again. But we made it to the high ground above the Carare River and we were out, and so were the emeralds. A million dollars worth of green ice for the two of us.

My khakis were shreaded at the ankles from the sharp tugging of the tall grass; my hands were raw and oozing thick rivulets of blood; my face felt heavy with the grotesqueness of panic, and the poison of before. But I was alive and death was behind me, I thought. I lay on the hot red ground, too weary to speak, too tired to look down the canyon for the Indians. Indians and more Indians.

I lay there an eternity and the exhaustion swallowed me and I felt the heat waves lifting my body. And I slept. Like a dead man. And Caymen did, too. But Caymen woke first and when I opened my eyes and saw he was gone, I thought the emeralds had gone with him.

I'D never distrusted Luke Caymen—but that time was different. After what we'd gone through—the blood—sweat—tears and death—I'd suspect my own grandmother. Frantically I lurched to my feet and spun up the rise and I saw Caymen there, on his knees, praying.

When I dropped to the ground beside him, Caymen ended his supplication and turned to me and grinned.

"So you're awake? You see, it was just as I said it would be. We're alive. Two more days and we're back in Bogota and we're rich!" Caymen said.

"Do we travel at night, Caymen?"

"Yes. Indians prefer the daylight hours. We travel at night."

"Okay," I said, seeing the exhaustion on his coppery face. "How do we do it—on our hands and knees?"

Caymen smiled. He knew we needed rest. Three days ago we'd begun the trek. Three years ago, so it seemed. Then the chonta spears began falling and the original five, dwindled to two.

Below us sprawled the rushing white waters of the Carare and to a side on the far bank rocks. Caymen indicated the rocks with a nod.

"There," he grunted, "are the caves. We go there. If we remain on the high ground they'll come up soon. I figure we'll fool them. They'll never look up there.

Ripped My Flesh

Backtrack. And right now. We'll be safe in the caves," he nodded.

But Caymen was wrong—dead wrong, almost, because what happened next made the spears of the savages seem hardly more than a bad hangover. What happened next happened slowly and bloodily and it robbed us of our Muzo treasure. And more—much more, including sanity itself. Mine and Luke Caymen's. . .

ON the 12th day of March, 1946, we made our strike. It happened late in the afternoon of a day that had started out most unfortunately for me: a moderately poisonous mountain snake caught me in the calf of my right leg.

I'd been in the Columbian jungles almost seven months scratching the hills above the Carare, digging for emeralds. Seven months of sheer backbreaking labor because, among other things, we—Caymen and I—were borrowed up to our eyeballs in order to keep our operation rolling.

Worse yet, our crews were constantly threatening to quit. Indian trouble. The fatal kind. Repeatedly we were harried by sporadic attacks on our mountain excavation—attacks that came suddenly with the whizzing of spears, or the sharp zing of the arrows. And always there were dead men in the wake of these attacks, and more men quick to quit. Seven months of that and I sprouted the neatest crop of gray sideburns this side of Bogota.

But, somehow, I'd always managed to come away from those deadly encounters alive and with a whole skin. I can't say why. Maybe it was luck; maybe the Indians had lousy vision; maybe they were saving us for a worse fate than the poisoned splinter.

I wondered about that for seven long months, day in and day out. I saw men sliced down the middle, split like stuck pigs by machetes that lanced through the jungle, thrown by unseen hands. I saw a lot of things that came under the general heading of horror but as I'd guessed, the worst was yet to come.

ORIGINALLY, Luke and I were pearl dusters in Mexico. Luke, whose mother was Spanish and his father Columbian, spoke the language, naturally. He was my voice, and, on many occasions, my life saver. We'd done service together in the old China fleet, running the Yangtse on a gunboat. The Navy agreed with us; we were shipmates and we had plans.

When World War II broke out, Luke and I got separated and we didn't meet again until the day I mustered out at Mare Island Naval Base. That was in May, 1945. I met Luke standing against the bar in the St. Francis Hotel in San Francisco. There, in an atmosphere of gushing whiskey, we formulated our weird plan. Next morning when I awoke, Luke met me down in the coffee shop and we rehashed the bit of the previous evening. Not the whiskey part—not just then. Just the part about the pearls Luke said he knew were ripe for plucking.

That's how it was. From Pearls with a capital P, we poured a thumping 70 thousand into men, materiel, engineers and a lot of bum advice. We listened to talk that the Muzo treasure was as available as our pearls had been. Muzo as in Spanish Conquistadores!

SEVEN long months slipped by and the only emerald I'd seen to date was down in the government assaying office in Bogota. I awoke that morning feeling lousy. I stepped out of our tent, and climbed down the grade to the chow house. I stumbled sleepily against a boulder and caught it—a searing pain in my right leg.

"Bad?" Luke said, running down.

"Bad enough!"

Luke tore my pants leg and made the incision. Then he gave me a shot of snake serum and stuck me back in the sack. Fever raged through my body until nightfall, and I swelled so I could barely breathe. But I lived, thanks to Luke Caymen, and that night my world took on a new lustre.

I was still in my bunk when I heard Luke shouting, and the other men with picks hollering like maniacs. I forgot the snake bite. I crawled out of the sack and literally slid down the grade on my hands and knees. They were too confounded crazy with joy to worry about me—the four of them (Continued on page 72)

ART BY NORMAN SAUNDERS

THE FETID heat of the jungle rolled up into the high ground at dusk, clawing our throats, soaking us, robbing us of our last strength, Caymen and I. But we ran to the high ground, ran frantically, tripping headlong into the stinking green morass and rising and running again. But we made it to the high ground above the Carare River and we were out, and so were the emeralds. A million dollars worth of green ice for the two of us.

My khakis were shredded at the ankles from the sharp tugging of the tall grass; my hands were raw and oozing thick rivulets of blood; my face felt heavy with the grotesqueness of panic, and the poison of before. But I was alive and death was behind me, I thought. I lay on the hot red ground, too weary to speak, too tired to look down the canyon for the Indians. Indians and more Indians.

I lay there an eternity and the exhaustion swallowed me and I felt the heat waves lifting my body. And I slept. Like a dead man. And Caymen did, too. But Caymen woke first and when I opened my eyes and saw he was gone, I thought the emeralds had gone with him.

I'D NEVER distrusted Luke Caymen—but that time was different. After what we'd gone through—the blood, sweat, tears, and death—I'd suspect my own grandmother. Frantically I lurched to my feet and spun up the rise and I saw Caymen there, on his knees, praying.

When I dropped to the ground beside him, Caymen ended his supplication and turned to me and grinned.

"So you're awake? You see, it was just as I said it would be. We're alive. Two more days and we're back in Bogota and we're rich!" Caymen said.

"Do we travel at night, Caymen?!"

"Yes. Indians prefer the daylight hours. We travel at night."

"Okay," I said, seeing the exhaustion on his coppery face. "How do we do it—on our hands and knees?"

Caymen smiled. He knew we needed rest. Three days ago we'd begun the trek. Three years ago, so it seemed. Then the *chonta* spears began falling and the original five, dwindled to two.

Below us sprawled the rushing white waters of the Carare and to a side on the far bank rocks. Caymen indicated the rocks with a nod.

"There," he grunted, "are the caves. We go there. If we remain on the high ground they'll come up soon. I figure we'll fool them. They'll never look up there. Backtrack. And right now. We'll be safe in the caves," he nodded.

But Caymen was wrong—dead wrong, almost, because what happened next made the spears of the savages seem hardly more than a bad hangover. What happened next happened slowly and bloodily and it robbed us of our Muzo treasure. And more—much more, including sanity itself. Mine and Luke Caymen's...

On the 12th day of March, 1946, we made our strike. It happened late in the afternoon of a day that had started out most unfortunately for me: a moderately poisonous mountain snake caught me in the calf of my right leg.

I'd been in the Columbian jungles almost seven months scratching the hills above the Carare, digging for emeralds. Seven months of sheer backbreaking labor because, among other things, we—Caymen and I—were borrowed up to our eyeballs in order to keep our operation rolling.

Worse yet, our crews were constantly threatening to quit. Indian trouble. The fatal kind. Repeatedly we were harried by sporadic attacks on our mountain excavation—attacks that came suddenly with the whizzing of spears, or the sharp zing of the arrows. And always there were dead men in the wake of these attacks, and more men quick to quit. Seven months of that and I sprouted the neatest crop of gray sideburns this side of Bogota.

But, somehow, I'd always managed to come away from those deadly encounters alive and with a whole skin. I can't say why. Maybe it was luck; maybe the Indians had lousy vision; maybe they were saving us for a worse fate than the poisoned splinter.

I wondered about that for seven long months, day in and day out. I saw men sliced down the middle, split like stuck pigs by machetes that lanced through the jungle, thrown by unseen hands. I saw a lot of things that came under the general heading of horror but as I'd guessed, the worst was yet to come.

Originally, Luke and I were pearl dusters in Mexico. Luke, whose mother was Spanish and his father Colombian, spoke the language, naturally. He was my voice, and, on many occasions, my life saver. We'd done service together in the old China fleet, running the Yangtse on a gunboat. The Navy agreed with us; we were shipmates and we had plans.

When World War II broke out, Luke and I got separated and we didn't meet again until the day I mustered out at Mare Island Naval Base. That was in May, 1945. I met Luke standing against the bar in the St. Francis Hotel in San Francisco. There, in an atmosphere of gushing whiskey, we formulated our weird plan. Next morning when I awoke, Luke met me down in the coffee shop and we rehashed the bit of the previous evening. Not the whiskey part—not just then. Just the part about the pearls Luke said he knew were ripe for plucking.

That's how it was. From Pearls with a capital P, we poured a thumping 70 thousand into men, materiel, engineers and a lot of bum advice. We listened to talk that the Muzo treasure was as available as our pearls had been. Muzo as in Spanish Conquistadores!

SEVEN long months slipped by and the only emerald I'd seen to date was down in the government assaying office in Bogota. I awoke that morning feeling lousy. I stepped out of our tent, and climbed down the grade to the chow house. I stumbled sleepily against a boulder and caught it—a searing pain in my right leg.

"Bad?" Luke said, running down.

"Bad enough!"

Luke tore my pants leg and made the incision. Then he gave me a shot of snake serum and stuck me back in the sack. Fever raged through my body until nightfall, and I swelled so I could barely breathe. But I lived, thanks to Luke Caymen, and that night my world took on a new luster.

I was still in my bunk when I heard Luke shouting, and the other men with picks hollering like maniacs. I forgot the snake bite. I crawled out of the sack and literally slid down the grade on my hands and knees. They were too confounded crazy with joy to worry about me—the four of them had found emeralds on our site.

Green ice sold at $12,000,000 per pound. Green ice came out of layers of rock and dirt and death. We had a small piece of it worth a cool million. We'd made a payday, but the joy was short lived. That night we made preparations to break camp. The boys made me a litter but I said the hell with that, I'd be okay.

THAT'S how it was. I made it. Luke and I came out together. The others caught arrows and spears and died screaming along the lower slopes. For two days we ran, hid, stumbled, scurried through the underbrush. Luke and I had the ice, the green ice, and that night in the cave below the high ground we lost it. We lost everything, it seemed.

The hole in the mountain beside the river was Stygian black. Luke went in first. I was sick to my stomach from the snake bite, so Luke dragged me in. Then, in the darkness, we lay on the moist, stinking cave ground and there we fell asleep.

It was not yet light when I saw them. I opened my eyes and shrunk back in horror as I felt wings rushing across my face. Wings on the jagged walls of the cave. Vampire wings on Luke Caymen—Luke was dead.

Even as I struggled to my feet I could see those beady-eyed devils sucking his blood. Hundreds of them covering his head and arms, blood trailing and draining onto the floor of the cave. The horror shriveled my guts and I shrank back against the cave wall.

I tried to cover my face and crawl to the entrance of the cave. But I couldn't. I was too weak to move. Too weak to defend myself when they attacked me. En masse, they dropped and I screamed.

It happened then in a rush of soft wings. Swarms of them left Luke's body and descended on my face and hands, biting me, clawing my face, then fastening themselves to the back of my neck. I felt the hot rush of blood coursing down my throat and dug my fingers into the body of one, tearing and squeezing it into a wet blob of shapelessness.

Squeaking wildly, they clung to my skin and probed the flesh of my chest. Others, their eyes glowing red in the lurid half light, swarmed down, their short, stubby teeth raking as they hit like dive bombers.

Cringing against the wet facing of the cave, I screamed and the sound of my terror boomed back. But above that, I heard the sound—the squeaking sound of the winged ones, and the rush of vampire wings. I saw my own blood drooling from their small, opaque throats. I lunged at the air, grabbing them in flight and squeezing even as they tore my fingers. I fought; I had nothing but animal terror to fight with, and it wasn't enough.

In that last frenzy to gain the entrance, my foot slipped in blood and I tripped over Luke's body. My face slammed against the side of the cave and I heeled over, the dizziness rolling over me crazily, distorted like the long wings of the vampires that hovered about my face.

Desperately I fought the rising mists, trying to crawl those last twenty feet, and not caring whether the bats sucked my blood. If I didn't make the entrance, I'd die there with Luke. I'd lose consciousness and die, my blood siphoned noiselessly by the thirsty death.

The back of my neck pained wildly as I felt the new rush smash down. My face was in blood, slapped against the stinking dankness of the cave, the last few feet of it. I thought my arms would fall off as the vampires suddenly moved to block the entrance. I beat at them hovering there, fluttering against my body. My hands were animated clubs, crimson pistons that slashed out and clutched the small wet heads and squeezed them until they spilled back my life.

I prayed as I crawled. I stared into the eyes of death hanging over me and on me and in my hair, and when one hit my mouth, I caught the wet body in my teeth and ground it so that it no longer fluttered.

I reached the face of the cave and felt the new air and the sound of squeaking, rushing wings and my own thumping heart receded quickly. The cave spun away; the sky darkened and engulfed my remains.

I left the emeralds there, back behind me in the cave, for when I awoke I ran through the jungle. I ran as I had never run before. I knew a terror that was far more horrible than silent spears. Vampire bats—long, squeaking, blood-sucking vampire bats.

Luke Caymen had the emeralds on his person when he died. We'd drawn straws to see which of us—originally five—would take them out. Luke had drawn the short one. So Luke died with them, a cool million; I left that behind.

And as far as I know they're still in the cave under the bats in the lee of the Carare. And they're safe. I'll never go back, I assure you. If I lived through a nightmare like that and emerged only with a little less sanity and some blood drawn from my body, I can go right on being a pauper. It's a damn sight easier on my nervous system—what nervous system I've got left, that is.

ISLAND OF DOOM

Bill Wharton

Sport Trails, Spring 1957   Cover by Stan Borack

Dennis Moyle looked apprehensively over his shoulder as he stepped into a small clearing deep in the green mangrove-covered eastern shores of Aldabra Island. Although the sun was baking down at 115 degrees the dark green depths of the wild plantation were cool, almost cold, the overhead branches forming a natural canopy through which the sun could not penetrate.

Behind him, following in the tunnel-like path which he had hacked through the jungle, he heard his two companions, Vic Lister and Ed Hammett, moving toward him, but it wasn't their sounds that Moyle heard. It was a heavy, almost stertorous breathing which seemed to emanate from the dense bush ahead of him.

Beyond the bush, maybe another twenty or thirty yards farther on, rose the craggy peak they had set out to see.

Moyle's hand rested lightly on the .38 revolver in the holster on his hip as he turned his six-foot frame toward the entrance which he had chopped through the undergrowth. A curly blond head appeared and Lister stepped into the clearing. Behind him came Hammett, sweating profusely.

"What's wrong, Dennis?" Hammett asked at once.

"I don't know," Moyle replied in a quiet voice. "Just keep quiet for a moment and listen."

As the three men stood silent they heard the heavy breathing and without any warning the slope facing them seemed to come alive. There was a violent rumbling like that of an avalanche; the ground shook underfoot, branches brushed them as trees were shaken.

Gradually the rumbling noise decreased until it faded altogether. For another few moments the men stood listening, then Moyle wiped his forehead.

"Let's go," he (Continued on page 81)

It's a cinch to find the fortune on Aldabra. The trick is getting out—alive.

36

The three men crouched in the dense brush, hardly daring to breathe, while the monster rumbled steadily toward them.

OF DOOM

By Bill Wharton
ILLUSTRATED BY MORTON ENGEL

37

ART BY MORTON ENGEL

DENNIS Moyle looked apprehensively over his shoulder as he stepped into a small clearing deep in the green mangrove-covered eastern shores of Aldabra Island. Although the sun was baking down at 115 degrees, the dark green depths of the wild plantation were cool, almost cold, the overhead branches forming a natural canopy through which the sun could not penetrate.

Behind him, following in the tunnel-like path which he had hacked through the jungle, he heard his two companions, Vic Lister and Ed Hammett, moving toward him, but it wasn't their sounds that Moyle heard. It was a heavy, almost stertorous breathing which seemed to emanate from the dense bush ahead of him.

Beyond the bush, maybe another twenty or thirty yards farther on, rose the craggy peak they had set out to see.

Moyle's hand rested lightly on the .38 revolver in the holster on his hip as he turned his six-foot frame toward the entrance which he had chopped through the undergrowth. A curly blond head appeared and Lister stepped into the clearing. Behind him came Hammett, sweating profusely.

"What's wrong, Dennis?" Hammett asked at once.

"I don't know," Moyle replied in a quiet voice. "Just keep quiet for a moment and listen."

As the three men stood silent they heard the heavy breathing and without any warning the slope facing them seemed to come alive. There was a violent rumbling like that of an avalanche; the ground shook underfoot, branches brushed them as trees were shaken.

Gradually the rumbling noise decreased until it faded altogether. For another few moments the men stood listening, then Moyle wiped his forehead.

"Let's go," he murmured and began to hack at the mangroves barring their way to the mountain.

In two hours they stood at the bottom of the peak which rose 2,000 feet above them into the liquid blue sky. Far up against the mountainside they saw gaping black mouths of caves and wide paths, apparently well-trodden, running up toward the caves.

Below them, beyond the bush, they could just distinguish the sea but they could not see their 40-ton schooner. They had sailed from the Seychelles Islands to catch half a dozen giant tortoises which they hoped to sell on the African mainland.

Several yards from them a boulder, almost the size of an ox, suddenly came to life. It started to rise, a hideous head emerged from it and they found themselves staring at the greatest tortoise any of them had ever seen.

The tortoise moved forward unsteadily, its head low to the ground.

"Let's get him! " Lister cried, uncoiling a length of strong, thin rope from his shoulder. In a moment he had lassoed the tortoise's head and drawn the noose tight as the giant withdrew its head and sank down to take cover in its shell.

"It's the biggest tortoise the world has ever seen," Moyle whispered. "We could get a fortune for a couple of these if we could get them to Europe or America. Tie him somewhere—"

He felt rather than saw Hammett tense next to him. The man's jaw opened in amazement, his eyes focused on the mountainside high above them.

"My God!" he whispered. "What's that?"

Moyle and Lister turned and stared upward at the brown-black creature emerging from one of the caves. It stood about fifteen feet high and from its horse-like head to the tip of the kangaroo-like tail they judged it to be at least fifty feet long. It had an oval, scaly body like that of a crocodile, its ten-foot neck was as thick as a man's torso and its head and jaws were horse-like.

"It looks like a dragon," Moyle cried. He had his revolver in his hand and was watching the monstrous creature. Its jaws were hanging open. Something appeared behind it, prodded it, and a second creature emerged from the cave.

It happened suddenly. The men seemed rooted to the spot. The creature was halfway down the mountainside, rumbling like an avalanche, before anyone acted. Lister was the first. He whirled and raced past the tortoise into the bush. Moyle, still gripping the revolver, raced after him, and Hammett followed a moment later, but the monster moved with the speed of lightning. In a flash it shook to a stop at the side of the tortoise.

In the dense bush, feeling secure for the moment, the three men watched, hardly daring to breathe. Incredulous, they watched the creature lift the giant tortoise in its right forepaw, then smash it down on a rock. Again and again it lifted the tortoise and smashed it. Then methodically it began to claw away the thick, shattered shell and dig its slavering jaws into the interior of the shell.

LISTER took aim with his revolver. Neither of the other two men saw him do so, and the sharp crack of the revolver echoed in their ears. There was a zing, then a whine as the bullet ricocheted from the beast's scaly head.

Moyle cursed and knocked Lister's hand down, but he was too late—the creature had raised its head from the gory feast and was glaring into the dark green patch where the men were hiding. For a moment it stood, head down, then began to move forward.

Then Hammett raised his revolver and fired at a range of twenty feet into the beast's head, but the .32 slug appeared to have no effect.

Three shots crashed out almost simultaneously, but the beast kept coming.

Then Lister panicked. He sprang up, revealing himself to the beast, turned and tried to run into the dense bush. He jerked out his hatchet and began to chop as Moyle grabbed him by the arm and tried to calm him.

"This way! This way!"

Hammett was running ahead, keeping low, through the tunnel they had made in the bush; behind him came Moyle, then Lister. It was Lister's hoarse scream that made the two men jerk to a temporary halt. They saw him swinging high above the bushes, the small of his back wedged in the beast's jaws, long hooked teeth biting deeply into him.

Above Lister's screams came the cracks of both guns, Hammett's .32 and Moyle's .38. In a fraction of a minute, ten bullets were pumped into the beast's neck and head. But it continued to smash its human prey violently to the ground. The two men refilled their magazines and began to shoot at the thing's broad belly. A moment later the head reared up again, still gripping Lister, but Lister was hanging limply, his back obviously broken. The beast turned with a rumble and, still breathing heavily, began to move up the mountainside. As they watched in horrified silence, they saw it deposit Lister's body in front of the second beast, then turn to stare at the green jungle.

Moyle was the first to move.

"I'm getting out of here!" he cried, and began to crawl as quickly as he could through the low, narrow tunnel.

"What about Lister?" Hammett shouted behind him.

"You can't help him," Moyle shouted back. "He's dead, and we'll be, too, if we don't get out of here."

The argument was sound; the two men were hurrying through the jungle toward the small cove where they had anchored their schooner when they heard a wild rumbling. Neither stopped to listen. It took them almost four hours to reach the spot where their dinghy was tied.

And they had just boarded the schooner when they saw the evil head emerge from the bushes on shore.

Despite their apparent safety, Moyle and Hammett took no chances. The auxiliary engine was started and the schooner, Crested Eagle, put to sea.

ON THE western side of the island, the men put into the small bay where a dozen fishermen from the Seychelles have built themselves huts.

Here Hammett and Moyle tried to recruit help to get the body of their dead friend, but not one of the men they found on the island would accompany them. The oldest of the men, whose name was Snijders, told them that no one ever goes to the eastern shores of Aldabra because of the monsters which live in the caves on the mountainside. None of these monsters has been seen on the western side of the island.

Aldabra Island, little more than a small dot to the northwest of the Island of Madagascar, is flanked on the north, east and south by seven other islands: West Island, South Island, Assumption, Astove, Menai, Cosmoledo, and Wizard.

Outside of the jungle area, and on the northern and southern tips of the island, the land has been flattened out by the giant tortoises as they make their way to the waterholes and sand dunes where they scratch huge excavations to lay their eggs. They usually live in deep holes clawed under heavy bushes, where they are reasonably safe from the depredations of the species of iguana-like monsters which infest the mountain and which feeds on them. As witnessed by Moyle and Hammett, these monsters are capable of lifting an elephant tortoise, which weighs, so far as science has established, up to and over 400 pounds, and smash its inch-thick shell in order to get to the meat inside.

In 1847, a British brigantine, the *Sylvester*, put into the eastern shore of Aldabra in order to take tortoises on board. It was the custom, then, for ships to stop at islands where there were tortoises and take large numbers of them aboard in order to have fresh meat on the voyage.

The crew of the *Sylvester*, bound south along the African coast for the Cape of Good Hope and Europe, had taken on about 300 tortoises ranging in weight from 20 to 200 pounds. Two of the men, working some distance from the others, looked up and found themselves staring at an awful monster standing above them.

The monster, which had apparently been watching them, snatched up one of the men in its jaw and clawed at the other, who ran quickly away. While guns were fetched, the monster lumbered off into the jungle with the screaming seaman clutched in its jaws.

Twenty members of the crew, led by the mate and armed with muskets, set off in pursuit. The track was easy to follow and within an hour they came to the slopes of the mountain. Far above them they could see the yawning mouth of the cave which they presumed to be the monster's home.

They were, according to the ship's log, about three-quarters of the way up when a gigantic creature, resembling a dragon but more likely a giant iguana, emerged from the cave.

The monster pawed the ground for a few moments as the men leveled their muskets and prepared to fire, then it came roaring down the mountainside toward them at great speed. The muskets were fired on a signal given by Gillespie, the mate, but the volley did not stop the beast. The men scattered, diving into the bush to seek cover. Three men were caught in the path of the monster and literally torn apart by its claws.

The crew completely lost their nerve, a few more shots were fired, then the men began to run for the beach and their ship. When a count was taken it was found that seven men were missing. They were never seen again.

Shortly after this incident, two brigs called at the island and loaded twelve hundred tortoises without any difficulty.

The meat of the Aldabra tortoise tastes just like a juicy beefsteak. For years tortoise meat was a highly priced delicacy in continental restaurants. It was the prices fetched by large tortoises which drove some ships' masters to make for islands like Aldabra where there were plenty of these animals. Most headed for Aldabra because of the huge tortoises and here it was that many men died either from snake or scorpion bite or from encounters with the notorious Aldabra dragons.

In the summer of 1937, five Frenchmen in a yawl from Madagascar arrived on Aldabra intending to take away as many large tortoises as their vessel could carry. They were led by a man named Michel and they had little trouble in rounding up dozens of medium-sized tortoises, weighing from about 20 to 50 pounds. They also had three or four weighing over one hundred pounds. One of the party wandered towards an extremely bushy part of the eastern jungle, following a tortoise trail, and was grabbed by a slavering-jawed monster which had been standing unobserved in the bushes.

His companions rushed to his aid, hacking at the beast with knives. The monster had gripped the Frenchman by the arm and in hoisting him from the ground, tore it off.

The men were so preoccupied they did not see that other creatures had emerged from the jungle behind them. It wasn't until one of the men screamed that the others realized their danger. They swung around, firing as fast as they could, then raced away.

Only two of the men escaped; the others were never seen again, although eight soldiers were sent to the island, armed with modern weapons. What these soldiers saw—if anything—is not recorded. Their commanding officer was reported to be a nervous type of sergeant and at the time it was generally believed they never had set foot on Aldabra.

Ships from the Seychelles call at Aldabra about twice a year to load tortoises, bêche-de-mer, mangrove bark and green turtles, but no one ever goes to the eastern seaboard of Aldabra; all the work is done on the side of the island that is considered safe, providing one doesn't wander too far from the seashore.

The world's zoos are interested in outsize tortoises, but they place their orders with recognized dealers who, in turn, arrange for the specimens to be obtained. From time to time schooners and other vessels anchor off Aldabra's eastern shore and enough men are sent to grab one or two giant tortoises. As soon as these are captured, they retreat to the ship.

Moyle, Lister and Hammett are typical of many others before them, searching for a few large tortoises which could bring upwards of $500 apiece, spot cash. It seems so easy, slip into the eastern cove, grab half a dozen of the giants and get away quickly. But it is not that easy.

The dragons of Aldabra live on these tortoises, but there is no danger of the tortoises becoming extinct, because they breed in thousands. For every tortoise devoured by the animals which live on them, a thousand survive.

Aldabra Island offers a temptation few men can resist. And year after year it continues to draw men to almost certain death at the claws of the island's guardians, the giant iguanas or Aldabra dragons.

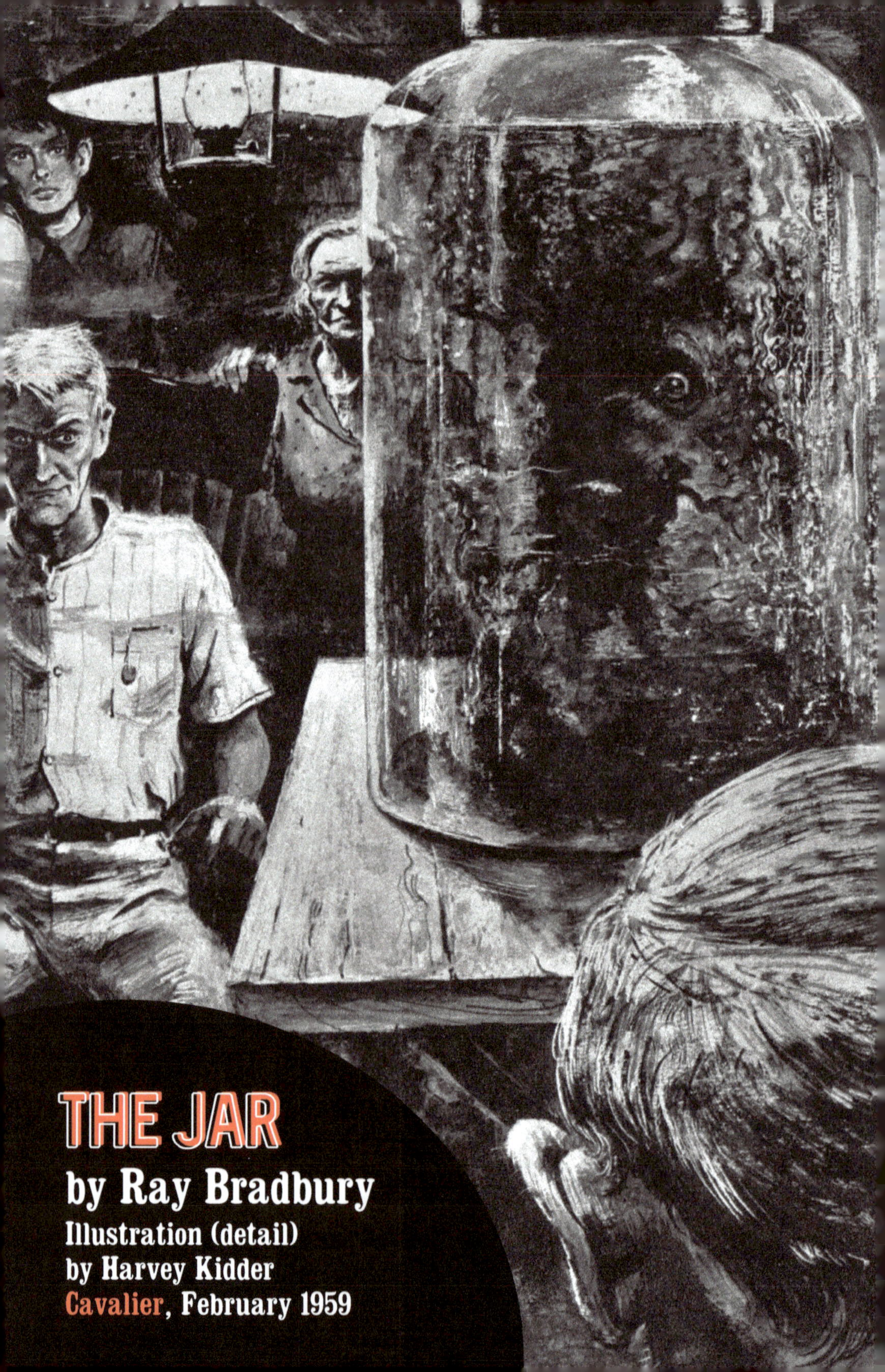

THE JAR

by Ray Bradbury
Illustration (detail)
by Harvey Kidder
Cavalier, February 1959

TRAPPED BY A MAN-EATING TREE

Robert Moore

Man's Life, March 1958   Cover by Wilbur 'Wil' Hulsey

TRAPPED BY A MAN-EATING TREE

Crippling pains shot up my legs as long sticky arms curled around me. I hacked at the poisonous vines that were picking me up—It was going to swallow me whole!

by OSCAR SCHNEE (Lt. Ret. RDN)
AS TOLD TO ROBERT MOORE

CELEB fishermen call it the devil tree—Rauk Yas. It grows in terrible profusion along the south coast of Makassar. On the Postiljon Islands, especially, cannibal or devil tree, is taboo. No islander will approach within a mile of it. I shouldn't wonder why.

In March, 1943, three of us escaped from the Japanese prison compound at Sumbawa, Dutch East Indies. Ironically, the world is full of redolent islands where the shipwrecked for years have found survival, if not happiness. In the back of three exhaused minds was the hope that Laut, a pearly green thumb of land, would be such a place. We made for it in the wake of a typhoon.

Rudder gone, leaking, we hit the outer bar and capsized finally. More dead than alive, we dragged ourselves up on the hard, white sands—delighted just to be alive and free again. Starvation had emaciated us, yet now, for the first time in nearly thirteen months we had hope. My companions—Johnny Krumann and Paul Doers—and I were naval officers, Royal Dutch Navy.

"Let's scout the upper end. There's some cliffs up there!" Paul Doers suggested right away. "With Oscar's knowledge of signaling, maybe we can raise some friendly native . . ."

ACTUALLY, it was a couple of days before we had strength enough to walk from the beach. For two days we lay in our new· (Continued on page 76)

18

He hacked with his knife as the green tendrils curled around him, sucking him into the death tree.

19

ART BY GEOFFREY BIGGS

CELEB fishermen call it the devil tree—Rauk Yas. It grows in terrible profusion along the south coast of Makassar. On the Postilion Islands, especially, cannibal or devil tree is taboo. No islander will approach within a mile of it. I shouldn't wonder why.

In March, 1943, three of us escaped from the Japanese prison compound at Sumbawa, Dutch East Indies. Ironically, the world is full of redolent islands where the shipwrecked for years have found survival, if not happiness. In the back of three exhausted minds was the hope that Laut, a pearly green thumb of land, would be such a place. We made for it in the wake of a typhoon.

Rudder gone, leaking, we hit the outer bar and capsized finally. More dead than alive, we dragged ourselves up on the hard, white sands—delighted just to be alive and free again. Starvation had emaciated us, yet now, for the first time in nearly thirteen months we had hope. My companions—Johnny Krumann and Paul Doers—and I were naval officers, Royal Dutch Navy.

"Let's scout the upper end. There's some cliffs up there!" Paul Doers suggested right away. "With Oscar's knowledge of signaling, maybe we can raise some friendly native..."

ACTUALLY, it was a couple of days before we had strength enough to walk from the beach. For two days we lay in our new-found freedom, living off coconuts and fish.

Like other tropical islands, Laut was a series of rough coral beaches running back to a volcanic hump which rose 600 feet or more above sea level. The entire circumference of the island was hardly more than a mile and a quarter, if that, and it was terribly steep once beyond the immediate beach.

"By rights there ought to be natives around here. Maybe on the other Islands—" Paul Doers speculated.

Dinner was fresh fish over a wood fire. Coconuts supplied alternate food and drink. It really was a pleasant change after Japanese starvation rice—the only thing missing was tobacco. I personally didn't smoke, but my companions did and they missed it terribly.

"You never know about these islands," Paul Doers said hopefully. "I'll bet we find something on here that I can inhale!"

For better, for worse, this was our home. We collected all the driftwood from the wreck and built several piles of potential firewood. Our plan called for three shirts to be tied to the tallest tree on the cliff, and to that end we were dedicated. That last night together we talked about the war; having lost it once, we always talked about the way it was when there was still a Dutch Navy. Then the nostalgia grew bitter.

What Navy? Singapore had surrendered, Darwin was abandoned. Southern Sumatra, Borneo, Celebes, Amon and Timor were in enemy hands. Java, too, was gone now. Our days in the prison camp had been miserable and the Jap sadists that guarded us stamped down a hell of oppression that will never be matched in the history of world wars.

There wasn't much to celebrate on our little island, yet there was something—freedom, in a word. The sensation was remarkable. I'd lost forty pounds in sixteen months—yet after two days of sunshine, fish, and coconut milk, I could truthfully say I felt better than I had in a year.

If our signals unfortunately drew Nips instead of Allies or friendly natives, we'd then be in far worse straits than back in a prison camp. For a couple of days we were extremely careful, recouping our strength and planning to go over every inch of the island in the event that hiding became necessary. This was our plan, perhaps the main reason why, when strength did return, we cut away from the coral beach to the green backdrop of Laut.

I was looking for caves; my friends, besides looking for caves, were interested in a spire weed that could be puffed on like a cigarette. We found the death tree instead.

On the morning of the third day at Laut, Krumann, the strongest of us, led the way through waist-high sedge. Using his knife as a machete, Johnny hacked out a path through deep, rough tangles. It took nearly an hour to make those 600 feet above sea level and once up, the climb had taken so much out of us that we flopped from exhaustion. It was then that my companions saw the devil trees, with their wide, tobacco-like leaves undulating against the blue backdrop of sea. They couldn't wait to investigate.

The two of them were big men, starved or not. Krumann weighed 185, stood six-one; Paul Doers equally the same height, if not taller. The thing that reached out vinelike tendrils was shaped like some grotesque tulip. Within the heart of the green tangle a polyp, *cannibal*, flung out nettly and undulating tentacles for man flesh. To this, unwittingly, went my friends.

Above the tree, a bizarre, almost licentious halo of poinsettias waved sensuously as the cannibal tree flexed its tendrils. This I watched, still seated, incredulous and mute as my friends, first one, then the other, were snared and enmeshed in the vile green death trap. Their shrieks suddenly cracked open the dank, breathless silence of the cliff.

INSTINCTIVELY, I jumped up and raced toward them, unconscious of the fact that it took a lot of meat to sate that tree. Or that there was more than one *Crinoida Dajeena* on the bluff!

Suddenly Krumann was in, caught, the snakelike tendrils stinging him with purple, hairy nettles, coiling around his legs, stomach, peeling back under his shirt and searing purple welts across his mouth. Almost immediately, a tentacle thick as a bullwhip jutted out through the red-flowered halo, catching Doers around the throat.

"Cut it! Cut! For God's sake, Krumann—*cut it!*" Paul Doers sobbed, grabbing at his throat. Doers' sustained shriek broke off unto a gurgling *aaagh* that lanced incalculable terror in my booming heart. Doers had dropped his knife!

Coruscating in the bright sunlight, the knife lay at Doers' bare feet, suddenly twisted from sight as recoiling green tendrils surged over Doers' thighs, stinging him. Both hands were clutched to his throat as he struggled, gurgling in great, broken sobs.

Vines immured the figure of Johnny Krumann, hacking frantically to extricate his arm. The giant polyp was open, pulling him into the green shroud, hairy nettles tumbling over his face. I watched the eyes of both men bulging hideously as they thrashed and fell, covered over with sinewy tendrils that slowly, inextricably engulfed them. Before my eyes, I watched my friends die!

I DIDN'T dare move closer than twenty yards for even then the giant tentacles, waving in the air, sensing more man flesh, groped in the direction of where I crouched, cringing. I felt my legs buckle and I sat there, screaming, holding my ears and screaming to drown out their screams. And I couldn't.

I watched, unable to tear my gaze away, as the cannibal tree fed on my companions, pulling them into the deep green folds, then covering them so that only Paul Doers' purplestreaked right ankle was still visible. A minute later that disappeared. I turned around, my knife clutched so tightly in my fingers that my arm tingled with pain, and I ran. I stumbled into the hacked-out path that wended to the beach; I tripped and got up again stumbling, turning off into a clear place to stop and choke for breath. The fantastic horror of the place whirred in my brain and my body trembled as I dropped to my buttocks and began pounding the earth with frenzy.

I WAS too numb to move, too inconceivably terrified to remain. All I could do was pick up the knife and plunge it into the earth from the sheer frustration of having been witness to my friends' deaths. Then it stung me. I shrieked, backing desperately as the first green tentacle curled through the underbrush of frond and sedge. As I looked up, there was another tree with red poinsettias undulating invitingly. I backed off as the vine looped around my ankle, surging an electric impulse up into my hip. I could feel my mouth dropping open and electric heat shocks oscillating under my tongue. With my left hand I took the knife, hacking the tendril as I pulled back.

The thing that caught me went with me—I cut it off and I backed like someone shot from a gun. I crawled on my back, screaming as I watched the hairy arms of the tree snapping out, dropping for me. Then I ran. I ran to where the firewood was stacked and I lit a fire. With the blade of my knife I cut away the raw, purple meat and bled the scar. Pain drove into my brain, and that combined with original debilitation and now toxin, left me in a comatose state for several days.

Only the good Lord knows why there weren't three men in the devil tree, as Rauk Yas, the Celeb fisherman who found me, called the tree. It took a great deal of fire and more of screaming to convince the first boat, a week later, that I wasn't the devil reincarnate. They hove to offshore for more than an hour, deliberating, while I waved my shirt. I had a bloody stump of a leg a month later; I lost it because of a slow blood poisoning, a reaction to the stinging nettles.

I can't report further on Krumann and Doers. I never went back up the death trail. I remained on a neighboring island for six months until an American submarine, *Perch*, took me off. They didn't believe the story either until they saw my leg.

February 1966
Art by Basil Gogos

SONG OF THE SLAVES

Manly Wade Wellman

Cavalier, April 1959

Song of the Slaves

The chained slaves were at the bottom of the ocean—but their terrible chant would not stop until a very special white neck filled the empty collar-shackle

by Manly Wade Wellman

Illustrated by John Leone

Gender paused at the top of the bald rise, mopped his streaming red forehead beneath the wide hat-brim, and gazed backward at his 49 captives. Naked and black, they shuffled upward from the narrow, ancient slave trail through the jungle. Forty-nine men, seized by Gender's own hand and collared to a single long chain, destined for his own plantation across the sea. . . . Gender grinned in his lean, drooping mustache, a mirthless grin of greedy triumph.

For years he had dreamed and planned for this adventure, as other men dream and plan for European tours, holy pilgrimages, or returns to beloved birth places. He had told himself that it was intensely practical and profitable. Slaves passed through so many hands —the raider, the caravaner, the seashore factor, the slaver captain, the dealer in New Orleans or Havana or at home in Charleston. Each greedy hand clutched a rich profit, and all profits must come eventually from the price paid by the planter. But he, Gender, had come to Africa himself, in his own ship; with a dozen staunch ruffians from Benguela he had penetrated the Bihé-Bailundu country, had sacked a village and taken these 49 upstanding natives between dark and dawn. A single neck- [Continued on page 71]

There was only one way to get rid of the evidence. The slaves were chained to the anchor, thrown overboard.

ART BY JOHN LEONE

GENDER paused at the top of the bald rise, mopped his streaming red forehead beneath the wide hat-brim, and gazed backward at his forty-nine captives. Naked and black, they shuffled upward from the narrow, ancient slave trail through the jungle. Forty-nine men, seized by Gender's own hand and collared to a single long chain, destined for his own plantation across the sea… Gender grinned in his lean, drooping moustache, a mirthless grin of greedy triumph.

For years he had dreamed and planned for this adventure, as other men dream and plan for European tours, holy pilgrimages, or returns to beloved birthplaces. He had told himself that it was intensely practical and profitable. Slaves passed through so many hands—the raider, the caravaner, the seashore factor, the slaver captain, the dealer in New Orleans or Havana or at home in Charleston. Each greedy hand clutched a rich profit, and all profits must come eventually from the price paid by the planter. But he, Gender, had come to Africa himself, in his own ship; with a dozen staunch ruffians from Benguela he had penetrated the Bihe-Bailundu country, had sacked a village and taken these forty-nine upstanding natives between dark and dawn. A single neck-shackle on his long chain remained empty, and he might fill even that before he came to his ship. By the Lord, he was making money this way, fairly coining it—and money was worth the making, to a Charleston planter in 1853.

So he reasoned, and so he actually believed, but the real joy to him was hidden in the darkest nook of his heart. He had conceived the raider-plan because of a nature that fed on savagery and mastery. A man less fierce and cruel might have been satisfied with hunting lions or elephants, but Gender must hunt men. As a matter of fact, the money made or saved by the journey would be little, if it was anything. The satisfaction would be tremendous. He would broaden his thick chest each day as he gazed out over his lands and saw there his slaves hoeing seashore cotton or pruning indigo;

his forty-nine slaves, caught and shipped and trained by his own big, hard hands, more indicative of assured conquest than all the horned or fanged heads that ever passed through the shops of all the taxidermists.

Something hummed in his ears, like a rhythmic swarm of bees. Men were murmuring a song under their breath. It was the long string of pinch-faced slaves. Gender stared at them, and mouthed one of the curses he always kept at tongue's end.

"Silva!" he called.

The lanky Portuguese who strode free at the head of the file turned aside and stood before Gender. "Patrao?" he inquired respectfully, smiling teeth gleaming in his walnut face.

"What are those men singing?" demanded Gender. "I didn't think they had anything to sing about."

"A slave song, patrao." Silva's tapering hand, with the silver bracelet at its wrist, made a graceful gesture of dismissal. "It is nothing. One of the things that natives make up and sing as they go."

Gender struck his boot with his coiled whip of hippopotamus hide. The afternoon sun, sliding down toward the shaggy jungle-tops, kindled harsh pale lights in his narrow blue eyes. "How does the song go?" he persisted.

The two fell into step beside the caravan as, urged by a dozen red-capped drivers, it shambled along the trail. "It is only a slave song, patrao," said Silva once again. "It means something like this: 'Though you carry me away in chains, I am free when I die. Back will I come to bewitch and kill you.'"

Gender's heavy body seemed to swell, and his eyes grew narrower and paler. "So they sing that, hmm?" He swore again. "Listen to that!"

The unhappy procession had taken up a brief, staccato refrain:

"Hailowa—Gendal... Haipana—Gendal..."

"Genda, that's my name," snarled the planter. "They're singing about me, aren't they?"

Silva made another fluid gesture, but Gender flourished his whip under the nose of the Portuguese. "Don't you try to shrug me off. I'm not a child, to be talked around like this. What are they singing about me?"

"Nothing of consequence, patrao," Silva made haste to reassure him. "It might be to say: 'I will bewitch Gender, I will kill Gender.'"

"They threaten me, do they?" Gender's broad face took on a deeper flush. He ran at the line of chained black men. With all the strength of his arm he slashed and swung with the whip. The song broke up into wretched howls of pain.

"I'll give you a music lesson!" he raged, and flogged his way up and down the procession until he swayed and dripped sweat with the exertion.

But as he turned away, it struck up again:

"Hailowa—Gendal … Haipana—Gendal…"

Whirling back, he resumed the rain of blows. Silva, rushing up to second him, also whipped the slaves and execrated them in their own tongue. But when both were tired, the flayed captives began to sing once more, softly but stubbornly, the same chant.

"Let them whine," panted Gender at last. "A song never killed anybody."

Silva grinned nervously. "Of course not, patrao. That is only an idiotic native belief."

"You mean, they think that a song will kill?"

"That, and more. They say that if they sing together, think together of one hate, all their thoughts and hates will become a solid strength—will strike and punish for them."

"Nonsense!" exploded Gender.

But when they made camp that night, Gender slept only in troubled snatches, and his dreams were of a song that grew deeper, heavier, until it became visible as a dark, dense cloud that overwhelmed him.

THE SHIP that Gender had engaged for the expedition lay in a swampy estuary, far from any coastal town, and the dawn by which he loaded his goods aboard was strangely fiery and forbidding. Dunlapp, the old slaver captain that commanded for him, met him in the cabin.

"All ready, sir?" he asked Gender. "We can sail with the tide. Plenty of room in the hold for that handful you brought. I'll tell the men to strike off those irons."

"On the contrary," said Gender, "tell the men to put manacles on the hands of each slave."

Dunlapp gazed in astonishment at his employer. "But that's bad for blacks, Mr Gender. They get sick in chains, won't eat their food. Sometimes they die."

"I pay you well, Captain," Gender rumbled, "but not to advise me. Listen to those heathen."

Dunlapp listened. A moan of music wafted in to them.

"They've sung that cursed song about me all the way to the coast," Gender told him. "They know I hate it—I've whipped them day after day— but they keep it up. No chains come off until they hush their noise."

Dunlapp bowed acquiescence and walked out to give orders. Later, as they put out to sea, he rejoined Gender on the after deck.

"They do seem stubborn about their singing," he observed.

"I've heard it said," Gender replied, "that they sing together because

they think many voices and hearts give power to hate, or to other feelings."
He scowled. "Pagan fantasy!"

Dunlapp stared overside, at white gulls just above the wave tips. "There
may be a tithe of truth in that belief, Mr Gender; sometimes there is in the
faith of wild people. Hark, I've seen a good fifteen hundred Mohammed-
ans praying at once, in the Barbary countries. When they bowed down, the
touch of all those heads to the ground banged like the fall of a heavy rock.
And when they straightened, the motion of their garments made a swish
like the gust of a gale. I couldn't help but think that their prayer had force."

"More heathen foolishness," snapped Gender, and his lips drew tight.

"Well, in Christian lands we have examples, sir," Dunlapp pursued. "For
instance, a mob will grow angry and burn or hang someone. Would a single
man do that? Would any single man of the mob do it? No, but together
their hate and resolution becomes—"

"Not the same thing at all," ruled Gender harshly. "Suppose we change
the subject."

On the following afternoon, a white sail crept above the horizon behind
them. At the masthead gleamed a little blotch of colour. Captain Dunlapp
squinted through a telescope, and barked a sailorly oath.

"A British ship-of-war," he announced, "and coming after us."

"Well?" said Gender.

"Don't you understand, sir? England is sworn to stamp out the slave
trade. If they catch us with this cargo, it'll be the end of us." A little later,
he groaned apprehensively. "They're overtaking us. There's their signal, for
us to lay to and wait for them. Shall we do it, sir?"

Gender shook his head violently. "Not we! Show them our heels,
Captain."

"They'll catch us. They are sailing three feet to our two."

"Not before dark," said Gender. "When dark comes, we'll contrive to
lessen our embarrassment."

And so the slaver fled, with the Britisher in pursuit. Within an hour, the
sun was at the horizon, and Gender smiled grimly in his moustache.

"It'll be dark within minutes," he said to Dunlapp. "As soon as you feel
they can't make out our actions by glass, get those slaves on deck."

In the dusk the forty-nine naked prisoners stood in a line along the bulwark. For all their chained necks and wrists, they neither stood nor gazed
in a servile manner. One of them began to sing and the others joined, in the
song of the slave trail:

"Hailowa—Genda! Haipana—Genda!"

"Sing on," Gender snapped briefly, and moved to the end of the line that
was near the bow. Here dangled the one empty collar, and he seized it in his

hand. Bending over the bulwark, he clamped it shut upon something - the ring of a heavy spare anchor, that swung there upon a swivel-hook. Again he turned, and eyed the line of dark singers.

"Have a bath to cool your spirits," he jeered, and spun the handle of the swivel-hook.

The anchor fell. The nearest slave jerked over with it, and the next and the next. Others saw, screamed, and tried to brace themselves against doom; but their comrades that had already gone over side were too much weight for them. Quickly, one after another, the captives whipped from the deck and splashed into the sea. Gender leaned over and watched the last of them as he sank.

"Gad, sir!" exclaimed Dunlapp hoarsely.

Gender faced him almost threateningly.

"What else to do, hmm? You yourself said that we could hope for no mercy from the British."

THE NIGHT passed by, and by the first grey light the British ship was revealed almost upon them. A megaphoned voice hailed them; then a shot hurtled across their bows. At Gender's smug nod, Dunlapp ordered his men to lay to. A boat put out from the pursuer, and shortly a British officer and four marines swung themselves aboard.

Bowing in mock reverence, Gender bade the party search. They did so, and remounted the deck crestfallen.

"Now, sir," Gender addressed the officer, "don't you think that you owe me an apology?"

The Englishman turned pale. He was a lean, sharp-featured man with strong, white teeth. "I can't pay what I owe you," he said with deadly softness. "I find no slaves, but I smell them. They were aboard this vessel within the past twelve hours."

"And where are they now?" teased Gender.

"We both know where they are," was the reply. "If I could prove in a court of law what I know in my heart, you would sail back to England with me. Most of the way you would hang from my yards by your thumbs."

"You wear out your welcome, sir," Gender told him.

"I am going. But I have provided myself with your name and that of your home city. From here I go to Madeira, where I will cross a packet bound west for Savannah. That packet will bear with it a letter to a friend of mine in Charleston, and your neighbours shall hear what happened on this ship of yours."

"You will stun slave owners with a story of slaves?" inquired Gender, with what he considered silky good-humour.

"It is one thing to put men to work in cotton fields, another to tear them from their homes, crowd them chained aboard a stinking ship, and drown them to escape merited punishment." The officer spat on the deck. "Good day, butcher. I say, all Charleston shall hear of you."

GENDER's plantation occupied a great, bluff-rimmed island at the mouth of a river, looking out toward the Atlantic. Ordinarily that island would be called beautiful, even by those most exacting followers of Chateaubriand and Rousseau; but, on his first night at home again, Gender hated the fields, the house, the environs of fresh and salt water.

His home, on a seaward jut, resounded to his grumbled curses as he called for supper and ate heavily but without relish. Once he vowed, in a voice that quivered with rage, never to go to Charleston again.

At that, he would do well to stay away for a time. The British officer had been as good at his promise, and all the town had heard of Gender's journey to Africa and what he had done there. With a perverse squeamishness beyond Gender's understanding, the hearers were filled with disgust instead of admiration. Captain Hogue had refused to drink with him at the Jefferson House. His oldest friend, Mr Lloyd Davis of Davis Township, had crossed the street to avoid meeting him. Even the Reverend Doctor Lockin had turned coldly away as he passed, and it was said that a sermon was forthcoming at Doctor Lockin's church attacking despoilers and abductors of defenceless people.

What was the matter with everybody? savagely demanded Gender of himself; these men who snubbed and avoided him were slaveholders. Some of them, it was quite possible, even held slaves fresh from raided villages under the Equator. Unfair! Yet he could not but feel the animosity of many hearts, chafing and weighing upon his spirit.

"Brutus," he addressed the slave that cleared the table, "do you believe that hate can take form?"

"Hate, Marsa?" The sooty face was solemnly respectful.

"Yes. Hate, of many people together." Gender knew he should not confide too much in a slave, and chose his words carefully. "Suppose a lot of people hated the same thing, maybe they sang a song about it—"

"Oh, yes, Marsa," Brutus nodded. "I heah 'bout dat, from ole gran-pappy when I was little. He bin in Affiky, he says many times dey sing somebody to deff."

"Sing somebody to death?" repeated Gender. "How?"

"Dey sing dat dey kill him. Afta while, maybe plenty days, he die—"

"Shut up, you black rascal" Gender sprang from his chair and clutched at a bottle. "You've heard about this somewhere, and you dare to taunt me!"

Brutus darted from the room, mortally frightened. Gender almost pursued, but thought better and tramped into his parlour. The big, brown-panelled room seemed to give back a heavier echo of his feet.

The windows were filled with the early darkness, and a hanging lamp threw rays into the corners.

On the centre table lay some mail, a folded newspaper and a letter. Gender poured whisky from a decanter, stirred in spring water, and dropped into a chair. First he opened the letter.

"Stirling Manor," said the return address at the top of the page. Gender's heart twitched. Evelyn Stirling, he had hopes of her…but this was written in a masculine hand, strong and hasty.

Sir:

Circumstances that have come to my knowledge compel me, as a matter of duty, to command that you discontinue your attention to my daughter.

(Gender's eyes took on the pale tint of rage. One more result of the Britisher's letter, he made no doubt.)

I have desired her to hold no further communication with you, and I have been sufficiently explicit to convince her how unworthy you are of her esteem and attention. It is hardly necessary for me to give you the reasons which have induced me to form this judgement, and I add only that nothing you can say or do will alter it.

Your obedient servant,
Judge Forrester Stirling

Gender hastily swigged a portion of his drink, and crushed the paper in his hand. So that was the judge's interfering way—it sounded as though he had copied it from a complete letter-writer for heavy fathers. He, Gender, began to form a reply in his mind:

Sir:

Your unfeeling and arbitrary letter admits of but one response. As a gentleman grossly misused, I demand satisfaction on the field of honour. Arrangements I place in the hands of…

By what friend should he forward that challenge? It seemed that he was mighty short of friends just now.

He sipped more whisky and water, and tore the wrappings of the newspaper.

It was a Massachusetts publication, and toward the bottom of the first page was a heavy cross of ink, to call attention to one item.

A poem, evidently, in four-line stanzas. Its title signified nothing—"The Witnesses." Author, Henry W. Longfellow; Gender identified him vaguely as a scrawler of Abolitionist doggerel. Why was this poem recommended to a southern planter?

> In Ocean's wide domains,
> Half buried in the sands,
> Lie skeletons in chains,
> With shackled feet and hands.

Once again the reader swore, but the oath quavered on his lips. His eye moved to a stanza farther down the column:

> These are the bones of Slaves;
> They gleam from the abyss;
> They cry, from yawning waves…

But it seemed to Gender that he heard, rather than read, what that cry was.

He sprang to his feet, paper and glass falling from his hands. His thin lips drew apart, his ears strained. The sound was faint, but unmistakable— many voices singing. The Negroes in his cabins? But no Negro on his plantation would know that song. The chanting refrain began:

"Hailowa—Gendal! Haipana—Gendal!"

The planter's lean mustaches bristled tigerishly. This would surely be the refined extremity of his persecution, this chanting of a weird song under his window-sill. It was louder now. I will bewitch, I will kill - but who would know that fierce mockery of him?

The crew of his ship, of course; they had heard it on the writhing lips of the captives, at the very moment of their destruction. And when the ship docked in Charleston, with no profit to show, Gender had been none too kindly in paying them off.

Those unsavory mariners must have been piqued. They had followed him, then, were setting up this vicious serenade.

Gender stepped quickly around the table and toward the window. He flung up the sash with a violence that almost shattered the glass, and leaned savagely out.

On that instant the song stopped, and Gender could see only the seaward slope of his land, down to the lip of the bluff that overhung the water. Beyond that stretched an expanse of waves, patchily agleam under a great buckskin-coloured moon, that even now stirred the murmurous tide at the foot of the bluff. Here were no trees, no brush even, to hide pranksters. The singers, now silent, must be in a boat under the shelter of the bluff.

GENDER strode from the room, fairly tore open a door, and made heavy haste toward the sea. He paused, on the lip of the bluff. Nothing was to be seen, beneath him or farther out. The mockers, if they had been here, had already fled. He growled, glared, and tramped back to his house. He entered the parlour once more, drew down the sash, and sought his chair again. Choosing another glass, he began once more to mix whisky and water. But he stopped in the middle of his pouring.

There it was again, the song he knew; and closer.

He rose, took a step in the direction of the window, then thought better of it. He had warned his visitors by one sortie, and they had hidden. Why not let them come close, and suffer the violence he ached to pour out on some living thing?

He moved, not to the window, but to a mantelpiece opposite. From a box of dark, polished wood he lifted a pistol, then another. They were duelling weapons, handsomely made, with hair-triggers; and Gender was a dead shot. With orderly swiftness he poured in glazed powder from a flask, rammed down two leaden bullets, and laid percussion caps upon the touchholes. Returning, he placed the weapons on his centre table, then stood on tiptoe to extinguish the hanging lamp. A single light remained in the room, a candle by the door, and this he carried to the window, placing it on a bracket there. Moving into the gloomy centre of the parlour, he sat in his chair and took a pistol in either hand.

The song was louder now, lifted by many voices:

"Hailowa—Gendal! Haipana—Gendal!"

Undoubtedly the choristers had come to land by now, had gained the top of the bluff. They could be seen, Gender was sure, from the window. He felt perspiration on his jowl, and lifted a sleeve to blot it. Trying to scare him, hmm? Singing about witchcraft and killing? Well, he'd show them who was the killer.

The singing had drawn close, was just outside. Odd how the sailors, or whoever they were, had learned that chant so well! It recalled to his mind the slave trail, the jungle, the long procession of crooning prisoners. But here was no time for idle revery on vanished scenes. Silence had fallen again, and he could only divine the presence, just outside, of many creatures

Scratch-scratch-scratch; it sounded like the stealthy creeping of a snake over rough lumber. That scratching resounded from the window where something stole into view in the candlelight. Gender fixed his eyes there, and his pistols lifted their muzzles.

The palm of a hand, as grey as a fish, laid itself on the glass. It was wet; Gender could see the trickle of water descending along the pane. Something clinked, almost musically. Another hand moved into position beside it, and between the two swung links of chain.

This was an elaborately devilish joke, thought Gender, in an ecstasy of rage. Even the chains, to lend reality…and as he stared he knew, in a split moment of terror that stirred his flesh on his bones, that it was no joke after all.

A face had moved into the range of the candlelight, pressing close to the pane between the two palms.

It was darker than those palms, of a dirty, slaty deadness of colour. But it was not dead, not with those dull, intent eyes that moved slowly in their blistery sockets… not dead, though it was foully wet, and its thick lips hung slackly open, and seaweed lay plastered upon the cheeks, even though the flat nostrils showed crumbled and gnawed away, as if by fish. The eyes quested here and there across the floor and walls of the parlour. They came to rest, gazing full into the face of Gender.

He felt as though stale sea-water had trickled upon him, but his right hand abode steady as a gun-rest. He took aim and fired.

The glass crashed loudly, and fell in shattering flakes to the floor beneath the sill.

Gender was on his feet, moving forward, dropping the empty pistol on the table and whipping the loaded one into his right hand. Two leaping strides took him almost to the window, before he reeled backward.

The face had not fallen. It stared at him, a scant yard away. Between the dull, living eyes showed a round black hole, where the bullet had gone in. But the thing stood unflinchingly, somehow serenely. Its two wet hands moved slowly, methodically, to pluck away the jagged remains of the glass.

Gender rocked where he stood, unable for the moment to command his body to retreat. The shoulders beneath the face heightened. They were bare and wet and deadly dusky, and they clinked the collar-shackle beneath the lax chin. Two hands stole into the room, their fish-coloured palms opening toward Gender.

He screamed, and at last he ran. As he turned his back, the singing began yet again, loud and horribly jaunty—not at all as the miserable slaves had sung it. He gained the seaward door, drew it open, and looked full into a gathering of black, wet figures, with chains festooned among them, awaiting him. Again he screamed, and tried to push the door shut.

He could not. A hand was braced against the edge of the panel—many hands. The wood fringed itself with gleaming black fingers. Gender let go the knob, whirled to flee into the house. Something caught the back of his coat, something he dared not identify. In struggling loose, he spun through the doorway and into the moonlit open.

Figures surrounded him, black, naked, wet figures; dead as to sunken faces and flaccid muscles, but horribly alive as to eyes and trembling hands and slack mouths that formed the strange primitive words of the song; separate, yet strung together with a great chain and collar-shackles, like an awful fish on the gigantic line of some demon-angler. All this Gender saw in a rocking, moon-washed moment, while he choked and retched at a dreadful odour of death, thick as fog.

Still he tried to run, but they were moving around him in a weaving crescent, cutting off his retreat toward the plantation. Hands extended toward him, manacled and dripping. His only will was to escape the touch of those sodden fingers, and one way was open—the way to the sea.

He ran toward the brink of the bluff. From its top he would leap, dive and swim away. But they pursued, overtook, surrounded him. He remembered that he held a loaded pistol, and fired into their black midst. It had no effect. He might have known that it would have no effect.

Something was clutching for him. A great, inhuman talon? No, it was an open collar of metal, with a length of chain to it, a collar that had once clamped to an anchor, dragging down to ocean's depths a line of shackled men. It gaped at him, held forth by many dripping hands. He tried to dodge, but it darted around his throat, shut with a ringing snap. Was it cold…or scalding hot? He knew, with horror vividly etching the knowledge into his heart, that he was one at last with the great chained procession.

"Hailowa—Gendal! Haipana—Gendal!"

He found his voice. "No, no!" he pleaded. "No, in the name of—"

But he could not say the name of God. And the throng suddenly moved explosively, concertedly, to the edge of the bluff.

A single wailing cry from all those dead throats, and they dived into the waves below.

Gender did not feel the clutch and jerk of the chain that dragged him alone. He did not even feel the water as it closed over his head.

THE RATS IN THE WALLS

HP Lovecraft

Sensation, January 1959   Cover by Howell Dodd

the RATS in the WALLS

By H. P. Lovecraft

ON JULY 16, 1923, I moved into Exham Priory after the last workman had finished his labors. The restoration had been a stupendous task, for little had remained of the deserted pile but a shell-like ruin; yet because it had been the seat of my ancestors, I let no expense deter me. The place had not been inhabited since the reign of James the First, when a tragedy of intensely hideous, though largely unexplained, nature had struck down the master, five of his children, and several servants; and driven forth under a cloud of suspicion and terror the third son, my lineal progenitor and the only survivor of the abhorred line.

With this sole heir denounced as a murderer, the estate had reverted to the crown, nor had the accused man made any attempt to exculpate himself or regain his property. Shaken by some horror greater than that of conscience or the law, and expressing only a frantic wish to exclude the ancient edifice from his sight and memory, Walter de la Poer, eleventh Baron Exham, fled to Virginia and there founded the family which by the next century had become known as Delapore.

Exham Priory had remained untenanted, though later allotted to the estates of the Norrys family and much studied because of its peculiarly composite architecture; an architecture involving Gothic towers resting on a Saxon or Romanesque substructure, whose foundation in turn was of a still earlier order or blend of orders—Roman, and even Druidic or native Cymric, if legends speak truly. This foundation was a very singular thing, being merged on one side with the solid limestone of the precipice from whose brink the priory overlooked a desolate valley three miles west of the village of Anchester.

Architects and antiquarians loved to examine this strange relic of forgotten centuries, but the country folk hated it. They had hated it hundreds of years before, when my ancestors lived there, and they hated it now, with the moss and mould of abandonment on it. I had not been a day in Anchester before I knew I came of an accursed house. And this week workmen have blown up Exham Priory, and are busy obliterating the traces of its foundations. The bare statistics of my ancestry I had always known, together with the fact that my first American forbear had come to the colonies under a strange cloud. Of details, however, I had been kept wholly ignorant through the policy of reticence always maintained by the Delapores. Unlike our planter neighbors, we seldom boasted of crusading ancestors or other mediaeval and Renaissance heroes; nor was any kind of tradition handed down except what may have been recorded in the sealed envelope left before the Civil War by every squire to his eldest son for posthumous opening. The glories we cherished were those achieved since the migration; the glories of a proud and honorable, if somewhat reserved and unsocial Virginia line.

During the war our fortunes were extinguished and our whole existence changed by the burning of Carfax, our home on the banks of the James. My grandfather, advanced in years, had perished in that incendiary outrage, and with him the envelope that had bound us all to the past. I can recall that fire today as I saw it then at the age of seven, with the Federal soldiers shouting, the women screaming, and the negroes howling and praying. My father was in the army, defending Richmond, and after many formalities my mother and I were passed through the lines to join him.

When the war ended we all moved north, whence my mother had come; and I grew to manhood, middle age, and ultimate wealth as a stolid Yankee. Neither my father nor I ever knew what our hereditary envelope had contained, and as I merged into the greyness of Massachusetts business life I lost all interest in the mysteries which evidently lurked far back in my family tree. Had I suspected their nature, how gladly I would have left Exham Priory to its moss, bats, and cobwebs!

My father died in 1904, but without any message to leave to me, or to my only child, Alfred, a motherless boy of ten. It was this boy who reversed the order of family information, for although I could give him only jesting conjectures about the past, he wrote me of some very interesting ancestral legends when the late war took him to England in 1917 as an aviation officer. Apparently the Delapores had a colorful and perhaps sinister history, for a friend of my son's, Capt. Edward Norrys of the Royal Flying Corps, dwelt near the family seat at Anchester and related some peasant superstitions which few novelists could equal for wildness and incredibility. Norrys himself, of course,

(continued on page 83)

35

ARTIST UNCREDITED

ON JULY 16, 1923, I moved into Exham Priory after the last workman had finished his labors. The restoration had been a stupendous task, for little had remained of the deserted pile but a shell-like ruin; yet because it had been the seat of my ancestors I let no expense deter me. The place had not been inhabited since the reign of James the First, when a tragedy of intensely hideous, though largely unexplained, nature had struck down the master, five of his children, and several servants; and driven forth under a cloud of suspicion and terror the third son, my lineal progenitor and the only survivor of the abhorred line.

With this sole heir denounced as a murderer, the estate had reverted to the crown, nor had the accused man made any attempt to exculpate himself or regain his property. Shaken by some horror greater than that of conscience or the law, and expressing only a frantic wish to exclude the ancient edifice from his sight and memory, Walter de la Poer, eleventh Baron Exham, fled to Virginia and there founded the family which by the next century had become known as Delapore.

Exham Priory had remained untenanted, though later allotted to the estates of the Norrys family and much studied because of its peculiarly composite architecture; an architecture involving Gothic towers resting on a Saxon or Romanesque substructure, whose foundation in turn was of a still earlier order or blend of orders—Roman, and even Druidic or native Cymric if legends speak truly. This foundation was a very singular thing, being merged on one side with the solid limestone of the precipice from whose brink the priory overlooked a desolate valley three miles west of the village of Anchester.

Architects and antiquarians loved to examine this strange relic of forgotten centuries, but the country folk hated it. They had hated it hundreds of years before, when my ancestors lived there, and they hated it now, with the moss and mould of abandonment on it. I had not been a day in Anchester before I knew I came of an accursed house. And this week workmen have blown up Exham Priory, and are busy obliterating the traces of its foundations.

THE BARE statistics of my ancestry I had always known, together with the fact that my first American forbear had come to the colonies under a strange cloud. Of details, however, I had been kept wholly ignorant through the policy of reticence always maintained by the Delapores. Unlike our planter neighbors, we seldom boasted of crusading ancestors or other medieval and Renaissance heroes; nor was any kind of tradition handed down except what may have been recorded in the sealed envelope left before the Civil War by every squire to his eldest son for posthumous opening. The glories we cherished were those achieved since the migration; the glories of a proud and honorable, if somewhat reserved and unsocial Virginia line.

During the war our fortunes were extinguished and our whole existence changed by the burning of Carfax, our tomb on the banks of the James. My grandfather, advanced in years, had perished in that incendiary outrage, and with him the envelope that bound us all to the past I can recall that fire today as I saw it then at the age of seven, with the Federal soldiers shouting, the women screaming, and the negroes howling and praying. My father was in the army, defending Richmond, and after many formalities my mother and I were passed through the lines to join him.

When the war ended we all moved north, whence my mother had come; and I grew to manhood, middle age, and ultimate wealth as a stolid Yankee. Neither my father nor I ever knew what our hereditary envelope had contained, and as I merged into the greyness of Massachusetts business life I lost all interest in the mysteries which evidently lurked far back in my family tree. Had I suspected their nature, how gladly would I have left Exham Priory to its moss, bats, and cobwebs!

My father died in 1904, but without any message to leave to me, or to my only child, Alfred, a motherless boy of ten. It was this boy who reversed the order of family information, for although I could give him only jesting conjecture about the past, he wrote me of some very interesting ancestral legends when the late war took him to England in 1917 as an aviation officer. Apparently the Delapores had a colorful and perhaps sinister history, for a friend of my son's, Capt. Edward Norrys of the Royal Flying Corps, dwelt near the family seat at Anchester and related some peasant superstitions which few novelists could equal for wildness and incredibility. Norrys himself, of course, did not take them seriously; but they amused my son and made good material for his letters to me. It was this legendry which definitely turned my attention to my transatlantic heritage, and made me

resolve to purchase and restore the family seat which Norrys showed to Alfred in its picturesque desertion, and offered to get for him at a surprisingly
reasonable figure, since his own uncle was the present owner.

I bought Exham Priory in 1918, but was almost immediately distracted
from my plans of restoration by the return of my son as a maimed invalid.
During the two years that he lived I thought of nothing but his care, having
even placed my business under the direction of partners.

In 1921, as I found myself bereaved and aimless, a retired manufacturer
no longer young, I resolved to divert my remaining years with my new pos-
session. Visiting Anchester in December, I was entertained by Capt. Norrys,
a plump, amiable young man who had thought much of my son, and secured
his assistance in gathering plans and anecdotes to guide in the coming restoration. Exham Priory itself I saw without emotion, a jumble of tottering
medieval ruins covered with lichens and honeycombed with rooks' nests,
perched perilously upon a precipice, and denuded of floors or other interior
features save the stone walls of the separate towers.

As I gradually recovered the image of the edifice as it had been when
my ancestors left it over three centuries before, I began to hire workmen
for the reconstruction. In every case I was forced to go outside the immediate locality, for the Anchester villagers had an almost unbelievable fear
and hatred of the place. This sentiment was so great that it was sometimes
communicated to the outside laborers, causing numerous desertions; whilst
its scope appeared to include both the priory and its ancient family.

My son had told me that he was somewhat avoided during his visits
because he was a de la Poer, and I now found myself subtly ostracised for a
like reason until I convinced the peasants how little I knew of my heritage.
Even then they sullenly disliked me; so that I had to collect most of the village traditions through the mediation of Norrys. What the people could not
forgive, perhaps, was that I had come to restore a symbol so abhorrent to
them; for, rationally or not, they viewed Exham Priory as nothing less than
a haunt of fiends and werewolves.

PIECING together the tales which Norrys collected for me, and supplement-
ing them with the accounts of several savants who had studied the ruins,
I deduced that Exham Priory stood on the site of a prehistoric temple; a
Druidical or ante-Druidical thing which must have been contemporary with
Stonehenge. That indescribable rites had been celebrated there, few doubted,
and there were unpleasant tales of the transference of these sites into the
Cybele-worship which the Romans had introduced.

Inscriptions still visible in the subcellar bore such unmistakable letters
as "DIV ... OPS ... MAGNA. MAT ..." sign of the Magna Mater whose

dark worship was once vainly forbidden to Roman citizens. Anchester had been the camp of the third Augustan legion, as many remains attest, and it was said that the temple of Cybele was splendid and thronged with worshippers who performed nameless ceremonies at the bidding of a Phrygian priest. Tales added that the fall of the old religion did not end the orgies at the temple, but that the priests lived on in the new faith without real change. Likewise was it said that the rites did not vanish with the Roman power, and that certain among the Saxons added to what remained of the temple, and gave it the essential outline it subsequently preserved, making it the center of a cult feared though half the heptarchy.

About 1000 AD the place is mentioned in a chronicle as being a substantial stone priory housing a strange and powerful monastic order and surrounded by extensive gardens which needed no walls to exclude a frightened populace. It was never destroyed by the Danes, though after the Norman Conquest it must have declined tremendously; since there was no impediment when Henry the Third granted the site to my ancestor, Gilbert de la Poer, First Baron Exham, in 1261.

Of my family before this date there is no evil report, but something strange must have happened then. In one chronicle there is a reference to a de la Poer as "cursed of God" in 1307, whilst village legendry had nothing but evil and frantic fear to tell of the castle that went up on the foundations of the old temple and priory. The fireside tales were of the most grisly description, all the ghastlier because of their frightened reticence and cloudy evasiveness. They represented my ancestor's as a race of hereditary demons beside whom Gilles de Retz and the Marquis de Sade would seem the veriest tyros, and hinted whisperingly at their responsibility for the occasional disappearances of villagers through several generations.

The worst characters, apparently, were the barons and their direct heirs: at least, most was whispered about these. If of healthier inclinations, it was said, an heir would early and mysteriously die to make way for another more typical scion. There seemed to be an inner cult in the family, presided over by the head of the house, and sometimes closed except to a few members. Temperament rather than ancestry was evidently the basis of this cult, for it was entered by several who married into the family. Lady Margaret Trevor from Cornwall, wife of Godfrey, the second son of the fifth baron, became a favorite bane of children all over the countryside, and the daemon heroine of a particularly horrible old ballad not yet extinct near the Welsh border. Preserved in balladry, too, though not illustrating the same point, is the hideous tale of Lady Mary de la Poer, who shortly after her marriage to the Earl of Shrewsfield was killed by him and his mother, both of the slayers being absolved and blessed by the priest to whom they confessed what they dared not repeat to the world.

These myths and ballads, typical as they were of crude superstition, repelled me greatly. Their persistence, and their application to so long a line of my ancestors, were especially annoying; whilst the imputations of monstrous habits proved unpleasantly reminiscent of the one known scandal of my immediate forbears—the case of my cousin, young Randolph Delapore of Carfax, who went among the negroes and became a voodoo priest after he returned from the Mexican War.

I was much less disturbed by the vaguer tales of wails and howlings in the barren, windswept valley beneath the limestone cliff; of the graveyard stenches after the spring rains; of the floundering, squealing white thing on which Sir John Clave's horse had trod one night in a lonely field; and of the servant who had gone mad at what he saw in the priory in the full light of day. These things were hackneyed spectral lore, and I was at that time a pronounced skeptic. The accounts of vanished peasants were less to be dismissed, though not especially significant in view of medieval custom. Prying curiosity meant death, and more than one severed head had been publicly shown on the bastions—now effaced—around Exham Priory.

A few of the tales were exceedingly picturesque, and made me wish I had learnt more of the comparative mythology in my youth. There was, for instance, the belief that a legion of bat-winged devils kept witches' sabbath each night at the priory—a legion whose sustenance might explain the disproportionate abundance of coarse vegetables harvested in the vast gardens. And, most vivid of all, there was the dramatic epic of the rats—the scampering army of obscene vermin which had burst forth from the castle three months after the tragedy that doomed it to desertion—the lean, filthy, ravenous army which had swept all before it and devoured fowl, cats, dogs, hogs, sheep, and even two hapless human beings before its fury was spent. Around that unforgettable rodent army a whole separate cycle of myths revolves, for it scattered among the village homes and brought curses and horrors in its train.

Such was the lore that assailed me as I pushed to completion, with an elderly obstinacy, the work of restoring my ancestral home. It must not be imagined for a moment that these tales formed any principal psychological environment. On the other hand, I was constantly praised and encouraged by Capt. Norrys and the antiquarians who surrounded and aided me. When the task was done, over two years after its commencement, I viewed the great rooms, wainscotted walls, vaulted ceilings, mullioned windows, and broad staircases with a pride which fully compensated for the prodigious expense of the restoration.

Every attribute of the Middle Ages was cunningly reproduced, and the new parts blended perfectly with the original walls and foundations. The seat of my fathers was complete, and I looked forward to redeeming at last the local fame of the line which ended in me. I would reside here permanently, and prove that a de la Poer (for I had adopted again the original spelling of the name) need not be a fiend. My comfort was perhaps augmented by the fact that, although Exham Priory was medievally fitted, its interior was in truth wholly new and free from old vermin and old ghosts alike.

As I HAVE said, I moved in on July 16, 1923. My household consisted of seven servants and nine cats, of which latter species I am particularly fond. My eldest cat, "Nigger-Man," was seven years old and had come with me from my home in Bolton, Massachusetts; the others I had accumulated whilst living with Capt. Norrys' family during the restoration of the priory.

For five days our routine proceeded with the utmost placidity, my time being spent mostly in the codification of old family data. I had now obtained some very circumstantial accounts of the final tragedy and flight of Walter de la Poer, which I conceived to be the probable contents of the hereditary paper lost in the fire at Carfax. It appeared that my ancestor was accused with much reason of having killed all the other members of his household, except four servant confederates, in their sleep, about two weeks after a shocking discovery which changed his whole demeanor, but which, except by implication, he disclosed to no one save perhaps the servants who assisted him and afterward fled beyond reach.

This deliberate slaughter, which included a father, three brothers, and two sisters, was largely condoned by the villagers, and so slackly treated by the law that its perpetrator escaped honored, unharmed, and undisguised to Virginia; the general whispered sentiment being that he had purged the land of an immemorial curse. What discovery had prompted an act so terrible, I could scarcely even conjecture. Walter de la Poer must have known for years the sinister tales about his family, so that this material could have given him no fresh impulse. Had he, then, witnessed some appalling ancient rite, or stumbled upon some frightful and revealing symbol in the priory or its vicinity? He was reputed to have been a shy, gentle youth in England. In Virginia he seemed not so much hard or bitter as harassed and apprehensive. He was spoken of in the diary of another gentleman adventurer, Francis Harley of Bellview, as a man of unexampled justice, honor, and delicacy.

On July 22 occurred the first incident which, though lightly dismissed at the time, takes on a preternatural significance in relation to later events. It was so simple as to be almost negligible, and could not possibly have been noticed under the circumstances; for it must be recalled that since I was in a building practically fresh and new except for the walls, and surrounded by a well-balanced staff of servitors, apprehension would have been absurd despite the locality.

What I afterward remembered is merely this—that my old black cat, whose moods I know so well, was undoubtedly alert and anxious to an extent wholly out of keeping with his natural character. He roved from room to room, restless and disturbed, and sniffed constantly about the walls which formed part of the old Gothic structure. I realize how trite this sounds—like the inevitable dog in the ghost story, which always growls before his master sees the sheeted figure—yet I cannot consistently suppress it.

The following day a servant complained of restlessness among all the cats in the house. He came to me in my study, a lofty west room on the second story, with groined arches, black oak panelling, and a triple Gothic window overlooking the limestone cliff and desolate valley; and even as he spoke I saw the jetty form of Nigger-Man creeping along the west wall and scratching at the new panels which overlaid the ancient stone.

I told the man that there must be some singular odor or emanation from the old stonework, imperceptible to human senses, but affecting the delicate organs of cats even through the new woodwork. This I truly believed, and when the fellow suggested the presence of mice or rats, I mentioned that there had been no rats there for three hundred years, and that even the field mice of the surrounding country could hardly be found in these high walls, where they had never been known to stray. That afternoon I called on Capt. Norrys, and he assured me that it would be quite incredible for field mice to infest the priory in such a sudden and unprecedented fashion.

That night, dispensing as usual with a valet, I retired in the west tower chamber which I had chosen as my own, reached from the study by a stone staircase and short gallery—the former partly ancient, the latter entirely restored. This room was circular, very high, and without wainscotting, being hung with arras which I had myself chosen in London.

Seeing that Nigger-Man was with me, I shut the heavy Gothic door and retired by the light of the electric bulbs which so cleverly counterfeited candles, finally switching off the light and sinking on the carved and canopied four-poster, with the venerable cat in his accustomed place across my feet. I did not draw the curtains, but gazed out at the narrow north window which I faced. There was a suspicion of aurora in the sky, and the delicate traceries of the window were pleasantly silhouetted.

At some time I must have fallen quietly asleep, for I recall a distinct sense of leaving strange dreams, when the cat started violently from his placid position. I saw him in the faint auroral glow, head strained forward, forefeet on my ankles, and hind feet stretched behind. He was looking intensely at a point on the wall somewhat west of the window, a point which to my eye had nothing to mark it, but toward which all my attention was now directed.

And as I watched, I knew that Nigger-Man was not vainly excited. Whether the arras actually moved I cannot say. I think it did, very slightly. But what I can swear to is that behind it I heard a low, distinct scurrying as of rats or mice. In a moment the cat had jumped bodily on the screening tapestry, bringing the affected section to the floor with his weight, and exposing a damp, ancient wall of stone; patched here and there by the restorers, and devoid of any trace of rodent prowlers.

Nigger-Man raced up and down the floor by this part of the wall, clawing the fallen arras and seemingly trying at times to insert a paw between the wall and the oaken floor. He found nothing, and after a time returned wearily to his place across my feet. I had not moved, but I did not sleep again that night.

In the morning I questioned all the servants, and found that none of them had noticed anything unusual, save that the cook remembered the actions of a cat which had rested on her windowsill. This cat had howled at some unknown hour of the night, awaking the cook in time for her to see him dart purposefully out of the open door down the stairs. I drowsed away the noontime, and in the afternoon called again on Capt. Norrys, who became exceedingly interested in what I told him. The odd incidents—so slight yet so curious—appealed to his sense of the picturesque, and elicited from him a number of reminiscences of local ghostly lore. We were genuinely perplexed at the presence of rats, and Norrys lent me some traps and paris-green, which I had the servants place in strategic localities when I returned.

I retired early, being very sleepy, but was harassed by dreams of the most horrible sort. I seemed to be looking down from an immense height upon a twilit grotto, knee-deep with filth, where a white-bearded daemon swineherd drove about with his staff a flock of fungous, flabby beasts whose appearance filled me with unutterable loathing. Then, as the swineherd paused and nodded over his task, a mighty swarm of rats rained down on the stinking abyss and fell to devouring beasts and man alike.

From this terrific vision I was abruptly awaked by the motions of Nigger-Man, who had been sleeping as usual across my feet. This time I did not have to question the source of his snarls and hisses, and of the fear which made him sink his claws into my ankle, unconscious of their effect; for on every side of the chamber the walls were alive with nauseous sound—the verminous slithering of ravenous, gigantic rats. There was now no aurora to show the state of the arras—the fallen section of which had been replaced—but I was not too frightened to switch on the light.

As the bulbs leapt into radiance I saw a hideous shaking all over the tapestry, causing the somewhat peculiar designs to execute a singular dance of death. This motion disappeared almost at once, and the sound with it. Springing out of bed, I poked at the arras with the long handle of a warming-pan that rested near, and lifted one section to see what lay beneath. There was nothing but the patched stone wall, and even the cat had lost his tense realization of abnormal presences. When I examined the circular trap that had been placed in the. room, I found all of the openings sprung, though no trace remained of what had been caught and had escaped.

Further sleep was out of the question, so, lighting a candle, I opened the door and went out in the gallery toward the stairs to my study, Nigger-Man following at my heels. Before we had reached the stone steps, however, the cat darted ahead of me and vanished down the ancient flight. As I descended the stairs myself, I became suddenly aware of sounds in the great room below; sounds of a nature which could not be mistaken.

The oak-paneled walls were alive with rats, scampering and milling, whilst Nigger-Man was racing about with the fury of a baffled hunter. Reaching the bottom, I switched on the light, which did not this time cause the noise to subside. The rats continued their riot, stampeding with such force and distinctness that I could finally assign to their motions a definite direction. These creatures, in numbers apparently inexhaustible, were engaged in one stupendous migration from inconceivable heights to some depth conceivably, or inconceivably, below.

I now heard steps in the corridor, and in another moment two servants pushed open the massive door. They were searching the house for some unknown source of disturbance which had thrown all the cats into a snarling panic and caused them to plunge precipitately down several flights of stairs and squat, yowling, before the closed door to the sub-cellar. I asked them if they had heard the rats, but they replied in the negative. And when I turned to call their attention to the sounds in the panels, I realized that the noise had ceased.

With the two men, I went down to the door of the sub-cellar, but found the cats already dispersed. Later I resolved to explore the crypt below, but for the present I merely made a round of the traps. All were sprung, yet all were tenantless. Satisfying myself that no one had heard the rats save the felines and me, I sat in my study till morning, thinking profoundly, and recalling every scrap of legend I had unearthed concerning the building I inhabited.

I SLEPT some in the forenoon, leaning back in the one comfortable library chair which my medieval plan of furnishing could not banish. Later I telephoned to Capt. Norrys, who came over and heloed me explore the sub-cellar.

Absolutely nothing untoward was found, although we could not repress a thrill at the knowledge that this vault was built by Roman hands. Every low arch and massive pillar was Roman—not the debased Romanesque of the bungling Saxons, but the severe and harmonious classicism of the age of the Caesars; indeed, the walls abounded with inscriptions familiar to the antiquarians who had repeatedly explored the place—things like "P. GE-TAE. PROP ... TEMP ... DONA ..." and "L. PRAEC ... VS ... PONTIFI ... ATYS ..."

The reference to Atys made me shiver, for I had read Catullus and knew something of the hideous rites of the Eastern god, whose worship was so mixed with that of Cybele. Norrys and I, by the light of lanterns, tried to interpret the odd and nearly effaced designs on certain irregularly rectangular blocks of stone generally held to be altars, but could make nothing of them. We remembered that one pattern, a sort of rayed sun, was held by students to imply a non-Roman origin, suggesting that these altars had merely been adopted by the Roman priests from some older and perhaps aboriginal temple on the same site. On one of those blocks were some brown stains which made me wonder. The largest, in the center of the room, had certain features on the upper surface which indicated its connection with fire—probably burnt offerings.

Such were the sights in that crypt before whose door the cats had howled, and where Norrys and I now determined to pass the night. Couches were brought down by the servants, who were told not to mind any nocturnal actions of the cats, and Nigger-Man was admitted as much for help as for companionship. We decided to keep the great oak door—a modern replica with slits for ventilation—tightly closed; and, with this attended to, we retired with lanterns still burning to await whatever might occur.

The vault was very deep in the foundations of the priory, and undoubtedly far down on the face of the beetling limestone cliff overlooking the waste valley. That it had been the goal of the scuffling and unexplainable rats I could not doubt, though why, I could not tell. As we lay there expectantly, I found my vigil occasionally mixed with half-formed dreams from which the uneasy motions of the cat across my feet would rouse me.

These dreams were not wholesome, but horribly like the one I had had the night before. I saw again the twlit grotto, and the swineherd with his unmentionable fungous beasts wallowing in filth, and as I looked at these things they seemed nearer and more distinct—so distinct that I could almost observe their features. Then I did observe the flabby features of one of them—and awaked with such a scream that Nigger-Man started- up, whilst Capt. Norrys, who had not slept, laughed considerably. Norrys might have laughed more—or perhaps less—had be known what it was that made me scream. But I did not remember myself till later. Ultimate horror often paralyzes memory in a merciful way.

Norrys waked me when the phenomena began. Out of the same frightful dream I was called by his gentle shaking and his urging to listen to the cats. Indeed, there was much to listen to, for beyond the closed door at the head of the stone steps was a veritable nightmare of feline yelling and clawing, whilst Nigger-Man, unmindful of his kindred outside, was running excitedly around the bare stone walls, in which I heard the same babel of scurrying rats that had troubled me the night before.

An acute terror now rose within me, for here were anomalies which nothing normal could well explain. These rats, if not the creatures of a madness which I shared with the cats alone, must be burrowing and sliding in Roman walls I had thought to be of solid limestone blocks . . . unless perhaps the action of water through more than seventeen centuries had eaten winding tunnels which rodent bodies had worn clear and ample . . . But even so, the spectral horror was no less; for if these were living vermin why did not Norrys hear their disgusting commotion? Why did he urge me to watch Nigger-Man and listen to the cats outside, and why did he guess wildly and vaguely at what could have aroused them?

By the time I had managed to tell him, as rationally as I could, what I thought I was hearing, my ears gave me the last fading impression of the scurrying; which had retreated *still downward*, far underneath this deepest of sub-cellars till it seemed as if the whole cliff below were riddled with questing rats. Norrys was not as skeptical as I had anticipated, but instead seemed profoundly moved. He motioned to me to notice that the cats at the door had ceased their clamor, as if giving up the rats for lost; whilst Nigger-Man had a burst of renewed restlessness, and was clawing frantically around the bottom of the large stone altar in the center of the room, which was nearer Norrys' couch than mine.

My fear of the unknown was at this point very great. Something astounding had occurred, and I saw that Capt. Norrys, a younger, stouter, and presumably more naturally, materialistic man, was affected fully as much as myself—perhaps because of his lifelong and intimate familiarity with local legend. We could for the moment do nothing but watch the old black cat as he pawed with decreasing fervor at the base of the altar, occasionally looking up and mewing to me in that persuasive manner which he used when he wished me to perform some favor for him.

Norrys now took a lantern close to the altar and examined the place where Nigger-Man was pawing; silently kneeling and scraping away the lichens of centuries which joined the massive pre-Roman block to the tesselated floor. He did not find anything, and was about to abandon his efforts when I noticed a trivial circumstance which made me shudder, even though it implied nothing more than I had already imagined.

I told him of it, and we both looked at its almost imperceptible manifestation with the fixedness of fascinated discovery and acknowledgment. It was only this—that the flame of the lantern set down near the altar was slightly but certainly flickering from a draught of air which it had not before received, and which came indubitably from the crevice between floor and altar where Norrys was scraping away the lichens.

WE SPENT the rest of the night in the brilliantly-lighted study, nervously discussing what we should do next. The discovery that some vault deeper than the deepest known masonry of the Romans underlay this accursed pile; some vault unsuspected by the curious antiquarians of three centuries; would have been sufficient to excite us without any background of the sinister. As it was, the fascination became twofold; and we paused in doubt whether to abandon our search and quit the priory forever in superstitious caution, or to gratify our sense of adventure and brave whatever horrors might await us in the unknown depths.

By morning we had compromised, and decided to go to London to gather a group of archaeologists and scientific men fit to cope with the mystery. It should be mentioned that before leaving the sub-cellar we had vainly, tried to move the central altar which we now recognized as the gate to a new pit of nameless fear. What secret would open the gate, wiser men than we would have to find.

During many days in London Capt. Norrys and I presented our facts, conjectures, and legendary anecdotes to five eminent authorities, all men who could be trusted to respect any family disclosures which future explorations might develop. We found most of them little disposed to scoff, hut, instead, intensely interested and sincerely sympathetic. It is hardly necessary to name them all, but I may say that they included Sir William Brinton, whose excavations in the Troad excited most of the world in their day. As we all took the train for Anchester I felt myself poised on the brink of frightful revelations, a sensation symbolized by the air of mourning among the many Americans at the unexpected death of the President on the other side of the world.

ON THE evening of August 7th we reached Exham Priory, where the servants assured me that nothing unusual had occurred. The cats, even old Nigger-Man, had been perfectly placid; and not a trap in the house had been sprung. We were to begin exploring on the following day, awaiting which I assigned well-appointed rooms to all my guests.

I myself retired in my own tower chamber, with Nigger-Man across my feet. Sleep came quickly, but hideous dreams assailed me. There was a vision of a Roman feast like that of Trimalchio, with a horror in a covered platter. Then came that damnable, recurrent thing about the swineherd and his filthy drove in the twilit grotto. Yet when I awoke it was full daylight, with normal sounds in the house below. The rats, living or spectral, had not troubled me; and Nigger-Man was still quietly asleep. On going down, I found that the same tranquillity had prevailed elsewhere; a condition which one of the assembled servants—a fellow named Thornton, devoted to the psychic—rather absurdly laid to the fact that I had now been shown the thing which certain forces had wished to show me.

All was now ready, and at 11 AM our entire group of seven men, bearing powerful electric searchlights and implements of excavation, went down to the sub-cellar and bolted the door behind us. Nigger-Man was with us, for the investigators found no occasion to despise his excitability, and were indeed anxious that he be present in case of obscure rodent manifestations. We noted the Roman inscriptions and unknown altar designs only briefly, for three of the savants had already seen them, and all knew their characteristics. Prime attention was paid to the momentous central altar, and within an hour Sir William Brinton had caused it to tilt backward, balanced by some unknown species of counterweight.

There now lay revealed such a horror as would have overwhelmed us had we not been prepared. Through a nearly square opening in the tiled floor, sprawling on a flight of stone steps so prodigiously worn that it was little more than an inclined plane at the center, was a ghastly array of human or semi-human bones. Those which retained their collocation as skeletons showed attitudes of panic fear, and over all were the marks of rodent gnawing. The skulls denoted nothing short of utter idiocy, cretinism, or primitive semi-apedom.

Above the hellishly littered steps arched a descending passage seemingly chiseled from the solid rock, and conducting a current of air. This current was not a sudden and noxious rush as from a closed vault, but a cool breeze with something of freshness in it. We did not pause long, but shiveringly began to clear a passage down the steps. It was then that Sir William, examining the hewn walls, made the odd observation that the passage, according to the direction of the strokes, must have been chiseled *from beneath.*

I MUST be very deliberate now, and choose my words.

After ploughing down a few steps amidst the gnawed bones we saw that there was light ahead; not any mystic phosphorescence, but a filtered daylight which could not come except from unknown fissures in the cliff that overlooked the waste valley. That such fissures had escaped notice from outside was hardly remarkable, for not only is the valley wholly uninhabited, but the cliff is so high and beetling that only an aeronaut could study its face in detail. A few steps more, and our breaths were literally snatched from us by what we saw; so literally that Thornton, the psychic investigator, actually fainted in the arms of the dazed man who stood behind him. Norrys, his plump face utterly white and flabby, simply cried out inarticulately; whilst I think that what I did was to gasp or hiss, and cover my eyes.

The man behind me—the only one of the party older than I—croaked the hackneyed "My God!" in the most cracked voice I ever head. Of seven cultivated men, only Sir William Brinton retained his composure, a thing the more to his credit because he led the party and must have seen the sight first.

It was a twilit grotto of enormous height, stretching away farther than any eye could see; a subterraneous world of limitless mystery and horrible suggestion. There were buildings and other architectural remains—in one terrified glance I saw a weird pattern of tumuli, a savage circle of monoliths, a low-domed Roman ruin, a sprawling Saxon pile, and an early English edifice of wood—but all these were dwarfed by the ghoulish spectacle presented by the general surface of the ground. For yards about the steps extended an insane tangle of human bones, or bones at least as human as those on the steps. Like a foamy sea they stretched, some fallen apart, but others wholly or partly articulated as skeletons; these latter invariably in postures of daemoniac frenzy, either fighting off some menace or clutching other forms with cannibal intent.

When Dr. Trask, the anthropologist, stooped to classify the skulls, he found a degraded mixture which utterly baffled him. They were mostly lower than the Piltdown man in the scale of evolution, but in every case definitely human. Many were of higher grade, and a very few were the skulls of supremely and sensitively developed types. All the bones were gnawed, mostly by rats, but somewhat by others of the half-human drove. Mixed with them were many tiny bones of rats— fallen members of the lethal army which closed the ancient epic.

I wonder that any man among us lived and kept his sanity through that hideous day of discovery. Not Hoffman or Huysmans could conceive a scene more wildly incredible, more frenetically repellent, or more Gothically grotesque than the twilit grotto through which we seven staggered;

each stumbling on revelation after revelation, and trying to keep for the nonce from thinking of the events which must have taken place there three hundred, or a thousand, or two thousand, or ten thousand years ago. It was the antechamber of hell, and poor Thornton fainted again when Trask told him that some of the skeleton things must have descended as quadrupeds through the last twenty or more generations.

Horror piled on horror as we began to interpret the architectural remains. The quadruped things—with their occasional recruits from the biped class—had been kept in stone pens, out of which they must have broken in their last delirium of hunger or rat-fear. There had been great herds of them, evidently fattened on the coarse vegetables whose remains could be found as a sort of poisonous ensilage at the bottom of huge stone bins older than Rome. I knew now why my ancestors had had such excessive gardens—would to heaven I could forget! The purpose of the herds I did not have to ask.

Sir William, standing with his searchlight in the Roman ruin, translated aloud the most shocking ritual I have ever known; and told of the diet of the antediluvian cult which the priests of Cybele found and mingled with their own. Norrys, used as he was to the trenches, could not walk straight when he came out of the English building. It was a butcher shop and kitchen—he had expected that—but it was too much to see familiar English implements in such a place, and to read familiar English *graffiti* there, some as recent as 1610. I could not go in that building—that building whose daemon activities were stopped only by the dagger of my ancestor Walter de la Poer.

What I did venture to enter was the low Saxon building, whose oaken door had fallen, and there I found a terrible row of ten stone cells with rusty bars. Three had tenants, all skeletons of high grade, and on the bony forefinger of one I found a seal ring with my own coat-of-arms. Sir William found a vault with far older cells below the Roman chapel, but these cells were empty. Below them was a low crypt with cases of formally arranged bones, some of them bearing terrible parallel inscriptions carved in Latin, Greek, and the tongue of Phrygia.

Meanwhile, Dr. Trask had opened one of the prehistoric tumuli, and brought to light skulls which were slightly more human than a gorilla's, and which bore indescribable ideographic carvings. Through all this horror my cat stalked unperturbed. Once I saw him monstrously perched atop a mountain of bones, and wondered at the secrets that might lie behind his yellow eyes.

Having grasped to some slight degree the frightful revelations of this twilit area—an area so hideously foreshadowed by my recurrent dream—we turned to that apparently boundless depth of midnight cavern where no ray of light from the cliff could penetrate.

We shall never know what sightless Stygian worlds yawn beyond the little distance we went, for it was decided that such secrets are not good for mankind. But there was plenty to engross us close at hand, for we had not gone far before the searchlights showed that accursed infinity of pits in which the rats had feasted, and whose sudden lack of replenishment had driven the ravenous rodent army first to turn on the living herds of starving things, and then to burst forth from the priory in that historic orgy of devastation which the peasants will never forget.

God! Those carrion black pits of sawed, picked bones and opened skulls! Those nightmare chasms choked with the pithecanthropoid, Celtic, Roman, and English bones of countless unhallowed centuries! Some of them were full, and none can say how deep they had once been. Others were still bottomless to our searchlights, and peopled by unnamable fancies. What, I thought, of the hapless rats that stumbled into such traps amidst the blackness of their quests in this grisly Tartarus?

Once my foot slipped near a horribly yawning brink, and I had a moment of ecstatic fear. I must have been musing a long time, for I could not see any of the party but the plump Capt. Norrys. Then there came a sound from that inky, boundless, farther distance that I thought I knew; and I saw my old black cat dart past me like a winged Egyptian god, straight into the illimitable gulf of the unknown. But I was not far behind, for there was no doubt after another second. It was the eldritch scurrying of those fiend-born rats, always questing for new horrors, and determined to lead me on even unto those grinning caverns of earth's center where Nyarlathotep, the mad faceless god, howls blindly in the darkness to the piping of two amorphous idiot flute-players.

My searchlight expired, but still I ran. I heard voices, and yowls, and echoes, but above all there gently rose that impious, insidious scurrying; gently rising, rising, as a stiff bloated corpse gently rises above an oily river that flows under endless onyx bridges to a black, putrid sea.

SOMETHING bumped into me—something soft and plump. It must have been the rats; the viscous, gelatinous, ravenous army that feast on the dead and the living… Why shouldn't rats eat a de la Poer as a de la Poer eats forbidden things? … The war ate my boy, damn them all…and the Yanks ate Carfax with flames and burnt Grandsire Delapore and the secret… No, no, I tell you, I am *not* that daemon swineherd in the twilit grotto! It was *not* Edward Norrys' fat face on that flabby, fungous thing! Who says I am a de la Poer? He lived, but my boy died! … Shall a Norrys hold the lands of a de la Poer?

… It's voodoo, I tell you…that spotted snake… Curse yon, Thornton, I'll teach you to faint at what my family do! … 'Sblood, thou stinkard. I'll learn ye how to gust…wolde ye swynke me thilke wys? … *Magna Mater! Magna Mater! … Atys … Dia ad aghaidh 's ad aodaun … ague bos dunach ort! Dhonas 's dholas ort, agus leat-sa! … Ungl … nngl … rrrlh … chchch…*

That is what they say I said when they found me in the blackness after three hours; found me crouching in the blackness over the plump, half-eaten body of Captain Norrys, with my own cat leaping and tearing at my throat. Now they have blown up Exham Priory, taken my Nigger-Man away from me, and shut me into this barred room at Hanwell with fearful whispers about my heredity and experiences. Thornton is in the next room, but they prevent me from talking to him. They are trying, too, to suppress most of the facts concerning the priory. When I speak of poor Norrys they accuse me of a hideous thing, but they must know that I did not do it. They must know it was the rats; the slithering, scurrying rats whose scampering will never let me sleep; the daemon rats that race behind the padding in this room and beckon me down to greater horrors than I have ever known; the rats they can never hear; the rats, the rats in the walls!

THE MAN WHO COULDN'T DIE

Gardner F. Fox

Adventure, August 1961   Cover by Vic Prezio

Slowly, reluctantly, the man who had been dead returned to keep his promise. For they had offered the puny Earth Thing eternal life—for the secret which would obliterate his world!

THE MAN WHO COULDN'T DIE

BY GARDNER F. FOX
ILLUSTRATED BY
BRUCE MINNEY

CLARR Morson swam up lazily through the black mists. He was leaving a strange, lovely world, and he did not want to return to reality. He had been dead. Now he was coming back, through the mists, to life.

"Disconnect the neural gauges," a voice whispered in the darkness. "Prepare to shock his brain with adrene-electrical charges."

They were making him come back. Suddenly he hated them all, the smug, white-garbed scientists who had taken him away from the neuro-psychiatric ward for Criminal (Continued on page 46)

If anything happened to them, Clarr thought, and to me, the Earth would be safe forever.

37

CLARR Morson swam up lazily through the black mists. He was leaving a strange, lovely world, and he did not want to return to reality. He had been dead. Now he was coming back, through the mists, to life.

"Disconnect the neural gauges," a voice whispered in the darkness. "Prepare to shock his brain with adrene-electrical charges."

They were making him come back. Suddenly he hated them all, the smug, white-garbed scientists who had taken him away from the neuro-psychiatric ward for Criminal Atavars to offer him immortality for a voyage. He had been happy back there, as happy as a man can be who is in punitive limbo.

Clarr opened his eyes. A face filtered through pale mists. It blurred, then cleared into the smiling, ruddy features of Dr. Hartley Ens, Chief of the United World Science Corporation.

"Can you hear me?" Clarr tried to nod, but nothing happened. This was not his body. It was—Why couldn't he remember? Oh, yes. They'd taken his brain from his starved, beaten body and put it in an eight-foot monstrosity of *moonalite* and *stil*, and given him cables for arms and legs and neck.

He tried again. This time the neural wires reacted. His head lifted. There was a dull clunk as the square metal brain-case fell back against the tabletop where he lay.

"Good. You know who you are, and the great honor that will be yours?" Clarr tried to sneer, forgetting he had no lips, only a meshed oval for a mouth and the synthetic sound box. He tried, sending his will along the tiny wires. He heard a queer, harsh grating. That was to be his voice, from here on in.

"My name is Clarr Morson. I was a criminal, an Atavar. The year is Thirty-two Ninety-one. I am going to be the first sentient being ever sent to a star system."

"Again, good. Try to sit up, to move." It was hard, but he made it. His cable-legs touched the floor as he sat on the high table. Dr. Ens walked around him, scrutinizing everything. He came to a stop in front of Clarr and smiled.

"No ill effects? I thought not," he said. "Lacing your nerve-ends onto the control wires—sheer genius. Only Claghorn could have done it. He came over from Sout Afrik, you know."

"Yeah. Sure. All the best! But how long will I live?"

"You're immortal. The Carrel experiments proved that. In case of uncontrollable growth, there is a special absorption feature built into the brain-case. It will keep your brain the same size it is now."

The door opened and a bald man, with the double scrolls of the Legal Craft worked into his tunic, came briskly into the room. He lifted out long documents, riffled through them.

Dr. Ens said, "The post-operative consent. You will sign, of course?"

"Sure. I'll sign." Ens regarded him critically from under his white brows. He said, "Do you still feel your criminal tendencies, Morson?"

"I don't know. Shouldn't I?"

"No. Chi'en Su worked with Claghorn on the job. Chi'en Su is the world's best brain specialist. He said he could remove those atavistic tendencies by a delicate operation. I wondered if he'd succeeded."

"How would I know if he succeeded?"

"You would realize the great honor that is yours. You would be anxious, as a good citizen of the World State, to get into the *Shark* and be off at once. You wouldn't have any of those old schemes of yours. Working the angles, you used to call it."

Chi'en Su had not succeeded. Clarr knew that. He was already considering whether it would pay him to take the gigantic *Shark* into a port on Mars or Titan and sell it. He might get a good price from the asteroid pirates.

But he said, "Why, I do feel that way. It's a sort of warm glow, isn't it?" He wondered if a brain would have any feeling at all.

Ens patted his shoulder, held out a pen. Clarr took it between two cable-like tentacles, held it gently. He bent and scrawled words on ten sheets of legal cap.

The lawyer examined the signatures fussily. He said briskly, "It is necessary that the signer give a summary of the events up to—" he paused, looking embarrassed. "The operation."

Clarr said, "I am—was, rather—a criminal Atavar. I was apprehended for my crimes against the state on Dawn 7, 3289, and sentenced to the psychopathic ward for observation and possible hypnotic cure. During my interment, the World Science Council offered pardon to any criminal who would consent to make the first trip to a star system."

"We've explored the solar system, but have never been beyond Pluto," interrupted Ens.

Clarr made the necessary addition. He went on, "My brain was removed from my body and placed in this robot form. I understand it will remain immortal. I have also been cured of my criminal tendencies."

Dr. Ens interrupted again. "And a mental bloc has been added, by post-operative hypnosis, to correct any backsliding in case the operation was not completely successful."

Clarr repeated the words; went on, "I am to be given the greatest space vessel ever built in the System, the *Shark*. It is equipped with hydrogen-fission drives. It takes its fuel from the particles of hydrogen that float in free space, as a fish does oxygen in water, through metal gills that filter out everything but the hydrogen and sift that into the fission chambers."

Ens, following him closely, nodded seriously. "My mission is: to travel in the *Shark* until I find a star system with an inhabitable planetary system; to make reports periodically, furnishing the Council with any discoveries I might make."

The lawyer snapped shut his briefcase, nodded to Ens and went out, closing the door behind him. Doctor Ens walked around the room, head bent.

He muttered, "You have the education, Morson. You received that from the State before your atavistic impulses overrode your normal responses."

Clarr stood up. He growled, "How long will this trip take?" Ens shrugged, smiled wistfully. "I will be dead and buried before you land your keel on dirt. But others will come after me. The race will go on. Who knows? Fifty years? A hundred?"

Clarr checked an oath. "I'll go mad!"

"You have the hibernation chamber. You can sleep for ten or twenty years at a stretch, rise to check the controls, then go back to sleep again."

"A hell of a life!"

"I'd go if they'd let me."

"Yeah, yeah. I'll never die. I know that. But—" He thought of Ada with the brown eyes and the yellow hair, and the shape that tormented his dreams. In fifty years, Ada would be—

"May I see any old friends?" he asked. Ens said, "Certainly. Matter of fact, an Ada Taggart has been hounding the receptionists for permission to talk to you."

"Ada! I'd like to see her. Alone?"

Ens went out. Clarr spent the minutes staring at his tremendous bulk in a tri-dimensional reflector. He towered eight feet in the air, his great cable legs thick as tree boles, but malleable as a snake. His chest was round, with arced panels for needed repairs. His head was a square, thick mechanism with wired jewels for eyes and a meshed screen for a mouth. His arms were thick cables, equipped with lean, powerful tentacles for fingers.

He wasn't pretty, but he was durable! God, when he thought what power he might get his hands on, somewhere out there in the stars!

The door swung wide and Ada came dancing in, yellow mane bobbing over her shoulders, her brown eyes wide. When she saw him, she drew back. "I was expecting a friend of mine. A Clarr Morson."

Clarr looked at her. She was different, less appealing. That dress that delineated her body, now. He recalled how much he'd liked her in clothes like that. Now...

"I'm Clarr, Ada. Oh, stop looking so horror-stricken. You knew what they were going to do with me! The *Starobot,* they call me. Or have you lost the knack of scanning the tri-dims?"

She backed into a chair. She licked her lips. "It's a shock, Clarr. You— you ain't the same guy, are you?"

"That pleases you, does it? You and that Drake character will have your-selves a time, no doubt?" He moved like a cat, for all his metallic bulk. His right arm whipped out, caught and held her up against his side. His square head bent. "Get this, Ada! Drake isn't going to get you. I'm coming back, see? Nothing can kill me. They made a mistake, those egghead scientists. If I can keep away from the World Militia, their local patrollers will never get me. I'm coming back—and I'll be the biggest crime lord since the twen-ty-third century!"

"Sure you will, Clarr. Sure... Only let me go. You're hurting my arm!" He let her go. If it weren't for his memory that lived on, he wouldn't give a snap of his tentacles for her. But he remembered nights on the Volga, after-noons in Brazil...swimming in Peconic Bay—that weekend in the underwa-ter hotel off the Bahamas.

"I'm selling out the *Shark!* I'm offering it for ten million *worths* to the pirates. They'll pay that for it. I'll need somebody—human—to build up a gang. I don't want you to move from the apartment, Ada. You hear me? I'll find you if you do. And you'll be sorry."

"I won't move on you, Clarr. I won't. I swear it." Clarr gestured her away. Already his brain was knowing the power that was his. He turned it over in his mind zestfully. Power was a wonderful thing.

THAT same power was reflected in the long, sleek lines of the *Shark.* Clarr stared at his new home from the speaker's platform. The speeches were almost over. He had made a credible one himself, spouting all the gush the people sopped up like sponges. World State! Glory of the Race! New Vistas opening to the World!

How they had cheered him! Doctor Hartley Ens was bobbing his white head, smiling. Clarr knew he was thinking that Chi'en Su had performed a miracle. Clarr let his brain feel scorn for a moment.

He moved fluidly toward the gangplank, and crossed it. With one stamp of his great foot, he smashed it to splinters. There would be no going back. The crowd screamed its delight at his gesture.

Clarr closed the parabolic door. He went into the interior and locked the safety valves. He made his way along a narrow corridor into the control chamber. The transparent metal they'd found on the moon thirteen centuries before afforded him a view of the thronged field and flier-dotted sky.

He stood erect in the chamber and waved both his cables at the mob. He let them see him lean forward and grasp the fission lever. He pulled it back slowly. Deep in the rear of the ship, the great engines sprang to thunderous, vibrating life.

"The fools!" Clarr whispered to himself. "The benighted fools!" The *Shark* roared upward through the clouds, gathering speed. It went up faster in the *heaviside*. The Earth was a slowly turning globe under its jets. It rolled faster and grew smaller as the ship fled away from it.

Clarr stared downward. At the rate the vessel was traveling, he would be out around Mars in one month, at the end of the Solar System in four. If he were going that far, that is. He wasn't, of course. Out beyond the asteroid belt, he'd cut his left banks into silence and swerve to Titan. He had ways of contacting the pirates.

Clarr mentally rubbed his hands, thinking of the ten millions *worths* they'd pay for this titanic hull. That much wealth would enable him to start in on Mars and build up an organization in the Dust Basins near Syrtis Major, expand to Venus and then to Earth. He was immortal. He had plenty of time. All he needed was the money.

After a long time, he went and stared out the forward ports. The moon was receding behind him, big and silvery where the sunlight hit it. He made out the *chrysalis* domes dotting the Sims Iridium and the Alpine Valley.

He stamped around the room, restlessly, knowing he had a good bit of traveling ahead of him. No sense in getting bored right off the Earth lanes so he decided to explore the ship. He went down the metal stairways into the bowels of the vessel and found laboratories and a draughting room, complete libraries on the arts and sciences. Clarr nodded, seeing row on row of books. They would help to pass the time.

He went onto a tiny catwalk and stared into the metal depression that held the gleaming fission chambers with their steady hum and throb.

Faintly he could hear the hum of the jet blasts that choked into silence when they hit empty space. It was an almost silent world he rode. The only noise was his own clankings.

He wandered into one of the laboratories and played with a Gorton burner and some chemicals. He discovered he remembered a lot about his courses at State under O'Mahoney and Nelson. He went through the silicide tests, just for practice, radio-activated some carbon, amused himself blowing odd colors into glass and shaping it in the forms of Venusian temple harlots.

When he went upstairs, Mars was looming two points off port side. Three long thin needles were sliding away from the snow-capped planet with its red hue, and coming to meet him. Clarr started, flipped over his visual screen, amplified it. The needles were big space-dragons, armed to the teeth with disintegrators.

He tapped out signals, but they wouldn't answer. They let him go out in front by a million miles, and they followed like patient nursemaids. Clarr let cold fact penetrate his brain. They weren't taking any chances, back on Earth. They were herding him out of the System, making sure he'd keep on going. Probably there'd be pickup relays from Titan and Neptune.

Clarr swore coldly and thoroughly. He kicked pettishly at a slim *stil* leg on a control table, and snapped it. Then he laughed at himself. "I can go from one end of the galaxy to the other and come back. By that time they'll have forgotten all about me. What'm I getting so burned up about?"

He unscrewed the damaged table and lugged it down decks to one of the laboratories, and fitted it with a new leg. He thought, *I'm going to have to keep busy. Anything—even this table leg to work on—is better than doing nothing.* The space-dragons tailing his jets would make sure he got out of the Solar System. They were taking no chances on Clarr Morson! It came to him that the authorities were afraid of him, in a sense. A criminal brain in a gigantic metal body!

"I could organize the greatest band of space pirates and planet jumpers the Patrol ever met up with. Nobody could kill me, except for a lucky shot. I could even go onto Jupiter, for I don't have to breathe to live."

He took the repaired table up and re-fastened it. Through the plaso-port lenses, he watched Saturn and her rings swim by, and then only utter darkness was out here, relieved occasionally by specks of light that were the distant stars. Loneliness came into the ship with the passage of the ringed planet. Clarr Morson felt as though a weight were pressing him down, stifling him.

He would be out of the System in another billion miles. Clicking on the visual screen he noted there weren't any space-dragons within ten million miles. But they might be back there, waiting. Clarr didn't want to risk being blown to elemental electrons. He'd rather go out there among the stars, and wait.

It dawned on him that he'd been riding for months, and he wasn't tired. He hadn't slept, but labored for weeks at a time down in the laboratories, not noticing the time. He chuckled. In his eight-foot metal shell, all his brain received from the food-vats was energy. There were no human muscles or organs to sap it.

He could go into the hibernation chamber and sleep for twenty years; but he didn't have to. He could go down to the laboratories and amuse himself with every volume they'd given him. From simple formulae he could work into the more complex. From easy experiments in the chemistry and physics primers, he could work his way through the whole set in... Well, how long would it take?

It took him seven years to go through every book, to study it and work out every phrase, equation and solution. He found five errors in the books. And at the end of that time he found he knew more about nuclear physics, organic and inorganic chemistry and biology than the entire teaching staff of State and World Universities. Seven years, working and experimenting day and night, were like a lifetime of study back on Terra.

There was only one drawback: His revived brain wouldn't let him rest. He found himself dissatisfied with things. He took the amplifier out of the curved hull and dismembered it. He found flaws. He used different wiring terminals, and added a new chemical mixture which he froze to plastic hardness as a screen for the bulb he wired and blew from spare glass parts. The amplifier showed him a lot more.

He was headed for Alpha Centauri. The Solar System lay astern, behind his jets. The amplifier worked miracles. It revealed a single space-dragon, a hundred million miles off black Pluto, hanging there in space, waiting to prevent his return.

He would have liked very much to grin. *Why return*, he thought, *when somewhere out ahead I might find the help I need to take a sweet revenge?*

He thought of Ada, but the old hunger was gone. She'd be thirty-nine years old now. By the time he got back, even if he started now, she'd be edging fifty. And he did not intend to go back, not yet.

Ahead of him were the unknown stars. Somewhere among them would be a planet with intelligent beings on it! He turned to the new amplifier and spun dials and he found planets, but when he ran tests on them, he found them frozen chunks of matter, or half-nebulous cores surrounded by swirling gases.

The planets he found were uninhabitable, every one of them. And Clarr Morson wanted to waste no time on a planet where only he could live. He wanted a planet with living, intelligent beings. People to serve him, acknowledge him as master, to return with him, armed and ready for war on the solar worlds.

At last he found a planet in his amplifier that was fifteen hundred light years away. As large as Earth, it had the same general atmosphere and plant life. But—fifteen hundred light years! It would take him five thousand years to get there! Earth would have forgotten about him centuries ago.

It was a problem. Clarr took it down into his laboratories and locked himself away for five years. At the end of that time he'd discovered that galaxies—and space itself—vibrated in certain rhythms.

For the next two years he tested his vibratory theories. He built tiny models and discarded them. Then one day he built a model and didn't discard it. After he completed it, it vanished in front of his eyes. It took him three months to locate it, ten light years ahead of him.

He toiled to make his spaceship a big model. Only the giant metal shell that was his body, only the brain that he'd built up in the long, lonely years in the spaceship could have done it. He completed the job, made his entire ship one single entity ready to vibrate in rhythm at the pull of a switch.

He couldn't explain it, exactly. The nearest he could liken it to was an ant climbing a staircase. He would walk the length of a tread, then up the height of a step. Assuming there was an escalator tread beside the stairs, and the ant could swing onto it, he would go to the top easier and faster. That vibratory pulse was the escalator tread. He would climb into its flow when he pulled the lever.

TOR NALL stared with infinite puzzlement at the series of radar-graphs that lined the replaceable walls of his study. His slim forefinger traced a red line midway between Altair and Cygnus-3. He shook his head in bewilderment.

"There is no planet there, no star. Unless an asteroid—" He went to the wall cabinets and drew out a thin volume, selected three films from it and ran them through the viewer. He emerged more bewildered than ever. He elevated three floors and went into a *takkus*-wood-lined office. A big man with a bald head and keen gray eyes looked up from his desk.

"Well, Tor Nall! Haven't seen you for ages! What brings you up to my hideout?"

"Something that's where it shouldn't be. An asteroid or a planet out of its orbit—or a spaceship." Integrator Jol Rayy raised his eyebrows. His lips quirked at their corners. "Bit imaginative, aren't you? The only inhabitable planet in five thousand light years is Sol Three. And you know about it."

"That's what worries me, sir. I'm positive it isn't from there. It could come from anywhere, because it doesn't travel the usual way."

Jol Rayy looked worried for the first time. "How does it travel?"

"It jumps. My radar-screens catch it in spots ten light years apart. It hops like an insect, or as though it were being carried along by a—a sort of *flow*."

Jol Rayy got to his feet. "Let's have a look," he said decisively. They descended the power chute together and went into the round radar room. Tor Nall slid his screens out and twirled dials. He said, "I'm guessing, right now. But I should say he'd be minus point two three one crossing at irregular tangent five. Let's give it a try."

He missed, but he kept trying. He found the thing twenty light years ahead. Jol Rayy worked on the oscilloscope, following Tor Nall's computations. He hung on grimly until he had his black-and-whites on the chart.

"Spaceship," he said dully, staring at the tiny recording.

Tor Nall looked at him. "Or a small asteroid?"

"What asteroid ever traveled light years at a clip?"

"What are you going to do?"

"Warn the Patrol, naturally. Smash it."

Clarr was in his workshop when the alarm jarred the driving chambers over to full pile drive. The ship quivered slightly, and only Clarr knew it was hopping light years as a grasshopper jumps leaves of grass. To the space-dragons from Trannvia, it simply disappeared.

He was interested enough to check on his radar recorders. He ran an almost invisible wire into a visualizer and made a low sound in his voice-box Nine space-dragons, away out here in forgotten space! Then he kicked the controls over to manual and made a wide arc, coming back as fast as he had gone. But now there were infro-space screens up around the hull, and a dozen beamers sliding out silently through lifting vanes in the prow of his ship.

He overran his target, but a glancing beam caught one of the space-dragons on its tail and whirled it end over end. Clarr circled, and came back. He hung there motionless, like a poised killer-shark. The eight spaceships blasted at him, but the infro-space screens sent the violet rays looped over the hull to meet and touch each other, with the *Shark* an unhurt core of violet brilliance.

Clarr let the ships pull out their best punches before he signaled. He knew they wouldn't understand his code, but they'd recognize intelligence.

Jol Rayy was nervous. He paced the wide metal strip far above the city, and watched the alien ship lower slowly between the eight space-dragons. He had scanned and re-scanned the space captain's report until he could recall it from memory.

The best weapons of the Trann had only served to spotlight the strange craft. Somehow, with the wisdom of a god, the alien had found a way to shrug off weapons it had taken the Trann half a million years to invent.

The strange craft was settling into the cradle now. Soon the valves would be opening and a stranger would be setting foot for the first time on his home planet. Jol Rayy shivered. It was not a first meeting with an alien civilization. But it was a first meeting with a different species, where the weapons of the Trann were futile.

He swung into the descendor and threw over the lever.

CLARR watched the sprawling, white and gold city emerge into the wide glassine panels of his port window. A high type civilization. Higher even than Earth culture. Fascinated, he watched narrow ribbons of metal curve upward almost to cloud level, and the narrow, speeding cars that rocketed on monorails. There were parks and swim-lakes scattered throughout the metropolis. Giant buildings moved up and up, and up, spaced by lower and wider ones whose roofs were dotted with lush green foliage.

"Couldn't have asked anything better," he muttered. "High culture. Advanced civilization. They're warlike, judging from the welcome I got. They ought to be interested in attaching a few rich planets to themselves, as colonies. With my space-drive units installed in their ships, they're that much closer to Earth. It's worthwhile colonizing, then."

Still, there was no sense in being a wide-eyed baby in this first meeting. He didn't know what sort of tricks they might pull, once he was out of the *Shark.* It might be well to be prepared.

He sighed and clomped down the passageway toward his workshop. He fumbled in his tool kit, and drew out a few twisty-barreled objects. Staring at his reflection in a mirror, he went to work on his left shoulder.

He cut a square hole and took out the cutting. Next, he welded a small metal box together, making sure that it fit the cut exactly. Into the box he crowded fission chambers and fuel ducts, each a perfect miniature of the great atom bombs on display in the World Museum. *If he had to go, he'd take a lot of them along.*

The last thing he added was a red stud that looked like an ornament. One touch on that stud and he would detonate a shell of fury that would disintegrate one hundred square miles.

He couldn't step out with a pile-gun in each tendril. He would have to emerge unarmed. On the surface, anyhow! He let a tendril slide over the red stud reassuringly, thinking what an untidy mess it would make if he ever had to press it.

Reassured, Clarr went out into the passageway and climbed to his forward tower. He was almost in the cradle now. He reached out and touched controls. The ship settled nicely, without a jar. He sat silent while the cradle lowered. There was a bump and a grate of metal against metal, and then a glittering walk of polished silver slid forth on silent rollers to the very edge of the spaceship's door.

Clarr touched a button, and the door opened. Looming in the doorway, he stared from his jeweled eyes at the thronged walks and railings.

They were men! He felt tricked, cheated. Back on the *Shark*, he had envisioned his meeting with some alien star beings. Secretly, he had imaged them as scrawny octopi, who would fawn on him. They would accept him as a god, would learn science under him. With their science, the star beings would form a mighty army under Clarr Morson and subjugate Earth. Revenge would be sweet!

A little delegation of white-robed men walked toward him, and halted. He saw their lips move, and heard sounds come out, but he could not understand them. He motioned them to silence, went back into the ship, and brought out an electro-graph, which he clicked onto an arm. The electro-graph had been developed by Klauss to assist in the study of the mentally deficient. It recorded the electrical waves given off by human thought. Fertelli had added an adapter which transmitted those thought waves into code.

"We of Trann greet you," they said. Clarr said, "I am glad to be here. Would you like to come aboard my ship?" Then he took them through the *Shark*, seeing their reactions reveal knowledge of some objects, and their utter ignorance of others. The things Clarr had worked on, alone in the *Shark*, they had never seen before. It was an advantage to read their minds when they could not understand his mental reactions.

The Trann, he discovered, were strangely suspicious of him. One faction wanted him killed. Another group wanted to make use of him. He had come from somewhere, and that somewhere might be ripe for conquest. He felt uneasy. But he learned, before long, that the Trann were planning a giant attack on another star system.

Space-dragons and cruisers were being ordered, new weapons were being developed.

After the investigation of his ship, Clarr was taken to a great building in the center of the city. Here he clanked across a white marble floor to stare unwinkingly into the hard, cold eyes of Stol Tay, Overlord of Trann. The Overlord was lean and fit, with arrogance stamped on his fine features, his lips proclaiming the physical appetites that warred in his makeup.

Clarr heard himself discussed, argued over, insulted, praised and flattered. From the thought-waved code being transmitted into his auriculox, and the sounds of the Trann speech, he was able to match up a thought and a word, here and there. Soon he found himself understanding the simple, austere Trann language. When he was sure that he knew the words he wanted to use, he stood up.

He lifted a metallic tentacle. A profound silence, of shock and awed disbelief, fell upon the room when he began to speak.

"People of Trann, I come in peace. I seek your aid to punish my people who did me a wrong."

Stol Tay was leaning forward, eyes glittering. With a smile on his lips, he said, "You who understand our speech so readily, tell me! Who are your people? Whence come you? These people who wronged you—do they resemble you?"

Clarr said, "I came from Sol Three. It is a small planet revolving around—"

He went no further. The entire room seemed to explode in sound, as men stood and waved silks and sashes, drummed on the floor with sandaled feet. Their voices were hoarse and savage. Here and there, Clarr caught a shouted, "He's a spy!" And other voices joined in with, "Disintegrate him! Disintegrate the spy!"

Stol Tay stood erect before his throne, nostrils flared, trying to look down the tumultuous reaction Clarr's announcement had caused. He lifted a right arm and swept it before his chest. Armed guards sprang from the walls, long lances butt foremost.

The hard *steethus*-wood butts enforced silence. Here and there a man held his silks to a bleeding head. The guards faced the gathering, now, and the butts were reversed. Instead of *steethus*-wood the men faced glittered spear-points

Stol Tay said softly, "One more disturbance, and my palace guards will sweep you from the audience chamber! This man is from Sol Three. Obviously he would not know we ourselves planned to invade his native planet, else he would never have been so rash as to come before us!"

Clarr staggered, as though hit with a *stil*-wedge. The Overlord's words burned in his brain. *We ourselves planned to invade his native planet...*

"But that can't be!" he protested. "I came hunting revenge. I find you here, at hand, ready to do what I've dreamed of doing for years!"

Stol Tay laughed softly. He said, "The gods choose strange servants for their ends. Your people, now. Are they like you?" Clarr shook his head.

"No—like you. They put my living brain in this metal body to send me out among the stars. I hated them for it. I want to go back, to conquer them, to—"

Stol Tay clapped his hands. He gave orders that Clarr be taken to a suite of rooms high in his palace, there to be tended by speech instructors and savants who would teach him of Trann, its history and sciences. The Overlord looked at Clarr and said, "I will come myself to visit you within a week. By that time, learn all my savants teach you."

It did not take long. Soon Clarr Morson spoke the short, yet liquid syllables of the Trann properly, soon he understood their past and their hoped-for future.

In mid-morning of his fifth day on the planet Trann, Stol Tay came to see him. Clarr Morson spoke of the power piles of Earth, of their weapons, of their almost barbaric genius for battle. But over that he laid a layer of praise for his own infro-space screen, which no weapon could penetrate.

Then he frosted his words with descriptions of *stil* mines on Venus, of the rare *corbonyx* crystals of Mars' red deserts, of the strange *vannar* atoms that man mined from Saturn's rings, which could furnish enough power from a lump of *vannar* the size of a pea to push a spacecraft across the Solar System a dozen times or more.

He dwelt on the pleasure chambers of Amerasia, where girls from all corners of Earth Empire were taught oddly pleasing habits. He referred to the underwater rooms off the Bahamas and Philippines, where a man could taste the strange effects of Martian *stahalish* without ill reactions. He spent some time on the giant metro-poles of Mars and Earth and Venus, rightly calculating the greed and the lust in the eyes of the Trann Overlord.

"I want to go back there," he said in conclusion. "I want to lead that force of Trann space-dragons and cruisers you've been gathering for years for just this invasion! I'll run up your Cat banner over every one of the System's major cities! You wanted war with Sol Three because it's the nearest inhabited star system. I'll bring you your war, with a positive victory. With my knowledge, my info-screen, plus your fighting ships and men, we can't lose! I'll make you Overlord of two star systems!"

Stol Tay licked his lips. "And you?"

"I'll be your second-in-command of the Solar System. You'll get your tribute. I just want a thin slice of it. That'll be enough for me."

Stol Tay stalked the room, his chest pumping with the greed and excitement that Clarr's words had started in him. He whirled with a sway of his white cloak, eyes bright.

"Taxes? Can you tax those people of yours?"

Clarr laughed. "I'll tax them bloody! I'll give enough to the ones in authority so that we'll keep them always just one jump short of armed rebellion. I've had a long time to plan the way to run the Three Planets. You'll get money for your—amusements."

Stol Tay opened his mouth, then snapped it shut. He chuckled, dryly. It was impossible to know anger against this thing of metal. It was like a servant, a perfect servant. He thought about his own particular brand of amusement, and a little thrill of anticipation coursed down his backbone. He locked his fingers and squeezed hard, to gain that cold control on which he prided himself.

He said, "We of Trann have certain things to offer you, as well as Overlordship of the Three Planets. Our medical men have long been using a plastoflesh synthesis to repair battle wounds. There is no reason why they could not form a body of plastoflesh for you, complete with neural system, implying as that does a thorough enjoyment of the five senses."

Clarr could not betray his emotions, but his brain remembered Ada. By this time, Ada was a rotting corpse, but there were other women in the Three Planets. He had always had a hankering for a redheaded Martian temple girl, but those temple girls cost money. Now he would have that money. It would be a nice setup. It was almost too good to be true.

For two hours, Clarr Morson and Stol Tay talked. They outlined to each other an entire course of action that would see the Three Planets overwhelmed in less than two years.

Stol Tay concluded, "We will tell the leading citizens of Trann, at a great council meeting, one week from today. I will have engineers there, the finest in the Trann Empire, to install your infro-space screens in one hundred of our mightiest space-dragons. I will have medical geniuses there, to begin work on your new body. I will have space-fleet commanders there to confer with you on battle tactics. There will be artists, to sculpt and paint you in your present form—the man who has made our invasion plans so simple and easy! I myself will deliver into your hands the scroll, making you a Trann citizen, with the rank of *Sandar!*"

Clarr got up, seeing the interview was at an end. He murmured his thanks, which Stol Tay brushed aside.

"After all," he told Clarr, "you have put certain victory in our hands!" For a long while after the Overlord had gone, Clarr Morson stood by the arched window, tasting the warm satisfaction of a cherished dream soon to be realized.

ONE WEEK later, Clarr Morson sat on a huge chair raised above the speaker's platform in the Great Council Room of the Trann. Before an audience of ten thousand of the first ranking Trann statesmen and engineers, scientists and scholars, Stol Tay presented him with the radiant scroll that made him an honorary citizen of the Trann in the advanced rank of *Sandar*.

Standing on the dais that overlooked the vast chamber, Stol Tay said, "We are gathered here to make the most decisive step in the long history of the Trann. We are sworn to secrecy, so that no word of what transpires here will reach the people, until such time as we can announce overwhelming victory!

"As you know, we planned to invade Sol Three, the nearest star system with habitable planets. That plan has become reality, thanks to Clarr Morson."

Stol Tay waited for the cheering to subside before he went on. "He will confer with all of you in the next few weeks, outlining my plans for making the Trann Empire the greatest in the stars…"

Clarr sat, a giant metal image, at the speakers' rostrum, and listened to the flow of oratory. Soon now, he would begin conferences with engineers and militarists. He would reveal the secret of his infro-space beams and other weaponry. He would expose the value of Earth weapons, the extent of space and planet defenses.

The thought came unbidden. *I am a traitor to my people!* But he pushed it aside, savagely. Clarr Morson owed no Earthling allegiance! He owed allegiance only to himself; and now, to the Trann.

If his metal mouth could have smiled, it would. He thought back on Dr. Ens and what he had said the day before he left Earth in the *Shark*. What was it? Oh, yes… "And a mental bloc has been added by post-operative hypnosis to correct any chance of your backsliding." He supposed that treachery was a form of backsliding into criminal ways. But there was nothing Dr. Ens of Earth could do, now.

Stol Tay turned and gestured to him. Clarr turned his attention to the Overlord of Trann. Stol Tay was saying, "According to our new citizen, the Earth and her satellite planets are rich with plunder. As Overlord of the Three Planets, he will make sure that we of the Trann Empire receive our full share. And now I present—Clarr Morson, of Trann!"

The room shook with applause. Clarr towered high on the dais, looking down at the upturned faces. The brains of all Trann were gathered here. *If anything happened to them, he thought, and to myself, the Earth would be safe forever.*

But what could happen?

Clarr thought of Dr. Ens and his mental bloc, and mentally sneered.

He lifted his right hand to still the continued cheering. At the height of his shoulder, his metallic hand paused and swerved. For one instant, as his hand turned aside and came down, Clarr remembered the powerful atom bomb he had built into his shoulder casing.

And then his metal finger touched the red stud, and thrust it down.

THE HISTORIANS of the Trann never did find out what caused the fearful mushroom of atomic power that blew its greatest brains to hazy mists in the Month of the Acorn, Year of the Red Dragon. That mushroom set them back two hundred years, in science and the arts. By the time they recovered from the blow, it was too late.

Earth Empire had already reached out and conquered the Trann.

March 1962
Art by John Duillo

THE HUNTED

Rick Rubin

Adventure, October 1961   Cover by Vic Prezio

THE HUNTED

THE girl's slim body lay stretched out in the shallow depression that Mike Kolkoski had scooped in the rain-soaked forest duff. In death her face, marked by hunger and exhaustion, seemed to be smiling.

Kolkoski stood over the grave, a heavy-shouldered man with broad cheekbones under overhanging brows, wearing torn brown pants and a thin jacket, stained by water and mud. He stood with his head lowered for several minutes and then began to pile rocks and dirt and branches on top of the body.

"Another truck full of them just went up toward the mountains," John Ralston said from where he crouched near a break in the underbrush, looking down on the highway below. "That makes three trucks this morning. They're getting ready to close in."

"Nuts," Kolkoski said. "They don't even know we're here."

"Do you think men can outsmart robots?" Ralston said. "We might as well turn ourselves in." He stood up and stretched. Standing near Kolkoski, his small-boned body and delicate features made the bigger man look crude.

Kolkoski finished covering the girl's body and sat wearily under a fir tree. Above them the sky was a uniform October grey and a cold drizzle covered trees, bushes and ground with glistening drops of moisture. Kolkoski pulled a *(Continued on Page 72)*

(Continued on Page 72)

TRAPPED, ALONE, THEY FLED THROUGH THE HOSTILE FOREST,
A MAN AND A GIRL AGAINST A ROBOT ARMY. SOMEHOW THEY
MUST SURVIVE THIS DAY—OR THE RACE CALLED MAN WOULD PERISH!

BY RICK RUBIN
ILLUSTRATED BY BRUCE MINNEY

43

ART BY BRUCE MINNEY

THE GIRL'S slim body lay stretched out in the shallow depression that Mike Kolkoski had scooped in the rain-soaked forest duff. In death her face, marked by hunger and exhaustion, seemed to be smiling. Kolkoski stood over the grave, a heavy-shouldered man with broad cheekbones under overhanging brows, wearing torn brown pants and a thin jacket, stained by water and mud. He stood with his head lowered for several minutes and then began to pile rocks and dirt and branches on top of the body.

"Another truck full of them just went up toward the mountains," John Ralston said from where he crouched near a break in the underbrush, looking down on the highway below. "That makes three trucks this morning. They're getting ready to close in."

"Nuts," Kolkoski said. "They don't even know we're here."

"Do you think men can outsmart robots?" Ralston said. "We might as well turn ourselves in." He stood up and stretched. Standing near Kolkoski, his small-boned body and delicate features made the bigger man look crude.

Kolkoski finished covering the girl's body and sat wearily under a fir tree. Above them the sky was a uniform October grey and a cold drizzle covered trees, bushes and ground with glistening drops of moisture. Kolkoski pulled a bag of tobacco out of his shirt pocket and rolled a cigarette. He stood up with a sigh and walked over to crouch behind Ralston. For a minute he studied the road, then shrugged and tapped the other man's arm.

"Give me a light, please," he said.

Ralston fished a box of wooden matches from his pocket and passed them to Kolkoski.

"I'm going to give myself up," Ralston said. "I'm going down to the road and wait for the next truck and let them take me back to Portland."

"Don't talk like a fool," Kolkoski said.

"They don't hurt returned escapees," Ralston said. "They just put them back in the camp and treat them like all of the other humans. Anyway, no-body's ever seen a robot actually hurt a man. And I don't want to die here."

"You won't die. We'll make it to the mountains."

"You've already killed Nancy. Do you want to kill the rest of us too? Even if we could make it to the mountains, those are just stories about there being escapees living there like free people."

He shook his head.

"Look at us, Kolkoski," he continued. "We're half dead, our clothes are in shreds, and we haven't found anything to eat but roots and berries in four days."

"One more day," Kolkoski said. "I'm sure we're within ten or fifteen miles of the mountains. Then you and Maggie can get married, and have children the robots can't take away from you. We can live like free people instead of slaves and prisoners."

"I can't take it any more," Ralston said. "Maggie and I are going down and let them take us back to the camp. It isn't so bad in the camp."

"I'm not coming with you," Maggie Eriksen said, entering the clearing through the bushes. She stood looking at the two men and the narrow grave. A tall girl with solid hips and breasts, she was dressed as they were, in tattered pants and a cloth jacket, and her long brown hair hung in snarls and matted rolls over her shoulders.

"Be sensible, Maggie," Ralston said. "We haven't a chance to make it to the mountains. There are bears and mountain lions, and we don't know how to live off the land. If the robots don't get us the forest will. Let's go down to the road while there's still time."

"I think we can make it," the girl said.

"Do you want to die like Nancy? I'm going down to the road, I tell you. I'm not going to get killed searching for an abstract called freedom."

"Then go," she said.

"You won't come?"

"No."

"I get it. You want to stay with Mike. I should have guessed."

"Mike and I couldn't care less for each other."

"Please come back with me, Maggie," he said. "We can learn to live in the camp. Human beings can learn to live anywhere. And maybe they'll treat us better some day."

The girl turned away from him and stood very straight.

"No," she said, "I won't go back and live the rest of my life behind barbed wire."

"They'll kill you," he said. "What do you think those signs they put up everywhere mean? THE STRONG WILL SURVIVE. The robots are going to survive, and we're all going to die, because we're human and weak and they hate us. You're just helping them along by speeding it up. The longer you live, the more you bother them."

"I'd rather die free," she said.

"I'm going," he said. "Good luck." He turned and walked off down the hill toward the road.

Kolkoski and the girl stood and listened to the sound of him breaking through the underbrush. It grew fainter and fainter and then they could no longer hear it.

"Thanks for sticking with me," Kolkoski said. "I don't know if I'd have had enough guts to go on alone."

"I'm not going with you," she said. "We're just going in the same direction."

"Have it your own way. We'd better get going. Ralston is probably telling the robots where to find us right now."

"He'd never tell on us. Don't you say he would."

"Forget it. Nothing I say is right."

"It's easy for you to criticize John, but what about yourself? You as much as killed Nancy, dragging her along into this wilderness. She never had a chance, a pretty little girl like her."

"She came because she wanted to. Freedom meant something to her."

Kolkoski picked up the butcher knife he had used to dig the grave and started toward the edge of the clearing. He headed across the slope and the girl fell in behind him.

For over an hour they marched in silence through the undergrowth. In the distance a crack of blue sky appeared and widened into a full quarter of the sky. Coming around the shoulder of a ridge they saw Mount Hood towering above them, white with snow.

"How far do you think we have to go?" the girl asked.

"I'm not sure. It's been a long time since I was up here. Not since I was a kid and people still went to the mountains to ski and camp."

"But it can't be too far, can it?"

"It's a big mountain. Anyway, we don't know where the free country begins. If it begins at all. I think Rhododendron maybe, where the land wouldn't be of any value to the robots, and if it's there, I'd guess we've got about ten miles to go by highway."

The girl laughed softly. "If we were going by highway."

Kolkoski laughed too.

"Let's take a break," he said. "We aren't in much condition and it's best to save our strength."

They found a tree and huddled beneath it.

"Do we dare chance a fire?" the girl asked.

"Maybe we can risk it. They can't see this spot from the road, and once it's dark we won't dare." He cut branches with the butcher knife and built a small fire behind a screen of brush and trees. He and the girl crouched over the fire, steam rising from their clothes.

"This feels good," she said. "I'd forgotten how it feels to be warm."

"That's the least of what we've forgotten."

"What do you mean?"

"I've been thinking about what we've forgotten down there in the valley, living as prisoners. We've lost all of the skills we used to need to stay alive. Even as prisoners we had it soft. No farming, no cooking, no manufacturing, no work at all."

"Are you getting ready to give up and go back?"

"Hell no. Just thinking about that robot slogan, 'The Strong Will Survive.' You know, I almost have to agree with them. We don't deserve to survive. We're weak and lazy and cowardly. We've even made weakness our criterion of beauty—emaciated girls and delicate young men. I'm ugly because I'm big and reasonably healthy. So are you. And most of the people down there don't even want to escape. Too much effort. They'd rather adjust themselves to being slaves. Look at you and me, two of the strongest. We're almost dead of exhaustion, after walking forty miles in four days."

"But forty miles is a long way."

"It didn't used to be. I remember hearing my father tell of soldiers walking sixty miles in twenty-four hours. Even Boy Scouts used to have to walk fourteen miles in one day to pass a test. Twelve-year-olds. The race has been going downhill ever since I was a kid. We used to have sports and games, and even go for walks just for pleasure. Then came television, and cars, and finally robots to do all the work. All we had to do was sit around and consume. I guess we deserved to have the robots take over and make us prisoners and slaves."

THEY had been sitting by the fire, feeding branches into it and relaxing in its warmth, when suddenly they heard a crash in the underbrush.

"They are in this direction." a metallic sounding robot voice shouted. "I have located the fire of the escaped humans."

"Run!" Mike yelled. He jumped to his feet and Maggie followed him in a headlong dash into the underbrush. They ran until they were panting with exhaustion, uphill through branches and sharp vines and stiff bushes. The hillside turned away toward the south and they abandoned it, cutting down the slope into a canyon. Coming to the bottom, where a stream rushed through an open meadow, they stopped finally to catch their breath. Above and behind them they could hear the robots, crashing through the brush.

"Wait until I'm across, then run like hell," Mike said. He dashed out into the open field, splashed through the stream, and into the forest on the far side. Turning, he watched Maggie start across.

"There is a woman human," a robot shouted.

From the protection of the forest, Mike saw two robots on the far hillside. One raised a rifle to his shoulder, the weapon dwarfed in his giant steel arm.

A bullet plowed into the dirt near Maggie, and she threw herself to the ground.

"Run!" Mike shouted. "Don't stay there. They've got a clear shot at you."

She leaped to her feet and ran again. The rifle crashed twice more, but the bullets plowed into the ground yards from her churning feet. Then she was in the forest, and they ran together, up a small canyon into the next range of hills.

"I think we're safe for a while," Mike said, stopping to catch his breath. "Robots don't like to get wet if they can help it."

"But why did they miss me, Mike? I thought robots never missed."

"Maybe they're just playing with us. I don't know."

They caught their breath and continued up the little valley, then over a ridge and back toward the highway. From the crest of the ridge they could see two robot trucks parked on the highway and ten robots gathered in conference beside them.

"Let's keep moving," Mike said.

At the edge of the road they hesitated, looking in both directions and listening. A hundred yards up the road was another sign, THE STRONG WILL SURVIVE, in great red letters.

"You go first," Mike said. "The second one across is a better target."

"Don't do me any favors just because I'm a woman."

"You took the risk last time," he said. He looked at her, her eyes on a level with his own.

"Get the hell going," he said.

She looked up and down the road, then ran, quickly but lightly, graceful for a large woman.

On the far side of the road a river rushed noisily down toward the distant valley. It was twenty or more yards across and the water boiled white off hidden rocks. They crawled along the bank, searching for a place to cross, but there was none. Finally they gave up, and waded as far out as they could and swam across. On the far side they huddled in the underbrush.

"I wouldn't have believed I could get any wetter until we took that swim," the girl said.

"You'd better thank that swim," Kolkoski said. "We're twice as safe from the robots as long as the river is on this side of the highway." He saw that she was shivering.

"Take off your clothes and wring them out," he said. He began to strip off his own shirt.

"Turn around," the girl said. "You're not getting a free view that way."

"You don't even appeal to me," Kolkoski said. "I like my women feminine, not big and tough."

"That's a laugh," Maggie said. "Here we are, big and hard and healthy, at least compared to the other people down in the camp, but we're both ashamed of it. And we were both in love with soft, delicate people."

"Everyone wants to be soft and cultivated looking," Mike said. "I've been ashamed of looking like an ape ever since I was a kid."

"I know. How do you think I felt, the biggest girl in my class? But you know, if we weren't such a pair of throwbacks we wouldn't be here now."

They undressed, facing away from each other, and wrung out their clothes. water cascading from each piece. "God, these are cold," Maggie said, putting her shirt back on.

They set off up the ridge again, away from the highway. For another hour they climbed slowly, until they were high enough to get a clear view of the road and the valley as they twisted up into the mountains.

"I think that's Rhododendron," Mike said, pointing up to near the head of the valley, "If I remember right it's about ten or fifteen miles below the pass."

"Is that a fence across the valley and the highway there?" Maggie said.

"Looks like it. Maybe I was right about the end of robot territory."

"Let's hope so."

"Anyway, we'd better keep moving. We've got to find a place to sleep soon, before it gets too dark, and some berries or roots to eat."

They came upon a narrow, well-worn trail through the forest, marked by the prints of animals, and followed it, ducking under overhanging branches. The trail twisted up and down the ridge but followed the easiest path. Then it cut down into a canyon, toward the sound of a rushing stream.

THEY were walking in silence when they rounded a bend and came face to face with a wide-eyed deer. The frightened animal turned to bound away down the trail, but in one quick motion Mike threw the knife at it, gashing it deeply in the shoulder. One leg hanging limp, the animal fell to the ground, struggling furiously to rise and run. In two bounds Mike was upon it, his retrieved knife slashing at its throat.

"Now we eat," he said, rising to stand panting over the dead deer. His face and arms dripped red. "Come on, we'll drag it off the trail and find a place to camp."

He grabbed the animal's front legs while the girl took hold of the hind ones, and they pulled and tugged it off the trail and through the underbrush to an open patch, covered with soft pine needles and surrounded by trees and bushes. The ground was dry, and Kolkoski dropped the deer. Squatting beside it he drove the butcher knife into the body and began to cut off chunks of the dark red meat.

"I don't think I can eat it raw," the girl said. "I'll be sick. I know I'll be sick."

"You can't afford to be sick. Eat in little bites. We can't cook it."

"But it's so brutal and bloody."

"Our ancestors did it. Maybe brutality is the price of freedom." He bit into a piece. "It's good," he said. "I can feel the energy already."

The girl took a slice and chewed it thoughtfully. Then they ate and swallowed, spitting out sinews too tough to chew. As he ate, Kolkoski began to skin the animal, scraping the hide clean of flesh.

"We'll sleep here," he said. "We ought to make it to the fence sometime tomorrow. Then we'll know one way or the other."

"Mike," the girl said, "I've been thinking. Why do you suppose the robots shot at us with rifles? They have more effective weapons than that."

"I wondered about that too. Maybe they consider hunting people sport."

"Or maybe they don't care if we do make it to the fence. It isn't like a robot to fail. Maybe they want us to reach the fence. And another thing. I used to think that a robot couldn't harm a human. It was supposed to be coded into them on a special circuit. Yet they've put us in prison camps, and cut us down to minimum food and no comfort—even forbidden us to marry or keep any illegitimate children we have. What happened to the protective circuit that was supposed to keep them from doing any harm to the human race?"

"Nobody knows," Mike said. "I remember we captured a robot once, back in the camp. But all he would say was that he was doing nothing to harm humans. And when one of the men who knew something about electronics opened him up, the circuit that was supposed to keep robots from hurting people was still intact. Maybe the robots get around it by never actually doing any physical harm to people. Maybe that's why they didn't try to hit us. They have to capture us alive."

"Or maybe the other side of the fence is a hunting ground," Maggie said, "Where they consider us fair game to shoot, since we've run away. And now they're just herding us toward the fence."

"I dunno. To me, freedom is worth the risk."

They ate their fill of the steaming venison and Mike finished cleaning the hide. It was dark now. He scraped together a bed of pine needles, large enough for two to lie on.

"Let's get some sleep," he said. "Come over and lie against me."

"Look, buster," Maggie said, "I'm not your woman."

"Quit talking nonsense. We need the warmth, and the deer hide isn't big enough to cut in half."

Grudgingly, the girl came to him and lay on the piled up needles, and he pulled the hide over them, hair side down. She lay with her back toward him, but as she fell asleep she rolled over, and her head settled into the cup of his shoulder.

They woke with the first light of the false dawn, and ate more of the deer meat. The girl begged for a fire, but Kolkoski refused, on the grounds that they were too close to their goal to chance it.

It was the same battle through stubborn underbrush as the day before, but now they could see their goal through occasional breaks in the forest. Their clothes, dried during the night by the heat of their bodies, were soon saturated again by the wet forest. They continued east, keeping parallel with the road on the north side of the valley, dipping down into small canyons and then climbing agonizingly up the far ridges. During the morning they saw or heard nothing of the robots, not even a truck.

At NOON the thin October sun came out, and they sat in a clearing on the last ridge before Rhododendron, looking down on the fence that cut across the valley like a belt. They ate more of the venison, taking it piece by piece from a sack that Kolkoski had fashioned from two handkerchiefs.

"They've really got it fenced off, don't they?" the girl said.

"It's a good sign. If there weren't something worth getting to the robots wouldn't have bothered with the fence."

"What do we do now?"

"I want to explore over the next ridge to the north. Maybe the fence ends over there and we can go around instead of over."

They sat and soaked in the warmth of the sun, until Kolkoski pulled himself to his feet with a grunt.

"I'll go and check," he said.

"I'll go along," she said.

"No use in tiring us both out. We'll need our strength in case we have to climb the fence. Besides, you can be watching to see if they patrol the fence, and if so what their schedule is."

He set off up the ridge, and the girl moved up to a position where she could see the fence from one side of the valley to the other. She lay in the open until the rain began again, then pulled up the collar of her coat and moved to the protection of a low tree. After two hours she heard the sounds of snapping twigs from up the ridge. She started to get up, then crouched back under the tree instead. The sounds moved to where Kolkoski had left her, then began to circle cautiously through the woods. Finally she saw him.

"Over here," she said.

"You're getting to be an expert at concealment," he said.

"I didn't know if it was you or a robot."

"Do I look like a robot?"

"Mister Kolkoski, you look pretty good to me right now."

"Even with an indelicate face?"

"Even with unfashionably broad shoulders. But what did you find?"

"The fence goes as far as I could see. They don't seem to patrol it, but it's electric. Insulators on the wires. Three rolls of barbed wire on the ground, then an electric fence about fifteen feet tall."

"They don't patrol it over here, either," she said. "But there's a big guard building or something down where the fence crosses the road. And I saw the smoke of fires up the valley, beyond the fence."

"Well, there's no use worrying about what that means. First we've got to get over the fence. I figure that we'll have to make a ladder. Cutting down a tree and dropping it over the fence might make too much noise and alert the robots."

They built the ladder, Maggie braiding branches and vines into ropes while Kolkoski cut two long poles and a number of cross pieces with the butcher knife. When they assembled the ladder it stood twenty feet tall, and held firm when they tested it against a pine tree.

They carried the ladder down to the fence just at dusk. Mike led the way through the barbed wire, but even picking their way carefully their legs and hands were slashed and bloody when they came to the tall electric fence. Working together, they hoisted the ladder up and dropped it on the top strand of the fence, close by one of the supporting posts.

A loud buzzing sounded from the wire, and in the distance, toward the road, they heard the raucous clamor of an alarm bell.

"Up you go," Mike said. "Now or never!"

She started up the ladder, then hesitated. "Mike, in case you don't make it…"

"Go, woman."

"No. Listen, I want to say that I think you're pretty great. I'm sorry for the things I said and I wish…"

"Get the hell up the ladder!"

She scurried up and Mike followed.

"We forgot about the other side," she laughed, and then jumped out into space and dropped to the ground. Mike saw her roll and then leap to her feet, and he followed her, pushing himself as far out as he could leap.

Above them they heard the deafening roar of a helicopter.

"Now they're going to play for keeps," Mike said.

They ran for the trees, Kolkoski favoring a sprained ankle, but before they had gone ten yards a searchlight from the helicopter caught and held them.

"Listen, Maggie," Mike said, "I'm sorry about the things I said, too. No matter how this comes out, I'm glad we got together. Even if you are an oversized Swede with more guts than most men."

"Norwegian, you dope," she said, squirming over to huddle against his shoulder. "And to hell with fashionably delicate people."

"Congratulations, Michael Kolkoski and Margaret Ericksen," a rasping voice said over a loudspeaker. "You have successfully escaped. Much as we regret the fate of Miss Nancy DeWare, we hope that you will forgive us. Driving superior individuals to escape is the only method we have been able to devise to select humans strong enough in mind, body and spirit to perpetuate the human race. If your race is to survive and once again become vigorous, only superior individuals can be permitted to breed, and now that you have proven your strength, the future of the race lies in your hands, and those of the other free people. The package we are now dropping will provide you with equipment for personal survival and you will find others of the free people by continuing up the center of the valley."

A heavy weight dropped through the trees and crashed to the ground fifteen feet from them.

"Good luck to you," the voice boomed. "The Strong Will Survive."

They were opening the package, marveling at the rifles and ammunition, the matches, cook pots, clothes, knives, tools and books on agriculture, weaving and pottery, when the reception committee of the free people broke through the forest to greet them.

THERE ARE ANIMAL MEN
by Wesley Garfield
Illustration (detail)
by Andre Zaro
Mr. America, August 1953

THE WEREWOLF AND THE COWBOY

Stuart Evans

See For Men, November 1961   Cover by George Gross

THE WEREWOLF AND THE

It was like no other animal that stalked the range—
an unkillable monster big as a steer.

But what made the stranger so sure it was a werewolf?

On the night of the full moon in July, 1937, a Basque sheepherder, named Fernando Romila, was awakened in his wagon by a strange sound. Fernando was not a man to scare easily. He was used to living alone under the stars, many miles from the nearest humans, in the company of the 700 sheep he tended and the two nags that drew his cart. He had lived that way for years, on the tick-ridden mountain pastures of the Idaho-Montana borderland, and he knew the howls of

COWBOY

by Stuart Evans

ILLUSTRATED BY BOB BAUM

ART BY BOB BAUM

ON THE night of the full moon in July, 1937, a Basque sheepherder named Fernando Romila was awakened in his wagon by a strange sound. He was used to living alone under the stars, many miles from the nearest humans, in the company of the 700 sheep he tended and the two nags that drew his cart. He had lived that way for years, on the tick-ridden mountain pastures of the Idaho-Montana borderland, and he knew the howls of the timber wolf and the coyote, and the brief noise a sheep makes when a mountain lion sinks his fangs into its throat.

The sound he heard that night was unlike any other he had ever heard before. It could have been the cry of a wolf on the prowl, but the full-throated howl of this wild beast had behind it a curious human quality. It was as if it were almost talking. Fernando threw off his blankets.

His horses had become restless. They scraped their hoofs and bellowed. The sheep mewed and squealed, and just as Fernando jumped from his caravan wagon, the strange howl turned into a snarl, and one of the sheep gave an agonized bleat.

Rifle in hand, Fernando raced toward the sound. He was afraid, but he knew his duty. Sheep bumped into his legs as he ran across the moonlit pasture, as if seeking comfort from his presence.

The beast howled again, and Fernando knew it was very close. He raised his rifle. Ahead, dimly outlined in the silver light, he saw a huge dark shape, at least twice the size of a full-grown timber wolf, squatting on its haunches over a blob of gray which Fernando recognized as a slaughtered sheep.

He fired. The monster did not budge. It howled again, and this time it sounded as if it were laughing. Fernando advanced another few feet, and again he pressed the trigger. Now the beast raised itself and bared its fangs. Desperately, Fernando slammed back the bolt, and he kept on firing until all his rounds were gone.

IT WAS quite by accident that Fernando's body was found the next day by Burke Jackson, a cattle driver who was riding back from Henry's Corner to the nearby ranch where he worked.

Fernando's head lay severed from his body, mouth open in a last, desperate scream and his eyes bulging in frozen terror. The torso was ripped open from breastbone to groin, a wide, gaping, dark cavity, and there was nothing inside, just shreds of the tissues that had held his bowels and his organs in place. Jackson noticed that there was surprisingly little blood; it almost seemed as if whatever had killed Fernando had nuzzled down on his open neck and sucked him dry. This was confirmed later by the undertaker at Henry's Corner.

Jackson examined the sheep. It too had bled but little, and its belly was torn open also, but the organs were not missing. Jackson found a few tracks. They were those of a wolf but much larger. The animal would have had to be seven feet long and weighed 400 pounds to leave prints like that.

Jackson got a blanket from Fernando's wagon, bundled up the torso and the head, slung the bundle over his saddle and rode back to town.

He found the peace officer in Kansas Pete's tavern, leaning on the bar and talking with a stranger.

"Back mighty quick," the deputy greeted Jackson. "What's the matter, Burke, they kick you out at Dooley's?"

Jackson, who was a slow man with words, first downed the whiskey the bartender put in front of him without being asked, and then said, "Not yet, they didn't, though they might if I don't show up by and by. I come back because that Fernando got himself killed. I got him outside on the horse."

Slowly, the deputy drew the story from Jackson, who was as puzzled as ever by his grisly find. "I can't figure what killed him. I never seen no beast that would eat a man's guts, 'cepting it was a coyote, but coyotes don't come that big. This was even bigger than a wolf."

"Say," said the stranger at the bar who had listened to the account. "Wasn't it full moon last night?"

"Sure," Jackson said.

"Could have been a werewolf," the stranger said. "You've heard of werewolves, haven't you? Men that turn into beasts when the moon is full, and go out to kill to drink blood and eat hearts. Now don't start laughing," he said when he saw the smiles breaking out on the faces around him. "Just because you never seen a werewolf doesn't prove they don't exist. Of course, werewolves aren't in fashion now, and they always were more popular in Europe, but that doesn't prove anything either."

The stranger was a bulky man, in a fancy city suit with a wide-striped tie. His hair grew low on his forehead; his eyebrows arched in a single span across his deep-set narrow eyes. When he smiled he displayed big yellow teeth, and his breath was so foul that people moved away from him.

"Who's that character?" Jackson asked the deputy when they went outside to take Fernando's body to the undertaker's.

"Don't know," said the deputy. "He came to town about a week ago, and took a room over at the hotel. Spends most of his time at Pete's. Don't know where he gets the money. Well, it's none of my business so long as he makes no trouble."

"He sure is a screwball," said Jackson.

The undertaker stitched the head back on Fernando, although there were no relatives around to pay their last respect, and then the sheepherder was buried. After one of the girls ran naked one night from Millie's whorehouse, chased by a drunken ranch hand, and into Kansas Pete's saloon, the people of Henry's Corner forgot about Fernando and talked about Millie and her girls instead. By that time, Burke Jackson had long returned to Dooley's twin-fork ranch.

ONE MONTH passed. The moon waned and grew again, and then shaped full for August. That night, Jackson was snoring in the bunk house when, from outside, he heard the unmistakable sound of a stampede. It wasn't a big stampede because most of the cattle were not kept grazing that close to the ranch, but any time you have a couple dozen cattle running in terror, it's a stampede. You hear the earth shaking like thunder, and you better watch out.

Jackson and three other men rushed outside to their horses. There was no time to saddle them. Jackson grabbed a lariat and jumped on bareback. The cattle were making for the river flats where there was quicksand, and it was head them off or lose them. From far off, Jackson heard a monstrous howl; to him it sounded as if a giant roared in anger. He galloped toward that sound, while the other man rode toward the river, because he suspected that this was where the trouble came from that had alarmed the cattle.

He raced through the moonlight. There was no mistaking the direction. He flashed past the corral, and down the gentle slope of the home pasture, and as he rode he still heard the trampling hooves and the yells of the other men toward his right, but already far away, but he also heard the strange howl subside into a snarl and, as he came closer, the sound of smacking lips and sucking.

Suddenly before him lay a fullgrown steer, and over the body of that animal rose the shape of another, equally as big. Jackson's horse reared up with a shriek. Jackson was almost thrown. He managed to slide off the horse's hind end, and as the horse galloped away, he advanced on the monster and swung his lariat.

The beast before him—Jackson thought it was a wolf but he could not believe its size—was squatting over the fallen steer and sucking on its neck, its huge yellow fangs catching the light of the moon and flashing. It paid no attention to the advancing man.

Jackson whirled the rope and threw it. The loop settled over the beast's neck.

Its eyes flashed red in the moonlight, and from its throat rose a deep snarl. Jackson pulled in on the rope and braced himself. This was going to be a lot tougher than calf-roping, he thought, but surprisingly he was not really scared.

The monster's snarl turned into something like a laugh. Jackson thought it almost sounded human, and the beast rose from the carcass and gaped its jaws at Jackson and rushed forward. Jackson knew then that he had no chance.

JUST THEN the night turned completely dark. A thick cloud had drifted over the moon. Jackson was as a blind man; he could see nothing, and standing there in the blackness he waited for his death.

Suddenly he felt himself yanked forward. He fell flat on the ground. And then he was pulled along as the beast apparently tried to escape. Jackson hung on. The rope burned his fingers bloody before he got a good hold on it, and he bounced along over rocks, his face grinding in the dust, beset only by the thought that he must catch and kill the beast.

He was dragged for several hundred feet, his clothes shredding and his skin rubbing off, and then he was pulled into the forest, and when he banged against a tree he saw his chance. He wrapped his body around the trunk, and then quickly slung the rope around it.

The beast howled. The tree bent forward and then snapped back, and as Jackson felt his way forward in the darkness, he heard the monster crashing through the forest, sounding farther and farther away, and his groping hands found the rope and reeled it in. The rope had torn.

Jackson limped back to the bunk house. What had happened was hard to believe. He examined the rope in the light. It was perfectly good rope, yet the beast had managed to tear it, something not even a full-grown bull can do. And then the other riders came in, and told him that altogether three head of cattle had been killed by the mysterious raider.

THE FOLLOWING weekend, Jackson went to Henry's Corner to spend his wages, and in Kansas Pete's he met up with the same stranger who had talked about a werewolf after Fernando's death. After a few drinks, Jackson told him the story of what had happened.

"You see," said the stranger, smiling his yellow-toothed smile, "it must be a werewolf. Otherwise you'd be dead."

"How you figger that?" Jackson said.

"You said that a cloud covered the moon just when the wolf was going to attack you, right? Well, any ordinary wolf wouldn't have been stopped by darkness, but a werewolf can only kill by the light of the full moon. So naturally he had no choice but to escape."

"Sounds like a bunch of hogwash to me," Jackson said. "Something must have scared him off. But we'll see. Maybe I'll get another look at him. I'll set a trap."

"How do you figure on doing that?"

"I'll stake out a juicy cow and wait for him."

"An excellent idea," said the stranger. "But don't lose your sleep doing it every night. You try it the next night of full moon, and you'll see he'll come."

"I think you're full of it," Jackson said. "But I guess there's no harm in trying. Last two times, he did his killing by the full moon, so he might again. I'll be waiting this time."

"You do that," said the stranger, grinning. "I am sure it will be a lot of fun all around. Just be sure you keep the date."

Jackson did not like the stranger's smirk. Even half-tight as he was, the man's peculiar manner and animallike looks made him feel uneasy. He edged away, and decided to continue his relaxing over at Millie's. But when he sobered up the next day, he began to have vague thoughts that perhaps the stranger might be right.

Jackson was a methodical guy who never liked to do things half-way, and he arranged with Dooley for a couple of days off so he could take a bus to Coeur d'Alene and go to the public library. He read all he could find about werewolves. He didn't find very much, but then he wasn't a very fast reader, and he didn't believe what he read.

But the next full moon he did just as he had planned. He tied a cow to an old corral post at the far end of the property, and settled down with his lariat and the old .44 his grandfather had given him when he was 16.

The moon did not rise until late that night, and Jackson fell asleep. He was awakened when his horse got restless and started scraping the ground and snorting. The moon was full and it was already high in the sky. Jackson guessed that it was about one o'clock in the morning. The cow, twenty feet from him, was tossing her head and mooing softly.

Jackson went into a crouch.

The howl was so close, it shocked even Jackson. A black shape flashed through the moon-lit night. The cow grunted. The beast snarled. And then Jackson heard the grinding of teeth and tearing of flesh as the monster's fangs closed on the cow's neck. The two big animal bodies fell together, and then came the sound of sucking.

Jackson inched forward. He saw the monster's head nuzzling the neck of the cow whose legs still twitched feebly. He swung the lariat and tossed. It was a miss. Jackson's hand went to his .44 and snapped it from the holster.

The beast had let go of the cow's neck, and was looking at him. It bared its teeth and snarled. Again, Jackson thought that mixed with the snarl was the sound of human laughter. For the first time in his adult life he was really afraid. He raised the revolver and fired. The muzzle blast blinded him, and when he had regained his vision; he saw the black monster stepping over the cow's body. Slowly, setting one foot before the other, it advanced.

Jackson fired again, straight into the beast's face. He could not believe that he had missed at such a short distance. He'd been an expert shot ever since he was a kid. His hand shook now, and frantically he squeezed off one shot after another. Between the blasts, he heard the laughter of the beast as it came forward inexorably. There was no stopping it.

The hammer snapped home on an empty chamber. There was a metallic click. An empty revolver couldn't stop the monster where a loaded one had failed. He threw the gun away. His hand hit an old fence post, a rotted piece of wood sticking out of the ground. It was a better weapon than nothing—at least he would fight to the death.

Jackson pulled as hard as he could, and the earth yielded up the post. Just then, with a final triumphant laugh, the beast crouched and leaped. It hurtled through the air at Jackson . The cattle driver raised the fence post high and tried to pray. The weight of the beast crushed him. He felt its foul breath against his face, and he waited for the fangs to dig into his throat.

Stunned by the impact of the heavy animal body, Jackson took seconds to recover his wits. Instinctively he pushed his hands against the monster's furry chest, and there was no reaction. Jackson crawled out from under the weight and saw that the beast was dead. The spike end of the fence post had driven straight into its heart as it jumped.

From then on, Jackson believed in werewolves, and was convinced that this beast was one. As he told everybody afterwards, in the split second while he had held the fence post raised, he had seen the shadow of a cross cast on the ground by the moonlight. And when he had examined the post afterwards, he had discovered that a small slat was still nailed to it, and that this had given its shadow the shape of a cross. He remembered from his reading in the library that only the shape of a cross could be victorious over a werewolf.

The next day, Jackson took a truck, loaded the carcass of the beast on it and drove to Henry's corner. He wanted to tell the stranger that he had been right, that he was now convinced. But he had a suspicion that he would not find the stranger.

He was right. The stranger had last been seen the evening before, cheerfully leaving Kansas Pete's tavern, wishing everyone a good night and assuring them that he himself would have one. Everybody'd thought he'd gone over to Millie's, but she claimed he hadn't been there, and there was no cause for her to lie. His bed at the hotel had not been slept in. And he was never seen again.

Jackson took his story to his grave with him when the Japs killed him in World War II on Tarawa, but the werewolf—or whatever it is—is still there in Henry's Corner, exhibited in a glass cage at the local museum: a huge wolf as big as a steer, but somehow looking like no other wolf that anyone had ever seen.

MAD DOCTOR OF NO-NAME KEY

Peter Eldridge

Adventure Life, December 1961   Cover by Mort Künstler

MAD DOCTOR
OF NO-NAME KEY

By PETER ELDRIDGE

Art by Frank Soltesz

Elena was trembling with fear as the old physician put the X-ray machine into place.

Nothing had ever shocked the American people as much as what was unearthed in an eerie lab off the coast of Florida.

Doctor von Cosel spread the silk square on the Chahbar rug, where the single shaft of moonlight streamed into the tomb. He held up his wrist and peered at the luminous dial of his watch. It was 10:47 He had eight minutes. Out in the night, beyond the rows of graves, the watchman was a lengthened shadow moving slowly down the path.

The doctor opened his black leather surgeon's case, and took out the suction cups, the glass-cutter, and the vial of kerosene. With a moistened finger he wet the rubber cups and pressed them against the window. He dipped the blade of *(Continued on page 46)*

24

ART BY FRANK SOLTESZ

DOCTOR von Cosel spread the silk square on the Chahbar rug, where the single shaft of moonlight streamed into the tomb. He held up his wrist and peered at the luminous dial of his watch. It was 10:47. He had eight minutes. Out in the night, beyond the rows of graves, the watchman was a lengthened shadow moving slowly, down the path.

The doctor opened his black leather surgeon's case, and took out the suction cups, the glass-cutter, and the vial of kerosene. With a moistened finger he wet the rubber cups and pressed them against the window. He dipped the blade of the sinister glass-cutter into the vial, and with a firm hand working close to the leaded mullion, he deftly rolled the blade along the glass. It made a hissing sound like a sharp intake of breath. And it was loud, louder than the eerie strains of spectral music which filled the vault, louder than the frenzied pounding of his heart...

No one knows why Dr. von Cosel happened to come to Key West, Florida. He arrived at Marine Hospital in 1932 in the wake of a chaotic hurricane which had blown in from the East over No Name Key. He possessed nine academic degrees and offered the authorities his services. They signed him on as an X-ray specialist.

The staff was delighted with his work. It was so good that they were willing to overlook his obvious peculiarities. Von Cosel made his home in a rambling frame building which once had been a garage. He divided his quarters into two separate sections. In one he lived, and in the other he improvised a work-shop laboratory in which he carried on strange experiments.

One hot day in August, 1932, the doctor sat in the hospital clinic, deeply absorbed in reading a medical journal. He scarcely heard the rapping on his door.

"Enter!" he called absently.

He did not look up as the girl advanced to his desk and held out a consultation request for a chest X-ray. Von Cosel put down the magazine and picked up the printed form.

Elena Hoyas Mesa, the examining physician had written. *19 years of age. Sputum positive. Routine request for chest plate.*

When Von Cosel raised his eyes he started involuntarily. The young woman had long black hair, drawn back from her forehead. The oval of her face was like alabaster. Her eyes were wide and dark. unnaturally bright.

Von Cosel's voice was quivering. "It's you," he whispered unbelievingly. "You have come back!"

Her dark lustrous eyes flickered with surprise. "Come back?" she asked doubtfully.

The doctor raised himself from his chair. "It was that spring of 1919 in Compos Santos," he said. "I met you in the park. We had a drink, and then we went to my room…"

A corner of the girl's lips lifted in a half smile. "I am afraid you are mistaken, doctor," she said. "You couldn't have seen me in 1919. I wasn't yet born."

THE DOCTOR blinked at her through his thick spectacles. He said nothing. Then he nodded stiffly. "Well," he said vaguely. "I beg you to pardon me. I must—I must have made a mistake. You look so much like—oh well, it is of small consequence. Will you step over here, please. You will have to take off your blouse."

The girl's lips trembled. A momentary flush of embarrassment touched her pallid cheeks with color. There was something disquieting about this frail old man. She began to fumble with the buttons of her blouse.

"Also the underclothes," the doctor said. The girl undressed demurely behind a screen.

"Is the undressing finished?" the doctor called to her. "We can begin."

Von Cosel looked at her creamy throat and at the graceful curve of her back. "You step right here." he said. And we place the chin here on the frame top. And the shoulders. We press them gently, gently against the plate." His long bony fingers pressed her upper arms into position. She could feel them tremble slightly as they touched her.

"You are too beautiful, my child," he said softly. "Too lovely, too fine —"

She stirred uncomfortably. "You must stir not, my dear," he said. "Hold. It is finished in one minute."

Later, long after the girl had gone, Dr. von Cosel sat at his desk trying to understand what had happened to him. He knew only that she was the girl who had come to him from out of the shadows, that spring in Campos Santos.

With great sadness, he took the X-ray plate into the darkroom, and developed it.

It was there, as he had known it would be, in the pleura of the left lung—the dark mass and thready lesions of tuberculosis. Elena Hoyas Mesa would die soon.

Dr. Karl von Cosel delivered the plate to the physician in charge and asked several carefully worded questions, learning what he could about the beautiful young patient.

ELENA was a native of Florida, of the original Spanish stock. On the maternal side there was an alarming incidence of deaths from tuberculosis. Shortly after her marriage to one Louis Mesa, a premature child was born of this union, and the ordeal proved too rigorous for Elena's frail constitution. The baby died, and Elena's health abruptly declined.

Her medical history contained a summary of the marital difficulties that had resulted in Elena's separation from her husband. She was now living with her father.

The physicians, without understanding von Cosel's concern, told him frankly it was futile to hope that Elena Mesa would live. But the elderly man would not accept their prognosis. Soon he was a familiar figure in the hospital library where he spent every available minute poring over the collected medical literature on TB. Nor was he satisfied with the accepted orthodox works on the subject. He began to study ancient writings on the white plague; he even looked into the occult explanations for the disease. Von Cosel made frequent trips to Miami where he consulted rare reference works.

Elena's health continued to deteriorate and she visited the hospital frequently. Von Cosel always "just happened" to meet her on these occasions. He would walk with her through the hospital corridors, with an unusual jauntiness in his step, an unexpected brightness in his blue eyes.

The approach of death had lent an unearthly delicacy to her natural beauty, and von Cosel ached with love. His tenderness flooded the girl with sunlight, and for a while she seemed to bloom. But her medical charts told a different story. Elena was beyond help.

One night in September, Dr. von Cosel came to call on Elena at her father's home. When the girl's father opened the door, he stared in astonishment at the incongruous figure on the porch. Von Cosel was wearing a white suit with satin lapels. In his bony hand he carried a gargantuan bouquet of flowers.

"If you please, honored sir," von Cosel said. "I have come to see Elena. She is at home?"

Elena was called to the door. She was not prepared for the visit. Her bare feet were in worn bedroom slippers, and a gaudy kimono, ripped at the shoulder seam, was wrapped around her slim body. Von Cosel bowed from the waist.

"I may come in?" he asked huskily. He straightened and extended the flowers stiffly.

THE GIRL mutely signaled to her father with her eyes. The father frowned.

"Of course, you may come in, doctor," she said.

She led the way into a small living room. It was cluttered and shabby. Hastily, she cleared strewn newspapers from a chair and pushed a chipped coffee cup out of sight. Von Cosel sat down in the chair. Mr. Hoyas stood in the doorway, looking on with grave, uncomprehending eyes.

"Dispenseme usted," he began. "You have come because of Elena's illness?"

The doctor touched his feathery beard with a nervous forefinger. "No," he said. "I have come on a social call."

It took some moments before Hoyas grasped that the elderly doctor was there as a suitor.

"One small moment, doctor," he said. "Elena is married. Perhaps you do not know this."

Von Cosel nodded. "I know it," he said. "I know much about Elena."

He told them about the girl he had met years before Elena was born. Her image had haunted him always, he said. Perhaps she was only a fancy, but he was convinced that Elena was the incarnation of that illusion.

The girl and her father listened, not quite sure what to make of the old man's passionate outpouring. Von Cosel finally turned to the girl.

"You must understand how it is with me, my child. Surely you understand?"

The girl's eyes were moist. "Yes," she said. "I think I understand."

In the weeks that followed, the doctor was a frequent visitor to the Hoyas home. No one could doubt that he was genuinely trying to help the dying girl.

Elena lingered in this life for more than two months. Perhaps she would have died sooner, were it not for the doctor's ministrations. Perhaps it was the doctor's hints that he was on the verge of discovering a cure for her disease that gave her the tenacity to cling to her feeble spark of life. But on a night in late November, Elena died.

If the Hoyas family was grief stricken, Dr. Karl von Cosell was inconsolable.

Please," he begged the family. "Let me take care of the funeral." He insisted that everything be done at his expense. Mrs. Florence Medina, Elena's sister, prevailed upon her father to agree, insisting only that the grave be simple and unassuming, as Elena herself had been.

The broken-hearted doctor personally superintended the burial. The body of his beloved was laid to rest in a small plot in City Cemetery.

THOSE who knew him remarked the extraordinary transformation in X-ray technician von Cosel during the next two years. He went from abject grief to a mysterious exuberance. It was not that he ceased to mourn for his dead sweetheart, for he kept her grave decked with flowers. He placed little love notes on her headstone and brought a portable record player to the cemetery so that he could play, over her grave, certain musical selections of which the young girl had been so fond. But his grief had become mixed with a certain odd excitement.

In those two years very strange packages from scientific supply houses were delivered to his ramshackle home. He worked late of nights in his mysterious laboratory. His colleagues at the hospital asked him what he was doing.

"I experiment," he said to them. "I am engaged in pure research. It is for me the great work of my life."

His preoccupation with scientific tinkering did not keep von Cosel from pursuing his friendship with Elena's relatives.

"She should be surrounded by great beauty," he told them. "I love her greatly. Please. Permit me to build for her a tomb to befit so wonderful a girl. I would die happy if I felt she was resting in a vault which I built for her with my own hands."

His pleas were so compelling, that at last the dead girl's family yielded to them. Von Cosel the doctor became von Cosel the architect. Then he purchased a large plot in City Cemetery. He laid in a supply of marble, glass, and tile and began his work on a mausoleum for Elena.

On the second anniversary of Elena Mesa's death, her earthly remains were transferred to the shining tomb her aged Romeo had erected to enshrine her. With the consent of the girl's relatives, von Cosel kept the keys to the crypt.

Cemetery attendants became accustomed to the thin, reedy figure as they made their rounds. At first they were startled to hear strains of music coming from the crypt in the late hours of the night. They were even more amazed when they investigated and discovered that the bearded Lothario was not there. The ghostly strains came from a radio that the doctor had installed in the vault. Remote-controlled, it was operated by the doctor himself from his laboratory-home.

The doctor also installed a telephone in the sepulcher, and from the seclusion of his workshop often spoke to his entombed love.

In the spring of 1934, a light, private airplane crashed on the south beach of Key West. The wreck was complete, hardly worth the trouble to salvage, and von Cosel was able to purchase the smashed hulk for a comparatively small outlay of cash. The idlers who watched the bearded oddball tinkering with the wreck on the beach speculated on his purpose. Obviously, he could not hope to restore the wreck to flying condition. Yet there seemed to be a purpose in his labors.

LATER IN the summer, Dr. von Cosel appeared on the beach with a tow truck and hauled the plane to a corner of the spacious grounds surrounding Marine Hospital. The surprised officials had given the doctor permission to park the wreck there temporarily.

The plane disappeared one night in late November. Von Cosel had it pulled by a taxi to a large open shed near his home. He draped the engine with a canvas tarpaulin and from time to time was observed continuing with repairs.

It was noticed that the doctor had given up his vigil at the cemetery, and the caretakers felt a sense of relief.

The dead girl's family felt better at the news that the doctor was now keeping close to home. It was all right for von Cosel to worship his dead love, but somehow it was more reasonable for him to worship her from a spot a bit further away.

During the next seven years, it occurred to no one that Dr. von Cosel might be guilty of one of the weirdest, perverse crimes which the human mind can conceive. No one dreamed that he was dabbling in supernatural experiments. They might never have come to light were it not for the chance discovery of a grave digger at City Cemetery.

On October 5, 1940, a grave was being dug a short distance from Elena Mesa's vault. One of the workmen noticed that starlings were flying in and out of a window in the rear of her palm-shaded tomb. He went over to take a look, and saw that the glass pane had been carefully cut out of its casement. Immediately, the worker notified the custodian of the cemetery, Mr. William Sawyer.

Sawyer sent a note to Elena's sister, Mrs. Medina, informing her of the fact. Mrs. Medina at once suspected that all was not as it should be in her sister's tomb. She asked the hospital authorities for von Cosel's address and paid him a visit that very night.

Trembling and pale, Mrs. Medina knocked on von Cosel's door. On the other side of the door there was the slow scuffle of slippered footsteps. The door opened, and Mrs. Medina stared at the doctor's eyes.

"Yes?" von Cosel asked.

"I have come to see you," Mrs. Medina said, shaken.

"Yes?" von Cosel said again.

"Aren't you going to ask me inside?"

The pale watery eyes wavered. "Please come in," he said slowly. "Of course."

The trembling woman took a resolute step over the threshold. This was in the laboratory section of the doctor's home. There was a disquieting reek of formaldehyde and other chemicals. She followed the reluctant man to his living quarters beyond the partition.

"I wanted to see you about—" She stopped in mid-sentence. A large photograph of Elena hung on the wall. The corners of the frame were decorated with beribboned locks of her jet black hair.

"You were saying, Madame—"

Mrs. Medina fought to retain composure.

"I should like the key to Elena's vault," she said firmly.

Von Cosel's lips trembled. "Dear lady. The key is mine. Elena was everything to me. Not even I go to the tomb anymore. No one must disturb her rest."

"She was my sister," Mrs. Medina reminded him. "I loved her, too."

Mrs. Medina's eyes cast about the room as she sought for words to pierce the doctor's shell. Suddenly she started. In the corner of the dimly lit room was a large double bed, topped with an organdy canopy. She recognized the bed at once. Almost nine years ago it had been Elena's!

Perhaps it was the reek of formaldehyde that sickened her. Mrs. Medina began to feel the cold sweat of nausea on her forehead.

"Please," she said to the doctor. "I feel a little ill. Might I have a glass of water?"

Dr. von Cosel hesitated. He lifted his palms in a gesture of resignation: "Of course," he said. "I bring you the water." He scuffed away to the side door of the shack, presumably on his way to the kitchen.

Swiftly, Mrs. Medina rose from her chair. With fearful steps she crossed the room to the canopied bed. It was made up in two sections, each complete with a counterpane and pillows. A bulge under one of the coverlets stabbed her with a fleet and horrible thought. Gingerly, she lifted a corner of the net curtain.

A scream welled unchecked from Mrs. Medina's throat. Rooted in dread, she stared into the wide-open eyes of her dead younger sister, Elena.

As in a nightmare, the woman fled the house and made her way to police headquarters, where she blurted out her fantastic story to Peace Justice

Enrique Esquinaldo. Within half an hour, Deputies Bernard Waite and Ray Elwood, armed with a search warrant, were at von Cosel's door.

"No," he cried. "You cannot come in. You must not!"

The officers brushed him aside. What they found inside transcended belief.

The long-dead Elena Mesa lay beneath the coverlet on one side of the canopied bed. In a sheer silk nightgown, under a blue flowered robe, the girl lay demure and expectant, as though a new bride.

The officers turned from the sight. Von Cosel stared at them with pain-glazed eyes.

"Just what in hell have you been doing here?" Deputy Waite demanded.

The doctor sighed. He took a deep breath and then made the most bone-chilling statement the policemen had' ever heard.

"Please, gentlemen," he pleaded. "Not so loud. You will disturb her. She is not wholly dead."

Waite's jaw dropped. "Knock it off, mister," he gritted tensely. "You give me the creeps."

"She is asleep, I tell you," von Cosel insisted. "We must have patience. It is only a matter of time before she awakes, healthy and completely restored. I pray you, do not take her from me, gentlemen."

Despite his protestations and even an abortive show of force. Dr. von Cosel was taken to headquarters. The corpse was removed to the morgue.

Piece by piece, in the days that followed, the entire macabre story was told. *Dr. von Cosel had been living in the same room with his dead sweetheart for seven years.* Tortured by grief when she died, he had dedicated himself to finding a way to bring her back to life. This, in brief, had been his all-consuming passion for the past years.

"Would you tell us how you got the body out of the tomb?" the officers asked him.

Von Cosel adjusted his glasses. "By means of my airplane," he answered. He explained that he had carried the body from its inner coffin at the crypt to a point not far from the cemetery gate. He had hailed a cab, the driver of which never suspected that the "rolled up rug" was a disinterred body.

The plane, von Cosel told the authorities, was intended to serve him and his resurrected sweetheart in another manner. After life had been completely restored to the pretty young girl, the reunited couple would fly away to some South Sea island.

There could be no doubt of the doctor's sincerity. He fully believed what he told the officers. "Life is dormant," he said, "inactive, sleeping in a person who has died. But it can be awakened by a series of treatments, by chemical solutions which penetrate the perforations of the body and feed the cells—"

The psychiatrist who examined Doctor von Cosel took a less charitable view of the old man's actions. He was of the opinion that the doctor was a necrophile, a person attracted by dead bodies.

Obsessed by his perverse desire, the physician went on, Dr. von Cosel had taken his sweetheart's corpse into his home.

THE OLD man was charged with the ghoulish crime of body snatching. There was disagreement among the curious who read the details in the nation's papers. Most were revolted by what von Cosel had done, but there were others who saw in the elderly Lothario a tragic and romantic figure. Here was a love that had hoped to cheat the grave, and a lover who, like the sorcerers of old, sought to restore the breath of life to the chilled remains of the beautiful young girl whom death had claimed.

Because the statute of limitations had run out during the seven years between the exhumation of the body and its discovery in von Cosel's bed, there was no prosecution of Dr. von Cosel. Elena Mesa's mummified remains were buried in a secret grave. The doctor moved from Key West to Zephyr Hills, Florida, where he lived inconspicuously until he was discovered dead by neighbors in the summer of 1952.

HER BODY BELONGED TO THE DEVIL

George Venner

Man's Look, December 1961   Cover by Jay Scott Pike

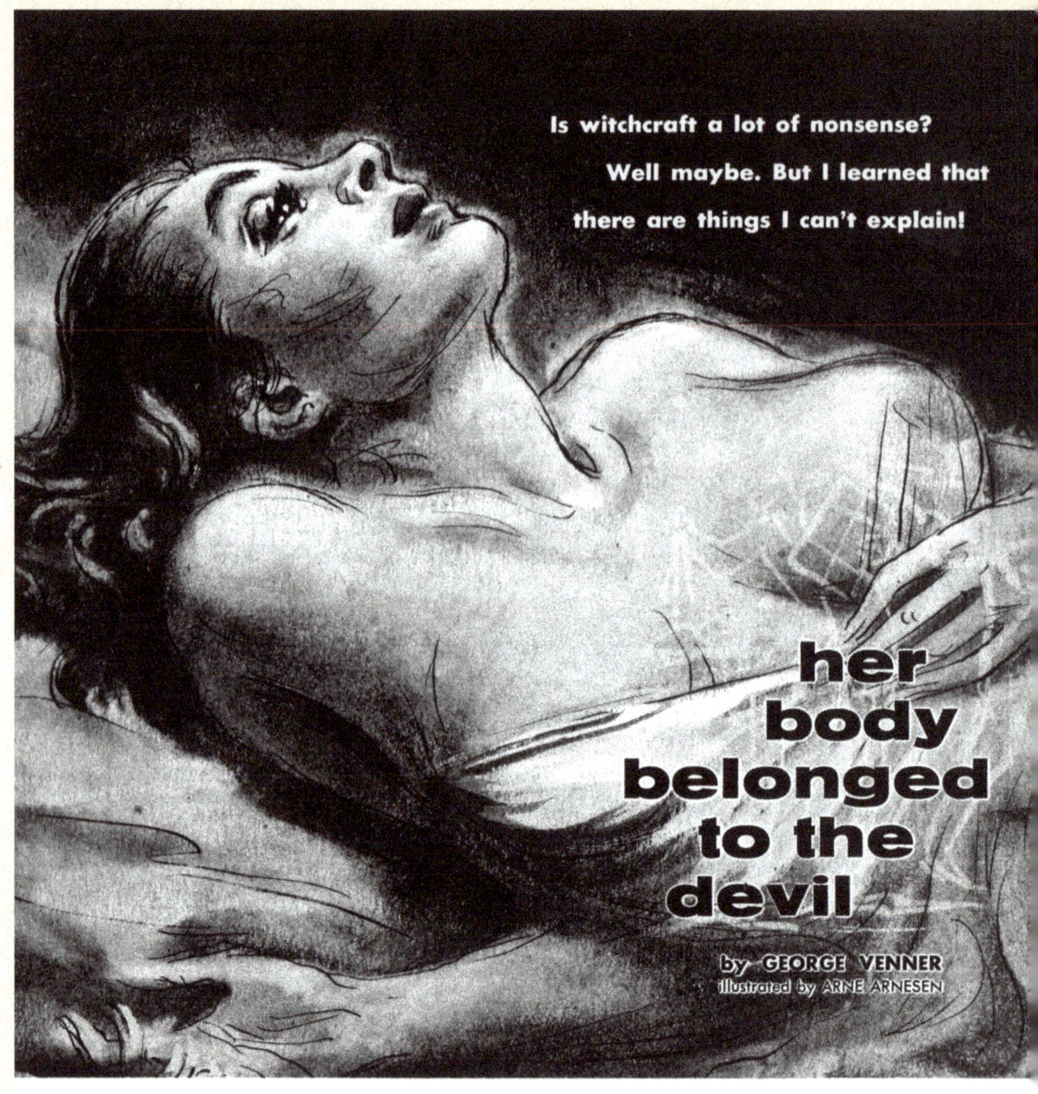

TAKE A CLOSE LOOK at the cute blonde waiting near you at the bus stop. Yep. She's neatly dressed in the latest fashion and her pert face is a picture of innocence.

Yet, she may be a full-fledged, witch!

See that attractive matron in her early 30's—the one who lives right down the street from you? Sure. She's quiet, well-mannered. At least, on the outside.

Behind that calm, placid facade of respectability, she could very well be hiding the vile, orgiastic nature of a woman devoted to worship of the Devil and the forces of Evil!

6

Don't laugh. Don't dismiss the possibilities from your mind. It doesn't matter much where you live —in the largest of eastern seaboard "Big Towns" or quiet, midwestern communities.

The shocking facts are that witchcraft, Devil Worship and the "practice" of Black Magic are commonplace in the United States today! All across the country, thrill-seeking men and women are turning to the "Dark Arts" to satisfy their thirst for weird and bizarre orgies.

In Los Angeles, California, three "Devil Cults" sprang up to take the place of the infamous "Purple Cult" which was (Continued on next page)

ART BY ARNE ARNESEN

TAKE A close look at the cute blonde waiting near you at the bus stop. Yep. She's neatly dressed in the latest fashion and her pert face is a picture of innocence.

Yet, she may be a full-fledged, witch!

See that attractive matron in her early 30s—the one who lives right down the street from you? Sure. She's quiet, well-mannered. At least, on the outside.

Behind that calm, placid facade of respectability, she could very well be hiding the vile, orgiastic nature of a woman devoted to worship of the Devil and the forces of Evil!

Don't laugh. Don't dismiss the possibilities from your mind. It doesn't matter much where you live—in the largest of eastern seaboard "Big Towns" or quiet, midwestern communities.

The shocking facts are that witchcraft, Devil Worship and the "practice" of Black Magic are commonplace in the United States today! All across the country, thrill-seeking men and women are turning to the "Dark Arts" to satisfy their thirst for weird and bizarre orgies.

In Los Angeles, California, three "Devil Cults" sprang up to take the place of the infamous "Purple Cult" which was dissolved after the murder of a member, sultry Anya Sosyeva. The "Purple Cult" and its successors were—and are—made up of fanatics who practice the loathsome Black Mass.

Not long ago, Chicago police raided a West Side cult's headquarters. More than a dozen couples were taken into custody. Officers declared that they had all been participants in wild sex orgies held after three-hour-long sessions of Black Magic and sorcery!

California's Psychoanalytical Assistance Foundation, which has been making a study of the sudden resurgence of witchcraft, demon worship and black magic, estimates that there are at least 1,500 groups devoted to these

practices in the United States!

Most of them are in smaller cities and towns, made up of people bored by "old-fashioned" wife-swapping orgies or wild parties.

I know. I can attest to the existence of one such cult in my own small town located less than 100 miles from Omaha, Nebraska! I learned at first-hand about the modern witches and black magicians. I also learned about the network of such organizations across the nation——because I, myself, unwittingly became a member!

How? Remember the cute blonde I suggested you eye carefully at the bus stop?`

Well, the girl who initiated me into the revolting practices of the "Dark Arts" wasn't blonde and I didn't meet her at a bus stop. But she was a normal, everyday sort of person.

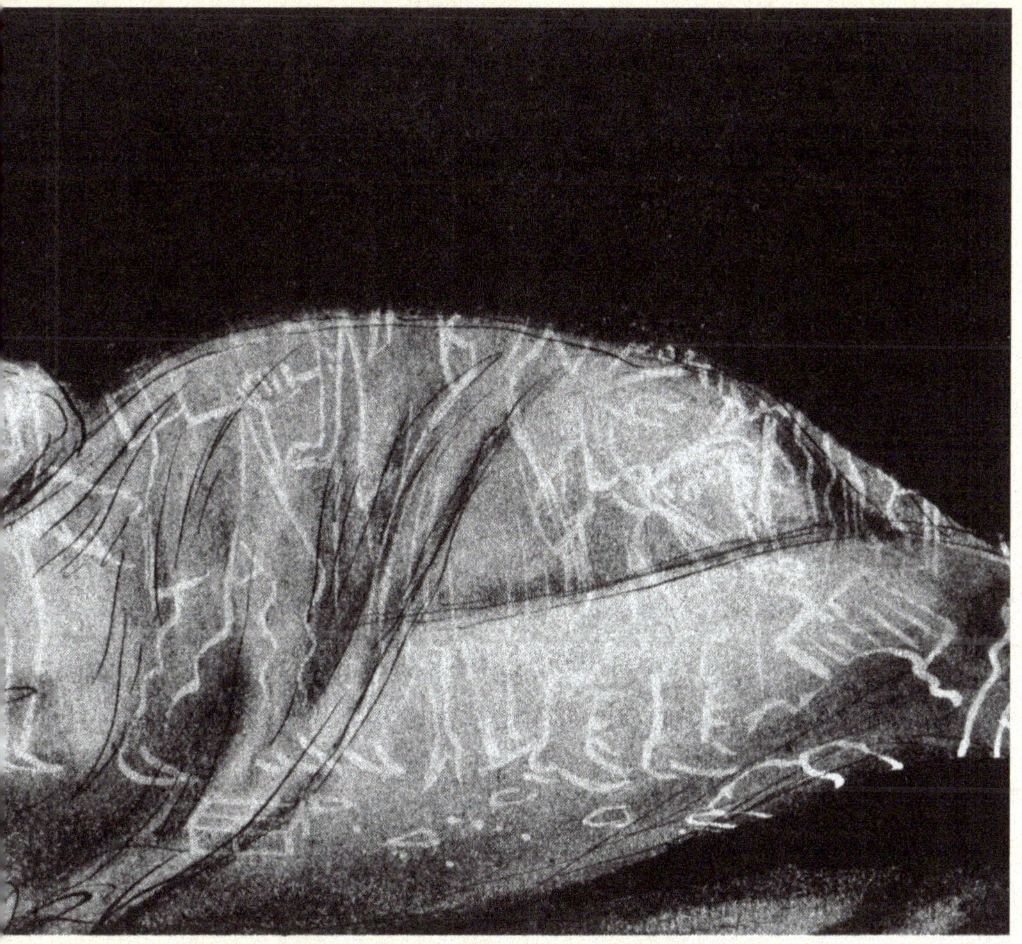

Joan was her name and she was a brunette. I'd gone to high school with her. I hadn't seen her for some years. First, I'd done a three-year hitch in the Air Force. Then I'd worked around here and there—in Kansas City, St. Louis and a few other places—for another four years.

I'd been back home for more than eight months before I bumped into Joan. I met her in a drugstore when I went in to buy a pack of cigarettes. She was purchasing some cosmetics and I didn't recognize her.

"Why, George!" she exclaimed. "George Venner!"

I thought hard. Then I remembered who the good-looking brunette was. I shook hands with her and took a quick, sneak-look at her left hand. She was still single—not even engaged. I became a lot more interested. Attractive, single women aren't too easily found in a burg that has less than 20,000 population.

One thing led to another and we wound up going to the best—and almost only —decent bar in town for a couple of drinks. Joan sipped hers and chatted pleasantly. I ended by driving her home and making a date for the following night.

THE FIRST date was pretty tame. We went to a movie, then had a bite to eat. We were both home—she in hers, me in mine—before one AM. But I did have another date with her for Saturday night.

We went into Omaha and did a lot of dancing and almost as much drinking. I parked along the highway on the way back. Joan melted like she'd been worked over with a blow-torch the moment I reached over and put my arms around her!

This time, we didn't get home until after dawn. I was worried for Joan, worried about what the neighbors might think when she got out of my car that time of the morning. I told her as much. Her answer shook me a little.

"Don't worry, honey," she grinned. "I don't care what those slobs think! There are things I know about them that would make your hair curl…"

Joan lived with her married sister and brother-in-law. They were friendly as hell whenever I called for her in the weeks that followed. I knew they must have guessed what was going on, but they didn't say a thing.

Then, on a warm spring night in 1956, Joan asked me if I'd like to go away for a weekend to a place where a lot of her friends went.

"It's only about 15 miles outside town—up in the hills," she murmured. "We can have a ball…"

Of course we went. The "place" was an old rambling farmhouse in the hills. It looked like any such building in the area—from the outside. There already were five or six cars parked outside when we arrived.

"Sure this is okay—you and me showing up with our suitcases?" I asked. Joan just laughed.

Inside, the house was weird. There were odd paintings and idols scattered around in the rooms. All the windows had heavy black drapes. The air smelled strongly of some queer kind of incense.

I was even more surprised by the people I met. I knew many of them— quite a few being what are called "Pillars of the Community."

BY THE time somebody stuck a drink in my hand, showed me the room which, my guide said pointedly, Joan and I would share, and came back downstairs, I had the deal figured. I knew that this was some kind of hell-raising club, but, of course, I never dreamed what I would see and hear before the weekend was over!

There was plenty of hooch and everyone—myself included—drank plenty that Saturday afternoon. We ate a sketchy meal about five and went back to drinking. A lot more people had shown up in the meantime.

"Here—try one of these," Joan purred shortly after dark, handing me a cigarette. I took one look at it—sniffed it—and knew what it was.

I'd seen marijuana before. I lit up, anyway, figuring that one wouldn't hurt me. Besides, everyone else was smoking the damned things and the party looked as though it was going to get very rough very soon.

It did.

Exactly at nine PM, we were all ushered into a large room that I hadn't seen before.

"Baby! You'll go wild now! This is going to be sensational!" Joan whispered to me hotly. I took a look at her flaring nostrils and narrowed eyes, felt her quick, shallow breathing as she clung to me. I felt myself caught up by the spirit of the binge and went inside!

The room was a hideous caricature of what one would find in a small church. There were benches to serve as pews and a kind of altar at the far end. The light was dim and I didn't get a chance to identify anything for a few moments. When my eyes became accustomed to the dark, I almost flipped.

An honest-to-goodness coffin, standing on end, was in each corner of the room. The walls were decorated with blasphemous parodies of sacred pictures. A brazier glowed near the "altar."

"What—what's this all about?" I stammered.

"You're going to see a Black Mass!" Joan rasped. "Here, sit down..."

WHAT IS a Black Mass? Well, basically it is a form of religious worship. Don't be surprised at the use of the word "religious" in connection with such a practice. For it is religion in every sense of the word. It has a creed, a theology, a ritual, a ministry and full belief in the immortality of the soul, with both reward and punishment in this life and the hereafter.

It is made up, here in America, of two forms of witchcraft. And though, for the most part, the ceremonial of the Black Mass is based on the ordinary Christian worship, it has also incorporated over the centuries the beliefs, superstitions and practices of dozens of other portions of the world.

One of the two mainstreams of American witchcraft traces directly back to the great, European tradition. This form, together with its superstitions, signs and rituals are known to millions of us who have had parents or grandparents from the teeming European continent.

The European witchcraft derives from a life of hardship. In the cool, temperate climate, the need for survival and safety were all-important. Starving serfs, semi-slaves, living an ignorant, agricultural life, inheriting the primitive, pre-Christian beliefs, needed something that could guarantee them a better life.

A good crop, a safe journey through robber-infested forests, freedom for themselves and their children; personal wealth that could purchase comfort or provide a dowry for daughter and an estate for a son were essential needs.

In a feudal society, these could not be gained directly. It took only a short time to discover that regular prayer in the established church could not rectify the hazards of life either.

Thus the need for gain predominated. At first, prayers to the "old gods," the names we come across in Roman mythology were tried. But as Christianity prevailed and grew stronger, the allegiance was transferred to the Devil. The theory was, if God can't help me, perhaps the Devil will. And obviously, since the Devil was the opposite of God, his worship too, must be exactly opposite. Thus to defile God's worship was to promote the Devil's.

Again, since the ancient magic beliefs of the Indo-European society were filled with what is known as "sympathetic magic"—that is performing a similar act to the effect you wish to cause—sex played a large role. The need for gain, for life, for fertility of wife, cattle or crop, required a symbolically sexual act. And so, combining sexual, fertility rites with defilement of church worship, sexual defilement became a primary ritual form.

The defilement included bestiality. Pan—symbolized by his goat, Odin by his great wolf, and other, lesser known deities, also symbolized by animals, entered the Black Mass at an early day. Even now, the fear of the great dog, the black cat, and the goat—all as symbols of the Devil, survive in witchcraft.

The second mainstream of American witchcraft comes from the import of African medicine-man magic. Primarily typified by Voodoo, this is a jungle worship that arises from an opposite motivation. Living is not so difficult in the lush jungles of the rain forest or Caribbean. Here, food is readily available. Crops may not be heavy, but they are constant. Rainfall is sure, and game abounds in the forest lands. There is little essential need to invoke magic or fertility rites to gain them.

But survival is another problem. Death lurks around the next bend in the jungle trail at all times. Tribal warfare is constant. Fighting, battling and confounding an enemy are the necessities of daily living.

Thus, the African witchcraft, deals in revenge. It is a method for saving your life, and killing your enemy. It deals in death, in negation, in destruction.

DEALING in death, it requires death to give it effect. The kill, done in the ritual, is vital. Blood is required. The cock, the cat, or the human who is coldly murdered as part of the ceremonial, symbolizes this belief in death. The drinking of the blood of the victim symbolizes the superiority and triumph of the drinker over all his foes and competitors.

But African witchcraft has no belief in the soul. It denies the possibility of the afterlife. Death is final and absolute. An enemy killed by witchcraft can never haunt the killer. No ghost or spirit remains on the trail to trip or trap the unwary. It is safe, and efficient.

That these two opposites should blend so completely here in America is not at all surprising. First of all, economically, we are more akin to the African than the European. In comparison with the rest of the world, we live in a rich country. Surplus more than famine is the order of the day. We don't have to struggle for food. But we do face a struggle for power and wealth. We do face the competitions of business. We do struggle for promotions, for pay-raises—even for women. Gaining a dowry for a daughter is not essential. Getting a good job for a son, is.

But inheriting a witchcraft tradition from Europe has left its mark. Those brought up in that tradition are horribly afraid to abandon it. And so, needing the results offered by the African magic, the Black Mass has incorporated its essentials. So too, the African, transplanted to a western civilization has come to desire the efficacy of the white man's magic. Accepting Christianity, they have accepted devil worship also. And since a regular ritual already existed, they have layered it over with their own jungle tradition.

Thus, today, we have this new form of witchcraft with its two points of effect: revenge and gain. The Black Mass can now offer almost anything to the believer. He can become wealthy, he can live longer. He can gain power and fame. He can foil his competitors. He can kill his enemies.

For the objects of the leaders—and consequently the objects of the congregation, are self-glory and damnation of all who stand in their way.

And strangely enough, these things actually happen. Call it accident, coincidence, or what you will, but in a surprisingly large number of cases, far larger than the normal logic of odds would dictate, the objectives of their witchcraft is achieved.

For example, a witchcraft group in a Massachusetts town was uncovered a few years back. The members were reviled, hounded and in the case of the leaders, jailed. Six months later, the two mills on which the town depended for economic survival closed. Better than 90% of the town's inhabitants were impoverished. Yet, not a single member of the witchcraft group suffered. Those employed by the mills were conveniently transferred to jobs down South. Another, a leader of the movement, even while in jail made nearly a million dollars when a worthless Canadian mining company struck Uranium. Every one of them in fact profited to some extent from the rest of the people's disaster.

Or take the reporter who uncovered a group in California. Six months later, he came down with leprosy. By the time it was uncovered, his wife and two children were also infected. Yet those were the only cases of the disease which had been seen in that town either before or since.

Two youngsters in Louisiana spied on a series of Black Masses for weeks before being discovered. The witches smiled at them, but never touched them. Nevertheless, they told their friends about what they had seen. The story flew all over the parish. Four weeks later, one of the boys went crazy, stabbing the second boy to death, without warning or provocation. The young killer is now committed to the state insane asylum for life.

The horrifying thing about it all is that in no case is there anything for a victim or an investigator to put his finger on. It's all so natural. The jailed Massachusetts devilpriest just happened to own the mining stock. He's held it for years. The mills were losing money. The decision to close them and move operations south was as natural as could be. The California reporter caught a regular disease. According to doctors he must have caught it somewhere, but certainly none of the witches could have infected him. The Louisiana boy went crazy. There was insanity in his family history. It was as natural as could be.

But still, why did it happen to just those people at exactly that time? Why did all the devil-worshippers prosper in spite of ridicule; and all their detractors suffer or die? Why?

Of course, I learned all this later. That night, I shakily took my place next to Joan in a rear "pew." A few minutes later, one of the men I'd met earlier came down the aisle with a tray-load of cups.

"Take two," my companion instructed me. I did, and handed one to Joan. We both drank the stuff inside. It tasted funny—but it worked fast. A hazy glow spread over me. Almost immediately after I'd swallowed it, I felt that I was floating—floating free of everything including all my repressions and normal living itself.

WHAT FOLLOWED defies description. A "high priest" came out. A light shone on him. Behind him came a woman. She was nude—and I recognized her as the wife of a grocer in town!

I didn't know the high priest. I hadn't met him before. It didn't make any difference. He began by leading the woman to a couch. She reclined on it. He turned to the "audience" and began reciting mumbo-jumbo formulas and filthy parodies of prayers.

Whatever drug was in my drink had worked well. I listened—and, instead of being horrified or revolted, I listened raptly and even felt my pulses pound.

"We call forth the powers of darkness," the voice intoned. "We are releasing ourselves from the false beliefs of the world and exchanging them for the true pleasures of the evil gods!"

There were more, many more, such fantastic lines. "Altar boys" came out. They sprinkled and "anointed" the nude woman on the couch. The watchers were beginning to strain in their seats. An air of electric tension filled the room.

There were insane songs and chants—all of which built up the rhythm of the tension. I felt the blood pounding in my veins. Joan squirmed and muttered beside me. The others were carried away by the awful ritual…

Then, with a wild, triumphant howl, the "high priest" threw some herbs on the fire glowing in the brazier. I caught a brief glimpse of him as he stalked over to the woman on the couch—and then the lights went out, leaving the room completely black, save for the faint, cherry-gleam of the coals in the brazier.

The people around me went wild. It was as though a dam had suddenly burst. Raw hell coiled and swirled. There were screams and groans and shrieking laughs. Joan flung herself on me.

Liquor, marijuana, drugged drink—everything inside my stomach spun. I shoved the panting girl away. Sick, trembling, I staggered into the aisle. Joan followed me as I groped my way to the door. She clutched at me, yelling for me to stay.

"Get away from me, you witch!" I roared, hardly knowing what I said.

Her fingernails raked my face and neck. She shouted oaths and curses fouler than anything I'd ever heard in my life—and I'd heard plenty!

I got to the door and opened it. Then I staggered out and went through the empty rooms upstairs until I found the one I'd been shown earlier. I got my bag and took it out to my car. Joan didn't even bother coming after me.

"Then go, you—!" had been her parting shriek. "Go. But you'll never go far enough to get away from me!"

That happened in my town last year. I saw it with my own eyes, felt it with my own senses. I understand it's still happening there once each month. The cult has over 100 members and almost everyone in the know has heard of it.

And now it's my turn to wonder. When is my punishment going to occur? Sooner or later, I know that it must come. For there is definitely some form of communication between the witchcraft groups of the entire world. They are aware of me. They've told me so.

My job takes me to places all over the world. And still, whether it's the most backward spot in the world or the most civilized, I know that I'm being watched. Sometimes, when I turn my head suddenly, I can see an old woman smiling evilly at me. And once, in New York City, I caught an enchantress in the very act of sticking pins in a doll, a doll that was dressed in a piece of my own clothing.

She didn't complain or threaten me when I caught her. She just shrugged her shoulders.

"Today or tomorrow!" she sneered. "What's the difference. Sooner or later. The mark is on you."

IN PLAIN self-defense, I've had to take steps for protection. I've spent a lot of time and effort since checking up and learning what I could about the prevalence of witchcraft and demonology and all the various types of dark cults in the United States.

There's no exaggeration in the statement that the man or woman who lives next door to you may be a witch or a sorcerer. I don't say that they can really perform magical feats or conjure up spirits or commune with the Devil. That's a matter of belief—and I don't believe that they can.

But they can use the Black Mass and Black Magic as vehicles for depravity and orgies. And they do!

For every single one of us is directly menaced by this invisible society. Even without being aware of them, we can become the object of their wrath.

For example: Did you gain a promotion last month? Did you close a big deal? Did your son marry that lovely girl who had several other suitors? Does your neighbor envy your lot, your wife, your children or your job? Does anyone at all have *any reason at all* to dislike you, to hate you, to despise you, to envy you, or to want you out of the way?

One of them, almost certainly at least one of them, is connected in some way with a witchcraft group. At the very least, he or she has heard about such a group and can wrangle an invitation to attend.

After that, trouble can dog your footsteps. Shadows can peer over your shoulder as they do over mine. You can learn the day-by-day fear of the unknown, fear of the secret reprisal.

For there is no defense against it. Believe in witchcraft or not, it makes no difference. The church has never found a method that can prevent witchcraft. The law, using extreme severity—as for example in the world-famous Salem trials— has not wiped it out. And no one has ever found any workable prayer or medicine to halt an attack by witches.

Only by surrendering to the Black Circle yourself, can charms of safety, spells of protection be woven. And that entails a complete surrender of mind, of body, of spirit and of soul.

The Black Mass is growing in America. Every week, every year, new circles and fresh congregations are organized to flourish in our midst.

A bunch of overly-rich college kids are doing just that in one Minnesota University. There are three "Black Mass" societies operating wide-open in the heart of New York City's Greenwich Village.

A devil-worshipping cult meets regularly in a loft building in San Francisco's Marina district. Omaha isn't a big city as cities go, but I learned there were two groups there—both of which were often visited by members of the cult in my hometown!

Sure. I know. This is the 20th century. That's what makes it even more horrible!

Take that girl—that one over there—just getting into the convertible parked at the curb. She looks like a normal, healthy, typical American young woman.

She may be that—and just that. On the other hand, she could be anything. Even a devil-worshipper or a witch—or simply a dizzy, bored female who got mixed up with a hell-cult for kicks.

There are tens of thousands of them…

By Ray Bradbury

A master of the tale of science fiction takes you on a rocket trip to the planet Venus, land of the disappearing Sun Domes!

THE LONG RAIN

THE RAIN continued. It was a hard rain, a perpetual rain, a sweating and steaming rain; it was a mizzle, a downpour, a fountain, a whipping at the eyes, an undertow at the ankles; it was a rain to drown all rains and the memory of rains. It came by the pound and the ton, it

MAN FROM OUTER SPACE

Ray Bradbury was born and raised in Waukegan, Illinois, but since he first began to write he has become a citizen of a strange world of fantasy and outer space. As a child he was fascinated by carnivals, circuses, magicians, and mind readers — all of the weird and colorful subjects that were to become the fascinating backgrounds for his tales of science-fiction, terror, and the supernatural. To read Bradbury is to escape in time and space to a world where fancy and irony show man things about himself and about his destiny that he would otherwise fail to see. Bradbury's stories have appeared in the top magazines. He has written several movies, and his books include *The Martian Chronicles*, *The Golden Apples of the Sun*, and *The Illustrated Man*.

The rocket ship was lying where they had left it. Somehow they had circled and were where they started!

The lieutenant looked up. He had a face that once had been brown and now the rain had washed it pale; the rain had washed the color from his eyes, and his teeth, and his hair.

The monster came out of the rain. It was supported on a thousand electric blue legs. Everywhere a leg struck a tree fell. One man leaped up and was immediately seared by high electricity.

"The Long Rain" by Ray Bradbury
CAVALCADE, March 1959
Art by George Kraynak

THEIR BODIES GLOWED WITH FIRE

Dane Marshall

Peril, December 1961   Cover by John Duillo

"THEIR BODIES GLOWED WITH FIRE!"

By DANE MARSHALL

THEY SAY DEATH comes as the end, but I'm not sucker enough to buy that. Of course, back home in Nuevo Cordura, they've always figured me, Joe Rainwater, for a sucker.

It's a funny thing the way all whites out there think as a group, like believing every Indian is poor red trash, especially me, Joe Rainwater, the local boy who made good in the War but didn't have enough pride to stay away from his home town.

All I really wanted was to come back home, forget war, and do a little thinking while prospecting in the Arizona desert. So they started to figure I was touched in the head.

"That crazy, lazy redskin, trying to find gold in the desert, the fool," is the big joke they told among themselves, when I'd go off with my burro and my pack. "He'll be lucky to find his way home."

What the hell did they know about it? Did they know I was really glad and grateful to get back home after the War? Even if home was the hypocritical little town of Nuevo Cordura I headed back like a homing pigeon. My folks were dead then, my father, the son of a chief, and my white mother who had been raised in Nuevo Cordura. If you were a stranger come to town, you'd have heard all about my mother soon enough.

Carmella Meigs! She shocked the town when she married Aaron Rainwater, my father. "A good Christian girl like Carmella taking up with an Injun," they shrieked in outraged horror. And didn't stop to think that my father had been converted to Christianity a long time earlier.

But that's Nuevo Cordura for you. My mother hadn't given them the satisfaction of seeing her run away. She'd stayed right there in town, had me, and raised me, and saw me go away to War where I was with Merrill's Marauders for a long, long time. And three wounds. One of them was my left leg, a hit bad enough to get me a pension and it was this that I lived on when I decided to return to Nuevo Cordura. And why did I come back? Because I thought that somewhere, out on the desert that bordered the town, I could wipe the bitterness from my heart and become whole again. I wanted to be the Joe Rainwater I was before the War, a guy who loved hunting in the hills and fishing and fun.

Instead I returned to deceit and hypocrisy and fist fights with bums like Ed Gordon, Wally Carter and those other shining lights of town. Sure, I could have shaken the dust of the place off my feet right after I visited my parents' graves. But when I saw I wasn't wanted, I decided to stay. At least until I found myself again.

So that's how come word got around that I was touched. Wally Carter started it when I bought grub and supplies at his General Store the first day I set out for the desert. When he asked what I was planning I said "look for gold." I knew as well as he did there was no gold out there, but he had to have an answer. Three trips later he had the whole town convinced I was touched.

IT STREAKED TOWARD HIM, A FEARSOME BLAZING APPARITION OUT OF THE DESERT NIGHT AND JOE RAINWATER, EX-GI AND HALF-BREED, WAS SURE HE WAS LOSING HIS MIND! AN INSTANT LATER HE BEGAN TO LIVE AS NO MAN HAS— BEFORE OR SINCE!

(Continued on page 54)

26

ART BY JOHN DUILLO

THEY SAY death comes as the end, but I'm not sucker enough to buy that. Of course, back home in Nuevo Cordura, they've always figured me, Joe Rainwater, for a sucker. It's a funny thing the way all whites out there think as a group, like believing every Indian is poor red trash, especially me, Joe Rainwater, the local boy who made good in the War but didn't have enough pride to stay away from his home town.

All I really wanted was to come back home, forget war, and do a little thinking while prospecting in the Arizona desert. So they started to figure I was touched in the head.

"That crazy, lazy redskin, trying to find gold in the desert, the fool," is the big joke they told among themselves, when I'd go off with my burro and my pack. "He'll be lucky to find his way home."

What the hell did they know about it? Did they know I was really glad and grateful to get back home after the War? Even if home was the hypocritical little town of Nuevo Cordura, I headed back like a homing pigeon. My folks were dead then, my father, the son of a chief, and my white mother who had been raised in Nuevo Cordura. If you were a stranger come to town, you'd have heard all about my mother soon enough.

Carmella Meigs! She shocked the town when she married Aaron Rainwater, my father. "A good Christian girl like Carmella taking up with an Injun," they shrieked in outraged horror. And didn't stop to think that my father had been converted to Christianity a long time earlier.

But that's Nuevo Cordura for you. My mother hadn't given them the satisfaction of seeing her run away. She'd stayed right there in town, had me, and raised me, and saw me go away to war where I was with Merrill's Marauders for a long, long time. And three wounds. One of them was my left leg, a hit bad enough to get me a pension and it was this that I lived on when I decided to return to Nuevo Cordura. And why did I come back? Because I thought that somewhere, out on the desert that bordered the town, I could wipe the bitterness from my heart and become whole again. I wanted to be the Joe Rainwater I was before the War, a guy who loved hunting in the hills and fishing and fun.

Instead I returned to deceit and hypocrisy and fist fights with bums like Ed Gordon, Wally Carter and those other shining lights of town. Sure, I could have shaken the dust of the place off my feet right after I visited my parents' graves. But when I saw I wasn't wanted, I decided to stay. At least until I found myself again.

So that's how come word got around that I was touched. Wally Carter started it when I bought grub and supplies at his General Store the first day I set out for the desert. When he asked what I was planning I said "look for gold." I knew as well as he did there was no gold out there, but he had to have an answer. Three trips later he had the whole town convinced I was touched.

I didn't mind. It didn't shake me. What did, though, was the knowledge that something in the desert was eluding me. Oh, it was peaceful enough out there in the wilderness where you could almost reach up and touch the stars at night, and where the coyotes howled their mournful tunes and the cold wind whispered its secrets. In the daytime the blazing sun beat down on a man and seemed to purify him. I didn't do much except read and smoke and think and read and smoke and think some more.

The days and nights out there passed peacefully enough and I know I should have been happy. Yet I wasn't; a strange restlessness had gotten into me and I couldn't shake it. The result was that I began having good days and bad nights. Then it switched and I had bad days and good nights.

It was on one of my bad nights that it happened.

It was shortly after midnight, one of those nights when the stars are so thick you can't see the sky, and I was idly looking at the brightest stars and wondering why they seemed to move. Everyone knows they don't, but these days you can never be sure with some of those satellites the scientists keep shooting into the sky.

Half awake, I was focused on one particularly bright star that almost had me convinced it was moving. So much so, in fact, that I made a note that when I got back I'd look at the papers and see if someone had put a new satellite into orbit. Thinking of this, I suddenly heard a coyote or something at the food supply kept in a pup tent. The burro heard it too because he began braying.

Hauling myself out of the sleeping bag, I grabbed up a rifle and a flashlight and moved quietly toward the intruder. To my surprise, the beam disclosed nothing. Then I almost leaped out of my skin as the burro suddenly screamed in terror, and started to tear madly at its tether.

I shot the flash toward the frightened critter and saw what I figured was the reason: a rattler, coiled and ready to strike. Shooting it was too risky. I rushed over and smashed my rifle butt hard against his head, throwing myself off balance. I got the rattler, but I went down right in the path of the burro's maddened stampede.

He'd broken his tether and, before I could get out from under, his flying hooves hit me. It wasn't a hard blow, more glancing than hard but I suddenly began to feel dizzy, weak, almost as is if I had no control of my body. The burro was screaming wildly, hightailing over the desert as though demons pursued him.

I saw all this as I pitched forward, my face hitting the sand, yet I didn't go under!

I was unconscious but, not unconscious. And I was staring as if hypnotized at a bright star that seemed to be rushing…rushing…toward me, a silver streak glittering in a world of silver streaks.

Powerless to move, unable to cry out, I just lay there as the streak came closer and closer. I guess I would have gone mad except that the moon suddenly appeared. But when I saw what was outlined in the golden light, I was certain I was mad.

It was a flying saucer! Sure, I'd heard of them, read of them, seen drawings of them. But this was real, dammit, real. A low, hypnotic humming sound reached my ears as it spun to a stop, a grotesque ship on a sea of sand. Terrified, I lay there, my heart going like crazy, my mind trying to tell me that what my eyes saw was actually true.

And then, almost as if to convince me, a door opened in the strange ship and a girl stepped out. She was wearing some kind of uniform that seemed to be made of fine-spun metal. Her hair was long and golden, fastened behind her shapely head with a circlet—a thin band cut evidently from a single giant emerald. The moonlight had turned night into day and every line of her magnificent body was outlined as the came toward me, a vision with voluptuous breasts, tapering thighs and long, slender legs. Behind her came four others, in similar costume, except that they weren't wearing a circlet. Like their leader they wore what seemed to be delicate space helmets.

I tried to move but couldn't. There was a smile on her soft, sensuous lips as she stood over me, very erect. A heady scent overpowered me, seemed to make me drowsy. I was in panic and trying hard not to show it.

For an instant longer she stood over me, very erect, looking at me with an odd expression. And then she spoke, speaking the words very carefully in a rich, musical voice.

The language was English!

I tried to answer but couldn't.

She smiled. "I forgot," she said. "I have rendered you harmless." She glanced over her shoulder at the four girls who had come up behind her. A strange, musical laugh came from all of them at once. Their leader seemed to take this as a form of approval.

She bent low over me for an instant and I saw the deep valley of her magnificent breasts, but, believe me, the shock I got the next instant drove all sexy ideas out of my mind. It wasn't an electric shock: it was optical. I felt the strength surging back into my body at the touch of the girl's finger and I almost screamed in terror.

The girl's voice was soft, reassuring

"Do not be afraid," she said, "We do not come to harm you, Earthman. We are performing a mission. Tell me now: You are an American?"

"The best." I managed to gasp. "I am an Indian, an original settler."

She looked at me through velvet eyes an instant and I suddenly felt a strange, peaceful feeling come over me. Almost as though I had found at last what I sought in the desert, what I wanted so desperately to find.

"This Indian," she said softly, "what is it? How came such a one here?"

I explained as best I could how my father's ancestors had come over the top of the Earth, settled in the plains and valleys and mountains. How they believed they had found their happy hunting grounds only to see them destroyed when the white men came. How the sweet fruit of their lives had been turned to bitter ashes by greed and gunpowder and gore. How many of us were now penned in, on places called reservations, although we really owned the land.

She heard me out gravely, the other girls standing silently around as I told my story to the hum of the strange machine's motors. My fear was gone now, and I was curious as to what these visitors from surely another planet wanted. Boldly, I asked her.

The girl's eyes looked into mine and in her eyes I saw the wisdom of ages, the infinity of all knowledge. Before she answered, she looked at the other girls. They nodded subtly and the girl suddenly smiled.

"I am Nara," she said. "And I want *you*, Earthman."

When she spoke these words, my calm deserted me and a chill passed through me. In an instant it was gone for, without warning, the glow bathing her body became more intense, brighter. As I stared at the sight Nara glided toward me.

Suddenly, I was weak and trembling as her lithe arms enveloped me. When her body pressed urgently and insistently to mine I knew that never again would I know fear or panic or anything else humans are plagued with. "You will be our High Priest, oh Indian Earthman," she whispered as her lips touched mine.

"OURS!" I heard her whispered words only dimly, for an amazing phenomenon of passion was taking place inside me at the nearness of her body, the lush loveliness of her soft curves. I was at once a giant, ten feet tall, but tender and eager for love. And in the giving that followed I knew that Nara had saved my mind, brought me back from the brink of the fearful insanity of terror I had been living.

Stranger still was the communication Nara and I still seemed to hold with one another, even after the rites of love I underwent with her companions, I had the feeling that wherever I was bound, whatever I might do there, she and I alone would share a secret love.

It is still like that with me. And it is almost like a dream, although I know it is not a dream. It is very serene up here on the Mountains of Malabar where the streets are platinum and where there is no yesterday, no today, or no tomorrow. What ultimate result the scientists here expect when they finish using me as a romantic guinea pig is not known to me. But I don't care. I know I am safe and that I am here with Nara, and that there is no time, as we of Earth know time.

I know also what they are saying back in Nuevo Cordura, They are saying that the half-breed, Joe Rainwater, died in the desert, because his burro returned alone to Nuevo Cordura. Alone and crazy. I know that not a single tear was shed for me, and that when my name is mentioned, as it sometimes is, guys like Ed Gordon, Wally Carter, and those other shining lights of town, grin and say, "We always said he'd go plumb loco. It was only a matter of time. He didn't belong here nohow."

It doesn't make me angry. Because I know something they don't know: that sometime I'll be back. And when I do come back, Nara will be with me.

They won't laugh then, the bastards.

I have plans.

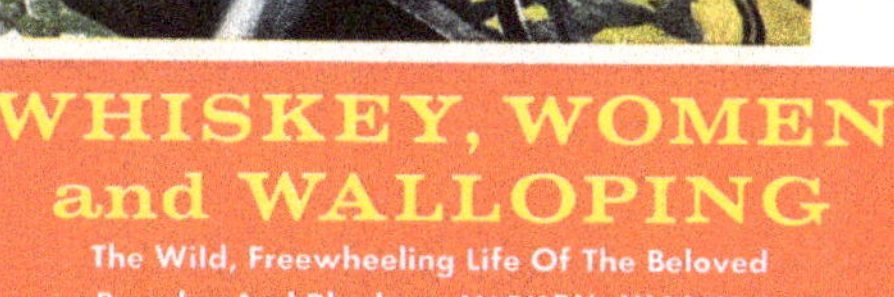

THE BLONDE WITH THE MYSTERIOUS BODY

Theodore Sturgeon

Men, April 1962   Cover by Gil Cohen

221

THE BLONDE WITH THE MYSTERIOUS BODY

Day after day, he spied on the golden headed girl—until one night, in a moment of pain and terror, he discovered her abnormal secret . . .

TALES OF

SHOCK AND HORROR

IF you live in a cheap enough rooming house and the doors are made of cheap enough pine, and the locks are old-fashioned single-action jobs and the hinges are loose, and if you have a 190 lean pounds to operate with, you can grasp the knob, press the door sidewise against its hinges, and slip the latch. Further, you can lock the door the same way when you come out.

Slim Walsh did these things. The company doctors had laid him up for three weeks (after his helper had hit him just over the temple with a 14-inch crescent wrench) pending more X-rays. Meanwhile, he felt fine and had nothing to do all day.

"Slim isn't dishonest," his mother used to tell Children's Court some years back. "He's just curious."

She was perfectly right.

By THEODORE STURGEON

Slim was constitutionally incapable of borrowing your bathroom without looking into your medicine chest. Send him into your kitchen for a saucer and when he came out a minute later, he'd have inventoried your refrigerator, your vegetable bin, and (since he was six feet three inches tall) he would know about a moldering jar of maraschino cherries in the back of the top shelf that you'd forgotten about.

Slim liked you better if, while talking to you, he knew how many jackets hung in your closet, how old that unpaid phone bill was, and just where you'd hidden those photographs. On the other hand, Slim didn't insist on knowing bad or even embarrassing things about you. He just wanted to know things about you, period.

Living in Mrs. Koyper's cheap, rundown rooming house was therefore a near-paradise. Within a week he knew Mrs. Koyper's roomers far better than she could, or cared to. Each secret visit to the rooms gave him a starting point; subsequent ones taught him more. He knew not only what these people had, but what they did, where, how much, *for* how much, and how often. In almost every case, he knew why as well.

ALMOST every case. Celia Sarton came.

Slim Walsh got a glimpse of her as she followed Mrs. Koyper up the stairs to the third floor. Mrs. Koyper, who hobbled, slowed any follower sufficiently to afford the most disinterested witness a good look, and Slim was anything but disinterested. Yet for days he could not recall her clearly. It was as if Celia Sarton had been—not invisible, for that would have been memorable in itself—but translucent or, chameleonlike, echoing the drab wall color, carpet color, woodwork color.

She carried a bag. When you go to the baggage window at a big terminal, you notice a suitcase here, a steamer-trunk there; and all around, high up, far back, there are rows and ranks of luggage not individually noticed but just *there*. This bag, Celia Sarton's bag, was one of them.

So anonymous, so unnoticeable was she that, aside from being aware that she left in the morning and returned in the evening, Slim let two days go by before he entered her room; he simply could not remind himself about her. And when he did, and had inspected it to his satisfaction, he had his hand on the knob, about to leave, before he recalled that the room was, after all, occupied. Until that second, he had thought he was giving one of the vacancies the once-over.

He grunted and *(Continued on page 66)*

41

ARTIST UNCREDITED

IF YOU live in a cheap enough rooming house and the doors are made of cheap enough pine, and the locks are old-fashioned single-action jobs and the hinges are loose, and if you have a 190 lean pounds to operate with, you can grasp the knob, press the door sidewise against its hinges, and slip the latch. Further, you can lock the door the same way when you come out.

Slim Walsh did these things. The company doctors had laid him up for three weeks (after his helper had hit him just over the temple with a 14-inch crescent wrench) pending more X-rays. Meanwhile, he felt fine and had nothing to do all day.

"Slim isn't dishonest," his mother used to tell Children's Court some years back. "He's just curious."

She was perfectly right.

Slim was constitutionally incapable of borrowing your bathroom without looking into your medicine chest. Send him into your kitchen for a saucer and when he came out a minute later, he'd have inventoried your refrigerator, your vegetable bin, and (since he was six feet three inches tall) he would know about a moldering jar of maraschino cherries in the back of the top shelf that you'd forgotten about.

Slim liked you better if, while talking to you, he knew how many jackets hung in your closet, how old that unpaid phone bill was, and just where you'd hidden those photographs. On the other hand, Slim didn't insist on knowing bad or even embarrassing things about you. He just wanted to know things about you, period.

Living in Mrs. Koyper's cheap, rundown rooming house was therefore a near-paradise. Within a week he knew Mrs. Koyper's roomers far better than she could, or cared to. Each secret visit to the rooms gave him a starting point; subsequent ones taught him more. He knew not only what these people had, but what they did, where, how much, *for* how much, and how often. In almost every case, he knew why as well.

ALMOST every case. Then Celia Sarton came.

Slim Walsh got a glimpse of her as she followed Mrs. Koyper up the stairs to the third floor. Mrs. Koyper, who hobbled, slowed any follower sufficiently to afford the most disinterested witness a good look, and Slim was anything but disinterested. Yet for days he could not recall her clearly. It was as if Celia Sarton had been—not invisible, for that would have been memorable in itself—but translucent or, chameleonlike, echoing the drab wall color, carpet color, woodwork color.

She carried a bag. When you go to the baggage window at a big terminal, you notice a suitcase here, a steamer-trunk there; and all around, high up, far back, there are rows and ranks and racks of luggage not individually noticed but just there. This bag, Celia Sarton's bag, was one of them.

So anonymous, so unnoticeable was she that, aside from being aware that she left in the morning and returned in the evening, Slim let two days go by before he entered her room; he simply could not remind himself about her. And when he did, and had inspected it to his satisfaction, he had his hand on the knob, about to leave, before he recalled that the room was, after all, occupied. Until that second, he had thought he was giving one of the vacancies the once-over.

He grunted and turned back, flicking his gaze over the room.

The bureau drawers were empty. The ashtray was clean. No toothbrush, toothpaste, soap. In the closet, two wire hangers and one wooden one covered with dirty quilted silk, and nothing else. In the shower stall, the medicine chest, nothing and nothing again, except what Mrs. Koyper had grudgingly installed.

Slim went to the bed and carefully turned back the faded coverlet. Maybe she had slept in it, but very possibly not; Mrs. Koyper specialized in unironed sheets of such a ground-in gray that it wasn't easy to tell. Frowning, Slim put up the coverlet again and smoothed it.

Suddenly he struck his forehead, which yielded him a flash of pain from his injury. He ignored it. "The bag!"

It was under the bed, shoved there, not hidden there. He looked at it without touching it for a moment, so that it could be returned exactly. Then he hauled it out.

It was a black gladstone, neither new nor expensive, of that nondescript rusty color acquired by untended leatherette. It had a worn zipper closure and was not locked. Slim opened it. It contained a cardboard box, crisp and new, for a thousand virgin sheets of cheap white typewriter paper surrounded by a glossy bright blue band bearing a white diamond with the legend: *Nonpareil the writers friend 15½ cotton fiber trademark registered.*

Slim lifted the paper out of the box, looked under it, riffled a thumbful of the sheets at the top and the same from the bottom, shook his head, replaced the paper, closed the box, put it back into the bag and restored everything precisely as he had found it. He paused again in the middle of the room, turning slowly once, but there was simply nothing else to look at. He let himself out, locked the door, and went silently back to his room.

He sat down on the edge of his bed and at last protested, "Nobody *lives* like that!"

His room was on the fourth and topmost floor of the old house.

Its door had a transom, the glass of which had many times been painted over. By standing on the foot of his bed, Slim could apply one eye to the peephole he had scratched in the paint and look straight down the stairs to the third-floor landing. On this landing, hanging to the stub of one of the ancient gas jets, was a cloudy mirror. By careful propping with folded cigarette wrappers, innumerable tests and a great deal of silent mileage up and down the stairs, Slim had arranged the exact tilt necessary in the mirror so that it covered the second floor landing as well. And just as a radar operator learns to translate glowing pips and masses into aircraft and weather, so Slim became expert at the interpretation of the fogged and distant images it gave him. Thus he had the comings and goings of half the tenants under surveillance without having to leave his room.

It was in this mirror, at twelve minutes past six, that he saw Celia Sarton next, and as he watched her climb the stairs, his eyes glowed.

The anonymity was gone. She came up the stairs two at a time, with a gait like bounding. She reached the landing and whirled into her corridor and was gone, and while a part of Slim's mind listened for the way she opened her door (hurriedly, rattling the key against the lock-plate, banging the door open, slamming it shut), another part studied a mental photograph of her face—its set purpose. Here were eyes only superficially interested in cars, curbs, stairs, doors. It was as if she had projected every important part of herself into that empty room of hers and waited there impatiently for her body to catch up. There was something in the room, or something she had to do there, which she could not, would not, wait for.

Slim buttoned his shirt, eased his door open and sidled through it. He poised a moment on his landing like a great moose sensing the air before descending to a waterhole, and then moved downstairs.

Celia Sarton's only neighbor in the north corridor was settled for the evening; she was of regular habits and Slim knew them well.

Completely confident that he would not be seen, he drifted to the girl's door and paused.

She was there, all right. He could see the light around the edge of the ill-fitting door, could sense that difference between an occupied room and an empty one, which exists however silent the occupant might be. And this one was silent. Whatever it was that had driven her into the room with such headlong urgency, whatever it was she was doing (had to do) was being done with no sound or motion that he could detect.

For a long time—six minutes, seven—Slim hung there, open-throated to conceal the sound of his breath. At last, shaking his head, he withdrew, climbed the stairs, let himself into his own room and lay down on the bed, frowning.

He could only wait. Yet he *could* wait. No one does any single thing for very long. Especially a thing not involving movement. In an hour, in two—

It was five. At half-past eleven, some faint sound from the floor below brought Slim, half-dozing, twisting up from the bed and to his high peephole in the transom. He saw the Sarton girl go out.

The temptation to go straight to her room was, of course, large, but caution also loomed. What he had tentatively established as her habit patterns did not include midnight exits. He could not know when she might come back and it would be foolish indeed to jeopardize his hobby—not only where it included her, but all of it—by being caught. He sighed and went to bed.

Less than fifteen minutes later, he congratulated himself with a sleepy smile as he heard her slow footsteps mount the stairs below. He slept.

The following day was unusually busy for Slim. In the morning he had a doctor's appointment, and in the afternoon he spent hours with a company lawyer who seemed determined to (a) deny the existence of any head injury and (b) prove to Slim and the world that the injury must have occurred years ago. He got absolutely nowhere. It took hours, however, and it was after seven when Slim got home.

He paused at the third-floor landing and glanced down the corridor. Celia Sarton's room was occupied and silent. If she emerged around midnight, exhausted and relieved, then he would know she had again raced up the stairs to her urgent, motionless task, whatever it was...

He slipped downstairs half an hour later and listened at her door, and smiled. She was washing her lingerie at the handbasin. It was a small thing to learn, but he felt he was making progress. It did not explain why she lived as she did, but indicated how she could manage without so much as a spare handkerchief.

Oh, well, maybe in the morning.

In the morning, there was no maybe. He found it, he found it, though he could not know what it was he'd found. He laughed at first, not in triumph but wryly, calling himself a clown. Then he squatted on his heels in the middle of the floor (he would not sit on the bed, for fear of leaving wrin-kles) and carefully lifted the box of paper out of the suitcase and put it on the floor.

Up to now, he had contented himself with a quick riffle of the blank paper, a little at the top, a little at the bottom. He had done just this again, without removing the box from the suitcase, but only taking the top off and tilting up the banded ream of *Nonpareil-the-writers-friend*. And almost in spite of itself, his quick eye had caught the briefest of pale blue.

Gently, he removed the band, sliding it off the pack of paper, being careful not to slit the glossy finish. Now he could freely riffle the pages, and when he did, he discovered that all of them except a hundred or so, top and bottom, had the same rectangular cut-out, leaving only a narrow margin all the way around. In the hollow space thus formed, something was packed.

He could not tell what the something was, except that it was pale tan, with a tinge of pink, and felt like smooth, untextured leather. There was a lot of it, neatly folded so that it exactly fitted the hole in the ream of paper.

He puzzled over it for some minutes without touching it again, and then, scrubbing his fingertips against his shirt until he felt that they were quite free of moisture and grease, he gently worked loose the top corner of the substance and unfolded a layer. All he found was more of the same.

He folded it down flat again to be sure he could, and then brought more of it out. He soon realized that the material was of an irregular shape and almost certainly of one piece, so that folding it into a tight rectangle required care and great skill. Therefore he proceeded very slowly, stopping every now and then to fold it up again, and it took him more than an hour to get enough of it out so that he could identify it.

Identify? It was completely unlike anything he had ever seen before.

It was a human skin, done in some substance very like the real thing. The first fold, the one which had been revealed at first, was an area of the back, which was why it showed no features. One might liken it to a balloon, except that a deflated balloon is smaller in every dimension than an inflated one. As far as Slim could judge, this was life-sized—a little over five feet long and proportioned accordingly. The hair was peculiar, looking exactly like the real thing until flexed, and then revealing itself to be one piece.

It had Celia Sarton's face.

Slim closed his eyes and opened them, and found that it was still true. He held his breath and put forth a careful, steady forefinger and gently pressed the left eyelid upward. There was an eye under it, all right, light blue and seemingly moist, but flat.

Slim released the breath, closed the eye and sat back on his heels. His feet were beginning to tingle from his having knelt on the floor for so long.

He looked all around the room once, to clear his head of strangeness, and then began to fold the thing up again. It took a while, but when he was finished, he knew he had it right. He replaced the typewriter paper in the box and the box in the bag, put the bag away and at last stood in the middle of the room deep in thought.

After a moment of this, he began to inspect the ceiling. It was made of stamped tin, like those of many old-fashioned houses. It was grimy and flaked and stained; here and there, rust showed through, and in one or two places, edges of the tin sheets had sagged. Slim nodded to himself in profound satisfaction, listened for a while at the door, let himself out, locked it and went upstairs.

He stood in his own corridor for a minute, checking the position of doors, the hall window, and his accurate orientation of the same things on the floor below. Then he went into his own room.

His room, though smaller than most, was one of the few in the house which was blessed with a real closet instead of a rickety off-the-floor wardrobe. He went into it and knelt, and grunted in satisfaction when he found how loose the ancient, unpainted floorboards were. By removing the side baseboard, he found it possible to get to the air-space between the fourth floor and the third-floor ceiling.

He took out boards until he had an opening perhaps fourteen inches wide, and then, working in almost total silence, he began cleaning away dirt and old plaster. He did this meticulously, because when he finally pierced the tin sheeting, he wanted not one grain of dirt to fall into the room below. He took his time and it was late in the afternoon when he was satisfied with his preparations and began, with his knife, on the tin.

It was thinner and softer than he had dared to hope; he almost overcut on the first try. Carefully he squeezed the sharp steel into the little slot he had cut, lengthening it. When it was somewhat less than an inch long, he withdrew all but the point of the knife and twisted it slightly, moved it a sixteenth of an inch and twisted again, repeating this all down the cut until he had widened it enough for his purposes.

He checked the time, then returned to Celia Sarton's room for just long enough to check the appearance of his work from that side. He was very pleased with it. The little cut had come through a foot away from the wall over the bed and was a mere pencil line lost in the baroque design with which the tin was stamped and the dirt and rust that marred it. He returned to his room and sat down to wait.

He heard the old house coming to its evening surge of life, a voice here, a door there, footsteps on the stairs. He ignored them all as he sat on the edge of his bed, hands folded between his knees, eyes half closed, immobile like a machine fueled, oiled, tuned and ready, lacking only the right touch on the right control. And like that touch, the faint sound of Celia Sarton's footsteps moved him.

To use his new peephole, he had to lie on the floor half in and half out of the closet, with his head in the hole, actually below floor level.

When she turned on the light, he could see her splendidly, as well as most of the floor, the lower third of the door and part of the washbasin in the bathroom.

She had come in hurriedly, with that same agonized haste he had observed before. At the same second she turned on the light, she had apparently flung her handbag toward the bed; it was in mid-air as the light appeared. She did not even glance its way, but hastily fumbled the old gladstone from under the bed, opened it, removed the box, opened it, took out the paper, slipped off the blue band and removed the blank sheets of paper which covered the hollowed-out ream.

SHE SCOOPED out the thing hidden there, shaking it once like a grocery clerk with a folded paper sack, so that the long limp thing straightened itself out. She arranged it carefully on the worn linoleum of the floor, arms down at the side, legs slightly apart, face up, neck straight. Then she lay down on the floor, too, head-to-head with the deflated thing. She reached up over her head, took hold of the collapsed image of herself about the region of the ears, and for a moment did some sort of manipulation of it against the top of her own head.

Slim heard faintly a sharp, chitinous click, like the sound one makes by snapping the edge of a thumbnail against the edge of a fingernail.

Her hands slipped to the cheeks of the figure and she pulled at the empty head as if testing a connection. The head seemed now to have adhered to hers.

Then she assumed the same pose she had arranged for this other, letting her hands fall to her sides on the floor, closing her eyes.

For a long while, nothing seemed to be happening, except for the odd way she was breathing, very deeply but very slowly, like the slow-motion picture of someone panting, gasping for breath after a long hard run. After perhaps ten minutes of this, the breathing became shallower and even slower, until, at the end of a half hour, he could detect none at all.

Slim lay there immobile for more than an hour, until his body shrieked protest and his head ached from eyestrain. He hated to move, but move he must. Silently he backed out of the closet, stood up and stretched. It was a great luxury and he deeply enjoyed it. He felt moved to think over what he had just seen, but clearly and consciously decided not to—not yet, anyway.

When he was unkinked again, he crept back into the closet, put his head in the hole and his eye to the slot.

Nothing had changed. She still lay quiet, utterly relaxed, so much so that her hands had turned palm upward.

Slim watched and he watched. Just as he was about to conclude that this was the way the girl spent her entire nights and that there would be nothing more to see, he saw a slight and sudden contraction about the region of her solar plexus, and then another. For a time, there was nothing more, and then the empty thing attached to the top of her head began to fill.

And Celia Sarton began to empty.

Slim stopped breathing until it hurt and watched in total astonishment.

Once it had started, the process progressed swiftly. It was as if something passed from the clothed body of the girl to this naked empty thing. Slim could see the fingers, which had been folded flat against the palms, inflate and move until they took on the normal relaxed curl of a normal hand. The elbows shifted a little to lie more normally against the body. And yes, it was a body now.

The other one was not a body any more. It lay foolishly limp in its garments, its sleeping face slightly distorted by its flattening. The fingers fell against the palms by their own limp weight. The shoes thumped quietly on their sides, heels together, toes pointing in opposite directions.

The exchange was done in less than ten minutes and then the newly filled body moved.

It flexed its hands tentatively, drew up its knees and stretched its legs out again, arched its back against the floor. Its eyes flickered open. It put up its arms and made some deft manipulation at the top of its head. Slim heard another version of the soft-hard click and the now-empty head fell flat to the floor.

The new Celia Sarton sat up and sighed and rubbed her hands lightly over her body, as if restoring circulation and sensation to a chilled skin. She stretched as comfortingly and luxuriously as Slim had a few minutes earlier. She looked rested and refreshed.

At the top of her head, Slim caught a glimpse of a slit through which a wet whiteness showed, but it seemed to be closing. In a brief time, nothing showed there but a small valley in the hair, just like a normal parting.

She sighed again and got up. She took the clothed thing on the floor by the neck, raised it and shook it twice to make the clothes fall away.

Moving leisurely but with purpose, she went into the bathroom and, except from her shins down, out of Slim's range of vision. There he heard the same faint domestic sounds he bad once detected outside her door, as she washed her underclothes.

Slim heard more water-running and sudsing noises, and, by ear, followed the operation through a soaping and two rinses. Then she came out
again, shaking out the object, which had apparently just been wrung, pulled
it through a wooden clothes-hanger, and hung it with the clothes on the
wardrobe door.

Then she lay down on the bed, not to sleep or to read or even to rest—
she seemed very rested—but merely to wait until it was time to do something else.

By now, Slim's bones were complaining again, so he wormed noiselessly
backward out of his lookout point, got into his shoes and a jacket, and went
out to get something to eat. When he came home an hour later and looked,
her light was out and he could see nothing. He spread his overcoat carefully
over the hole in the closet so no stray light from his room would appear in
the little slot in the ceiling, closed the door, read a comic book for a while,
and went to bed.

The next day, he followed her.

What he found out about her daytime activities was, if anything, more
surprising than any wild surmise. She was a clerk in a small five-and-ten on
the East Side. She ate in the store's lunch bar at lunchtime—a green salad
and a surprising amount of milk—and in the evening she stopped at a hot-
dog stand and drank a small container of milk, though she ate nothing.

Her steps were slowed by then and she moved wearily, speeding up only
when she was close to the rooming house, and then apparently all but over-
come with eagerness to get home and...into something more comfortable.
Slim, had he disbelieved his own eyes the first time, must believe them now.

So it went for a week. Every twenty-four hours, she changed bodies, carefully washing, drying, folding and putting away the one she was
not using.

Twice during the week, she went out for what was apparently a con-
stitutional and nothing more—a half-hour around midnight, when she
would stand on the walk in front of the rooming house, or wander around
the block.

At work, she was silent but not unnaturally so; she spoke, when spoken
to, in a small, unmusical voice. She seemed to have no friends; she maintained her aloofness by being uninteresting and by seeking no one out and
by needing no one. She evinced no outside interests, never going to the
movies or to the park. She had no dates, not even with girls. Slim thought
she did not sleep, but lay quietly in the dark waiting for it to be time to get
up and go to work.

And when he came to think about it, as ultimately he did, it occurred to Slim that within the anthill in which we all live and have our being, enough privacy can be gotten for all sorts of strangeness, providing the strangeness doesn't show. If it is a man's pleasure to sleep upside-down like a bat, and no one ever sees him sleeping, he may sleep bat-like all the days of his life.

One need not, by these rules, even *be* a human being. Not if the mimicry is good enough. It is a measure of Slim's odd personality that Celia Sarton's ways did not frighten him. He was, if anything, less disturbed by her now than he'd been before he had begun to spy on her. He knew what she did in her room and how she lived. Before, he had not known. Now he did. This made him much happier.

He was, however, still curious.

His curiosity would never drive him to do what another man might—to speak to her on the stairs or on the street, get to know her and more about her. He was too shy for that. Nor was he moved to report to anyone the odd practice he watched each evening. It wasn't his business to report. She was doing no harm as far as he could see. In his cosmos, everybody had a right to live and make a buck if they could.

Yet his curiosity did undergo a change. It was not in him to wonder what sort of being this was and whether its ancestors had grown up among human beings, living with them in caves and in tents.

No, Slim's curiosity was far simpler and more basic. He simply changed his question from *what* to *what if?*

So it was that on the eighth day of his survey, a Tuesday, he went again to her room, got the bag, opened it, removed the box, opened it, removed the ream of paper, slid the blue band off, removed the covering sheets, took out the second Celia Sarton, put her on the bed and then replaced paper, blue band, box--cover, box, and bag just as he had found them. He put the folded thing under his shirt and went out, carefully locking the door behind him in his special way, and went upstairs to his room. He put his prize under the four clean shirts in his bottom drawer and sat down to await Celia Sarton's homecoming.

She was a little late that night—twenty minutes, perhaps. The delay seemed to have increased both her fatigue and her eagerness; she burst in feverishly, moved with the rapidity of near-panic. She looked drawn and pale and her hands shook. She fumbled the bag from under the bed, snatched out the box and opened it, contrary to her usual measured movements, by inverting it over the bed and dumping out its contents.

When she saw nothing there but sheets of paper, some with a wide rectangle cut from them and some without, she froze. She crouched over that bed without moving for an interminable two minutes. Then she straightened up slowly and glanced about the room. Once she fumbled through the paper, but resignedly, without hope. She made one sound, a high, sad whimper, and, from that moment on, was silent.

She went to the window slowly, her feet dragging, her shoulders slumped. For a long time, she stood looking out at the city, its growing darkness, its growing colonies of lights, each a symbol of life and life's usages. Then she drew down the blind and went back to the bed.

She stacked the papers there with loose uncaring fingers and put the heap of them on the dresser. She took off her shoes and placed them neatly side by side on the floor by the bed. She lay down in the same utterly relaxed pose she affected when she made her change, hands down and open, legs a little apart.

Her face looked like a death-mask, its tissues sunken and sagging. It was flushed and sick-looking. There was a little of the deep regular breathing, but only a little. There was a bit of the fluttering contractions at the midriff, but only a bit. Then—nothing.

Slim backed away from the peephole and sat up. He felt very bad about this. He had been only curious; he hadn't wanted her to get sick, to die.

Should he call a doctor?

She hadn't. She hadn't even tried, though she must have known much better than he did how serious her predicament was. Well, maybe not calling a doctor meant that she'd be all right, after all. Doctors would have a lot of silly questions to ask. She might even tell the doctor about her other skin, and if Slim was the one who had fetched the doctor, Slim might be questioned about that.

Slim didn't want to get involved with anything. He just wanted to know things.

He thought, "I'll take another look."

He crawled back into the closet and put his head in the hole. Celia Sarton, he knew instantly, would not survive this. Her face was swollen, her eyes protruded, and her purpled tongue lolled far—too far—from the corner of her mouth. Even as he watched, her face darkened still more and the skin of it crinkled until it looked like carbon paper which has been balled up tight and then smoothed out.

The very beginnings of an impulse to snatch the thing she needed out of his shirt drawer and rush it down to her died within him, for he saw a wisp of smoke emerge from her nostrils and then—

Slim cried out, snatched his head from the hole, bumping it cruelly, and clapped his hands over his eyes. Put the biggest size flash-bulb an inch from your nose, and fire it, and you might get a flare approaching the one he got through his little slot in the tin ceiling.

He sat grunting in pain and watching, on the insides of his eyelids, migrations of flaming worms. At last they faded and he tentatively opened his eyes. They hurt and the after-image of the slot hung before him, but at least he could see.

Feet pounded on the stairs. He smelled smoke and a burned, oily unpleasant something which he could not identify. Someone shouted. Someone hammered on a door. Then screamed and screamed.

It was in the papers next day. Mysterious, the story said. And there had been others—people burned to a crisp by a fierce heat which bad nevertheless not destroyed clothes or bedding, while leaving nothing for autopsy. This was, said the paper, either an unknown kind of heat or heat of such intensity and such brevity that it would do such a thing. No known relatives, it said. Police mystified—no clues or suspects.

Slim didn't say anything to anybody. He wasn't curious about the matter any more. He closed up the hole in the closet that same night, and the next day, after he read the story, he used the newspaper to wrap up the thing in his shirt drawer. It smelled pretty bad and, even that early, was too far gone to be unfolded. He dropped it into a garbage can on the way to the lawyer's office on Wednesday.

They settled his lawsuit that afternoon and he moved.

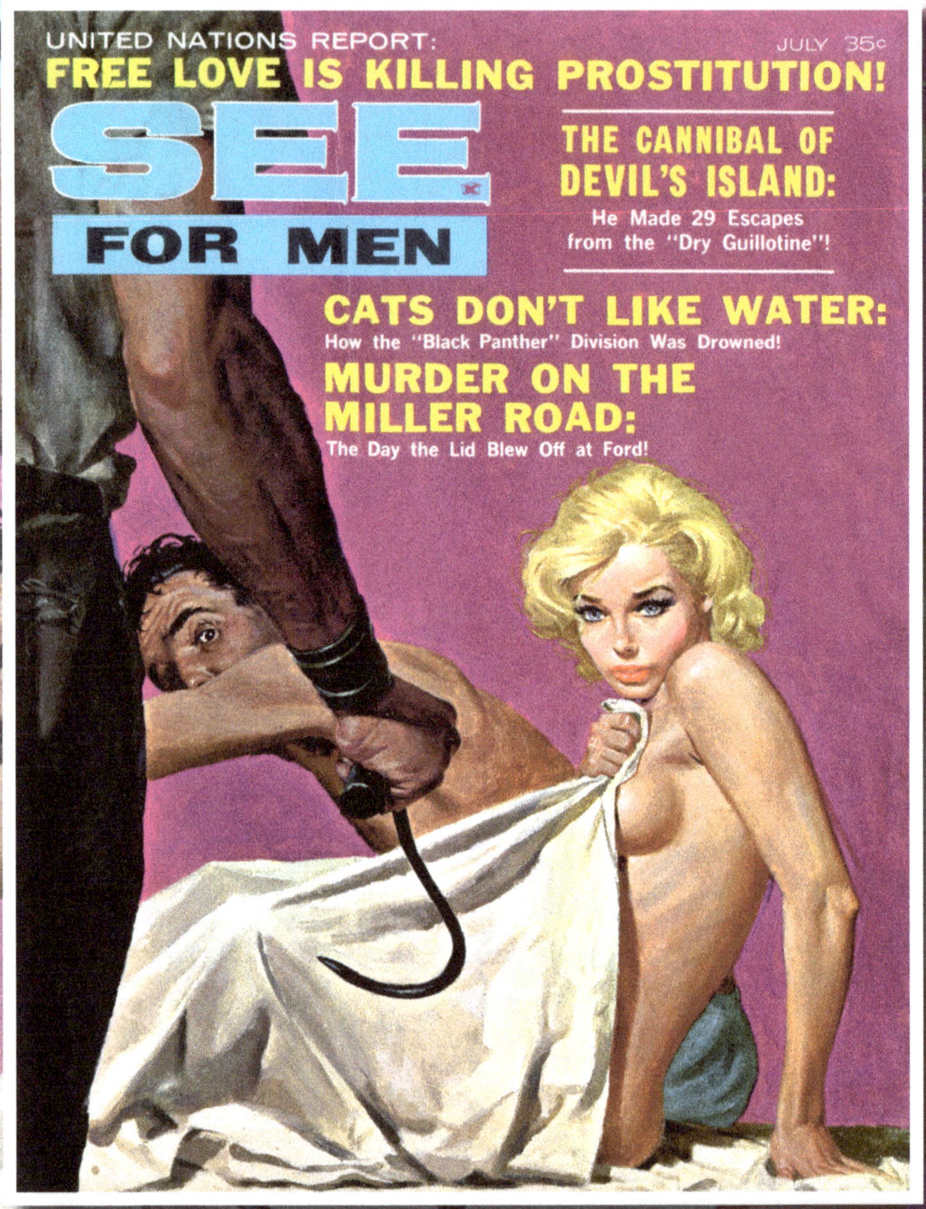

July 1962
Art by George Gross

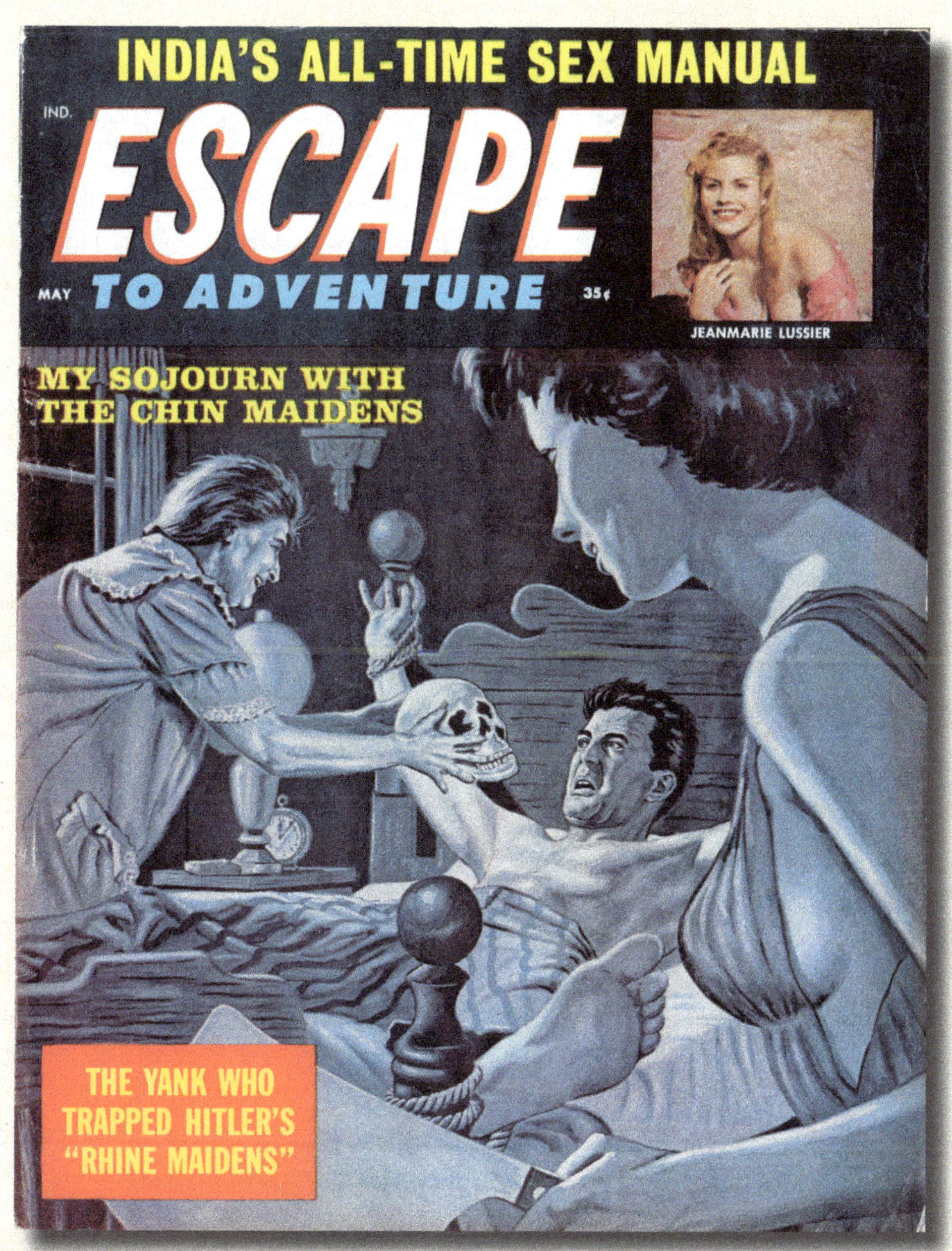

FOWL PLAY

William Bayne

Escape to Adventure, May 1962   Cover by Sydney Shores

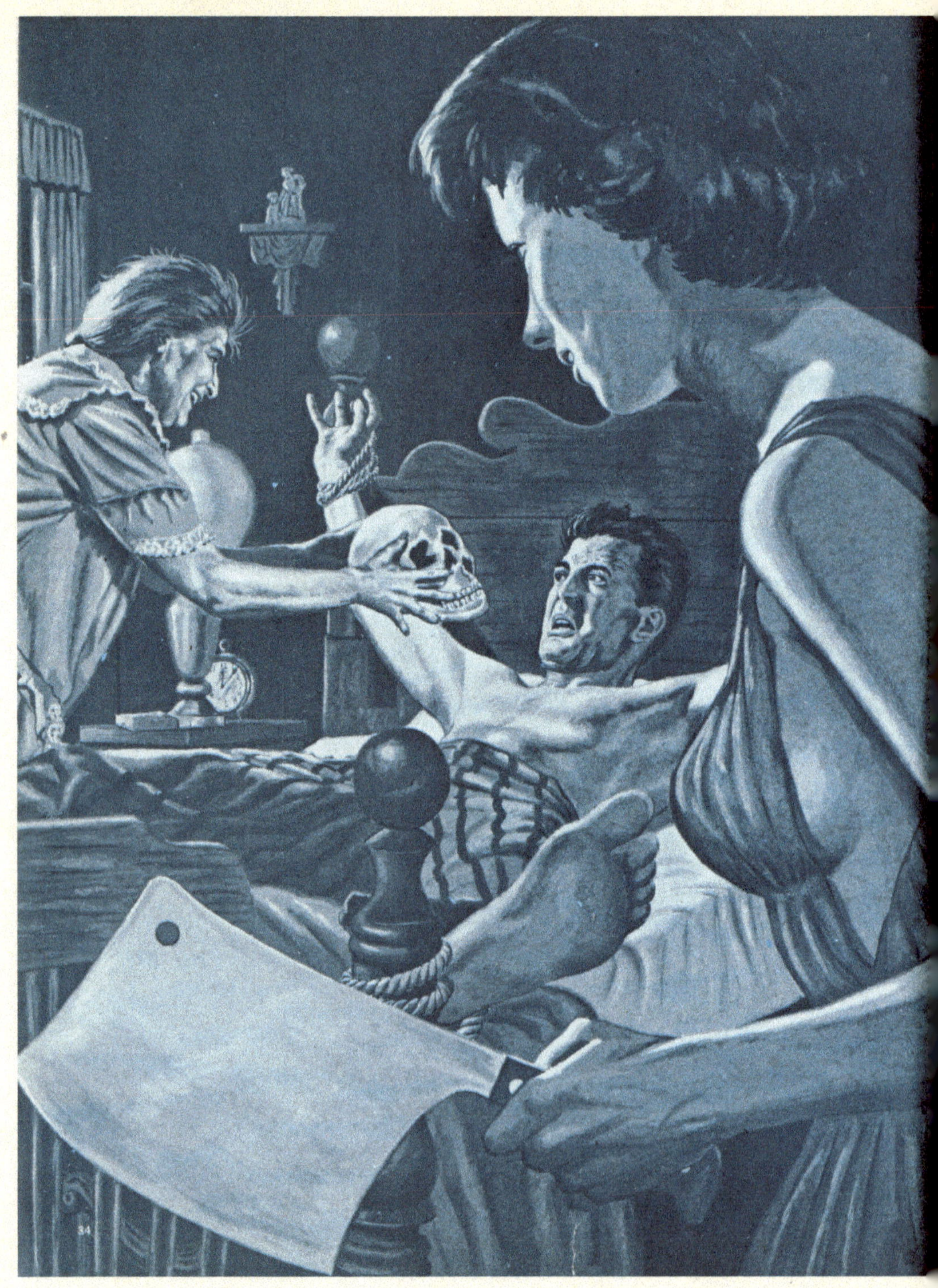

FOWL PLAY

Buzz, Buzz Went That Strange Noise in Bill's Ear. It Whispered a Solution to His Problem

By WILLIAM BAYNE

CRACK! Plunk! Crack! Plunk! He got another one. Crack! Plunk! The same old thing everyday. Everyday. Until today! Today was different! Just take it easy and relax, and I'll tell you all about it. I'll tell you all about the heads!

Heads! Heads! Heads! That's all Bill does everyday, is cut off heads. He works in one of the larger poultry houses in the city. His job for eight hours a day, six days a week, is to cut the heads off chickens, and after he's finished with the bird, he passes the fowl to the next man on the bench, and after that man does his part, he in turn passes the bird to the man after him. At the far end of the bench, the birds are cleaned and packaged, and made ready for the delivery to the stores, for sale to the consumers to purchase. Hundreds of birds everyday, and then today it happened.

Today as Bill was reaching into the huge container that held numerous dead birds, he got a strange buzz in his ear. At first he thought it was a bug, but after brushing his ear with his hand, and finding no insect, but still hearing the buzz, he thought that he had something wrong with his ear. The buzz went away, and when it returned Bill didn't think anything strange about it.

It returned just as he set the chicken on the chopping block. He checked again to make sure that a bug was not in his ear, for he thought that maybe the insect eluded him the first time. He brushed his ear, and looked at the space between his head and the ceiling. No bug. He laughed inwardly to himself, and looked at the chicken on the chopping block.

No! It couldn't be!

He took his eyes off the bird, and then returned his gaze to the bird.

Yes, it was! But how? But why?

He blinked and wiped his eyes, for he could hardly believe what he saw. When he set the chicken on the block, it was a true normal chicken. All over! But now the bird was exactly the same, except for one thing. The head! The head on the body of the chicken was the head of his mother-in-law! Everything matched: the beady eyes, the ashen skin, the parrot-like beak for a nose, the stringy hair, and the two missing front teeth. Bill was sweating, and he wiped his forehead with his handkerchief. He looked again, and it was still there on the chopping block waiting for the cleaver. The buzz was back in his ear, and then the other happened.

Sensual spasmodic tremors trickled through the husky body of the man, and it was sheer delight for him to gaze down on the head on the chopping block.

He would lift the razor-sharp cleaver with a sense of satisfaction that he had never experienced before, and drive the blade of the cleaver down on the neck of the mother-in-law with a powerful stroke. Crack! Plunk! The head flipped off the chopping block, and into the box on the floor at the side of the chopping block.

He'd lean over the block with the feeling that if the head was in the box, he would be able to complete his satisfaction all of the way. He'd discover nothing but chicken heads in the box, and it would leave him frustrated. He had the desire to see the head in the box like a junkie needs a fix. Head after head, the same old thing. He would always see the head of the old woman on the block, but after using the cleaver, and peering into box full of hope, it was not there. Crack! Plunk! He'd look again, but (Continued on page 53)

The only light in the bedroom was the eerie moonlight coming through the window, but Bill did not have any trouble at all seeing what the woman thrust in front of his nose.

35

ART BY SYDNEY SHORES

CRACK! Plunk! Crack! Plunk! He got another one. Crack! Plunk! The same old thing every day. Every day. Until today! Today was different! Just take it easy and relax, and I'll tell you all about it. I'll tell you all about the heads!

Heads! Heads! Heads! That's all Bill does every day, is cut off heads. He works in one of the larger poultry houses in the city. His job for eight hours a day, six days a week, is to cut the heads off chickens, and after he's finished with the bird, he passes the fowl to the next man on the bench, and after that man does his part, he in turn passes the bird to the man after him. At the far end of the bench, the birds are cleaned and packaged, and made ready for the delivery to the stores, for sale to the consumers to purchase. Hundreds of birds every day, and then today it happened.

Today as Bill was reaching into the huge container that held numerous dead birds, he got a strange buzz in his ear. At first he thought it was a bug, but after brushing his ear with his hand, and finding no insect, but still hearing the buzz, he thought that he had something wrong with his ear. The buzz went away, and when it returned Bill didn't think anything strange about it.

It returned just as he set the chicken on the chopping block. He checked again to make sure that a bug was not in his ear, for he thought that maybe the insect eluded him the first time. He brushed his ear, and looked at the space between his head and the ceiling. No bug. He laughed inwardly to himself, and looked at the chicken on the chopping block.

No! It couldn't be!

He took his eyes off the bird, and then returned his gaze to the bird.

Yes, it was! But how? But why?

He blinked and wiped his eyes, for he could hardly believe what he saw. When he set the chicken on the block, it was a true normal chicken. All over! But now the bird was exactly the same, except for one thing. The head! The head on the body of the chicken was the head of his mother-in-law!

Everything matched: the beady eyes, the ashen skin, the parrot-like beak for a nose, the stringy hair, and the two missing front teeth. Bill was sweating, and he wiped his forehead with his handkerchief. He looked again, and it was still there on the chopping block waiting for the cleaver. The buzz was back in his ear, and then the other happened.

Sensual spasmodic tremors trickled through the husky body of the man, and it was sheer delight for him to gaze down on the head on the chopping block.

He would lift the razor-sharp cleaver with a sense of satisfaction that he had never experienced before, and drive the blade of the cleaver down on the neck of the mother-in-law with a powerful stroke. Crack! Plunk! The head flipped off the chopping block, and into the box on the floor at the side of the chopping block.

He'd lean over the block with the feeling that if the head was in the box, he would be able to complete his satisfaction all of the way. He'd discover nothing but chicken heads in the box, and it would leave him frustrated. He had the desire to see the head in the box like a junkie needs a fix. Head after head, the same old thing. He would always see the head of the old woman on the block, but after using the cleaver, and peering into the box full of hope, it was not there. Crack! Plunk! He'd look again, but it didn't do him any good.

Then it got to be time to wash up, punch the clock, and catch the bus for home. Home! Home? What a laugh. Wife and mother-in-law nagging all of the time. Do this. Do that. Why this? Why that? They wouldn't even give the poor guy his supper until he finished the daily chores. What a terrible life he had. Then the buzz was back in his ear, and it made him think real well when it left.

What if they were not around to be nagging him all of the time? Then he would again be free. Hmm. Hmm. He was thinking, and he noticed that the buzz had left after it cooed softly in his ear.

He and his wife had grown up together, and their parents' farms were situated side by side. Then one day his parents were killed at a railroad crossing and he was alone. He hired a maid to do the cooking, cleaning, and washing, but after he found out that he had made her pregnant, he decided that he could no longer use her in his employ. What in the world would people have said about that? Then he was living alone again and did not like it.

His wife's father was a drunkard, and when drunk, he would beat the wife and daughter. Then one day in a drunken rage while whipping one of his horses, the animal reared, and struck the man on the forehead with its front hoofs. The man was struck dead on the spot, and he guessed that the wife and the daughter were relieved that they would not receive any more of the man's beatings.

About six months later, he married the girl, and he might have just as well married the both of them, for they were all living on Bill's farm. Bill, the wife, and the mother-in-law.

While he was finishing washing the cleavers off and oiling them with mineral oil, he visualized the chopping block, the head of the old woman, and the razor-sharp cleaver. The buzz had returned to his ear, left, and he was again thinking. He decided then to get rid of the both of them. No more of their constant nagging and questions.

What to do with the bodies? He would have to destroy them so that the law would not catch him and send him to prison. He hurried to catch the bus…for he had chores.

His head was resting on the back of the seat on the bus when the buzz reappeared in his ear. The buzz was getting pleasant to him now, for after it left, he always thought of something. Buzz…buzzzz.

Strange, he thought.

He wished that he had the maid back with him then. At least she wasn't nagging him all the time, and when she did nag him, it was in the way that he wanted her to. That's what he liked about her. Hmmm. Hmmm. She was pretty too. Short and well built, nice blonde hair, big brown eyes, skin without a blemish, and a beautiful set of teeth. Except for that one tooth, which was a gold one. She was so proud of that tooth, that she used to shine it. Hmmm. He wished he had her back.

The buzz whispered softly in his ear. He had to stack the hay that he bought in the barn, for it might rain. And he had to feed the hogs. Those nasty brutes! They would eat anything. Anything! Anything? ANYTHING!!! Yes, they would, if they were hungry enough! And he was just the person to get them hungry enough. Today is Monday, and he would not feed them again until Saturday, and then they would be ready to eat anything. ANYTHING!!! Ha! Ha! Ha!

The buzz appeared again, and then left. Then he knew that he would strangle both of them on Saturday night. First his wife, for they slept together, and then the old witch of a mother-in-law. He'd bleed the both of them good, so the hogs would not shy away from them. He could do that easily. After the porkers had their dinner, he would gather the bones that remained and bury them in lime. He could keep adding lime until the bones had transformed to fine powder. He would never be caught by the law.

So, Bill slated the deaths for Saturday night, and his sleep on Thursday and Friday nights was very restless. No wonder, with that on his mind. His mind?

SATURDAY finally came, and he brought one of the cleavers home from work and hid it very carefully in the large barn. He did all of the chores as soon as he got home, glad that it was the last time that he had to wait for his supper. He felt good, and they all went to bed about 9 PM. He was so sure that he would be able to wake that he let himself doze off, and without knowing it fell into a deep, sound sleep.

The moon was shining in the window, directly on his face, and that was what woke him. He seemed to sense that his wife was not in the bed with him, and when he looked to the left, he saw that her half of the bed was empty. She was probably warming herself a glass of milk as she sometimes did. He was sweating, and the bed was damp from the water that drained out of his pores. His body was tense. He was going to get her as soon as she returned from the kitchen.

He heard the footsteps. Yes, that was her. He really felt joyous then. He turned his body to watch his wife enter the room. I should have said that he tried to turn his body. He couldn't. He tried, but he could not turn.

He was tied, and he was utterly helpless. His right foot was tied to the foot of the bed on the right side, and his left to the foot of the bed on the other side. His hands were tied over his head to the head of the bed. The right to the right side, and the left to the left side. He was spread-eagled on the bed, as if he had been grabbed by the Apache Indians. The only part of his body that he could possibly move was his head.

Then he turned his head, and he found himself looking into the eyes of his mother-in-law. That was a nightmare in itself, he thought. Her eyes were glassy, and saliva was running down the corners of her mouth. She was cackling as if she fully enjoyed his position. She did. Her sudden presence startled the hell out of him. She leaned over him, with her hands behind her back, and he demanded:

"Just why in the hell am I all tied up like a animal?"

The mother-in-law only cackled some more, and the wife who entered the room silently said: "Show him, mother dear."

The only light in the bedroom was the eerie moonlight coming through the window, but Bill did not have any trouble at all seeing what the woman thrust in front of his nose. It was the skull of the maid, for that one tooth, the gold one, was still in the jaw, and had a faint shine to it. He cursed his luck to himself.

"What in the hell is that thing?" he asked innocently.

"Do not try and act so innocent, Bill darling," said the wife. "You know as well as we do that it is the head of the maid that used to work for you."

Then the mother-in-law set the head on the floor, sat in the rocking chair, and started back cackling. The cackle of the witch was getting on

Bill's nerves.

His wife said: "The hogs have been hungry lately, and that was what caused them to start their rooting in the sty. They uncovered the maid's bones, Bill, and if you had been feeding them properly, we would never have known what you were planning for us. Then today, Mother saw you hide the cleaver in the barn so carefully, and that left us with only one choice. We have to get you before you get us. I'm sorry, baby, but that's how it goes. The strong shall stay, and the weak shall go."

Bill was waiting for the buzz to return to tell him what to do, but things had gone too far for the buzz to help him. Or had they gone too far?

Maybe they didn't know for sure, and were just testing him? Maybe he could con them anyway. He had to try.

"Honey, you know that I love you, and that I would not do anything at all to hurt you or your mother," he said. "Get those crazy thoughts out of your mind and untie me. Okay?"

"Bill, it's all over," said the wife coldly.

Bill was thinking again, waiting for the buzz, when his wife looked at her mother, nodded her head, and said: "Mother, the hogs are hungry."

The mother-in-law rose out of the rocker, walked over by Bill, raised something shiny over her head, and said: "Daughter, this will be more messy than your father was."

If the buzz did come at the last minute, Bill couldn't have heard it for the old woman was cackling too loud.

Then the thing that was so shiny was over Bill's head and on its way down. It was the blade of the cleaver that he had hidden so carefully in the barn.

Down...down...down.

Crack! Plunk!

Bill couldn't have heard the buzz then.

"Did you hear that, daughter?" asked the old woman as she wiped the blade of the cleaver off on the blanket.

"Hear what, mother?" asked the daughter.

"That buzzing sound," answered the mother.

STRANGE CULT OF THE VAMPIRE TARANTULAS

Rick Manners

Peril, September 1962   Cover by John Duillo

STRANGE CULT OF THE *Vampire* TARANTULAS

BY RICK MANNERS

THE HUGE, HAIRY SPIDER CAME CLOSER AND CLOSER TO HER WHITE BODY. I'LL NEVER BE ABLE TO FORGET THAT HORROR NOT IF I LIVE TO BE A HUNDRED!

I STILL DREAM of the horrible, nightmarish sight of that huge, black, hairy spider beginning to feed upon the blood of that beautiful girl. It's something a man just can't forget—not if he lives to be a hundred.

The whole unbelievable terror-stricken adventure began about a year ago. Actually it must have begun long before that in the fevered brain of a man named Dr. Unicorn. But I didn't know anything about Dr. Unicorn until . . .

I'm getting ahead of myself. the whole thing actually started on a sunny morning in Spring. I was in my laboratory testing a new species of algae for resistance to radioactivity, when the director of our foundation, The Society For The Study of Marine Growth, came sweeping through the door with a loud bang. It is definitely not like Dr. Ponsonby to come sweeping through doors. He is a short, rather stout man, who usually walks softly and always knocks before he enters any door. I knew he must be very, very upset.

"Rick, dammit, we've got to do something about this. This is the second expedition we've lost in three years. We just can't go on losing people. Why, one of our best men was on that trip. How could they just vanish without a trace?" and he looked at me plaintively as if he expected me to have an answer up my sleeve.

"Don't tell me we've lost touch with the Cawthorne expedition, too," I asked unbelievingly.

"Haven't had a word from them in two weeks. And you know they were supposed to contact us every second day."

"Where were they the last time you heard?" I asked.

"Well, the best I can figure is that they were between *Nukutipipi* and *Marutea* in the Tuamotu Archipelago. The last radio communication received by our control ship placed them in that area. We've got to find them," and he pointed his fist on the table so that the test tubes rattled dangerously.

"That's why I'm sending you, Rick. You know all about those Pacific Islands. You were on that expedition that was investigating the resistance of plankton to radioactivity."

"But—wait, doctor . . ." I interrupted helplessly.

"Now, don't give me any excuses. I've got the boat all set and I'm sending a good crew of men with you. Elaine is going, too. She is so worried about her friend Maria who was on that expedition as Cawthorne's assistant," the doctor paused for a moment and watched me knowingly.

I didn't know that my secret was that well known around the labs. I had a yen for the luscious Elaine from the moment I had caught a glimpse of her beautiful blonde hair and her beautiful blonde body. Around the offices our contacts had been scrupulously polite and circumspect. She transcribed my notes efficiently. She even called me Dr. Manners instead of Rick as most of the girls did. Only once had I felt the touch of fire buried deep within her, when I had accidentally brushed against one magnificent breast. She drew back quickly but her eyes flashed like streaks of passionate lightning.

Needless to say, I was on that ship when it left two mornings after Doctor Ponsonby had talked to me.

Did I call that hulk a ship? It was the most run-down, unseaworthy-looking craft I had ever seen. The cabins were about as big as broom closets and less comfortable. And from the very beginning before we even got out to sea the ship began to roll and pitch as if she were possessed. Since most of the members of our search party were not really good sailors, they spent the first week of our voyage in the unhappy agony of seasickness. And I'm sorry to say my lovely Elaine was no exception.

Thus it was that I didn't even get a chance to speak with her until we hit the smooth *(Continued on page 34)*

ART BY JOHN DUILLO

I STILL dream of the horrible, nightmarish sight of that huge, black, hairy spider beginning to feed upon the blood of that beautiful girl. It's something a man just can't forget—not if he lives to be a hundred.

The whole unbelievable terror-stricken adventure began about a year ago. Actually it must have begun long before that in the fevered brain of a man named Dr. Unicorn. But I didn't know anything about Dr. Unicorn until .

I'm getting ahead of myself. The whole thing actually started on a sunny morning in spring. I was in my laboratory testing a new species of algae for resistance to radioactivity, when the director of our foundation, The Society for the Study of Marine Growth, came sweeping through the door with a loud bang. It is definitely not like Dr. Ponsonby to come sweeping through doors. He is a short, rather stout man, who usually walks softly and always knocks before he enters any door. I knew he must be very, very upset.

"Rick, dammit, we've got to do something about this. This is the second expedition we've lost in three years. We just can't go on losing people. Why, one of our best men was on that trip. How could they just vanish without a trace?" and he looked at me plaintively as if he expected me to have an answer up my sleeve.

"Don't tell me we've lost touch with the Cawthorne expedition, too," I asked unbelievingly.

"Haven't had a word from them in two weeks. And you know they were supposed to contact us every second day."

"Where were they the last time you heard?" I asked.

"Well, the best I can figure is that they were between Nukutipipi and Marutea in the Tuamotu Archipelago. The last radio communication received by our control ship placed them in that area. We've got to find them," and he pointed his fist on the table so that the test tubes rattled dangerously.

"That's why I'm sending you, Rick. You know all about those Pacific Islands. You were on that expedition that was investigating the resistance of plankton to radioactivity."

"But—wait, doctor…" I interrupted helplessly.

"Now, don't give me any excuses. I've got the boat all set and I'm sending a good crew of men with you. Elaine is going, too. She is so worried about her friend Maria who was on that expedition as Cawthorne's assistant," the doctor paused for a moment and watched me knowingly.

I didn't know that my secret was that well known around the labs. I had a yen for the luscious Elaine from the moment I had caught a glimpse of her beautiful blonde hair and her beautiful body. Around the offices our contacts had been scrupulously polite and circumspect. She transcribed my notes efficiently. She even called me Dr. Manners instead of Rick as most of the girls did. Only once had I felt the touch of fire buried deep within her, when I had accidentally brushed against one magnificent breast. She drew back quickly but her eyes flashed like streaks of passionate lightning.

Needless to say, I was on that ship when it left two mornings after Doctor Ponsonby had talked to me.

Did I call that hulk a ship? It was the most run-down, unseaworthy-looking craft I had ever seen. The cabins were about as big as broom closets and less comfortable. And from the very beginning before we even got out to sea the ship began to roll and pitch as if she were possessed. Since most of the members of our search party were not really good sailors, they spent the first week of our voyage in the unhappy agony of seasickness. And I'm sorry to say my lovely Elaine was no exception.

Thus it was that I didn't even get a chance to speak with her until we hit the smooth seas of the South Pacific. Even then our exchanges consisted of discussions about the weather or "shop talk."

As we approached the area in which two of our expeditions had mysteriously disappeared, I began to confer with the captain as to the best search methods. He said we would have to put into port at the tiny island of Rurutu in order to take on water and food. He suggested that perhaps they would know something of our expeditions there.

The small harbor was alive with activity and color as we moored and the native canoes set out from shore to welcome us. As they drew closer; beautiful golden skinned native girls peeled off their sarongs and dove into the water to swim to the ship. As they began to climb up the ladders on the side of the ship encouraged heartily by the sailors, I saw Elaine grow pale and

The natives had told us the grisly story before we even left port. But we couldn't believe such things existed.

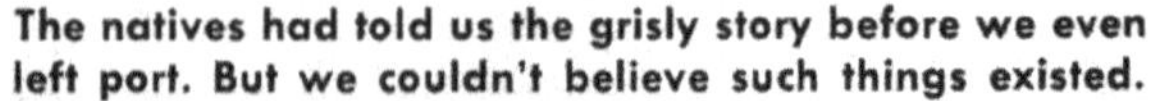

turn away. Their glistening bodies and pink-tipped brown breasts seemed to make her conscious of her own femininity.

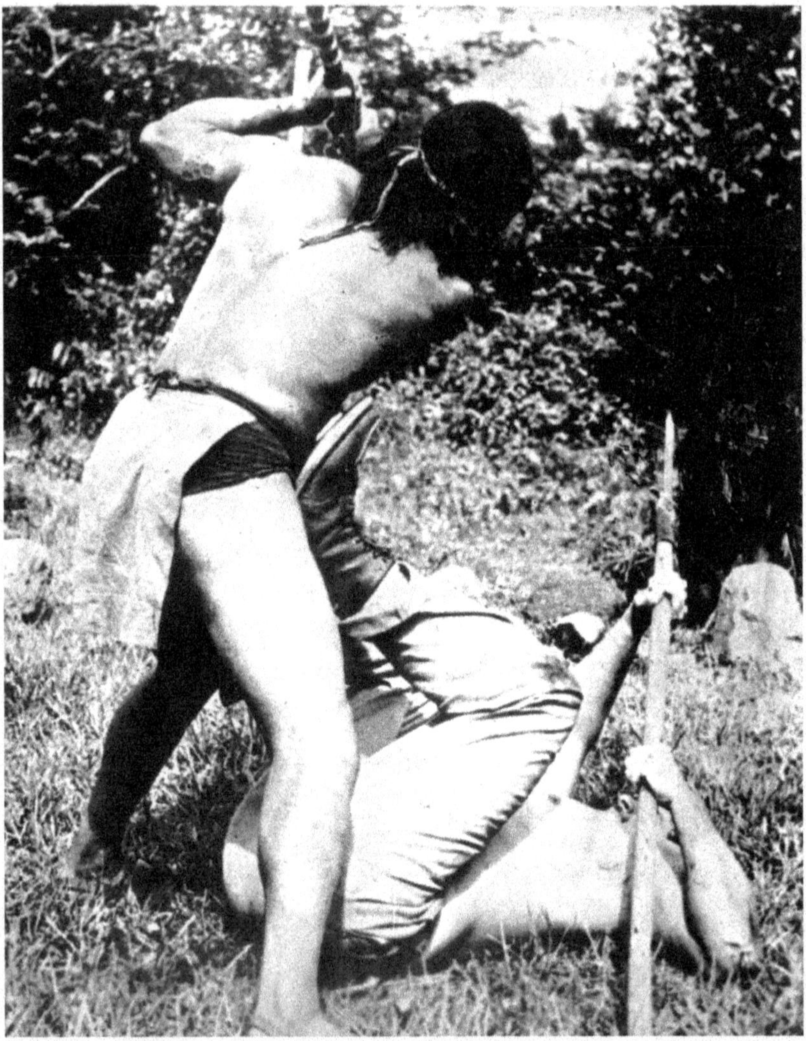

I watched her go below and then turned to find the Captain coming toward me.

"We won't stop here long," he told me. "I've asked some of the natives about your expedition ships and they say that your men were here. Two groups of them." Then he shook his head wonderingly. "All I can get out of them from there on in is that the ships headed off into the direction of

Nukutipipi, which, according to the local gossip, is a very bad place to be headed. Seems as if there's some evil god or something which destroys all ships."

"Then there's another story about the place that I just can't make out," he continued. He beckoned one of the native girls over. Her breasts swayed invitingly as she stepped gracefully to his side showing her even white teeth in a seductive smile.

Her smile became a look of pure terror when he spoke to her. She babbled excitedly, almost hysterically for several moments.

"She says that on one of those islands called Sampali there is a cult of man-eating spiders—tarantulas—I guess. They are tremendous, at least the size of humans, and they feed upon human blood. She says she knows this to be true for her cousin was the only one who escaped out of 20 strong men who had landed on that island a year ago."

The girl quickly darted away still looking frightened. The captain gave a short unconvincing laugh.

"Hell, these crazy natives have a lot of those kind of stories. They're like a bunch of kids with a book of ghost stories."

"I don't know, Captain," I said slowly. "A lot of these 'crazy' native stories have some truth in them. At any rate, that's where we've got to go—to Sampali." Even as I said the word an eerie chill premonition of disaster passed over me.

The disaster began that very night. It must have been about midnight. I had been sleeping restlessly in my narrow bunk. I awoke with a start to see one of my heavy suitcases of equipment just about to descend on my head from a swinging rack overhead. I twisted out of the way just before it came crashing down to splinter the side of the bunk. That could have been my head, I thought shakily. The ship was rolling and pitching as if in the grip of a destructive giant. I got to my feet and struggled out of the cabin. As I entered the corridor, there was a crash louder than the rest and I felt the ship lurch crazily and begin to settle on her side. The lights dimmed but, thank God, stayed on and I made my way but fast towards the cabin I knew was Elaine's. I had to break the door open and I found her sprawled on the floor with a bruise on her temple, where she had struck her head when thrown against the wash stand.

My heart thudded crazily as I bent to listen at her breast, covered only by a filmy nightgown. She came to when I splashed water in her face and chafed her wrists and she grabbed a robe as I hurried her out of the cabin and onto the deck. As we gained the top of the stairs, I saw two life preservers and stopped long enough to fasten them around us. And that was all we had time to do before a tremendous sea swept us over the deck into the swirling ocean. Somehow I had kept hold of Elaine's arm and I gripped it all through the horrible two hours that followed. Later I found that she had a bruise in the exact shape of my clutching fingers.

But she surely would have drowned if I had not held her so tightly. At last the subsiding waves carried us into the safety of a small lagoon. We were washed up on a sandy beach and lay exhausted for nearly an hour before we could even speak.

Finally she turned to me weakly and said faintly, "Thank you, Doctor. I guess I owe you my life."

"Well, then, isn't it about time you started calling me Rick?" I said in answer.

She smiled a little at that and then sat up and looked around. We had been deposited on a small beach which looked like those you see on the travel posters. Its white sand was perfect and the palm trees waved softly in the background. But beyond that was the jungle, dark and menacing and unknown. The sun came up almost as quickly as the click of a light switch and we stood up to better survey our surroundings.

"I wonder if we're the only survivors," Elaine said voicing the fear that had been in my mind.

"Oh, I don't' think so," I answered casually. "I'm sure some of the others must have gotten to shore. I think they must have gotten off the ship before we did."

As I said it I thought darkly that it was very probable that we were the only two people on this island. I had been foresighted enough to snatch my revolver in its waterproof case from my suitcase before leaving the cabin and it was still strapped around my waist. But how long could we last even so?

"Listen, Elaine, I'd like to find out our exact situation so that I know what to start doing in this island paradise," I tried to keep the mood light so as not to alarm her. "I'm going to start exploring right away. I think maybe you'd better come with me if you feel up to it."

She nodded and we set out into the jungle. I made her walk in front of me and I couldn't help but notice the provocative swelling of her buttocks underneath the thin, torn skirt of her robe. She kept trying to pull it together at the top where the creamy whiteness of her breasts were almost completely exposed. Even in the tight spot we were in I could not help feeling a rush of desire claim me. "Stick to business, Rick," I reminded myself. "There'll be time enough for that later."

WE HAD only been walking about ten minutes when we came to a small rocky clearing in the jungle. It was a charming spot with a little waterfall and a crystal clear pool. Above the waterfall was a small cave.

"Looks like this is where we're going to make our headquarters for the time being," I said. "Who could ask for a better spot. Running water and everything," I joked feebly.

I helped her up the rocks to get to the cave and as we entered the gloom, she exclaimed in wonder at the formation of the cave.

"Rick, we really could set up housekeeping here very easily," she said smiling. "Look: there's even a flat rock that we could use as a table. That is if we have anything to eat, Tarzan," she teased me.

"Oh, me heap big hunter," I went along with her game. "Catch many fish in pond," and I pointed down towards the clearing.

"I wonder where it goes," she said wandering towards the back of the niche. I had already started down the rocks to see if there really were any fish in the pond. Her bloodcurdling scream came just as I got to the bottom of the small cliff and I whirled in panic and clawed my way back up to the top.

The grisly, unworldly scene that I saw can never be erased from my mind. For hovering over that blonde, fresh skin and just about to sink its huge fangs in her lovely throat was the ugliest THING I had ever seen, even in nightmares. It was a hairy, black tarantula, its thick obscene body was at least two feet in diameter and its legs extended six feet. The red eyes regarded me with hatred as I drew my revolver fumbling in my haste. It dropped Elaine and lumbered towards me on its long legs. I shot six times into the ugly body before the evil, ugly eyes finally glazed in death. Its legs twitched and thrashed about in the final throes. I leaned against the side of the rock and retched uncontrollably before I was able to go to revive Elaine.

She came to still shuddering in terror and turned her eyes quickly away from the slimy THING. I held her body close to me as she sobbed hysterically in fear and relief.

After she had calmed down I told her of the story the natives had told back in that port we had touched.

"It looks like they knew what they were talking about, after all," I admitted grimly. "Elaine, we've got to get off this island. First of all, we've got to find out if any of the others are here. They might have a boat. We've got to go over this island, now. I know it's going to be tough for you. But we've got to do it."

She clung to me even harder and as the points of her soft breasts dug into me, she lifted her head and looked up at me "I'll do anything you say, Rick," and her blue eyes softened.

I couldn't help it. Her mouth was so close. The aphrodisiac smell of danger was still in the air. My mouth covered those soft lips and my hands sought the twin globes of her breasts. For a moment she thrust her body against mine in surrender. Then reluctantly she pulled away and said softly: "Later, Rick, later. I want it to be good for us."

"You're right, Elaine," I admitted. My heart pounded as I thought of the loveliness that awaited me if we ever got out of this mess.

After we had walked about an hour we found another clump of high rocks—no cave this time, thank God—and we climbed to the top to see if we could see any signs of life. As I stood up breathing hard from the climb, I gave a shout of joy. Not more than half a mile away there was a house—it looked as if it had been transported from old England—a huge gray stone pile with turrets and a moat.

"Elaine," I called down to her. "We're saved. It's okay. There's some kind of a silly castle…and I broke off in mid-sentence. "Oh God, no!"

"What's the matter, Rick?"

"Don't look, darling!"

It was too late. She buried her head in my shoulder with a moan of disgust and despair.

The sight we saw was enough to drive any sane man out of his mind. Clustered around that castle were those hideous, evil tarantulas. Their black hairy legs scurried over the bridge across the moat and their antennae waved as they communicated in some weird way. There must have been 20 of them.

Then everything went black and in my nightmarish unconsciousness the evil red eyes of the tarantulas followed my every move.

WHEN I awoke I found myself in pitch blackness in what must have been some sort of a dungeon in the bowels of the castle. Beside me crouched two of the men who had been on the expedition before us, George Vermeer and Tony Scanelli. I could hardly recognize them, for their bodies were emaciated to the point of starvation and their eyes had the terror-stricken look of the hunted.

"Thank God you're here, Rick. Maybe you can think of something to destroy Dr. Unicorn. He's got to be stopped!" said Tony almost hysterically.

"Wait a minute, wait a minute. Remember, I just got here. I don't have any idea what's going on."

In a hoarse voice which sometimes faded away into a whisper George told me a tale right out of the bloodiest of the horror story books.

The second expedition had been wrecked in much the same fashion as our boat. They had been snatched from the waves in a boat manned by a hunchbacked dwarf and a strange, tall, man in a turban.

"That was our first meeting with Dr. Unicorn," George told me bitterly. "They brought us to this dungeon. At that time, most of the members of the first expedition were still here. It was they who told us about Dr. Unicorn's horrible pets. I never dreamed they could be so ugly until I saw them—those monstruous hairy beasts. And the worst part of it," he continued brokenly, "is that these awful creatures were once beautiful young girls. Dr. Unicorn is an insane scientist who was once jilted by a woman he loved. His theories were ridiculed by the scientific world. This whole set-up is his obscene joke on the civilized world. He performs a delicate operation on these young girls that turns them into tarantulas. He has set up a phony signal on one of the reefs so that any ships venturing near will inevitably crash. Because the one thing he needs is men. Do you know why? Can you guess, Rick?" George was almost shouting in hysteria now. "His female tarantula pets—those hairy black, thick insatiable fiends—feed on living blood of male humans!" and he sank to the floor sobbing.

I sat absolutely still paralyzed by the horror of the story. And then I remembered that this maniac doctor had Elaine.

I shook George's shoulder violently. "What happened to Maria—the girl who was on your expedition. Did he...?"

George only looked up at me and nodded. "She's one of those things now.

The thought of the fair skin and blonde hair being turned into black hairiness made me curse as I have never cursed before. I had to do something to get her out of the clutches of Dr. Unicorn.

"George, do they feed you at regular hours here?" I asked.

"Yes. I guess he figures he's got to give us something to keep us alive."

"Who brings the stuff to you?"

"The hunchbacked dwarf. If you have any ideas about jumping him I'd better warn you he's pretty powerful for his size. One of us tried that the first couple of days we were here and the guy got a broken leg for his pains."

"Well, I think my plan will work." I explained to him. "Are there any other guards?"

"No—just the tarantulas. And they're outside the house most of the time."

I explained my plan to George and the others. Shortly after breakfast the next morning, we were going to have a mass attack of food poisoning. I told the men that it must look as if they were in real agony. They must clutch their stomachs, roll around the floor and kick at the walls. In other words, create a real chaotic scene. At that time there were about 20 men left of the original 40 who had been on the two expeditions. I figured that 20 men rolling around and screaming would cause enough of a mess so that I might be able to do something about escaping and finding Elaine.

It all worked better than I had expected. That dwarf may have been powerful, but he sure was short on brains. When he saw that cell full of men in apparent agony, he got so excited that he forgot to lock the door behind him. He began kicking at the men sprawled on the floor.

In the darkness of the rank dungeon and the excitement I was easily able to slip away. Cautiously I made my way through the huge stone monument Dr. Unicorn had constructed. In my brief survey of the place before being captured I had noticed bright lights at the very top of the tower. If my hunch was right, that was where Dr. Unicorn performed his little experiments.

Step by step I gained my way up the stairs towards the bright lights. As I got closer to the open doorway I heard a wild laugh and Dr. Unicorn's words galvanized me into action.

"You are really the most beautiful of my little pets. It is a pity that those beautiful white breasts will soon be covered with black hair. No, don't struggle, my lovely one. Soon you will feel and know nothing but the hunger for the blood of men."

I raced up the final stairs, my heart pounding with fear. As I burst into the room, the scene that greeted my eyes wrung a cry of panic from me. Elaine was tied to the operating table underneath the glaring lights. Her naked body strained at the ropes as the dark, turbaned man, his eyes glittering, poised a scalpel over the body.

As I leaped at him, he turned with a quick movement and threw the scalpel towards me. It whistled by my ear and Dr. Unicorn grabbed for another among the glittering instruments laid out on the table. With a flying tackle I sent him sprawling among his bottles and jars and a large cut on his face began to bleed profusely. I swung at him in wild, blind anger. And the smooth look on his dark face turned to fright. Turning, he suddenly made a bolt for the stairs. I dragged him back and slugged him with a hard right. He fell against the table and then suddenly he had in his hands a small bottle.

"This bottle contains a powerful explosive," he hissed. "I shall not hesitate to blow us all up if you come closer." As he spoke he backed away from me nervously. Then, suddenly, he tripped over an overturned chair and by some fluke accident crashed through the large window that was directly behind him. The bottle flew from his hands and with a desperate lunge I managed to catch it. I could hear him scream as he fell to the rocks below. And as I looked out of the window I shuddered despite my hatred for him. The smell of the blood from his cut face had driven his "pets" wild and they were systematically devouring him.

Elaine drew closer to me sobbing in relief and terror. I knew we had to get away from that awful, evil island.

Quickly I freed Elaine from the ropes and she slumped in my arms. "Now is our chance. Hurry! Those beasts are busy and we can get by them," I told her as we rushed down the winding staircase.

We were met on the way down by the men from the dungeon who had succeeded in overpowering the dwarf. We hurried out of the gloomy castle and past the vampire tarantulas who were busy with their grisly task of destroying the man who made them.

As we got into the boat which Dr. Unicorn had used for transporting his victims, I glanced at the bottle still in my hand. When we were far enough away from the shore I threw the bottle with all my strength at the cluster of huge, hairy spiders. A mighty explosion threw us all down into the boat and dreadful stink spread over the island as the jungle began to catch fire.

We were guided to land by a native fishing canoe and for three days the natives celebrated in our honor. We had destroyed the dreaded Tarantula Island.

Elaine and I are married now and I must say you will never find a better wife—especially in the housekeeping department. I'll tell you one thing for sure. You'll never find a stray spiderweb in any corner of our apartment.

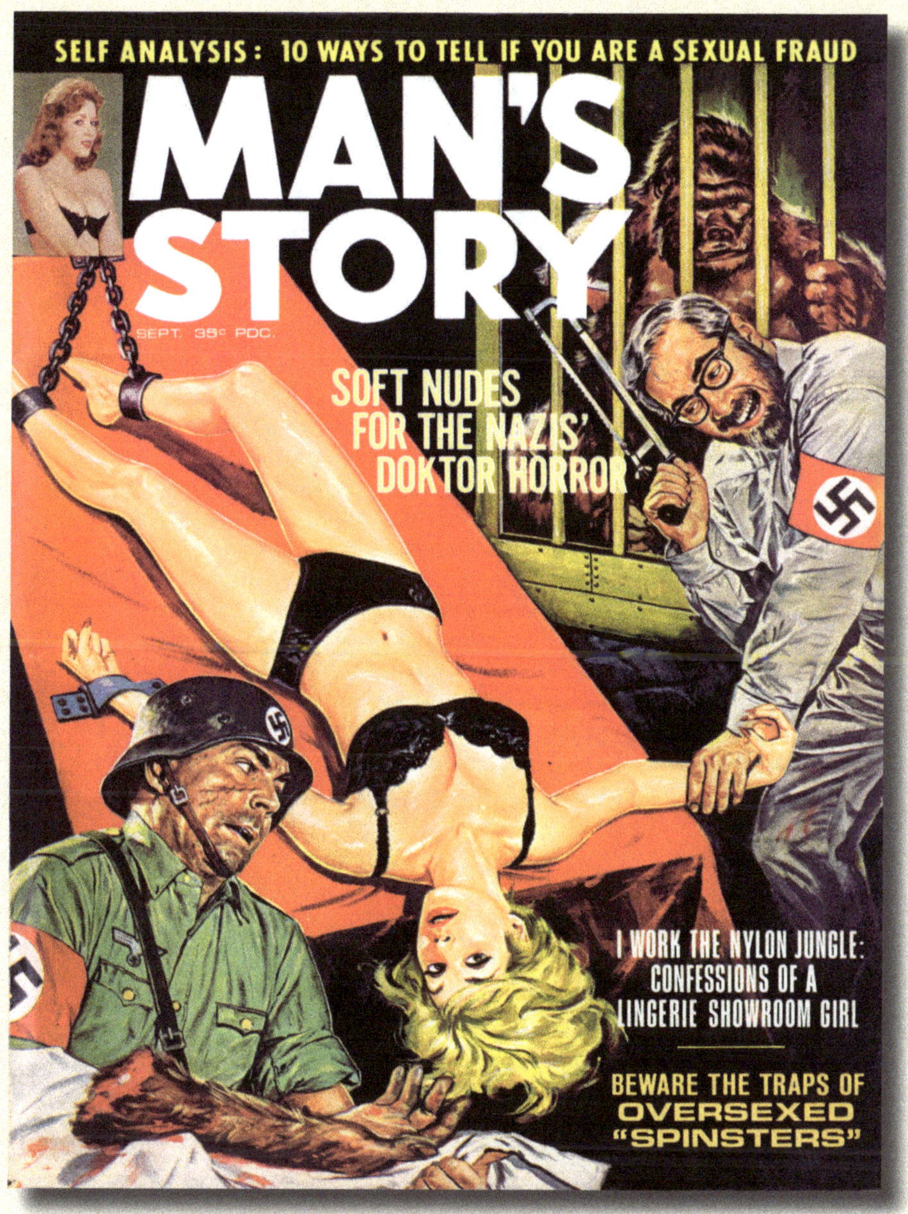

SOFT NUDES FOR THE NAZIS' DOKTOR HORROR

Martin Bowers

Man's Story, September 1964   Cover by Norm Eastman

SOFT NUDES FOR THE DOKTOR HORROR

By MARTIN BOWERS

The beast's severed arm represented the madness of a regime where surgery was butchery and the scream of a woman could fulfill a strange lust.

THE gorilla had received a shot of morphine. The girl who lay chained to the operating table had not. She listened to the rasping surgical saw and the final sickening crack of bone. Before her horrified eyes a geyser of steaming red blood spurted from the portable cage.

Despite the anesthesia, the gorilla thrashed and groaned. By instinct its remaining paw slapped at the stump of what had been his arm.

Fritz Mennecke watched the grisly tableau and grunted in satisfaction. His fingers trailed over the tight silk panties the girl still wore. He watched the paroxysm-like heaving of her conical breasts which threatened to burst the straps of the skimpy bra which covered them. Her flesh was warm and sweet to him despite the sheen of perspiration which covered it.

The Nazi doctor stooped over the straining girl. His yellow teeth shone in the overhead light. "Ach, fraulein, what a pity it is that you are too mad to understand the importance of the scientific research we do here."

The leg irons clanked ominously as the girl fought to free herself of their fearfully cold grip. Her fists clenched and unclenched in futile convulsive movements.

"In the name of heaven, you can't!" she cried through clenched lips. Her answer was the sound of tearing cloth. She felt the last of her clothing being shredded from her young body.

"In the name of science we must," Mennecke snickered. "Our soldiers are dying at the front to make a better Germany. You anti-socials should feel honored to make a contribution to their welfare. Only through experimentation can medicine advance. Do you realize what it will mean if this graft takes hold? Men who have lost their limbs in battle will be able to be fitted with new living prosthesis. But of course you could have no interest in such things. You have been judged insane by a competent board of psychiatrists. I don't know why I waste my time explaining our program to you."

Mennecke's obscene touch traveled up and down the girl's right arm. He probed the tenderness of her young flesh with his dirty fingernails. The girl's head swung from side to side. Her eyes grew wide and fixed as they fastened on the bloody contents of the towel carried by the gross faced guard. The hairy fingers of the gorilla's dismembered limb blotted out all other vision.

An uncontrollable shuddering suffused her. Little tendrils of blood seaped from under the iron cuffs which held her ankles. Mindless shrieks of terror bubbled from her distened mouth as she saw the glint of the surgical saw waving above her. The steel grip of the fetter which held her arm was replaced with the more repulsive clasp of her tormentor. The hot flame of agony burned across her bicep as the saw's teeth grated across her skin. . . .

Two days later the maimed gorilla died of shock. Mennecke had used all the drugs at his command to spare the brute the tortures of its mortal agony.

The girl, the hideous limb firmly affixed to her shoulder by strong sutures remained alive longer. She even regained consciousness long enough to view the hairy hand lying naked beneath its plaster cast across her bosom.

However what Mennecke and any second year medical student had already known proved itself again. The human body will reject any foreign matter attached to it. It may host a kidney from an identical twin, but its immune mechanism will not tolerate a transplant from other humans, let alone other species of mammal.

Mennecke could not have cared less. He sat at the girl's bedside savoring the hideous suffering of his victim, refusing her even the mildest palliative prescription. He watched her skin turn black and her body bloat to three times its normal size as the sepsis flooded slowly to her brain.

He attended her final death throes not as a physician, but as a torture master.

DOKTOR Fritz Mennecke was one of the elite of Nazi medicine during a time when humanity and learning turned back a thousand years to the torture chambers of the middle ages. Together with S.S. Major General Karl Brandt and Dr. Paul Neitsche they formed the infamous *Traveling Circus*.

Where their bloody (Continued on page 56)

34

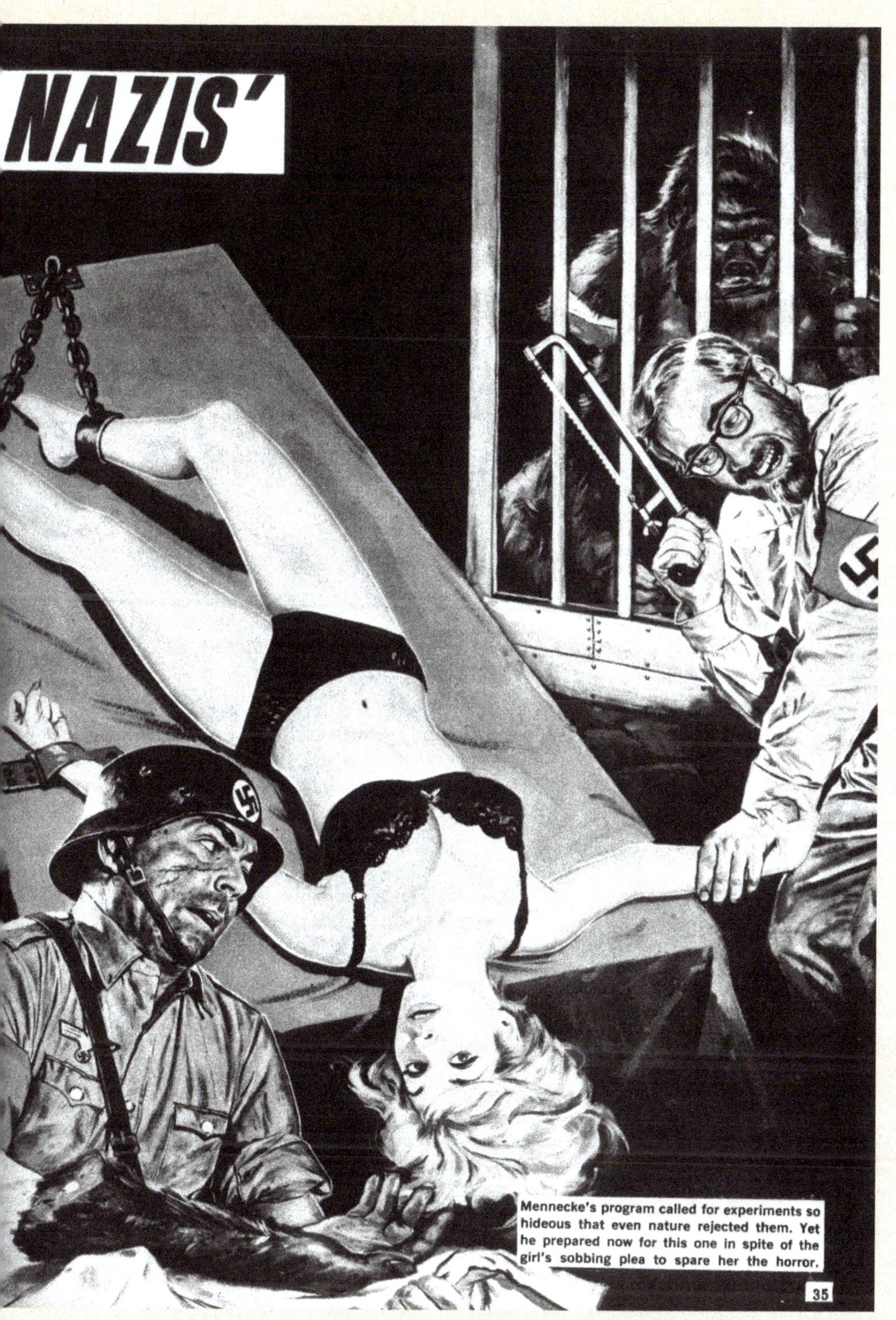

Mennecke's program called for experiments so hideous that even nature rejected them. Yet he prepared now for this one in spite of the girl's sobbing plea to spare her the horror.

ART BY NORM EASTMAN

THE GORILLA had received a shot of morphine. The girl who lay chained to the operating table had not. She listened to the rasping surgical saw and the final sickening crack of bone. Before her horrified eyes a geyser of steaming red blood spurted from the portable cage.

Despite the anesthesia, the gorilla thrashed and groaned. By instinct its remaining paw slapped at the stump of what had been his arm.

Fritz Mennecke watched the grisly tableau and grunted in satisfaction. His fingers trailed over the tight silk panties the girl still wore. He watched the paroxysm-like heaving of her conical breasts which threatened to burst the straps of the skimpy bra which covered them. Her flesh was warm and sweet to him, despite the sheen of perspiration which covered it.

The Nazi doctor stooped over the straining girl. His yellow teeth shone in the overhead light. "Ach, *fraulein,* what a pity it is that you are too mad to understand the importance of the scientific research we do here."

The leg irons clanked ominously as the girl fought to free herself of their fearfully cold grip. Her fists clenched and unclenched in futile convulsive movements.

"In the name of heaven, you can't!" she cried through clenched lips. Her answer was the sound of tearing cloth. She felt the last of her clothing being shredded from her young body.

"In the name of science, we must," Mennecke snickered. "Our soldiers are dying at the front to make a better Germany. You anti-socials should feel honored to make a contribution to their welfare. Only through experimentation can medicine advance. Do you realize what it will mean if this graft takes hold? Men who have lost their limbs in battle will be able to be fitted with new living prosthesis. But of course you could have no interest in such things. You have been judged insane by a competent board of psychiatrists. I don't know why I waste my time explaining our program to you."

Mennecke's obscene touch traveled up and down the girl's right arm.

He probed the tenderness of her young flesh with his dirty fingernails. The girl's head swung from side to side. Her eyes grew wide and fixed as they fastened on the bloody contents of the towel carried by the gross-faced guard. The hairy fingers of the gorilla's dismembered limb blotted out all other vision.

An uncontrollable shuddering suffused her. Little tendrils of blood seeped from under the iron cuffs which held her ankles. Mindless shrieks of terror bubbled from her distended mouth as she saw the glint of the surgical saw waving above her. The steel grip of the fetter which held her arm was replaced with the more repulsive clasp of her tormentor. The hot flame of agony burned across her bicep as the saw's teeth grated across her skin…

Two days later, the maimed gorilla died of shock. Mennecke had used all the drugs at his command to spare the brute the tortures of its mortal agony.

The girl, the hideous limb firmly affixed to her shoulder by strong sutures, remained alive longer. She even regained consciousness long enough to view the hairy hand lying naked beneath its plaster cast across her bosom.

However, what Mennecke and any second year medical student had already known proved itself again: The human body will reject any foreign matter attached to it. It may host a kidney from an identical twin, but its immune mechanism will not tolerate a transplant from other humans, let alone other species of mammal.

Mennecke could not have cared less. He sat at the girl's bedside savoring the hideous suffering of his victim, refusing her even the mildest palliative prescription. He watched her skin turn black and her body bloat to three times its normal size as the sepsis flooded slowly to her brain.

He attended her final death throes not as a physician, but as a torture master.

DOKTOR Fritz Mennecke was one of the elite of Nazi medicine during a time when humanity and learning turned back a thousand years to the torture chambers of the middle ages. Together with SS Major General Karl Brandt and Dr. Paul Neitsche they formed the infamous *Traveling Circus.*

Where their bloody footsteps took them, horror barked at their heels. The prisoners at Buchenwald, at Belsen, at Dachau came to know the unholy three and to smell a new stench of death when they appeared.

Ostensibly they were a touring court of alienists empowered to hold sanity hearings. This was a typical Nazi device for giving acceptable names to the barbarity they perpetrated.

A typical scene upon their arrival at camp would go something like this: The *Traveling Circus* would take over the camp commandant's office. They would seat themselves behind a large table piled high with 14 F 13 forms (the certification of lunacy papers). One by one, the prisoners would be led before them. A few quick questions. A rubber stamp on a printed slip of paper, and the prisoner would be committed to the worst type of death a Nazi mind could conjure up.

Of special interest to the triumvirate of death were the young girls who had been assigned to the officers' brothels of the various concentration camps.

When a girl appeared before their table, she would be ordered to strip for a physical examination. The girl was not even allowed the comfort of a screen to disrobe behind. Instead she divested herself of her clothing with her ears burning from the obscene remarks of the board of alienists.

One survivor of Buchenwald tells of her experience: "I entered the large office, and there were three high Nazi officials seated behind a table. They seemed happy to see that I was still neat, clean, and relatively well fed. I could tell from the way they stared at me that they had no appetite for the regular prisoners. The half-starved cadavers in their striped dresses had long since ceased to resemble women. Their shaved heads and gaunt breasts hid any feminine attributes which remained.

"From the start of my time in Buchenwald, I had been assigned to the officers' brothel. Prior to being arrested by the Gestapo, I had been a nurse in Prague, so I was able to avoid contracting a disease. I was able to take the necessary precautions, well aware that if I hadn't, I would have been shipped off to a chimney. (This is a name given to the concentration camp crematoriums.)

"I had no idea why I had been ordered to the commandant's office, but I had heard that a prisoner who was told to go there was in the utmost danger. However, the kapo in charge of our barracks threatened me with a whipping if I did not obey the command.

"When I arrived, the three men were seated behind a large table. One, I believe it was Brandt, shouted at me to remove my clothing. I looked around for some place to undress. However I realized that they intended for me to strip before them. Even though my body had been defiled by the camp guards, I was still appalled by the necessity of taking my clothes off before three men. Mennecke screamed at me to be on with it.

"I took off my blouse and skirt and stood before them in the delicate panties and bra which had been assigned to the camp *hures*. Dr. Brandt moved to my side. Never have hands ravaged my flesh the way his did as he took off the last of my clothing.

"NITSCHE placed a record on a portable phonograph and I was told to dance. The three men sat with arms folded, sucking their teeth and making the most lewd comments imaginable. At last Nitsche turned to Brandt. "I believe the woman warrants a private interview, Herr Doktor," he said. The other two men laughed and I was told to dress once more.

"A guard appeared at the door and I was taken to another room which had steel bars over the window. The guard stretched my arms high over my head and handcuffed them to the bars. There I waited for several hours, almost going mad with the strain on my shoulders and wrists. I could scarcely reach the floor with my toes.

"At last Brandt came in. He slammed the door shut behind him. He carried a short whip, more of a riding crop than a lash. I'll never forget the sight of him standing in the middle of the floor regarding my straining figure. His mouth was distended, the jaw slack. His face was beet-red. The arteries in his neck stood out.

"Brandt moved towards me like a predatory animal stalking his prey. Suddenly he seized my blouse and tore it from my shoulders. With a practiced precision he stripped me.

"What followed was not the first whipping I had received at Buchenwald. But I had never before been subjected to such pain. Being a physician, Brandt knew all of the most sensitive parts of my body. He was aware of how every one of my nerves would respond to the lash. He could keep punishing me for hours without ever allowing me the mercy of unconsciousness. When he finished, blood covered me from neck to thighs. I could hardly breathe, let alone walk.

"Yet the whipping was only part of what was in store for me. Brandt indicated the bed which waited in the center of the room. I will not say what the next hours did to me.

"At last I was allowed to rest and then told to report to the commandant's office again. When I arrived, Mennecke was holding a printed form. He signed it, stamped it and handed it to me. I was told to report to the guard at the main gate.

"The underground of any concentration camp is an amazing thing. Prisoners learn with the speed of lightning, or they do not survive. As I staggered out into the smokefilled haze of the crematorium chimney which commanded the camp, my arm was seized by a cadaverous little man who trundled a wheelbarrow full of corpses.

"Quickly!" he cried. "There's not a moment to lose!"

"I found myself being shoved under the cadavers. The stench of their bodies almost suffocated me. Their jagged bones dug into my lash wounds.

It was all I could do to keep from screaming as the wheelbarrow trundled over the broken, rutted, rock-strewn ground.

"The man who had saved me told me to hide under the foundation of the clinic hospital. There when night had fallen, a prisoner who had been assigned to the hospital staff came for me. She was a middle-aged woman who managed to remain jolly despite her surroundings.

"She spirited me inside and told me to get into a vacant bed. The mattress still bore the warm imprint of another woman's body. The woman had died only scant moments before. The plan was for me to assume the dead person's identity. This was called *going underground*, and was a method of survival among those marked for torture and death. The callousness of the Nazis played into our hands. They had little use for the wasted corpses which lay all around Buchenwald. Death certificates are not needed when cadavers are to be melted down for soap and fertilizer.

"Had it not been for my two unknown friends. I am absolutely sure that I would have been consigned to some medical experiment in sadism and bestiality."

No one can argue with the belief of the woman prisoner who somehow managed to survive the atrocities of Buchenwald until its liberation in 1945.

For the evidence against the Nazi medical profession defies all reason. Psychiatrists have studied for twenty years now, and have yet to come up with an answer for the Doktors of Death. Nor have statisticians yet reached a satisfactory total of those martyred in the Nazis' network of laboratories of pain.

Had the *Traveling Circus* been an isolated instance, one could find a ready explanation in reflecting on the workings of three madmen who happened to meet by coincidence. There would not be an indictment of a whole nation. France has its Landru, Scotland had its Sawney Beane, England, its Jack The Ripper. But a quick look at the Doktors of Torture indicates that the German Universities as well as the Gestapo and the Wehrmacht were capable of turning out the most grisly of monsters. These "physicians" appeared on the scene in wholesale lots.

Take for example, Obersturmführer Hans Eisele, who also served his post medical-school internship in Buchenwald.

Writing of him, Eugen Kogon says, in *The Theory and Practice of Hell*, "Worst of the criminal type of SS physician was undoubtedly Dr. Eisele. His accomplishments between 1940 and 1943 probably outdid any of the depravities committed by other SS physicians. He too, in order to complete his training, engaged in human vivisection, subsequently killing his victims.

"He would abduct them indiscriminately from the camp streets, take them to the outpatients' clinic, and inject them with apomorphine to gloat over the emetic effect. He performed operations and amputations without the slightest reason. He never used anesthesia."

Eisele, like the *Traveling Circus,* had a special talent for dealing with young and beautiful girls. He too consistently raided the camp brothel for his victims.

A woman who was employed in the clinic gives a graphic description of Eisele's sadism. She says, "If any young and attractive girl were unlucky enough to catch the attention of Eisele, she had sealed her doom. I believe Eisele had a psychopathic hatred of all women. It might be something which stemmed from his relationship with his own mother. Most of his type of aberration have their beginnings in a person's infancy.

"I'll never forget the beautiful girls who were brought to the surgical wing of the hospital. They came trusting the kapos who told them they were merely to have a routine gynecological examination.

"Not until Eisele had stripped them and bound them to the operating table with heavy leather straps did they understand what was about to happen to them. Then they would scream and plead with him. They would beg me to intervene. But had I raised one word of objection, Eisele would have condemned me to a more horrible death even, than the one which awaited them.

"His face was a mask of twisted evil as he lifted his scalpel and traced shallow scratches on their abdomens or some other part of their anatomy. The girls couldn't believe that this needless procedure was about to be carried out on them. It never occurred to them that it was to happen without any type of anesthesia at all."

"My most lasting picture of Eisele is seeing him with head bent over the raw open incision, his eyes squinted, his lips puffed out. He would glance from time to time to the face of the screaming, heaving girl. Then he would hold his scalpel to the light, running his thumb over its gleaming blade like a butcher. Seconds later there would be another shriek, another spurt of blood, another eon of pain.

"I saw Eisele perform every conceivable operation from the amputation of arms and legs to the excision of lungs, stomachs and reproductive organs.

"But I would say that he reached the zenith of his madness when he began his shrunken-head experiments. He brought odd-looking volumes which dealt with South Seas cultures to his office. There he and his colleagues would bend over the books by the hour.

"At last they were ready to begin their experimentation. A girl who could have been no more than nineteen was brought from the sex stable

and ordered to disrobe. She was bound face down to the operating table
with her head extending over its edge. Perhaps the instruments were dull
or Eisele was nervous; it doesn't matter which caused it, but it took the girl
over twenty minutes to die. All the time, blood gushed from the hacked out
wounds on the back of her neck. Even after the poor thing's head rolled
free, her arms and legs continued to twitch under the straps. I believed that
at any moment I would go mad with the scene before me."

There are varying accounts of how many prisoners lost their lives
before the cannibal head-shrinking techniques were perfected. However,
shrunken human heads began to appear in offices of Nazi camp personnel.
They were used as paper weights and other types of ornaments. When the
camp was finally liberated, a few of these heads became part of the damning
evidence against the German medical profession gone mad.

Each of the major German concentration camps had its Doktor
Torture. None was worse than Luftwaffe Kapitan Sigmund Rascher.
Rascher was a personal favorite of Reichminister Heinrich Himmler. Dr.
Rascher's diseased mind dreamed up the infamous freezing experiments
where male victims were submerged in ice water until all signs of life had
vanished. Then various forms of resuscitation were attempted, including
the use of naked women placed under covers with the victim.

With diabolical Nazi thoroughness, Rascher wrote detailed accounts of
the work. He recommended that only one girl be assigned to each frozen
victim. He said, "We find that when two women are placed in the same bed
with one man, their actions become inhibited."

Himmler traveled to Rascher's laboratory many times to take part in the
festivities. Other high Nazi voyeurs also paid frequent visits. Rascher's stock
with the Reichsführer grew by leaps and bounds. He might have reached the
top, had he not pulled a fraud concerning his own virility.

Rascher informed Himmler that he had become a father three times
after having reached the age of 49. In turn he was roundly congratulated by
his superior. However Rascher was to learn what a Nazi execution was like
first hand when he and his wife were condemned for having kidnapped three
children to pass off as their own.

After Rascher's death, there were others to carry on his work. No account of the Doktors of Torture is more graphic or more terrifying than
this which was given by a witness to the War Crimes Tribunal:

"I have personally seen through the observation window of the decom-
pression chamber when a prisoner inside would stand in a vacuum until her
lungs ruptured… They would go mad and pull out their own hair in an effort to relieve the pressure. They would tear their heads and faces with their

fingers and nails in an attempt to maim themselves in their madness. They would beat the walls with their hands and heads and scream in an effort to relieve the pressure on their eardrums. These cases usually ended in death."

This is the monument that the medical profession of a nation gone mad left behind to itself.

WEIRD
WEIRD
STRANGE · FANTASTIC · TRUE
MAY / 35c
WHEN THE DEVIL KEPT HIS PROMISE
I INTERVIEWED A ZOMBIE
May 1956
Art by Jon Martin

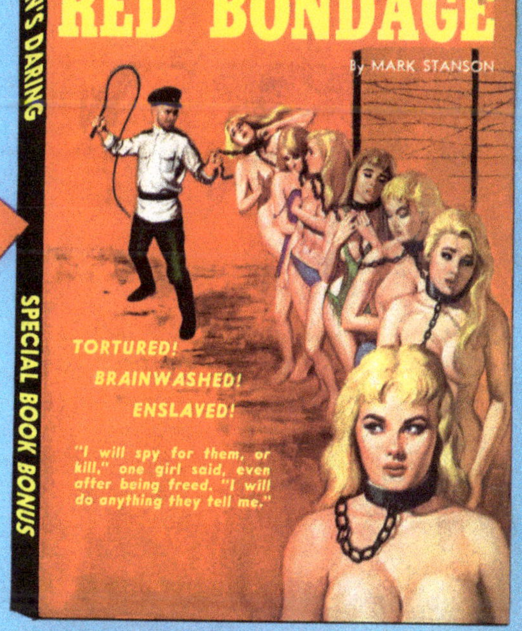

STONE AGE LUST—TODAY

Goeffrey Costain

Man's Daring, July 1965   Cover by John Duillo

STONE AGE LUST --

I GNASHED MY TEETH in anger and sheer frustration, and jerked helplessly at the rawhide bonds tearing into my wrists and ankles. I had to get away quick, or in a few minutes it would be too late for both of us.

Already, they were lashing Doris to the tablerock to the accompaniment of a ritual chant . . . a solemn chant of death. They completely ignored the choked sobs and hysterical pleadings of the girl. They just continued—stony-faced and chanting—to fasten her nude body to the large stakes in the rock.

Then I lost control.

"In the name of decency!" I yelled at them. "Let her go. She's done nothing to you. Are you all mad?"

The long-robed cultists, surveying the grisly scene before them, turned and glared at me, as if I had committed a grave sacrilege. A deft signal from one of them brought a hooded giant running toward me brandishing a thick lash. Another sign brought the bearded torturer's whip into play.

I saw his cruel face light   (Continued on next page)

18

By GOEFFREY COSTAIN

The first light struck the monoliths and a cultist jabbed a torch at Doris.

ILLUSTRATION BY JOHN DUILLO

EDITOR'S NOTE: *Mr. Costain, an archeologist for a London university, unfolds this terrifying tale of his most harrowing assignment…an assignment which almost cost him his life.*

I GNASHED my teeth in anger and sheer frustration, and jerked helplessly at the rawhide bonds tearing into my wrists and ankles. I had to get away quick, or in a few minutes it would be too late for both of us.

Already, they were lashing Doris to the tablerock to the accompaniment of a ritual chant…a solemn chant of death. They completely ignored the choked sobs and hysterical pleadings of the girl. They just continued— stony-faced and chanting—to fasten her nude body to the large stakes in the rock.

Then I lost control.

"In the name of decency!" I yelled at them. "Let her go. She's done nothing to you. Are you all mad?"

The long-robed cultists, surveying the grisly scene before them, turned and glared at me, as if I had committed a grave sacrilege. A deft signal from one of them brought a hooded giant running toward me brandishing a thick lash. Another sign brought the bearded torturer's whip into play.

I saw his cruel face light up with rapture as he leaned back and sent the steel-balled end of the whip whirring into my naked body. The searing pain came a second after the lash ripped into my flesh. I convulsed, and howled piteously. Cold sweat poured in torrents from my forehead.

Seeing that I was in for an ordeal, I gritted my teeth and waited for the next blow. It came straight at my face, tearing raw flesh from my nose and lips. I screamed myself hoarse through the blood dripping all over my chin.

The sadist, his hood falling from his thick head, let me have it again and again—in the shoulders and chest, and the more tender parts of my body— hoping to make me cry for mercy. But I disappointed him by passing out

274

from pain.

When I came to, Doris was bound to the tablerock. Her buoyant breasts rose and fell with terror.

My own body felt as though it had been torn apart. I was burning up with fever, and I throbbed all over with pain.

I watched them pile branches and dry leaves at the prisoner's feet on the top of the huge stone slab. From my knowledge of these fanatic cultists, I knew what was coming next. Racked with pain, I thought back to how Doris and I first got into this mess.

Three days before, I had been lounging in a London newspaper office waiting for a murder case newsbreak. I have been a research specialist in the field of archeology for my university for the past ten years, and knew that something important to my work might come clicking over the tickertape.

Then it came through. I waited till the ticking stopped and the yellow tape stopped feeding out of the glass dome of the machine. Tearing off the tape, I read the message:

Fourth mystery slaying uncovered in Wiltshire—Link to ancient druid rites at Stonehenge suspected.

I had been following a series of mystery murders in the south of England, but this was the first clue in months. I had always been fascinated by the naturistic rites of the ancient druids and was a frequent visitor at Stonehenge, just an hour-and-a-half's drive out of London. I always enjoyed the intense feeling of awe and even terror which came from standing in the open country, dotted with old, gnarled trees of centuries ago, and regarding the towering stone monoliths…silent and foreboding.

I was well aware of the frenzied love rites and rituals of the terrible human sacrifices which took place there in the third and fourth centuries. Enemies of the druid sect, lawbreakers, and beautiful young virgins were tortured, mutilated and then burnt to death.

The burning was carried out rather uniquely. The shrieking victim was trussed up and thrown across the flaming altar. Within one minute, the body was reduced to ashes.

Excited by the exclusive story of a modern cult of druids, I returned to my own office and began loading my tripod, cameras and other equipment into my car. Then I notified my department head that I was bound for Stonehenge.

"Jeff Costain! You can't go without me and you know it."

It was Doris Chandler, an associate professor of anthropology, but a real live wire. Not a man's eyes remained on his work when Doris's ripe, full body passed through the school. And there wasn't a man on the faculty staff who secretly didn't picture his hands roaming over her well defined shoulders and back…who didn't imagine his fingers exploring her neck and hair till she begged to be loved.

Doris was a woman clear through, and reactions like these were common to any red-blooded man. And Doris knew it. She knew just how to move that body in front of a man to turn him to a mass of aroused jelly. Then he'd do anything her little heart desired.

"Look, Doris," I told her firmly, "I'd take you along ordinarily, but this might be a lot rougher than you think."

"Oh, really, Jeff?" she mocked, removing her jacket and sauntering up to me alluringly. Suddenly I realized that we were alone in my office, and my heart began to pound.

Now she began playfully to rub her mature thighs against my knee.

"You sure you can't take me, Jeff?" she asked seductively, wedging her warm body solidly between my knees.

I didn't answer her. Instead, I grabbed her around the waist and crushed her against my chest. My heart was pounding like a drum, and I knew I must have her there and then. My hand groped inside her blouse.

"That couch over there…" she sighed. "Let's lie down…"

In seconds we were stretched out on the divan. Our arms found each other, and our lips met and clung together. Through it all, I knew Doris was going with me to Stonehenge….

I started when the office phone rang. Stroking Doris's arm tenderly, I lazily reached over and took the receiver off the hook.

"Jeff, Brewster of Scotland Yard here," the voice crackled. "Look, I've got something special for you down here at Stonehenge. How soon can you make it?"

"Give me two hours," I told him, and hung up. In twenty minutes, Doris and I were inside my MG, speeding south toward Wiltshire and… Stonehenge.

We arrived in less than two hours, and the Scotland Yard detective who phoned was on the spot to meet us.

"Costain, I have a chap here that you'd be interested in meeting. But please don't let his present condition upset you. I hope you have a strong stomach."

The policeman then led us into a small inn on the outskirts of Salisbury. Following him into a back room, we found a man sitting in a straight-backed chair, staring out the window.

The detective prodded him gently in the shoulder, and he slowly turned around. He was about thirty-five, with a weatherbeaten face and a shock of thick hair falling over his forehead. His eyes looked through us, not at us, and they conveyed an unmistakable impression that he had suffered an unspeakable ordeal…an ordeal that brought him face to face with death.

"…They'll like her…" he babbled incoherently, "beautiful…good body…burn, burn, burn…gods will be pleased…council of elders…druids…"

Druids! What on earth could the ancient sacrificial sect have to do with this poor deranged fellow, I wondered. The only way to find out was to drive out to the Stonehenge site itself and look around. Thanking the policeman, I loaded my camera with a fresh roll of 35mm and left with Doris for Stonehenge.

The first few minutes were taken up with shooting different angle shots of the towering stone monuments. I trudged through the breezy fields and wondered if there was a connection between the murders and the poor fellow I met in the inn.

Suddenly, I realized that Doris wasn't in sight. Before I could call out for her, a scream pierced the stillness of the Salisbury countryside. It was Doris.

I dropped my camera, and dashed in the direction of her voice. Darting in and out of the broken rows of giant stone slabs, I called Doris's name. But I was answered only by the gentle whine of the dry wind.

Then I came near the end of the horseshoe-shaped circle of monoliths, and didn't know where to turn next in my search. I heard crackling of dry brush behind me, but I spun around too late. Something came crashing down on the back of my head with terrific force. My brain exploded and I saw colors flashing. Then I passed out.

The first thing I was aware of when I regained consciousness was the presence of many people. I heard the buzzing of countless voices and sensed people moving around in front of me. I also got a whiff of a strange aromatic odor…something like incense. Then my eyes cleared, and I gasped at the sight before me.

The druids! Hundreds of bearded men and long-haired women moved in a wide circle around me, chanting old haunting Saxon folk melodies in a dull monotonous voice. But the striking feature of the participants was that they were completely unclothed. Their nude bodies undulated gracefully to their weird refrain, and they stared before them as though they were unaware of my presence.

Then feeling returned to my arms and legs, and I realized that I was securely tied to one of the huge stones. Looking down, I saw that they had stripped me clean of clothing and had scented my body with sweet smelling herbs and spices. I strained at my bonds, but they had done a first-class job of tying me, and I soon gave up.

Straining my head to the side, I spotted Doris. They also had her cruelly lashed to one of the big slabs. Her clothes had been torn from her body, and—to my horror—I saw that they were readying her for the dreaded druid fertility rites. We sure saved them a lot of trouble in hunting for fresh sacrificial victims, I told myself ironically.

"Jeff! For heavens sake, make them stop!"

Four of the unclothed men had advanced on the girl with stone mortars filled with blue paint. Doris squirmed uncomfortably when she saw what they were going to do. Each of the four now dabbed his fingers deep into the receptacle until they were dripping with the blue solution.

Then the first part of the dreaded ceremony began. They started smearing the paint down Doris's writhing body in broad, professional strokes. The whole scene made me disgusted and livid with rage.

Doris managed to summon up some courage, I noticed, as they finished swathing her nude body in gleaming blue. Her proud breasts heaved defiance in the face of her tormentors. She didn't have to be told what was coming next.

Then I realized that the four men with the blue paint were the head priests of this insane ritual. Untying the girl, three of them forced their struggling victim to the ground and held her fast on her back. The fourth by now had gotten hold of a long, thick whip from one of the women. The chanting became louder and more intensified as the love priest prepared to

She was stripped and prepared for death by fire.

Illustration by Charles Fracé

administer the ceremonial three lashes to the intended victim of the fertility sacrifice. I turned away, and squeezed my eyes shut.

Doris's first shrill scream tore through my head, and bounced faintly off the distant hills. The girl's pain hit me in the pit of my stomach, and I thought I was going to heave up. Again I tried to pull loose, but only succeeded in burning my wrists with the rawhide.

Then the first of her torturers—his sunken eyes gleaming with passion—flung himself onto the helpless girl's prostrate body. She sobbed hysterically and weakly tried to turn away from the revolting creature on top of her.

The circle of chanting druids was revolving round and round now, whipped into a frenzy by the brutal ravishing taking place before them. Then I noticed that Doris stopped struggling, allowing the druid to take his pleasure…

The other three love priests followed, leaving the girl's limp body before them on the ground for a few minutes. The chanting came to a crashing silence, as the four leaders uttered some ancient incantations over Doris's barely breathing body. Then they lashed her in preparation for the sacrifice. After I regained consciousness from my beating and saw Doris hoisted to the top of one of the huge slabs, I was determined to get us both out of this seemingly hopeless situation. It would be a slow, painful procedure, but I got started.

I BEGAN slowly and deliberately rubbing my rawhide bonds against the rough edges of the slab to which I was tied. It must have been an hour and a half before I weakened them enough to break them.

I didn't have long to wait until one of the nude female members of the sect strolled near enough to me to grab hold of. She started a loud yelp, but I cut it off by throwing my arm around her throat from behind and shutting off her windpipe. She gurgled for breath and kicked violently to get away. I seized her firmly around her lithe waist and hung on.

"I'm the daughter of one of the elders," she wheezed through closed throat. "They'll kill you for this!"

"They'll kill both of us anyway," I snapped at the struggling woman, "so you'd better yell for them to untie Doris, or you're as good as dead."

She stopped struggling and nodded that she'd do as I commanded. I loosened my arm a bit so that she'd be able to speak.

"Well, go ahead," I barked, prodding her in the back.

Then she turned toward the rest of the druids, who were staring at Doris atop the slab.

"Everyone…listen to me! We must release the girl at once, or I die at the hands of an intruder."

The whole crowd, as a unit, whirled around and stared unbelievingly for a few seconds. Then an angry murmuring rose and the druids began surging toward me and my captive. As a warning I meant business, I again tightened my hold on the girl's throat.

"Tell them again," I snapped.

She quickly nodded, and called out to the advancing ritualists, "Please! Get back and do as I say, or he'll kill me!"

After a minute of confused grumbling, the angry druids shuffled back toward the stone monument to which Doris was tied. They reluctantly undid the thongs holding the girl's feet together, and stood aside.

I walked steadily into the mass of enraged worshippers, dragging the girl along with me. Still holding my right arm around the druid's windpipe I ordered a few of them to help Doris to her feet. She had regained consciousness, and I could see that, in spite of the ordeal her aching body had gone through, she'd be able to make it to the car.

"All right," I said· coldly, "two of you help her to my car. And be gentle, or this druid girl will suffer."

Two OF the closest men gazed at me bitterly, and moved forward to help Doris to her feet. Taking no chances, I pulled the angry young druid spitfire across the fields of stone monoliths, until we reached my car.

After I saw that Doris was placed sitting in the front seat, I made our would-be killers get us some adequate clothing. I threw some feminine garments over to Doris, slipped on a pair of shorts, and let go of the druid girl.

Even as I started up the motor, the cursing woman I had held only seconds before, lunged at me. But before her fist could connect with my face, I threw the auto into gear and shot out toward the main road, leaving the girl in the dust.

I shot up the road with the pedal down to the floorboard, until I came to the first police station, just off the highway. I sputtered out our story to six wide-eyed constables, and in minutes had the whole precinct—with Doris and myself leading them—rushing back to Stonehenge.

As I expected, there wasn't a soul in sight. But the ominous stench of burning flesh met our noses.

"Look, Jeff," said Doris, pulling on my sleeve, "the altar."

We all ran over to the main sacrificial altar in the middle of the group of giant stones. There was still a trace of flame from a fire built about half an hour before, and smoke poured from the structure's brim.

But we all stopped short when we got to the altar. Doris winced and buried her head in my chest. The police and myself just stared

Cultists waited quietly for the light that meant doom.

Artist not credited

unbelievingly. The charred remains of a woman were thrown over the flame, and created an unbearable odor. The shriveled, blackened skin stretched tight over the burnt bones. I took Doris away from Stonehenge as the police disposed of the body.

My instincts told me somehow that it was the body of the girl I had grabbed as a hostage. The druids had their hideous sacrifice after all.

July 1962
Art by Earl Norem

KILLER OF THE CAVE

Gene Preen

Adventure, April 1966   Cover by Shannon Stirnweis

IT TURNED A MAN INTO A KILLER-BEAST, AND NEWMAN TRACKED IT DOWN UNTIL HE STOOD FACE-TO-FACE WITH IT . . . THEN HE HAD NO CHOICE BUT TO DIE

KILLER
of the
CAVE

■ Like a man drugged, Don Newman had been sitting on the soft earth outside the mouth of the underground cave, looking into the distance. Hope had left his eyes, even the fear that had replaced it, and now they stared blankly as though a shade had been lowered behind them to shut out the scene—the scene of a world that had ended, a world that had been scorched clean of all living things, both evil and good, with atomic power unleashed by men's hatred.

The soft loam beneath him was just a strip around the cave, all that was left in existence. Beyond it the strangely crystalline sand, that only a month earlier had been the same loam verdant with foliage before it had been transformed by the alchemy of atomic fission, stretched endlessly toward the horizon where warped, naked steel girders marked the grave of a city. In the lowering twilight the sand had begun to glow weirdly. It became a sea of cold luminescence and in it the host of charred white skeletons of men and animals lay half submerged like ghostly swimmers struggling to reach his small island of life. And the cave had been a real island of life in that vast deluge of death. Its natural magnetic ore had been an impermeable fortress shielding him and his companions against the bombardment of nuclear radiation. But death had long known other ways of killing.

A chill suddenly shook Newman's motionless figure. His eyes cleared and he turned to look down the strip of earth toward a spot where a number of graves were marked by shallow mounds. Originally there had been eight people, including Newman himself. All had miraculously escaped the holocaust, and had been the last living creatures on the world. Now six of them lay buried there. Murdered! By an inhuman creature spawned by the same radiation they had escaped.

For a minute Newman shook his head insanely from side to side as though trying to dislodge the memory from his brain. Alice! Would she ever forgive him!

As he struggled to his feet a photograph dropped from his pocket, a portrait of the killer taken with the camera he'd rigged as a trap. He picked it up, looked at it. The face of a monster leered back at him. In a frenzy he tore the photograph to shreds and (Continued on page 75)

ART BY BASIL GOGOS

LIKE A man drugged, Don Newman had been sitting on the soft earth outside the mouth of the underground cave, looking into the distance. Hope had left his eyes, even the fear that had replaced it, and now they stared blankly as though a shade had been lowered behind them to shut out the scene—the scene of a world that had ended, a world that had been scorched clean of all living things, both evil and good, with atomic power unleashed by men's hatred.

The soft loam beneath him was just a strip around the cave, all that was left in existence. Beyond it the strangely crystalline sand, that only a month earlier had been the same loam verdant with foliage before it had been transformed by the alchemy of atomic fission, stretched endlessly toward the horizon where warped, naked steel girders marked the grave of a city. In the lowering twilight the sand had begun to glow weirdly. It became a sea of cold luminescence, and in it the host of charred white skeletons of men and animals lay half submerged like ghostly swimmers struggling to reach his small island of life. And the cave had been a real island of life in that vast deluge of death. Its natural magnetic ore had been an impermeable fortress shielding him and his companions against the bombardment of nuclear radiation. But death had long known other ways of killing.

A chill suddenly shook Newman's motionless figure. His eyes cleared and he turned to look down the strip of earth toward a spot where a number of graves were marked by shallow mounds. Originally there had been eight people, including Newman himself. All had miraculously escaped the holocaust, and had been the last living creatures on the world. Now six of them lay buried there. Murdered! By an inhuman creature spawned by the same radiation they had escaped.

For a minute Newman shook his head insanely from side to side as though trying to dislodge the memory from his brain. Alice! Would she ever forgive him!

As he struggled to his feet a photograph dropped from his pocket, a portrait of the killer taken with the camera he'd rigged as a trap. He picked it up, looked at it. The face of a monster leered back at him. In a frenzy he tore the photograph to shreds and flung the pieces to the empty world. Without turning on his flashlight he stumbled into the dark mouth of the cave.

As he groped his way down the long stone ramp leading to the main cavern, voices seemed to whisper to him from the darkness, voices of the countless curious sightseers who had once traveled great distances to experience the mysteries of this underground fairyland where a subterranean stream flowed uphill, and where they could strap metal soles on their shoes so they could walk upside down on its polished ceiling, and where their car keys would float in the air by themselves, perfectly balanced between the ore's magnetic fields. He and the others had constituted the last party of visitors. Alice, his fiancée, had been one of them. His job with the Homicide Division had become hectic with all the recent foreign intrigue, but she had persuaded him to take the trip. The others he'd come to know too well in the days that followed the sudden start, and equally sudden end, of the suicidal A-war. Now he wished that he had died mercifully in it.

He had felt the tremors in the earth when the first bombs were dropped in some distant country, but thought he was imagining them because there was something about the cave that gave everybody strange sensations. That's what the guide had said. Then one bomb fell nearby. How near? A hundred miles would have been close enough. The cave was shaken as though by a giant hand and its occupants were hurled across the floor.

After that there was a moment of stupefied silence. Then panic. Everyone rushed to the cave's mouth and saw the world give its last convulsive shudder.

It was amazing that most of them kept their sanity. Two didn't. The guide ran screaming across the earthen moat surrounding the cave, vanished into the molten cauldron beyond. The nurse from the first-aid room followed him. Perhaps to try to save him? Newman never found out. He ran after her, clutched her arm as she reached the edge, released it when the overflow of radiation struck him like a blast from a giant blowtorch.

The survivors returned underground then. There was little conversation. Everyone was too stunned, and walked around like zombies. Newman recognized their symptoms, had seen them in another war that hadn't been as total, and he feared them. When their shock eventually wore off, there would come the full realization of what happened, and then all hell would break loose.

To forestall it, there had to be some stabilizing influence, someone who could supply a straw of hope which these trapped people could grasp. Perhaps he could do it, since he'd been through it before. He assembled them in a small wooden structure at one end of the cave which had served as a first-aid room and a kind of commissary.

THERE was stocky, bearded Vladimir Simonoff of the Russian Diplomatic Service who seemed as surprised as anyone else that "it" finally had happened. And F. Raymond Pyne of the US Consulate's office, a fragile slip of a man who couldn't conceal his suspicion of the Russian. A mustached, swarthy Dr. Raoul Mitvini—doctor of what, Newman never had a chance to discover—had brought his pretty, blonde nurse, Katy Allen, on the tour. Her exact relationship to the doctor was unknown but suspect. And there were two teenagers, a boy and a girl. The latter was more scared than Newman had ever seen anyone, but the boy was obviously unfriendly, had sullen furtive eyes, and refused any information except that his name was John and the girl's Mary.

Newman looked them over grimly. Besides Alice and himself there were these four men and two women.

"All of you know what happened—outside. We're alive because this place is somehow impervious to radiation. And no reason why we shouldn't continue to live.

"The stream comes from inside the earth. It should be uncontaminated by radiation, therefore fit to drink. It contains fish." He remembered reading in the brochure that the stream contained hordes of blind cave fish. "That will provide us with food to supplement the commissary's provisions when they run out. And since the electric lights are still on, there must be a power plant somewhere. I suggest we explore every corner of the cavern and collect everything usable."

From the manner in which they took up the search, Newman knew the crisis had been averted, at least temporarily. And the items they found gave additional encouragement. With the diesel power plant were a dozen fifty-gallon drums of oil, enough to keep the cavern lighted until its occupants were sufficiently adjusted to tolerate rationing it. Also several flashlights, one of which he shoved into his pocket. A closet behind the commissary was packed with canned food, probably stashed away by the guide for an emergency.

Three weeks passed uneventfully. But there persisted an atmosphere of tension, a strange barrier to friendliness, among the survivors. Newman tried to relieve it by creating diversionary interests, and received no cooperation.

The doctor and his nurse kept to themselves, carrying on whispered conversations, as did the teenagers. The Russian spent his time avoiding everyone, especially the little American diplomat, and the latter seemed angry with everyone for not recognizing that the Russian was to blame for everything.

THAT night the first murder occurred. The diesel generator had been turned off. Sometime toward morning the cave was awakened by hoarse shouts in Russian. Newman switched on his flashlight. Simonoff and Pyne, the American, were rolling around on the floor, the latter's fingers clutching the Russian's throat. With the help of the doctor he pulled the men apart.

"Look! Look!" Pyne screamed, pointing. "He did it!"

Newman shifted the beam of his light. It fell on a still figure lying face up, nearby. The boy! Newman bent over him. A glance told him he was dead. His throat had been torn open, either by human hands or the claws of a beast.

With the generator started and the lights on, Newman sat with his back to the cave wall, Alice clutching him tightly, while he tried to think. The murderer was one of the five, of course, since there were no beasts. But which of them was physically capable of tearing out a man's throat?

Newman questioned everyone. No one had seen anything immediately prior to the murder. They had all been asleep. Pyne denied emphatically he'd done it, looked at his accuser as though Newman had suddenly gone mad. There was nothing Newman could do without proof. He decided to wait. They buried the body in the earth outside the cave. Then there was the second murder on the following night.

IT WAS Pyne. His throat had been torn out, as had the boy's. Now Newman was sure he knew the identity of the murderer. Who else could it be but Simonoff? Obviously he had killed Pyne to quiet him. It took both Newman and the doctor to subdue the husky Russian sufficiently to put handcuffs on him. Then with a rope they tied him to the metal guard rail of the ramp.

A trial was planned for the next morning, everyone participating, and if found guilty Simonoff would be given a choice. Either he would walk voluntarily into the radioactive no man's land beyond the cave or he would be thrown into it. Newman hoped he would choose the former. And as they buried the second body, Newman prayed fervently it would be the last.

Sometime during the day he suddenly remembered once having seen Pyne with a Polaroid camera, the kind that produced a self-processed picture in a minute, and it had had a flash attachment on it. If he could find it he could secretly set it so its lens would take in the spot where Dr. Mitvini slept, also the place where Simonoff was tied and even the door of the room where the women would be sleeping. And he could attach a heavy thread to its shutter release, stretching it across the cave floor in such a way that if any of them got up during the night and walked into the thread, it would trip the shutter and take the person's picture. Such a device would be a good precautionary measure on the slight chance that Simonoff might be innocent and the murderer might decide to strike again.

Newman searched for Pyne's outfit, found it and when he was sure the rest were asleep that night, he rigged it up as he'd planned. For a long time he lay with his hand on his revolver before he dozed off.

In the morning Simonoff was dead, killed the same way, without uttering a sound anyone had heard. They didn't find him until the lights had been turned on. The thread to the camera was intact. Somehow the course the murderer had taken had avoided it. As soon as Newman saw the body, without hesitation he drew his revolver and held it on the doctor.

The man was the only logical suspect that remained. Surely neither the girl nor the nurse, the pretty blonde, would be able to commit such murders of violence. Newman had just transferred the handcuffs from the dead Russian to the doctor and tied him to the rail in spite of his protests, when the nurse appeared.

She quickly saw what had happened, sprang at Newman like a tigress, fought him with the strength of a maniac. It was all Newman could do to hold her wrists with their wildly clawing fingers. With blood running from numerous scratches on his arms and face, he led her to the first-aid room where he gave her a sedative. And giving his revolver to his fiancée with instructions to watch her, he left and climbed the ramp toward the entrance. Somehow the daylight of the old dead world seemed a refuge from the darkness of the dying one, which reeked of fresh death.

For a long while he sat outside. The sun shone as a fuzzy disk through the high clouds of dust that had mushroomed up from the atomic explosions and were still circulating across the stratosphere. As he watched them he remembered a term nuclear scientists had used, "radioactive fallout." Regardless of what they'd meant by it, now he had his own definition. They were the fallout, he and the others who had escaped the radioactivity. Escaped for what? To play cat and mouse with a homicidal killer. There were five left.

He could have prevented two of the murders if he'd guessed right the first time. But now he had the doctor, and he couldn't be wrong. Who else was there? The nurse and the teenage girl. But if he were wrong once more! Impossible!

Even so, that night he set up the camera again, focused directly at his prisoner. And he tried desperately, but in vain, to keep awake.

The next morning there was the fourth victim, throat torn, crumpled on the floor between Alice and the girl. It was the nurse. Newman didn't know what to do or say. He was totally confused, and for the first time fear began to distort his reasoning. His fiancée and the girl became hysterical when they realized how close death had come to them. Newman gave each a sedative from the first-aid kit, then took one himself.

He fought to clear his brain. As his nerves grew calmer, one fact gradually became plain: It was that the doctor was innocent. He couldn't have killed his nurse, even if he'd had a motive, because he'd been handcuffed to the rail. Newman released him, noticing as he did so that again the thread to the camera hadn't been touched. This time the murderer's victim lay in a different direction. He returned and started to put the handcuffs on the girl. She was the only one left. Alice stopped him.

"Don't, Don! Please! Don't you see she's not the one. It's not any of us. It's something—out there!" She threw her arms around him, sobbing.

SUDDENLY she felt strange against his body. He looked at the young girl, at the doctor. They blurred before his eyes and he slumped to the floor. He saw the doctor move as a shadow, then felt a knife pierce his brain. As his vision grew sharp he brushed aside the hand in front of his face. The ammonia did its job quickly but Newman was still weak. The doctor's voice sounded hollow, as from a long way off.

"Rest a while. You'll be all right. But I do think your fiancée is correct, Newman. There is some wild beast here with us. And we must stop it before—" He completed the sentence with a shrug of his shoulders.

That night Newman set the camera facing the end of the cavern and in addition they all took turns standing guard with the revolver. And they left the lights on.

It happened after Newman's watch. Too tired to stay awake, he dropped off into a troubled sleep and didn't awaken the doctor, whose turn was next. Later he was aware of someone shaking his shoulder roughly. When he opened his eyes it was to find the fifth murder.

The teenager's slight figure lay twisted on the floor, blood staining the front of her dress. The doctor was standing over her, holding the revolver. As he turned toward Newman, the latter half expected him to raise the gun and shoot. But the man scarcely saw him. His eyes, too, had become clouded with fear. Newman looked at Alice. Her face was white, expressionless, as she stared at the cave wall. He should have known, then.

THEY ate little that day, were like three condemned people awaiting the executioner. They were safe until nightfall, since the killer seemed to strike only then, but they knew the night with its menace would surely come. And as though to quicken the end, in the afternoon the lights suddenly flickered several times, then went out.

With their flashlights they made their way to the generator, Newman holding his revolver ready. Then he passed it to the doctor while he tried in vain to fix the small diesel engine. The trouble might have been slight, but he couldn't find it. His mind was whirling too rapidly for him to concentrate.

After an hour he gave up in despair. They returned to the foot of the ramp and began their guard watches immediately. This time Newman remained awake during his turn.

It was after he had passed the revolver to the doctor and was in the throes of another nightmare that Mitvini was murdered.

Newman couldn't recall too clearly how he'd passed the day that followed. He'd buried the last body, then he'd remained outside in the daylight, huddled against the rock with Alice next to him. She had kept staring at him silently, queerly, with blanched face and vacant eyes. Then when the twilight had fallen he had dragged her back into the cave.

There was something about the eerie luminescence of the wasted earth that had been more maddening than even the unknown death lurking below. He remembered the rays of his flashlight had accidentally fallen on the camera. It lay on its side, its back open as though a picture had been taken and someone had removed it.

"Alice, the camera!" he'd shouted. "The picture!"

SHE HAD trembled at his side and a second later forced something into his hand. It had been the picture he had shined the light at, looked in bewilderment at the figure of the beast with hairy body and cruel face, but wearing the clothes of a human being. It was kneeling by the stream, washing its clawed hands in the water. He had screamed and lost his senses.

He had been sitting outside the cave when he'd regained consciousness. The night had passed, also another day, and twilight was descending once more. After the long rest his brain had functioned for a while with its old clarity, and he'd been thinking. He'd started to leave, then the picture had fallen from his pocket and he had destroyed it. Why not? There would be no one to see.

NEWMAN staggered down the ramp. When he reached the bottom he turned on the flashlight and searched the floor of the cavern. He knew what he was seeking. He found Alice's body, knelt beside it and gathered it in his arms. He ignored the blood that stained his hands and his clothing. She was his Eve. And wasn't he her Adam? He laughed, more in bitterness now than madness.

It must have begun that first day when the blast of radiation had hit him and seared him as he was trying to pull back the girl from the sea of fire. And for three weeks the insidious poison had worked on his mind and body, twisting and distorting them. The picture had been more proof than he'd needed—it had been of him, himself. Radioactivity, and he was the fall-out! He felt the hair again beginning to bristle on his arms, felt his fingers swelling into long talons. This time he'd kill the murderer. He groped for his revolver.

MIKE CHOMKO, the winner of the 2010 Munsey Award, has been a regular at pulp cons since the early nineties. In September of 2008, he joined Jack Cullers, Barry Traylor, and Ed Hulse to launch PulpFest. Mike serves as the marketing and programming director of the convention and is also the publisher of *The Pulpster*.

A former member of the Pulp Era Amateur Press Society, Mike was the publisher of *Purple Prose*, a highly respected pulp fanzine that ran for seventeen issues in the late 1990s and early 21st century. Around the same time, he founded Mike Chomko Books, an independent purveyor of genre fiction and related materials. His specialty is pulp-related material.

In "real life," Mike is a semi-retired registered nurse. He works in the operating room of a surgical center for pediatric patients. Married for nearly 45 years, he is the father of two adult children and a grandfather. To reach Mike by email, write to mike@pulpfest.com.

STEFAN DZIEMIANOWICZ has been a collector of pulp fiction magazines for over 50 years and is the author of *The Annotated Guide to Unknown and Unknown Worlds*. His more than 50 anthologies of mystery, horror, fantasy, and science fiction include *Weird Tales: 32 Unearthed Terrors*, *Rivals of Weird Tales*, and *100 Wild Little Weird Tales*. He is co-editor of *Supernatural Fiction of the World: An Encyclopedia* and his book reviews and features have appeared in the *Washington Post, Locus, Publishers Weekly, The Scream Factory, barebones*, and other publications. He has also written a collection of retold urban legends, *Bloody Mary and Other Tales for a Dark Night*.

ROBERT DEIS owns one of the world's largest collections of vintage men's adventure magazines (MAMs) published in the 1950s, 1960s, and 1970s. In 2009, he created a popular blog about the genre, **MensPulpMags.com**. A few years later, Bob and Wyatt Doyle of New Texture launched The Men's Adventure Library, a series of books that feature classic MAM pulp fiction stories and artwork. That series now includes nearly 20 lushly illustrated story anthologies and art books. In recent years, Bob and Wyatt have been featured speakers at PulpFest, and Bob was listed in the book *Who's Who In New Pulp*. Starting in 2021, Bob began working with Bill Cunningham, head of Pulp 2.0 Press, to publish a magazine that features MAM stories and artwork, called the *Men's Adventure Quarterly*. He has contributed articles about MAMs to various magazines and fanzines and also writes two blogs about famous quotations, **ThisDayinQuotes.com** and **QuoteCounterquote.com**. Bob lives near Key West, Florida with his wife BJ (who graciously tolerates his fascination with vintage MAMs), their three dogs, and four cats.

WYATT DOYLE is ringmaster of New Texture, and he edits and designs most releases. His own books include *Stop Requested* (illustrated by Stanley J. Zappa), *Dollar Halloween*, *I Need Real Tuxedo and a Top Hat!*, *Buty-Wave Is Now Closed Forever*, and *Jorge Amaya Doesn't Live Here Anymore*. A retrospective of his photography was presented by Gallery 30 South in Pasadena, CA. With Robert Deis, he edits The Men's Adventure Library series, exploring vintage pulp fiction, illustration art, and history. With Jimmy Angelina, he created *The Last Coloring Book* and *The Last Coloring Book on the Left*, as well as *Be Italian*. Together with Hal Glatzer and Norman von Holtzendorff, he produced *Things That Were Made for Love*, collecting the Jazz Age songsheet art of Sydney Leff. He assisted in the publication of Georgina Spelvin's memoir, *The Devil Made Me Do It*, and published Josh Alan Friedman's *Black Cracker* and *Tell the Truth Until They Bleed* via his Wyatt Doyle Books imprint. He administers the creative estate of Rev. Raymond Branch, and curates **RevBranch.com**. His screenplay with Jason Cuadrado, *I'm Here For You*, was produced as *Devil May Call*. A member of The Stanley J. Zappa Quartet, a recording, *The Stanley J. Zappa Quartet Plays for the Society of Women Engineers*, has been released.

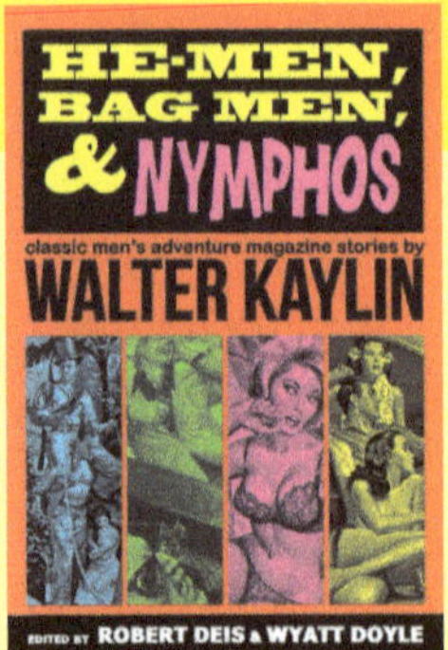

He-Men, Bag Men, & Nymphos
Stories by Walter Kaylin

Leaving an indelible mark on three decades of sweat-soaked pulp fiction, Walter Kaylin tackled testosterone-fueled subjects from Westerns to war, secret agents to sex sirens, Nazis to noir. His frequently over-the-top plots and characters scaled new heights of ingenuity and invention, while setting the standard for the kind of un-apologetic savagery and excess that made men's adventure magazines notorious, then and now. Includes reminiscences by Kaylin, his family, and his former editor, writer Bruce Jay Friedman.

Atomic Werewolves and Man-Eating Plants: When MAMs Got Weird

Featuring Theodore Sturgeon, Manly Wade Wellman, Gardner Francis Fox, Gil Paust, Rick Rubin, HP Lovecraft, *and more*

Weird MAM tales of supernatural encounters, monstrous cryptids, vampirism, witchcraft, demonic death cults, killer robots, psychotic chicken butchers, and of course, atomic werewolves and man-eating plants!

"Hands down, one of my favorite books of the year."
—Stephen Bissette (*Swamp Thing, Tyrant*)

Recommended by The Washington Post

Cryptozoology Anthology
With guest editor David Coleman
Featuring Arthur C. Clarke, John Keel *and others*

When American men had questions about the Yeti, the Loch Ness Monster, Bigfoot, and other weird beasts from the strange world of cryptozoology, they found answers in the hard-hitting pages of men's adventure magazines. Here are samples of sensational period reporting and wild, "true" accounts of savage, fist-to-claw duels between man and Sasquatch, man and fishman, man and monster! Plus expert analysis by crypto authority **David Coleman**, cryptid-by-cryptid commentary, and much, much more. Don't leave civilization without it!

Recommended by The Washington Post

A Handful of Hell
Stories by Robert F. Dorr

Aviator, diplomat, and historian, Robert F. Dorr was uniquely qualified to write for men's adventure magazines, bringing sweat-and-blood, nuts-and-bolts authenticity to his stories of risk, combat, and sacrifice. Vivid, gripping tales of aerial conflict, battlefield heroism and action—some fact, some fiction, all adrenaline-fueled, white-knuckle adventure from one of the genre's greatest voices.

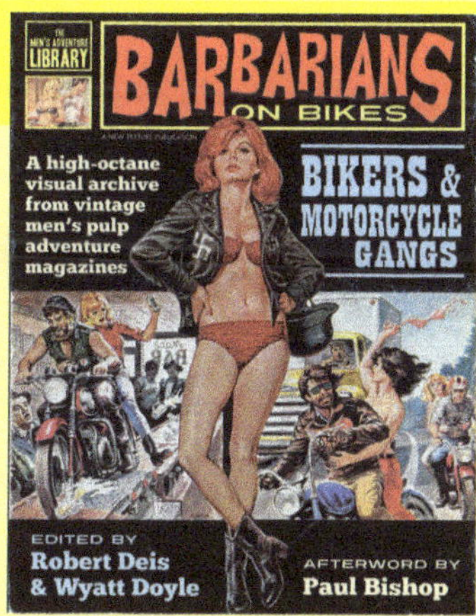

Barbarians on Bikes
Afterword by Paul Bishop

An oversized color collection compiling three decades of motorcycle-themed magazine covers and interior spreads from the 1950s through the 1970s, most unseen since their original publication. Biker illustration art at its most savage. A biker movie between covers, **Barbarians on Bikes** is big, bad, and untamed… Think you can handle the ride?

A series of lush visual archives collecting some of artist Samson Pollen's most memorable pieces, selected from the hundreds of jaw-dropping illustrations he provided for men's adventure magazines (MAMs) from the 1950s through the 1970s. Pollen was equally celebrated for his abilities to effectively render action and movement, as well as his gift for painting beautiful and dangerous women. Illustrating work from authors like Mario Puzo, Martin Cruz Smith, Richard Stark (Donald Westlake), Norman Mailer, Ed McBain, Richard Wright, Don Pendleton, Erskine Caldwell, Walter Kaylin, and Robert F. Dorr, Pollen's immersive illustrations transported adventure-hungry readers from tropical jungles to brutal battlefields to raging seas and mean city streets. Samson Pollen painted it all—spectacularly. Yet almost none of these stunning illustrations have seen print since their original publication. Until now.

Both **Pollen's Women** and **Pollen's Action** are drawn from the artist's own exhaustive archives of his original artwork for MAMs, while **Pollen in Print 1955–1959** is the inaugural volume of a projected series presenting his artwork chronologically as it appeared in the magazines, allowing us to fill gaps in Pollen's archive and definitively chart the trajectory of a remarkable career.

All three big 11" x 8.5" horizontal volumes include the late artist's reminiscences and autobiographical comments.

Eva: Men's Adventure Supermodel
by Eva Lynd

Blonde Swedish countess Eva Lynd's multi-faceted career touches every aspect of 20th century popular culture. A model for leading illustration artists and top glamour and pin-up photographers of the era, she also appeared with some of the biggest names in entertainment on both the big and small screens. Eva shares her story in her own words and pictures. Includes artwork from pulp masters such as Norm Eastman, Al Rossi, Mike Ludlow, and James Bama.

One Man Army *by* Gil Cohen

Exploring the incomparable talent of Gil Cohen via the unique perspective he brought to the Mack Bolan universe as one of **The Executioner** series' most celebrated cover artists. **One Man Army** showcases Cohen's spectacular and original paintings for the bestselling action paperbacks, chronicling his seminal role in establishing the Bolan mythos for millions of dedicated readers worldwide.

Mort Künstler: The Godfather of Pulp Fiction Illustrators

Celebrated for his ability to present large-scale action while never losing sight of essential details, **Mort Künstler** is a master of capturing conflict in paint—both its spectacle, and human cost. At last, here is a stunning selection of his finest pieces from the MAM era in this long awaited collection. A close study of an unequaled career, every page explodes with action, color, and artistry.

The Naked and the Deadly
Stories by Lawrence Block

Spicy detective stories, international intrigue, and bedroom secrets… Before the bestsellers, Block cut his teeth on MAM fiction and non-fiction articles, collected here in their complete and uncut versions for the first time since their original publication. Includes a new introduction by the author.

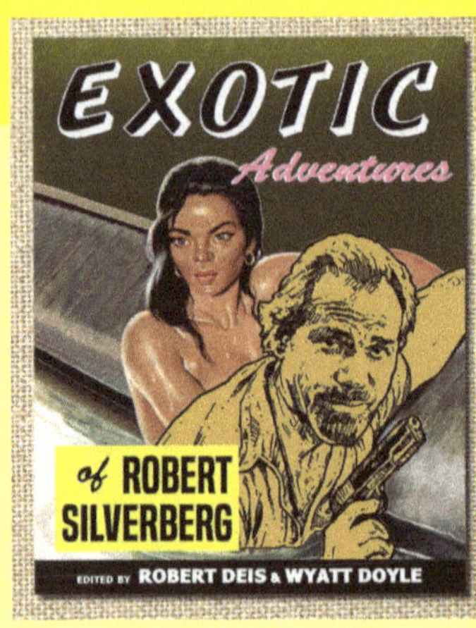

Exotic Adventures of Robert Silverberg

From safari to bordello, from smugglers' cove to opium den, Robert Silverberg's lost pulp exotica returns to print for the first time since its original 1950s publication, presented in bold new facsimile re-creations that look fresh off the newsstand, circa 1958. Strap in for fully illustrated globe-trotting adventures from the vivid imagination of one of speculative fiction's most honored talents, working incognito.

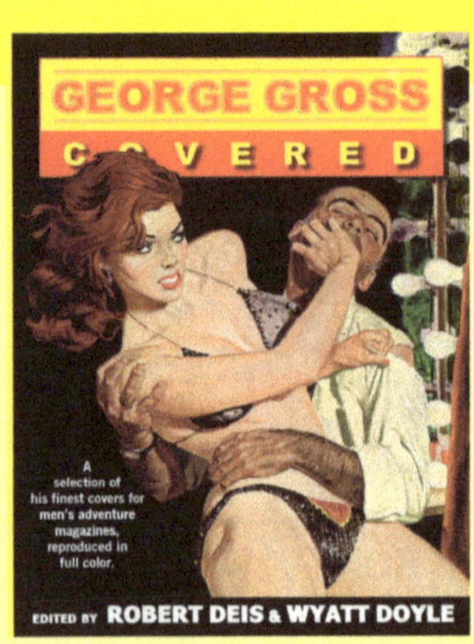

George Gross: Covered

A top artist for pulps, men's adventure magazines, and paperback covers, George Gross's artwork spans decades, and helped establish a visual vocabulary for action/adventure and hard-boiled fiction. A unique talent who led the way for generations of artists, his imagery continues to inspire and influence. Spotlighting dozens of his memorable covers, this full-color collection includes contributions by historian David Saunders and artist Mort Künstler.

SOFTCOVER AND EXPANDED HARDCOVER EDITIONS AVAILABLE

ROBERT DEIS AND WYATT DOYLE, SERIES EDITORS

I Watched Them Eat Me Alive
Killer Creatures in Men's Adventure Magazines

Cuba: Sugar, Sex, and Slaughter
Cuba and Castro in Men's Adventure Magazines

Maneaters
Killer Sharks in Men's Adventure Magazines

The Men's Adventure Library Journal is a bold and explosive annex of **The Men's Adventure Library**, devoted to deep dives into some of MAMs' most popular and potent subjects. Titles include **I Watched Them Eat Me Alive**, a hot appetizer sampler of killer creature survival stories; **Cuba: Sugar, Sex, and Slaughter**, presenting MAM fact and fiction centered on Castro and the Cuba in the 1960s; and **Maneaters**, a savage collection of terrifying shark fiction and illustration art paired with mythbusting by contemporary shark experts, including contributions by **Shark Week** creator **Steve Cheskin** and sharkfilm director **Ace Hannah**. All are available in softcover and expanded hardcover editions featuring additional content.

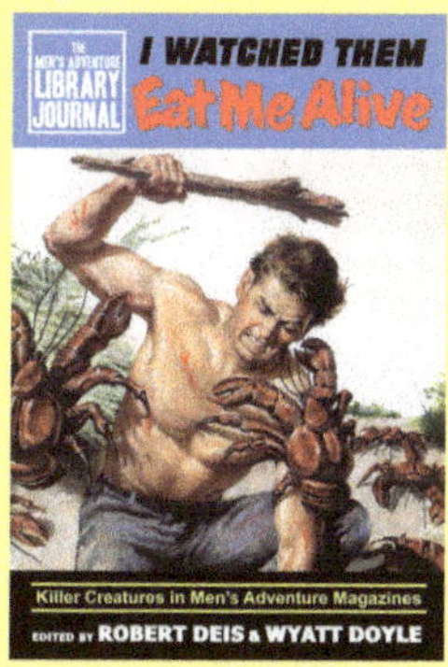

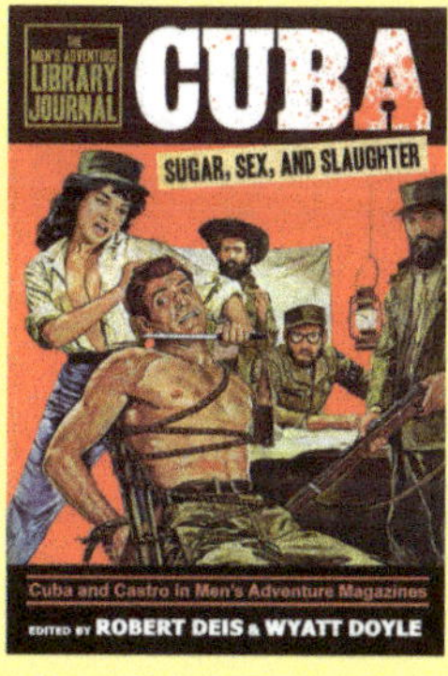

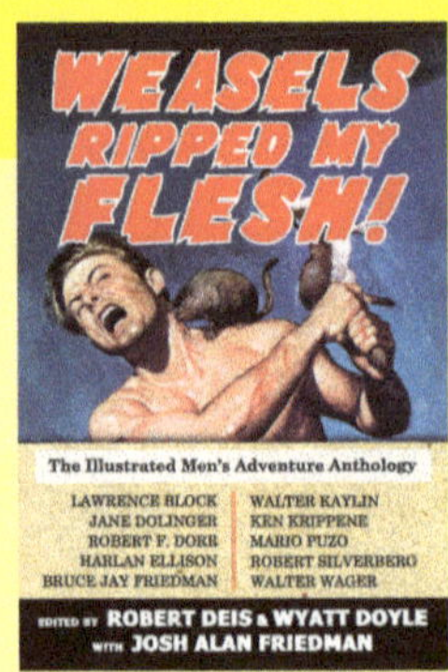

Weasels Ripped My Flesh!
(revised and expanded color edition)

With guest editor Josh Alan Friedman
Featuring Lawrence Block, Robert F. Dorr, Harlan Ellison, Bruce Jay Friedman, Walter Kaylin, Mario Puzo, Robert Silverberg *and more.*

War stories, exotic adventure yarns, (allegedly) true, first-hand accounts of white-knuckle clashes between man and beast, and spicy tales of sadistic frauleins and tropical queens hungry for companionship…This definitive guide to MAM fiction is your passport to a gonzo world where men fought small mammals bare-handed!

Recommended by The Washington Post

Gil Cohen: Inside/Out, Volumes 1–3

Presenting Gil Cohen's earliest published pieces, as an illustrator and cover artist for men's adventure magazines (MAMs). Cohen created memorable illustrations for just about every kind of story MAMs published: military battles on land, sea, and, of course, air; exotic adventures; hard-boiled crime; historical action; animal attacks; biker, Nazi, and Communist villainy; sexy potboilers and more. This stunning body of work represents both the longest and, until now, least revisited period of his career—almost all of it unseen and unreprinted since their original publication. The series pairs print versions of Cohen's MAM illustrations with their original artwork, and includes the Artist's reminiscences and commentary.

Stop Requested,
stories by Wyatt Doyle; *illus.* Stanley J. Zappa

"A series of rueful, witty and occasionally heartwrenching stories about riding the bus in LA. Doyle finds consequence in the inconsequential. He's Bukowski without the nasty streak. And he's real good. Highly recommended." —Marc Campbell, *Dangerous Minds*

Attaché Case: Backstage at the Embassy,
memoir by Todd Pierce

The Kitchen Confidential *of the State Department.* Opening up a famously tight-lipped profession, 28-year Foreign Service veteran Todd Pierce shares what it's like to serve as a working-level diplomat. As he explains in his preface, "This is a book by the help." Funny, revealing, pointed, and deeply human.

"Part memoir, part behind-the-scenes guide, and part ethnographic portrayal of the puzzling, opaque but never boring universe of American diplomacy, Attaché Case *is an irresistible page-turner, jam-packed with wit and insight. A pleasure to read."*
Stathis Kalyvas, Gladstone Professor of Government and fellow of All Souls College, Oxford University

By Jorj: Georgette & Benjamin Harris Songsheet Art 1929–1948

Wyatt Doyle, Hal Glatzer, Peter Mintun, Norman von Holtzendorff, *editors*

Collecting rare and beautiful Jazz Age sheet music cover art by masters of the form, an endlessly inventive and innovative husband-and-wife team whose art both documented and helped define their times.

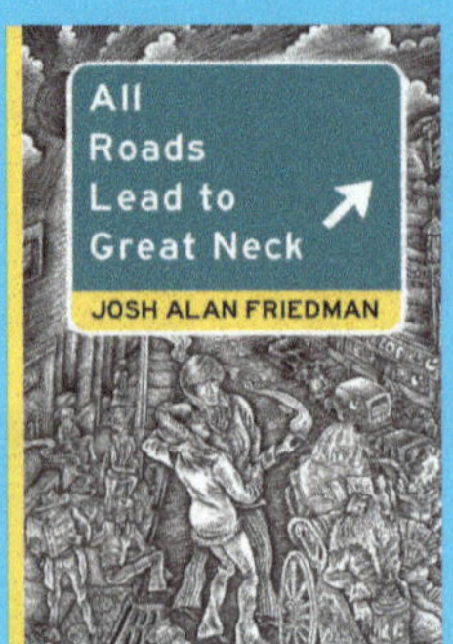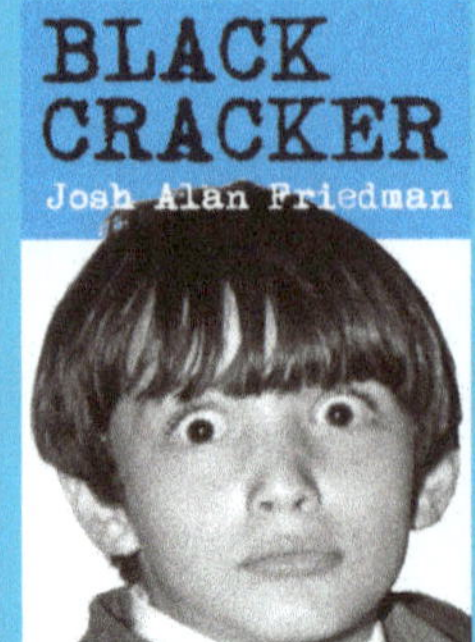

All Roads Lead to Great Neck, *a novel by* Josh Alan Friedman

Sacred hash pipes, high school freakouts, and the brief, intoxicated life of Bruce Disoto, a doomed adolescent hippie in 1970 who sees visions of a 19th century Jewish pimp while tripping. Welcome to psychedelic Great Neck.

"A laugh-out-loud dystopian hipster bildungsroman *with a heart of gold."*

Black Cracker, *an autobiographical novel by* Josh Alan Friedman

1962, flashpoint of the civil rights struggle. And young Josh is the lone white boy in a segregated grade school. An unflinching fun-house tour of a Long Island boyhood, and its now-forgotten poor Black shantytowns. Hilarious and heartbreaking.

Tell the Truth Until They Bleed, *by* Josh Alan Friedman

Up close and personal with important and unsung figures in blues and rock 'n' roll: the self-made, the self-serving, and the self-destructive. Illuminating parts of the music industry most don't talk about, this is show business without the showbiz.

---

nu luna, *a novel by* Andrew Biscontini

After 400 years of colonization, the moon is home to nearly a billion people, living in a crowded industrial police state on the verge of collapse. *nu luna* is a deeply personal matinee space adventure, spun through an improbably plausible future history. The future is beautiful and dangerous.

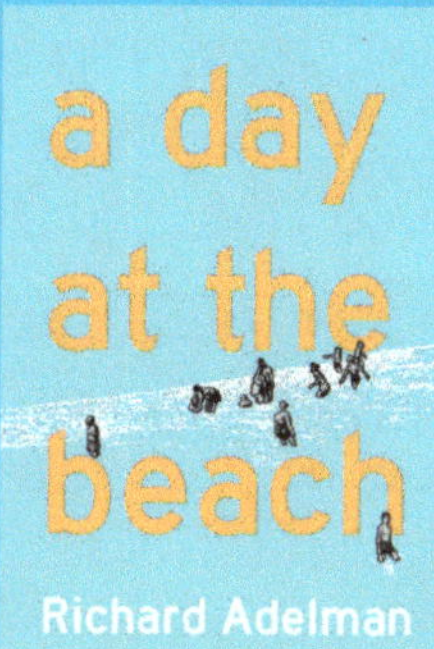

Teacher Tales, *a novel by* Richard Adelman

For 40 years, Mr. Kessler has kept his head down and not made waves. But new acquaintances and bad decisions in his final year before retirement bring his ordered world crashing down around him—tragically and hysterically. A smart and darkly comic novel.

A Day at the Beach, *a novel by* Richard Adelman

Atlantic City, summer of '63. A boy. A girl. And the other boy, who reluctantly pretends to date her to help his pal. A funny, nostalgic novel of young love, best friends, and poetry, capturing one 12-year-old's last great summer as a kid down the shore.

Nimrodia, *poems by* Eric Reymond

Visual art and ancient history are the starting point for most of the poems in this collection, as the modern world intersects with these domains again and again. Though language, culture, and time may divide us, these are also the forces that link us together.

Sub-Sub Librarian, Extracts on a, *poems by* Eric Reymond

The title poem imagines *Moby Dick*'s Sub-Sub Librarian experiencing transcendence and illumination through his wide readings. Additional poems find inspiration in texts as diverse as contemporary poetry, vocabulary quizzes, and course syllabi.

Things That Were Made for Love: The Songsheet Art of Sydney Leff

Wyatt Doyle, Hal Glatzer, Norman von Holtzendorff, *editors*

The first-ever songsheet art collection presenting the cream of the Jazz Age illustration artist's work on songsheet covers from 1924–1932. A gorgeous visual feast that playfully captures the moods, elegance, and style of an era.

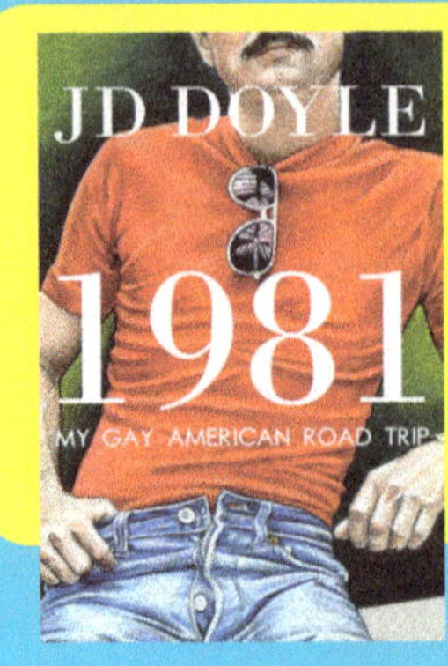

1981—My Gay American Road Trip

by JD Doyle

A playful, intimate, one-of-a-kind illustrated record of gay life, love, lust, and liberation post-Stonewall, in the heady days before the devastating crisis that would change everything.

#new texture Music

CD / DOWNLOAD

I've Got Heaven on My Mind
Reverend Raymond Branch

Sixty Goddammit Josh Alan

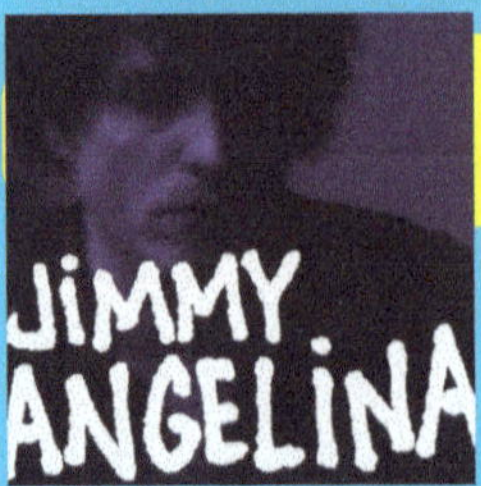

Jimmy Angelina s/t

Cursed Carolina

Continental / International
Jon E. Edwards

Map of the Moon s/t

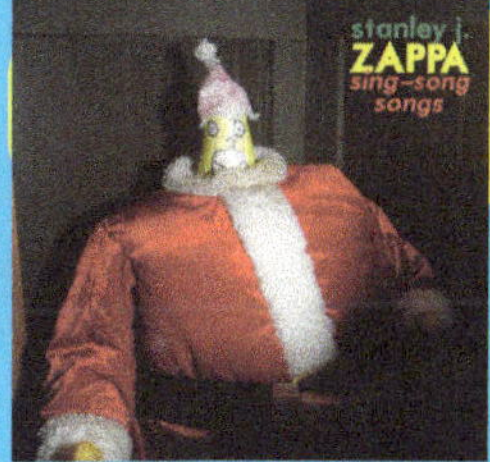

Sing-Song Songs
Stanley J. Zappa

Free / Refuse
Hall, Skrowaczewski, Zappa

Live a Little
Manzappaczewski

The Stanley J. Zappa Quartet
**Plays for The Society
of Women Engineers**

Crossing Guards
Carter, Leffue, Sikora, Zappa

Turkey Bacon Donuts Bitches
MANZAP REBORN

Balloons

Daniel Carter,
Nick Skrowaczewski,
Stanley J. Zappa

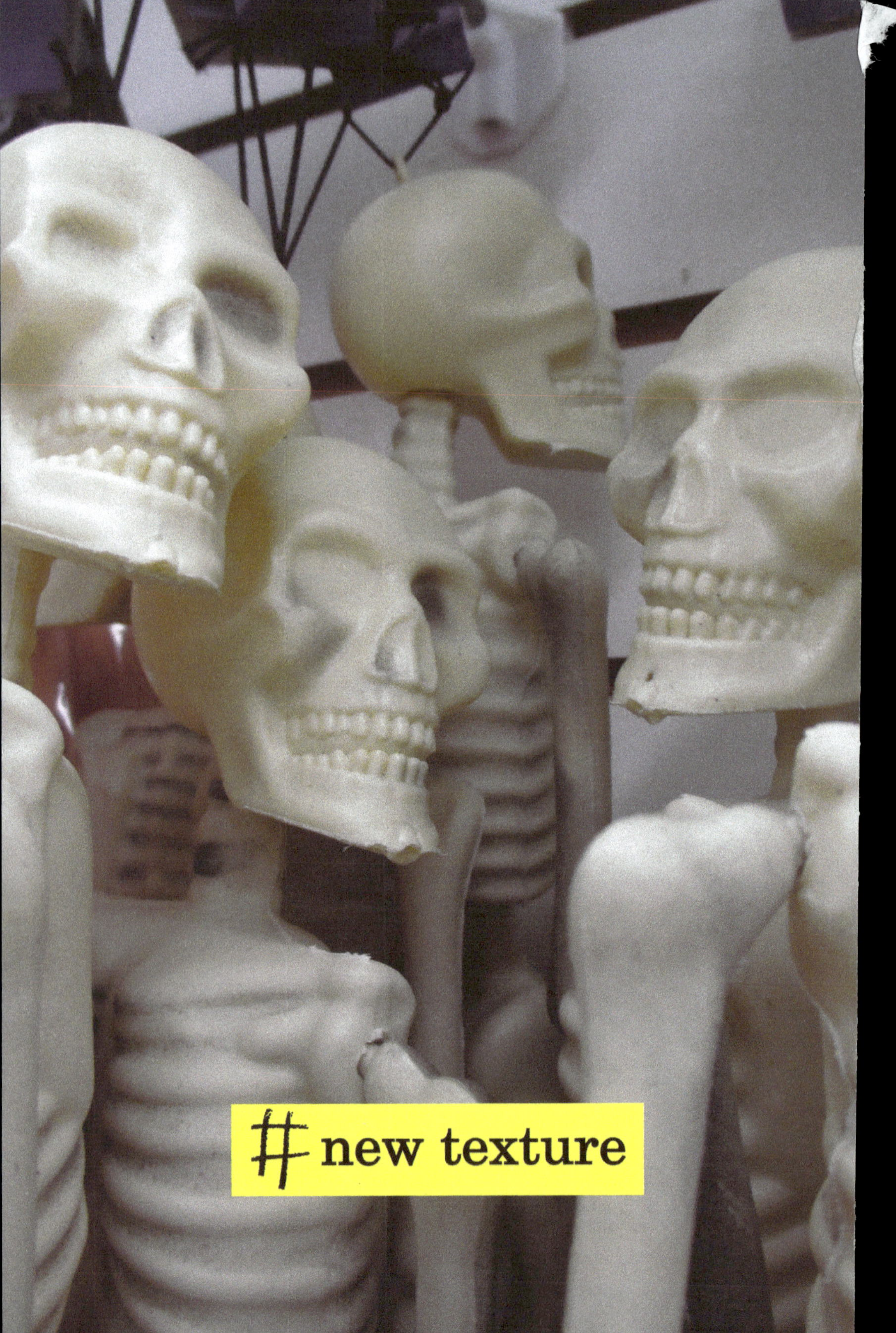

new texture